Soul Trader

By
Steve Bell

Eloquent Books

Eloquent Books
An imprint of Strategic Book Group
P.O. Box 333
Durham CT 06422
www.StrategicBookGroup.com

ISBN: 978-1-60911-904-1

*To the memory of my father, whose
guidance remains with me always*

1936—2007

Rest in Peace.

The events and characters within this publication are purely fictitious and any resemblance to actual events or people is purely coincidental. (However, there are certain traits related to the characters that have been 'borrowed' from those known to the author . . . that may keep some of you thinking.)

Chapter 1

The solitary figure stood motionless among the lightly wooded bank above the Essex lane that he was studying. The winter's air was cold yet stirring, allowing the light fog that enveloped his surroundings to gently swirl like some tantalising dancer light on her feet. Despite the eerie tranquillity, the activity in the small wooded area in which he was positioned, revealed the place to be active with wildlife. It could not be seen but he knew it was there, all around him. The sinister rustling of the few remaining leaves on the trees as the occasional breeze billowed through the canopy was an unnerving spectre, as it was neither quiet nor noisy. Both traits he could normally handle, but the observer felt uneasy in this twilight zone between the two.

It was an early November morning and the biting air was finding its way through his multiple layers of clothing. However, he revelled in the fact that soon he could return to the comforts of life that most people take for granted; such as a simple shower and decent food, both of which had eluded him these past few days as his research was being conducted. Tony Falconer (aka Falcon), had spent several nights outside his quarry's country mansion, surveying his target in readiness for the inevitable elimination that was to ensue. This was his profession and this was just another day at the office, although today's task was a little different from the usual portfolio he was assigned.

Falcon was no ordinary gun for hire. The fact that he was a trained killer was without question. He had been trained by the British Military and was proving a fine testament to his former teachers. However, he was not generally for hire on the open market. He was a specialist but also a closely guarded secret with his clientele, that being a somewhat exclusive list; essentially limited to the requirements of the British Secret Service and the American National Security Agency. Any works undertaken outside the realms of these chaperones would invariably be undertaken through them as a form of cross hire contract. Even people within these organisations were not aware of the existence of Tony Falconer, whose projects were often so heavily shrouded in secrecy only those with the highest clearance would ever get to know of their very existence, let alone be involved in any operational input.

Above the leafy lanes as the sun was still attempting to break through the English winter's morning gloom and light mist. However, today was the day was anticipating catching his prey within a couple of hours, so the surrounding atmosphere could not dampen his spirits. After all, he had done his homework over the past few tiring days and hopefully, all being well, his mark would be eliminated and the contract completed. It was still early morning, yet the shadowy figure lurking in the tree line on the high bank side knew he would not have long to wait. The still and eerie silence was almost deafening as he tried to listen for any approaching sound somewhere in the distance.

For Tony Falconer, this was nothing new - the elimination of a so called enemy of the state. However, what made this particular assignment so interesting was firstly the simplicity with which he could despatch his quarry yet the difficulty of this time ensuring that it was made to look like a complete accident; a sniper shot to the head could not be deemed as falling into this category. This was no straight forward assassination due to the political and commercial high esteem in which the target was held by so many. Unfortunately, the secret services had discovered that their man was also dirty and playing for the other side. Not for any misconceived perception over whether one nations ideals were better suited to mankind than another's, oh no; this time the player was working both sides for nothing other than money; the greatest evil of all.

Sir Charles Draper was the mark for the lone assassin. Draper was very well respected in many walks of life for his technical and consequently financial achievements, despite his humble origins; yet he had this insatiable flaw for greed and power. He was a wealthy industrialist and a member of the aristocracy albeit only by wealth and not birth right, who specialised in the design and manufacture of highly sophisticated micro processors. These were not for domestic use but formed part of the guidance systems for several modern surface launched missiles operated by a number of NATO countries. This was an exclusive club of customers for his company's most advanced piece of electronics, yet despite the rewards that was not enough. The urge was too great and the lure of the dollar too strong for him to patriotically stick with his existing clients, who had essentially funded his rise to power and fortune with a number of contracts for sophisticated avionics through the years. It was mutually beneficial . . . he was the best in his field. Unfortunately, as is always the case with military advancements, the opposition were also keen on getting hold of the technology and would pay any price to attain it. Stealing a rocket was clearly out of the question so they decided to go to the source itself. They too had done their homework and discovered that Draper would invariably be approachable.

The money in question was far too much for a briefcase full, oh no this was electronic transfer of many millions of dollars to Draper's numbered account with UBS in Geneva. Unfortunately Draper's business dealings even when legitimate, by their very nature attract regular surveillance and checks by the security services, simply for peace of mind by the state. Unfortunately for him, one such check was even more in depth than usual when prompted by his loyal man-servant Miles. Despite the myriad of accounts and companies used to effect the payment to Draper, it could still be tracked. For Miles, being around so much money and the predictable corruption that went with the territory associated with military contracts allowed him to get a taste for all the trimmings that went with this environment. He saw his way out and sold his artificial loyalty to Draper to the men of the American National Security Agency. He had been present at several meetings with the North Korean business men and minor diplomats who were brokering this deal to purchase the micro processors, so knew only too well what was going down. He had an out from Draper, a couple of million dollars, a new identity and a new start somewhere tropical. The decision was not that difficult. He was looked after handsomely by Draper despite spending much of his time having to clean up the personal life of his employer in his wake, even though never fully appreciated. That opportunity to escape his down trodden existence, whilst still having access to the trappings that came with it, was a great incentive for Miles to spill the beans to the agencies. Draper was often like some wayward Caribbean hurricane which showed no mercy for those around him whom he ridiculed, belittled, humiliated and eventually betrayed. Money had changed Draper and not for the better. Ultimately it would lead to his downfall. Money brings power which in the wrong hands breeds greed and contempt along with the quest for greater power. Draper was most definitely the wrong hands.

Clearly, neither the NSA nor their associates throughout the military alliance could allow their most advanced technology to fall into the wrong hands, national economies were prospering spending tax payers' money where best needed rather than fighting a spiralling cold war with a secretive enemy. No, the cold war could not resume that was effectively cast in stone, and the NATO powers were ever hopeful of that. Military budgets were already stretched fighting the War on Terror; the taxpayers did not want to see that pushed even further.

The NSA had used Falcon before on several occasions and found his services to be extremely useful. He was not one of theirs and was seen as an external expense, '*off balance sheet trading*' as the accountants would call it, but discrete all the same and very resourceful. Falcon covered all the exits so everything was clean and files closed, with very few questions. He earned his income from these guys, that fact was never in question. This assignment though had a twist, nothing he couldn't handle all the same but Draper and Miles had to be erased simultaneously. Why? Miles was in effect the inside man. The NSA on the other hand, could not be seen to have a hand in the demise of Draper. After all, he was also one of the Country's top military contractors. He was maybe not as big in budgetary terms as the hardware suppliers with their planes, missiles and tanks, but still equally important. He couldn't be exposed as a traitor as this would undermine internal confidence within the alliance, along with the creation of concerns over what else had leaked out of the organisation to the unseen enemy. Too many battles being fought on many fronts with the global push on fighting terrorism, another real worry about the few remaining communist states obtaining superior weaponry just could not be brought into the open. This predicament had to be rectified with discretion and without recourse.

The solution was simple and came from very high up within the corridors of power on both sides of the Atlantic. An executive order of this magnitude needed the highest approvals and utmost secrecy. An accidental death would eradicate the problem yet leave Draper's reputation, at least as a key supplier to the NATO countries arsenals, intact; causing no security concerns throughout the alliance. After all, if countries who had spent billions of dollars on strategic defences suddenly found they could be rendered useless if the technology was already available with the enemy, there would be at the very least some severe discord. Today that problem would be resolved. The unfortunate side effect though would be that Miles would also need to have the same fate bestowed upon him as his employer. He had already shown his willingness to sing like a canary when offered the golden lure of green backs; consequently the authorities could not run the risk of eradicating the source of the problem yet allowing its tributary to remain at large. Miles' own naivety would be his undoing.

The past few days, Falcon had been watching his mark both at home and en route to the main roads leading to London, a drive undertaken almost daily by Draper and Miles when he was in the country. Despite the results of any hangover he may have from his previous evenings over indulgence, Draper still enjoyed a visit to his empire's head office in the city as often as he could. Having observed the ease with which Miles swung the Daimler Sovereign around the country lanes with which he was eminently familiar; Falcon hatched a plot to force the vehicle off the road at a suitable location and down the steep rocky incline that bordered the carriageway opposite to where he was currently standing. It was hardly rocket science and scarcely the work of accomplished professionals; however the simplicity was the beauty itself.

As there was still very little daylight, Miles would be relying heavily on his instinct and knowledge of the roads for his navigation. They seldom encountered any traffic coming the other way on the early morning runs into the city, which allowed Miles to enjoy the full width of the road at many a sharp bend, minimising his need for speed reduction to an almost crawl in some parts, something greatly assisted by the road holding capabilities of the sturdy vehicle. Falcon had watched and traversed the route himself leading him to the current location; a particularly blind bend although not excessively sharp. The outer edge was manned by Armco crash barrier although beyond that was a severe drop down steep rocky moraine to a stream some distance below. Falcon had loosened the nuts from the barrier a few hours earlier during the real hours of darkness and had dragged some fallen tree branches into the carriageway adjacent to the bank side, effectively blocking off the inner lane. Having watched Miles' driving technique, Falcon felt that this should cause the chauffeur to swerve and hit the Armco, which on this occasion would not be able to perform as designed, thus leading the Daimler and its hapless occupants over the edge, after that it was out of Falcon's hands, although he was confident that the terrain would be sufficient cause for the desired effect. Planning is what had kept him ahead for all these years and despite how simple or difficult a project may be, Falcon knew planning was always the key. If there was no time for sufficient planning with at least two exit strategies, he would not take on the project. He had learnt that lesson the hard way in his early days, on his first assignment for the British in Africa, and it had served him well ever since.

There was not intended to be any imminent urgency to complete the mission as Draper was not scheduled to meet with his new found friends for several weeks. However, Falcon's employers had discovered that the first part of Draper's blood money from the North Korean's, a sum of five million dollars no less, had been deposited at the Chemin Louis-Dunant Branch of UBS in Geneva, so the game was definitely on. The biggest concern to the agencies was in reality where had the North Koreans secured five million dollars from to be able to spend in such a way, let alone the full amount which they understood to be nearer twenty five million dollars. No doubt there was some even greater evil behind the scheme that needed to be stopped. If there was a workable plan conceived, then Falcon's philosophy was to get on with the job and clear out. Why wait for chance tomorrow if today will suffice? Who knows, with so much money already out of pocket and committed, then maybe Draper's contacts would want to move faster. After all they had bared their backside now it was time for Draper to perform.

The time was fast approaching for the arrival of the prey to the snare. Falcon was trying to keep the cold and damp out as best he could but being stationary and hidden made this ever more difficult. He sat in the now ghostly morning silence as the night life seemed to have retired, so quiet considering the rest of the country was beginning to rise for work, yet here time seemed to simply stand still as nothing stirred. All this changed after about half an hour, but not to what was expected.

"Oh shit," Falcon muttered to himself as he observed a slow moving vehicle coming up at the hill towards him. "This can't really be happening now, not this time of the bloody morning."

A battered VW camper van was slowly crawling up the hill, a foreign vehicle with European plates, probably just on a tour of the British countryside simply itching to get away from the rat race that exists daily on the English motorway network, even so early in the morning. No direction whatsoever, yet today they were stumbling into a nightmare that has nothing to do with them. Falcon could not afford to reveal himself and jump into the carriageway and try and remove the debris, yet he had a strong belief in avoiding collateral damage. He prided himself on only targeting his objectives along with any of their equally atrociously associated comrades who get in the way of the mission; but innocent collateral damage he had never engaged in, and he was proud of that. Things may change now, he had to think fast. His analysis of the situation convinced himself that the vehicle was sufficiently slow moving that it should not suffer the fate of going over the edge; it was travelling in the wrong direction which should assist, so long as the driver keeps his nerve if he stumbles upon the blockage before the Daimler. Suddenly from behind, he heard the throaty purr of a finely tuned engine, the target vehicle was coming. This could solve the problem for the camper van but the target needed to get here fast. This would leave witnesses but so long as Falcon was not around this may be okay; in fact it would be superb if it all came together at the right time. He had no choice, the task at hand was all too important and he had to let the Daimler stumble upon its planned fate.

Suddenly the shiny chariot roared into sight around the tight bend and just as planned caught sight of the woodland debris. Miles yanked instinctively on the leather clad steering wheel veering the car across the road. It was all so quick but precisely as planned. The unanticipated obstruction lurching out of the mist at the ill-fated vehicle caused sheer panic inside the cockpit with Miles yanking left and right almost at random but all in timescales amounting to nothing more than split seconds. The result was the smashing of the front end of the gleaming luxury marque into the Armco barrier, forcing the barrier into sections as the remaining bolts sprung and popped in all directions, and the car hurtling off the edge of the road and down the steep incline. The rocky steep slopes and the bouncing of the vehicle caused it to overturn and roll over and over as it crashed into the icy stream below where it came to its final resting place. The car had rolled several times and by the time it made it to the watercourse, the roof had been flattened and the car almost damaged beyond recognition. No explosion of the vehicle but both occupants were surely no longer alive after that encounter. Falcon was convinced that his task was done. The VW camper van was still not in his sight on the stretch of road immediately downhill of the crash site but had pulled in some way down after they saw the car smash down the hill. Falcon had his chance, he quickly went to the road side and pulled the branches as best he could to the inside of the curve; he had no time to drag them back into the woods away from immediate view but at least they were off the road. He then smartly set off on his journey back cross country to his parked Vectra several miles away although well away by road from the incident location. He was originally hoping for more time before the damaged carriage of Sir Charles Draper was discovered such that he could clear from his hiding place and move on; but despite the early discovery, this should not blight Falcon's overall plan and would in fact lead to a swifter conclusion of this being nothing more than an accident.

Falcon had rented a holiday home only around ten miles away from Draper's palatial abode in Essex, a small converted farmhouse which served his needs perfectly. No prying neighbours to answer to with respect to his comings and goings. The old farm house had been arranged by others on his behalf as was usual, reducing any traceability back to him. He was there as a washed up executive having suffered financial meltdown with his investment company leading to subsequent meltdown in his private life. It was perfect cover for a loner should he make any contact with the locals, coming and going as he pleased adopting a dishevelled look when it suited. It was to here he returned after the apparent contract conclusion and commenced packing. It was time to move on.

After checking the rented property ensuring there were no personal traces left behind, he cleared everything away and completed packing his few belongings. He put on the TV and watched the satellite news channel, repeating itself almost every fifteen minutes to the point of boredom if you watched it too long, but Falcon still needed to be attentive. Then it happened. As the *breaking news* banner splashed across the screen in front of him in bold red letters, the female news reader advised viewers that she was interrupting her current story to announce some breaking news just received off the wires.

'We are receiving unconfirmed reports at this stage that Sir Charles Draper, renowned industrialist had been killed in a terrible road accident near his home earlier today. Sir Charles was never far from controversy with his involvement in some of the country's most sensitive and sizeable military contracts.' The newsreader sat stony faced declaring a man's death with just as much sentiment as the reporting on the latest football scores.

She went on: *'Sir Charles had been linked to numerous politicians and was known for his generous donations to both major parties. We shall bring you more on this story as it develops.'*

Falcon was a little dismayed that poor old Miles, seemingly easily led astray by money, didn't even get a mention in this breaking news. Such is life. He knew the truth and over the coming hours as further details were released Miles did finally make it into the bulletins, but more as an aside rather than the news item itself, simply the hired domestic help caught up in this terrible tragedy. It was unfortunate, but Miles would later be used as the official scapegoat for the incident, citing the levels of alcohol found in his blood stream as a probable cause. Politics is a dirty game . . .

Falcon's work was done here and he jumped into the car and headed for Heathrow. As he set off he called James Brown, his contact to the NSA and advised them that his work was done and the contract between them shall be concluded as arranged with the deposit of his fee into his corporate account in the Cayman Islands. Falcon knew damn well that James Brown was not his real name but that wasn't a bad thing. It provided a level of discretion between the client and the customer which satisfied both parties. Once this transaction was complete the number for James Brown would usually be discontinued as would that being used by Falcon on this mission. When they need to contact him again it would be an inconspicuous order or email through to his Caribbean corporation which was the front for all of his operations, as well as his financial arrangements. There were only a few people who had access to this arrangement, these chosen few were the agents who set up the contracts.

This transaction would net Falcon a cool quarter of a million dollars even though this one carried little personal risk, the only complication being the result needed to be an accident and clean. There was a lot at stake here so the Client needed to use a proven specialist and would happily pay for certainty. In hindsight, it was a good pay day for a very simple solution but simple is often the best. The simpler a project the easier it is to keep conspiracy theorists away from the works. He didn't command attention in his personal life and certainly did not need to attract any at work. The Client was happy and the defence industry lost a maverick to a terrible accident. The balance of power was, for the time being at least, restored.

Chapter 2

The Vectra was parked at Heathrow Airport and returned to the Hertz car rental stand as required. The car was clean, ordered and returned in the open, too deliberate to attract suspicion. Falcon knew his masters would take care of any issues if they arose at this end, he just throws the keys in and walks away. This is far better than the authorities finding a burnt out car or one abandoned in a quarry or river, which would itself open up an investigation.

He whistled as he strolled through the crisp cool air from the car park into the terminal. It may have been under cover but the openness still formed a channel for the icy blasts that passed through. Christ he thought, this place just gets busier and busier. He always liked to return to Italy after any project for the chill out phase of his unusual lifestyle, subject of course to any other scheduled operations. This was his own debriefing so to speak and to prepare for the next venture in his career.

First though, he needed to arrange suitable air passage. Where to? Can he get back to his villa in Northern Italy directly or does he need to take a detour? The latter seemed the best solution, a detour to Zurich would permit him to call in on his bank Credit Suisse where he held several numbered accounts in a variety of names, as well as several corporations, some of which were also established on his behalf by the bank. More importantly he also held there a safety deposit box with some key items inside. There was an assortment of currencies available at hand but more fundamental to his modus operandi was the selection of identities he owned, passports, social security numbers, driving licenses amongst other items and keys to various properties around Europe from which he operated. Most of these premises were rarely used as Italy was his preferred domicile and if in the UK he always had a place in London. The other addresses were really nothing more than an investment portfolio which at-

tracted seldom visits, but at least afforded an alternative retreat should one be required.

When returning home, home to Falcon was considered to
be Italy, he chose to operate under his real name of Tony
Falcon. He was not working there this was his R and R so
why not travel inconspicuously where he could indulge in
conversation and reveal significant parts of his history whilst
relaxed, and not have to think too hard about which lies to
tell to retain his cover. Back home in Italy Tony Falcon was
simply Tony Falcon. He was himself . . . and at peace.

First he needed to arrange the trip to Zurich. A flight by
Swiss Air left within three hours and he wanted to be on it.
He checked in at the Swiss Air counter under the name he
had been travelling on within the UK on his latest mission,
John Heaton.

The young Swiss Air attendant gazed at Falcon with a well
rehearsed smile and exuding an aura of beauty that many
men would die for. Her deep blue eyes transfixed him as he
put the past couple of weeks behind him and drifted into
fantasy land, not usual for him to lose focus but fatigue and
beauty momentarily got the better of the Englishman.

"Mr. Heaton sir," she repeated, "do you have any luggage
to check in?"

Falcon jumped out of his fixation as the young attendants
sweet voice echoed inside his head and apologised about
being exhausted, and advised the lady that he would travel
with hand baggage only. He only purchased an economy
ticket as he hadn't bothered changing into any finer clothes
than the denims he had been wearing these past few days.
Functional and practical for what he had been doing but not
lending themselves to business class travel without looking a little out of place. So for a flight of only a couple of
hours, economy travel and anonymity would have to suffice.
Very soon he would be once again Tony Falcon, indulging in
dialogue with his neighbours and fellow village occupants,
and breathing that crisp fresh mountain air. This was the best
tonic Falcon could ever hope for, good food, good wine, un-

spoilt scenery—hill walking in the summer and skiing in the winter. When not working he wanted for very little, except for the company that awaited him there.

Falcon decided to take a coffee from one of those numerous gourmet coffee houses that have sprung up as multi nationals all over the developing world prior to boarding. He had an hour or two to pass and didn't want to indulge the alcohol until he was away. He could wait, quality wine awaited him back home and he would soon catch up on his quota. He slouched into a well worn airport lounge chair and sipped his coffee, whilst undertaking another pastime of his, people watching. He wasn't sitting in fear; this was just habit after most of his jobs and as a creature of habit, would never be able to change this trait. As he sat in the airport he saw the early editions of the London Evening News being placed in the various news stands, the front of which borne the headlines about the accidental death of Sir Charles Draper. It was official, mission complete and the world knew. No mention of foul play and no conspiracy suggestions from any quarter despite his known, or at least implied, financial indiscretions with members of Westminster and the securing of lucrative contracts. He relaxed a little more now and waited for his flight to be called. After the gate was opened Falcon delayed boarding for another twenty minutes, another habit brought about by his career path. First and last boarders tend to be noticed, he tended to follow the masses and remain incognito whenever possible.

The wheels of the passenger jet left the ground and were tucked away under the wings as it soared into the darkening early evening skies above London. It had been a busy day after all as well as very successful. The efficiency with which the latest contract was executed would only further endear him to his employers. Now he could relax a little and enjoy a small scotch whiskey. He had a liking for fine whisky, both Scottish and Irish, and sported a fine collection back home in Italy. For now at least, a shot size of Glenfiddich on an airplane would have to suffice. Although he knew a true malt drinker would traditionally not take ice with a malt, he always felt there was something about a nicely chilled shot of scotch, so irrespective of protocol he would happily pour his malt whisky over a couple of rocks. Now Falcon shifted into holiday mode and began drifting away . . .

He was already relaxing by his pool as the plane came crunching down into the tarmac at Zurich Airport with the pilot, fighting cross winds and the onset of heavy mist at night, found the ground fractionally earlier than he was anticipating. The engines screamed into reverse thrust mode as the plane shuddered along the runway jerking and hopping to a walking pace as it yanked off the main runway onto the taxi way on its route to the parking stand. Everybody was alert now including Falcon, who was surprised at his dozing on such a short flight.

"Christ I must be ready for a rest," he uttered to himself as he rubbed his eyes gingerly whilst stretching his arms aloft, in the now chatter filled cabin. Soon be in a comfortable bed he thought.

As the plane came to its stand everybody arose almost in unison and scrambled for the overhead lockers to retrieve their hand luggage. There certainly had been some movement within the lockers as the plane landed but Falcon's baggage all remained securely intact. Not that he was travelling with a great deal of luggage but his cabin bag did afford him basic toiletries along with a change of casual clothes. Too late for the bank this evening he thought. His bank manager would surely wish to enter into social dialogue and use Falcon as his excuse to secure another all expenses paid meal in downtown Zurich with another one of his private clients. Falcon was in no mood for such pleasantries tonight, his only company was to be a comfortable double bed which tonight he would gladly occupy on his own, with the added benefit that he would arise once refreshed. No alarm clocks, no telephone calls; his body clock would tell him when he could face the world outside again tomorrow. What was needed now was a hotel down town but fairly close to the bank.

From the plane Falcon made his way through the airport. Customs officials glanced at his European passport and he was straight through as were most of the passengers who alighted ahead of him. This was the business mans flight and probably last of the evening. This flight was full of Swiss Financiers and high flyers returning home from a day at the office in the global financial centre that is London. Customs officials were used to this traffic and very rarely paid a great deal of attention to the travellers.

Falcon was familiar with his environment, take the escalator now downstairs and follow the crowds. No need for a taxi, the railway station was just below the terminal and was extremely efficient. Stick with the crowds when you can and become just another John Smith. He made his way to the ticket office on the lower level and joined the queues. The office was very efficient with numerous tellers so it would only be a matter of minutes.

"Bahnhofstrasse bitte," he said, as if it was his natural tongue. Being fluent in several languages had its advantages in many situations and greatly helps to blending in wherever you are, but Falcon had also found in the past that more importantly socially, it could be used in the right situations to impress the fairer sex. Unfortunately German was not a romantic sounding language and had never really helped him in this quest (with the exception of Maria), but the smooth sounding Italian which he spoke very efficiently and the little Spanish which he could use to indulge in basic conversation had proved highly successful in his more colourful past. Luckily he was not after picking up the fifty plus year old male teller so the use of the German tongue was for efficiency only, even though the teller would probably have been just as comfortable with the request in English. He paid for his ticket with a Swiss Ten Franc note which was fifty percent of the Swiss Currency he had with him at that time, but it was sufficient for his immediate needs.

He took the train for five or six stops, disembarking at the Northern end of Bahnhofstrasse and setting off down the road opposite for the Hotel Park Hyatt Zurich. An exquisite modern hotel used on many occasions by Falcon and always in his own name and nicely located for the commercial and business districts. He was a creature of habit in many walks of life, none more so than when he was playing the part of himself. This familiarity helped him in times of need, just like tonight. The streets were fairly quiet, probably as a result of the very damp mist that had descended on the darkening city, causing many of the lights to appear subdued as a result of the semi opaque haze. There was noise and lots of frivolity coming from the small bistros and bars that lined the streets as he strolled on past towards his hotel. He though to himself, just what a contrast these streets are when the sun is shining; people laughing and joking, wealthy people admiring the designer shops that are found in such magnitude of numbers in very few other locations around the world, and many attractive males and females looking as though they had just stepped from the cat walks of Paris or Milan and into the street. Yes, this was a city of plenty and there were a lot of players in it who had plenty, and liked to show it. Falcon never thought of this place as being homely, not to the extent where he could settle down. To Falcon this was a functional city, banking and business. It was always nice to visit because of the general beauty of the city as well as its hospitality, but it was too quick. It was always nice to leave when his business was done. His utopia would always remain his Italian retreat up in the mountains.

Falcon was breaking out in a light sweat as he rounded the top of the street on which his hotel lay prior to catching the welcome sight of his overnight accommodation as it loomed out of the dark vapour, a welcome sight. Due to his reasonably regular visits, there were often familiar faces amongst the staff.

"Guten abend, mein Herr." The voice lurched out of the darkness and brought a startled turn from Falcon as he approached the main entrance. The doorman sprang out of the darkness from nowhere as he had been sheltering as best he could from the night chill. However it was his job to welcome the guests, passing on that feeling of sincere caring from the hotel even before you enter, although tonight the doorman could have done with a task indoors.

"Good evening," replied Falcon preferring an exchange in English rather than German, after all he was playing an English man abroad. "Do you have any vacancies this evening?"

"Ah, English, may I take your bag sir and we shall check at the desk. I think we are quiet this evening so you should not have too much problem."

The doorman was overjoyed at the prospect of being able to get back into the hotel foyer, even for only a minute or so, it was still welcome relief from the biting night air.

Falcon declined the offer of letting his bag go but the doorman insisted on trying to make polite conversation as they walked to the main desk. There was another familiar face behind the desk trying to look occupied on what was obviously a sedate evening by any standards, but that face instantly recognised Falcon as a regular guest at the hotel.

"Mr. Falcon you have returned. How long this time?" asked Antoine, who had been the Deputy Manager at the hotel for as long as Falcon could remember.

"You should have called and we could have made reservations earlier, I may have to do some juggling now to get you a suitable room and with such a late booking I am not sure what I can do with the rate."

This type of banter with the manager in waiting was no stranger for Falcon and he often indulged the upstart with suitable banter in return.

"My good friend, you know very well what you can do with the rate and more importantly what I will do to you if you don't. As for busy, it's fair to say there is more life at the cemetery than there is in here this evening so can I just have a room for one night only without the dispute?"

"Mr. Falcon, you English never cease to amaze me with your strange little sayings. Luckily I have managed to squeeze you in," he continued with a wry grin whilst still banging away on his keyboard, but being unable to resist casting a glance upwards to see what reaction he would draw from the object of his repartee. "Will sir be requiring a reservation in the restaurant this evening?"

Falcon acknowledged that he would like to dine there but in an hour or so, first he needed to freshen up. Falcon was handed the key to his room, no 317 and off he wandered. No need for credit cards here at check in stage, there was enough trust between the parties to know that the bill would be settled either tomorrow or some time soon, but it would be settled. Besides, he was introduced to this hotel by the bank personally, so they would always have redress if any such reputable guest omitted to pay. However, such clientele seldom adopt such practices so the system works.

Room 317 was a pleasantly decorated room over-looking the front street. On a summer's evening it could be quite noisy but tonight it was not going to be. Falcon threw his bag on the two seat settee that was in the lounge area of the suite and proceeded to remove his change of clothes from it. As expected his change of attire was somewhat the worse for wear having not been packed formally in a suitcase, but that was no problem. Falcon being ex military had the ability to drive an electric iron over his shirt and trousers and very quickly it would be looking as though it had just been starched in an upmarket Chinese laundry. Time for a bath and try and get some of this tension out of my aching body he thought. A hot steaming bath was run with the added comforting touch of the complimentary bath milks that are free with such a room, as free as can be considered free in a room costing over three hundred pounds a night. Falcon sank into the silky waters and began cleansing his mind and body of fatigue. His body became limp as his thoughts drifted onto the gourmet food and wine menu that awaited him down stairs at the Restaurant Parkhuus and his knotted muscles began to ease. He felt he was back in civilisation at last.

Half an hour of semi consciousness gave way to a state of alertness for the guest as he suddenly felt rejuvenated. Time for a shower and shave for a full clean down then he was to be dressed in fresh clothes and almost a new man was born. He admired himself in his mirror in the bathroom, marvelling at the transformation that had taken place in the last hour, a splash of cologne then lights out and down to the restaurant. As anticipated it was not full although there was still plenty of activity. This was not just a dining experience but also one of entertainment as the diners are able to watch all the chefs at work in the centre piece show kitchen.

Down to the business at hand, he purveyed the wine menu and was once again planning an attack . . . how could he not with such a renowned cellar to assault?

When he awoke the following morning, the streets outside were already buzzing and thoroughly alive. He had slept well, better than he had for a long time. The double bed looked as though it had hardly been used, most of the crisp white Egyptian cotton sheets seemed unruffled, he could hardly have moved all night. Nevertheless it worked. Falcon was now ready to face the world, put his business affairs in order at the bank then off to his retreat in the Alps. It felt good to be alive. Despite having terminated the lives of two human beings only twenty four hours earlier, he felt no remorse. He didn't easily take pride in his profession but did take pride in how good he was at it. He was a real pro and the chosen few who had access to him were fully aware of that fact. He toyed with his own conscience safe in the knowledge that those he eradicated were nothing but scum: cheats, betrayers, traitors, gangsters, drug dealers and murderers in one way or another, and those who were above retribution for their crimes, a trait often brought about by wealth and improper connections. No, those who were erased were done so for the benefit of mankind. God would make his judgement call at some stage in the future and Falcon rehearsed regularly his defence in readiness for that day. He may win some technicalities in the final challenge but always suspected the choice of career would go against him and no defence lawyer's skilled rhetoric would be able to gain absolution from his crimes. Still, that was the challenge for another day. His role in life was to eliminate scum for a greater good, despatch their very souls to where they truly belonged . . . and for a greater pay day than sticking with the military or his various other forms of employment he had enjoyed since leaving military service. The hours were better too.

He dressed and decided that he could skip breakfast as no doubt his banker would arrange some pastries and coffee upon his arrival, notwithstanding the fact that it was probably nearer to lunch time than breakfast in any case. He strolled out of the hotel casting a casual wave to the desk clerk on his way and out into the bright sunshine. The air in Switzerland was always clean and fresh, it reminded him so much of his alpine refuge but with additional traffic and street characters. The air was cold and his breath was evident in it's stillness as he walked down the road towards his branch of Credit Suisse. He would be there in around ten minutes so decided a walk in the crisp air would be more palatable than a taxi ride, which would probably take longer in the city traffic. Besides that he probably didn't have enough cash in Swiss Francs on his person to be able to pay the fare. Decision made by default.

He entered the familiar building of Credit Suisse on Paradeplatz in the financial district of Zurich using the privileged access reserved for private banking customers. This was banking services that pander to the wealthy. Falcon had a significant sum of money in their bank through various fronts. His private banker, Heinrich Wilhelmson, never knew what Falcon's business was, but was savvy enough to accept at face value that Falcon was a maverick financier and financial trouble shooter for small companies. One of his corporations was established as a high tech security specialist organisation being involved in not only the obvious CCTV and the like but also forensic security securing sensitive data, a market place with a global audience. Wilhelmson probably suspected differently, but the attraction of Switzerland and its financial benefits were observed by the upper echelon of their banking fraternity. The skill of the bankers keeps them in this unique position and the rewards these specialists receive reflect their trust in their client's claims. They would make the deposits realistic; it's what they were paid for. Private accounts usually required a minimum balance of one million dollars, a sum which Falcon had exceeded some years earlier; however he also had a habit of spending it. Never outwardly flash but never buying cheap, especially if it was for himself. His property portfolio in various European cities added to his asset base, although his cash holdings with Credit Suisse were only a little over the million dollar mark at this moment in time. He had never sat down and tried to work out how much he needed on deposit to allow him to retire; he often wondered though if he ever could.

On introducing himself to the receptionist and advising who he wished to see, Mr. Wilhelmson was buzzed by the receptionist and Falcon was escorted to a private elevator which had already been programmed to travel to the third floor of the building where Wilhelmson's secretary would be waiting to greet him. Opulence always brought with it a sense of pampering by those around and Swiss bankers were experts at it. A shapely auburn haired receptionist met Falcon as he exited the lift on the third floor of the bank building, although from the outside it resembled nothing like a bank. The halls and corridors of the building were adorned with fine antiques and paintings which would not look out of place in any stately home. How much value was here he cared not to wonder, perhaps this is why there is so much security lurking around the place. One thing was for certain, no one was going to walk out with anything.

Falcon was shown into a small but well furnished reception room, akin to a drawing room but on a smaller scale, yet incredibly homely.

"Can I interest you in a coffee Mr. Falcon?" asked the ever attentive receptionist, "espresso or perhaps water?" she continued.

He enjoyed this type of service every time he came to the bank, just like being in an up-market city centre restaurant where the omnipotent staff just can't do enough for their over charged guests.

"Cappuccino would be very well received if that's at all possible," retorted Falcon playfully as he toyed with the young girl as this was not originally offered, although he was certain it would be no problem. Besides, he was not breaking with protocol this time of the morning partaking of cappuccino, so felt assured that his ignorance of local tradition would not shine through. It was his first of the day after all.

Predictably he was told that it would be with him in a little while so he could make himself comfortable and the receptionist backed out of the room and made her escape from the Englishman's charms. He chose not to sit just yet but instead casually walked around the small room admiring the fineries that were on show and occasionally gazing out of the windows through the laced curtains to the busy streets below. What a contrast to last night he thought, now the financial sector was alive and kicking and already the street bistros and cafeterias were filling. Only a couple of minutes had passed when the door flew open and the larger than life character of Heinrich Wilhelmson entered the room.

Wilhelmson was a stocky man, mid to late forties and with a complete head of dark hair. He was cleanly shaven and sported an Italian hand made suit that probably cost more than the average salaries of the counter staff that worked the front desks on the Bank's public face. Very well educated of course and very articulate and although German being his mother tongue, you could be forgiven for thinking that he was educated at Eton and Cambridge. He spoke English with a silver spoon already in his mouth. His position with the bank was to not only look after his private clients, but to attract more of similar status whenever possible and infer on them the type of service and security they sought. Whatever the needs of the customer, there would be someone within the banking network of this organisation who would be tasked with arranging it. Not necessarily simply arranging finance or moving cash but of you wanted a hotel, a chauffeur or reservations at a restaurant that you could not secure yourself, the bank would do it for you. If you had the cash, they were your on call Mr. Fix It. How far this service would lend itself Falcon never really tested as he was not of a mind to be overly beholden to anyone, right now they handled his finances appropriately and that was all that mattered.

"Good day Mr. Falcon, I was half expecting to see you some time soon, although I must admit . . . perhaps not this soon."

He was followed in the door by a waiter transporting a tray of two large cappuccinos as well as a couple of bottles of sparkling and still mineral water. This was hospitality, coupled with the usual amaretto biscuits, always a favourite with coffee drinkers.

"Oh really, I just thought I would call as I was passing this way back to Italy, hence no appointment."

"So you are not at all interested in the deposit received yesterday afternoon in the account of Apollo Holdings in the Cayman Islands?"

"Oh that deal, so they finally paid up, it's about time. Hell I restructured their security over a couple of months ago and saved them a packet since no doubt, maybe next time they need me I will take the cash up front."

Wilhelmson knew not to push on the origins of cash and both men knew this was just the standard style banter they were accustomed to but needed to get through the formalities. After all, how would it look for an international world top bank to ask its depositors how the assassination business is going or asking it's South American customers about the swings in the cocaine and heroin markets. The bank wanted their business and the customers wanted their assistance and discretion . . . everybody wins a little.

"Would sir like anything doing with his finances at the moment?" the banker cheekily asked.

Falcon hesitated a moment then asked that the banker create another half million dollar stake in a suitably secure investment hedge fund the bank was promoting. This took cash away from prying eyes out of an account to a simple growth fund. Sure the right people would be able to access his files and see the extent of his financial holdings, but not the everyday employees at the bank. This would reduce liquid cash in Apollo to below one million dollars but for a business account with very little outgoings and generally only incoming funds, this should suffice for the foreseeable future. It also meant that Falcon would now have investment funds in various forms totalling around one million dollars, ready for capitalisation whenever he decided it was time to hang up his guns, although in truth no hard and fast timescale had been set aside in his head for such an eventuality. He did not want to rush the ageing process and wondered whether he would simply vegetate if he ever stopped what he was doing, not that he particularly enjoyed it as such but it did give him his sanity. He did have other assets with regards to his properties and general liquidity but had not really decided at what level he would have sufficient financial security behind him to be able to maintain a chosen comfortable lifestyle and enjoy early retirement. There was always the other concern of course that as a result of his profession there could be those out there who would wish to retire him. It was a constant gamble and even if he did get to the stage of retiring there was the fear that because of his knowledge and lack of further use to previous patrons, he would need disposing of. These were the bad dreams that haunted him when on quiet stake outs, whilst working but not active and the mind begins to wander, yet strangely when in his own comfort zone for relaxation such concepts never invaded his space.

Wilhelmson agreed that he would make the necessary arrangements and within three days all formalities would be completed and Falcon could access his portfolio on the internet using the coded entry system all private clients enjoyed, virtually hack proof so long as you never lost your security random number key generator. Not really random as the algorithms that generated the six digit codes required for log on were tied to your account and your account only, but to an onlooker they were effectively meaningless. However this was only one step in the security access required for such a system as it also operated on a series of passwords held by the account holder.

Whilst the greater part of his assets were within the Credit Suisse banking arena in one format or another, there were others around Europe that he used and often transferred funds in small quantities through several corporations and names providing liquidity usually in advance of any planned operation . . . or vacation. This was generally cash holdings or deposits as well as some safe deposit boxes; the investment strategy was usually overseen by Wilhelmson, at least for the finances that he was aware of.

"Do you have time for lunch Mr. Falcon?" asked Heinrich almost on cue and just as anticipated by his guest.

"Of course," retorted Falcon grinning, "I deliberately haven't eaten today anticipating your hospitality, but let's make it quick as I would like to get back to Italy this evening; and by the way, I don't have any money on me, is that a problem?"

Both men grinned at one another.

"I think the bank will stand you on this one Mr. Falcon. I shall have the secretary make the reservations and see where we can eat." A strange situation but the bistros are always so busy from eleven o'clock in the morning that even top Swiss Bankers need to call in advance to see if there is availability at the street side establishments. Needless to say they seldom were refused, however they could not afford the embarrassment of arriving with a multi million dollar value client only to be told by some university student working their holidays or off days, that there was no room at the inn.

Food was taken literally two hundred metres away from the bank so these guys tend not to get much exercise over lunch time. Traditional Swiss lunch washed down with a small local beer would suffice Falcon and no doubt upset his banker friend who could happily have indulged three or four courses complete with fine wines and brandy at the banks expense, all in the name of business development. They said their goodbyes and the Englishman was soon on his way. First stop the hotel to check out then the railway station and find suitable travel back to the Vinschgau in Northern Italy.

Within the hour Falcon was aboard the Cisalpino service train to Italy from Zurich central station. Had he not taken lunch he may have caught the earlier train which would have cut an hour off the journey time, nevertheless he was aboard now and it was still only mid afternoon, a little after three p.m., and he would be in Milan in around four and a half hours going via Stuttgart. Not a problem he could again relax as the carriages were rather comfortable, a continental benefit he found which far outweighed their UK counterparts. The carriages were well catered for, clean and tables around each set of seats. He chose a first class car for additional solitude more than anything else, as the second class is often filled with tourists, invariably students trying to see as much of Europe as they can on a budget during a gap year. Nothing against students but he was in his relax mode and did not savour the prospects of being smacked in the face with an over-packed rucksack amid jostling youngsters. The journey was extremely picturesque and although he had travelled the route many times before both by car and train, the natural beauty never ceased to impress him, reminded him so much of his own refuge back in Mals.

Once in Milan it was a quick dash for the internal journey which would take him in the darkness through the Italian countryside to Bolzano and Merano where he would again need to change for a local train up to Mals. It seemed a slog in truth as he could drive from Zurich to Mals when he needed to in around three to four hours, but unfortunately today would not be one of those days. Still, he reached Mals local railway station around eleven p.m. As the train left the station quietness once more descended on to the area and had he not known any better Falcon would have been very wary of his strange surroundings. The place was dark and quiet, yet strangely familiar. He was ready for a bath once again, travelling half the day he felt uncomfortable in his clothes. He knew that a walk outside the station would find the occasional taxi to take him to his castle of replenishment where time stood still for him, days were irrelevant and time meant even less. Here he would simply recuperate until the next assignment arrived. Soon he would be home and could take another good night's rest before completing the next and final phase of his chill out time . . .

Chapter 3

"Hallo liebling," the husky voice whispered seductively down the telephone in the best Austro-German accent that could be mustered by an Englishman.

"My Tony, My Tony where have you been? You did not call, you did not tell me where you were going, you did not tell me when you would be back ," shrieked Maria secretly overjoyed at hearing from her lover once again.

"Well, I am glad to hear your voice also . . ."

"Don't you think I will sit around and just wait for you Mr. Englishman. Do you know how many men try to date me? I sit here alone night after night not knowing . . ."

"I'm outside!" Falcon cut her off in full flow. She hadn't realised he was calling from his mobile. Maria dropped the telephone without terminating the call and ran to the front door of the house she shared with her parents and sister. Yanking it open with great gusto only to reveal her beau outside sporting a clean shaven appearance, dressed in smart casual twill jeans and sports jacket but more importantly presenting his young lady with a bunch of deep scarlet red roses. He knew she was instantly putty in his hands.

Maria was the epitome of Italian beauty. Her long flowing dark hair, skin which resembled velvet and hazel brown eyes adorned with the inevitably long and highly groomed eyelashes that could beckon a turtle from its shell. She was athletically slim being a ski instructor and around one hundred and sixty five centimetres tall. Somewhat younger than Falcon at twenty eight, they still made a handsome couple. During the week Maria was a school teacher specialising in, amongst other subjects, teaching English to the local children, and on weekends and holidays in the winter months, she worked out at the choice of ski schools on the numerous mountain resorts that surrounded the village. Her services were always in demand as she was especially good with child skiers.

Her first encounter with the Englishman was on the slopes where he accidentally, he always alleged, ran across her path and they both ended up heaped in the snow, neither resembling the accomplished skiers that they both were. Maria, now that she knows the man so well, always remained suspicious about his tale of the chance meeting, but still gives him the benefit of doubt. She is convinced that fate has dealt her this hand of kindness and deep down she has never been so happy. There's only one thing really missing from her life now . . . and she waits patiently, for now at least.

"When you going to marry my daughter?" cried Maria's mother from behind the door using the very little English she actually spoke, and this she specifically learned from her daughter, solely to apply additional pressure on her daughter's suitor.

"Her cousins are all married. Her little sister will probably marry first if you are not quick Mr. Tony. I want my grandchildren."

This was rapidly escalating and Falcon was hoping it would come to a head quickly. To hear the old woman complaining that the rest of the family would all be in wedlock before Maria was now repetitive and he was used to it, although it did make this macho man somewhat uncomfortable. However this was the first time she had blurted out the need for grandchildren.

"Mamma!" cried Maria in pretend rage, whilst inwardly enjoying watching Falcon writhe in discomfort. She secretly longed for her Tony to request her hand in marriage but up to now it was not happening, any time the subject even came near it was changed. So, she decided that time would reward her in the end, patience.

As Mamma Gassinger departed from the scene and Maria knew she was alone, no longer could she retain her composure as she threw herself at Falcon as though he had just returned from the dead. He savoured these reunions after a business trip and always knew a warm welcome would be waiting from his beloved Rita Maria Gassinger, the eldest of two children both of whom were still waiting to be married off. They were not indigenous Italian people, and were technically only Italian due to the redrawing of Country boundaries following the war when the Vinshgau was annexed with the area being handed to Italy. Nevertheless, the people of the former South Tyrol prefer to remember their roots as non Italians, as such the first language remains German with only little Italian being in use at all. However, there was an opportunity to be multi lingual, especially for the more recent generations who had the added benefit of formal education, Maria of course, extending that prowess into English as well.

"So Johnny Englishman, are you going to tell me all about your trip? Where was it this time you said, boring old England? How come you never call?"

"Maria, you know my rules, no distractions permitted when I am working. Work long and hard so I can get back here as soon as possible. No delays whatsoever to take my mind off the job, mistakes in my business are costly and I rely on reputation by word of mouth. I have to show one hundred percent commitment. Corporate security is big business these days and I am at the front of the game which allows me so much time here with you, because I am good . . . and you know it."

"Oh, you are good Mr. Fancy Pants Englishman, but can you remember how to make a girl happy?"

"I may need some reminding. I thought perhaps a stroll around the village and a bite to eat then per . . ."

She cut in sharply "I hope you are kidding, I have not seen you for three weeks now so I think other things take priority. I can cook dinner at your place . . . after, if you're still hungry then."

Falcon knew exactly what she meant, and was obviously pleased. As ever meticulous planning would pay dividends. He had already started a lamb casserole which was slowly cooking along with selecting a fine bottle of Chianti from his stocks which would be waiting for them for dinner on the

already laid table for two, when they returned to his villa.
But his master stroke would be the bottle of Bollinger which
was currently set in a large ice bucket beside his bed in the
master suite at the villa. Pretentious perhaps, even presump-
tive, but he knew the efforts would be well received even if
Maria showed initial surprise and took offence, it would be
very short lived, experience had taught him that.

"Ich gehen für den abend aus," shouted Maria from the
doorway as she advised the household she would be out
for the evening. Everyone knew what this really meant, she
would not be back at all that evening, however the Gassinger's
were modern folk and despite the Catholic background appreciated that they had to move with the times and although
the elders may not have liked the idea of young love outside
of wedlock, knew it was inevitable these days. Besides, the
whole family admired Falcon as despite his disappearances
and air of mystery, he certainly cared for Maria and everybody hoped that one day they would be married.

Falcon could not bear the silence whilst awaiting the re-
tort from within the house. Only a few seconds passed before Mamma Gassinger found something in her heart to
reply with. The response sent a shiver down Falcon's spine
and he hoped that the threats were nothing more than good
humour from Maria's mother. Falcon really knew she was
joking, or at least hoped she was as if not he would need to
heed mother Gassinger's warning about keeping his hands
off her daughter.

Maria chuckled as she closed the door and watched
Falcon's face as he tried to make sense of what he had just
heard.

"She is joking, yes?" he asked, as they walked hand in
hand down the hill from Maria's house towards Falcon's
waiting car.

"What do you think superman, has mamma got you worried? Put it this way, if you do keep your hands off me tonight I will tell her you didn't . . ."

With that, it was all systems go and he poured Maria into the fiery red Alfa Romeo and sped back towards his own villa where a romantic evening for two would ensue. Maria was as ever impressed but not surprised at Falcon's preparation. The table was set for the job at hand ready for immediate dining should the diners so choose. The aroma of fresh casserole warmed the air of the rustic kitchen as they entered the villa, but both had only one thought on their mind at this stage so it was straight to the bedroom.

Following several hours of heated passion, interspersed with regular goblets of Bollinger, the two lovers lay in the four poster bed covered with a simple cotton sheet. It may be cold outside but internally the under floor heating in the villa was extremely efficient at keeping the whole place at a very pleasant temperature. Falcon cradled Maria in his arms and although he couldn't say so to her face at this time, he believed he couldn't live without her. He longed for a different life where he could spend lazy days and nights just with her, settle down and do what normal people do, but with his profession that was not that easily achieved.

He could hear her quietly and softly breathing as she lay asleep in his arms, exhausted but smiling and clearly content. Not that he had the gumption to rate himself as a Casanova, but there was something about this pairing that ticked all the right boxes. They were made for each other and they both knew it. It was now down to Falcon to decide when and how he could change his lifestyle. They both lay motionless for several hours whilst Falcon simply admired the view of the beauty in his arms. When Maria stirred he was already wide awake and had been now for several hours, they once again began their courtship rituals and started a repeat of the previous evenings athletics, although somewhat toned down now. The casserole would have to wait for another day.

Breakfast was taken in the shelter of the orangery on the North side of the villa. This still allowed heat from the low winter sun to penetrate the room continuing the cosy feel that the rest of the house gets from the heating system. The orangery was essentially a glorified deck extension, a veranda surrounded by glass and a solid wooden floor, so it could be contained in the winter yet doors opened in the summer. It did however allow one to gaze in wonder at nature's spectacle which greeted occupants of this property in almost every direction they looked. It was utopia for Falcon, no question about it, and with Maria by his side the house had a whole new feel. It was once again a home.

Falcon had decided that a simple continental breakfast with some good Italian coffee was required and then down to discussions on the order of the day. All trivia nothing really pressing although he was keen for the snows to be prepared on the mountains so he could get some over due skiing in. The mountains of Mals were turning white early this year although the slopes had not yet been groomed and opened for business as there had not been a sufficient snow covering. However another substantial covering overnight on the mountains meant that the time had to be near. Snow had not made its way to the village as yet as it was a couple of hundred metres below the visible snow line, but that was not necessarily all bad. Snow on the mountains however was good. Falcon persuaded Maria that she should escort him on the mountain to do some off piste skiing. This was always invigorating although not as enjoyable for Falcon as on piste skiing where he could simply hurtle down the mountain releasing his tensions through his speed. Luckily he was an accomplished skier because at the speeds he liked to travel the more difficult black runs could prove not very conducive to his health should he have a mishap. Reluctantly Maria agreed to the choice of activity for the day, her first day with her man for some time and whilst she just wanted to be with him closely for the time being, it was not quite what she had hoped for. Still, they would be together so they set about getting prepared for the day.

Maria decided she would take a shower as Falcon finished his morning coffee admiring the views and planning his coming challenge when the telephone rang. Not an unusual event per say, however, very few people had the number for Falcon at this residence as this was his fixed line, not his mobile. In fact, he could not think who would have the number as it was only used as an emergency line out when weather or climatic conditions, or system failure, prevented use of cellular phones in the high mountain areas. He also was not sure who would know he was here.

He reticently lifted the receiver slowly to his ear and waited. He decided not to speak simply to listen. There was traffic noise in the background drifting through the earpiece of the receiver yet for several seconds there was nothing else. He tried to drown out Maria's singing, lovely as it was, meandering out of the bathroom and resonating around the villa as he attempted to focus on the mystery caller. Eventually the silence broke and the stranger spoke.

"Mr. Falconer?" the voice asked.

This in itself was highly unusual as this name was one he thought would be reserved for judicial and ecclesiastical use only and perhaps on his headstone if he had no say in the matter when the time came. He had shortened it many years ago and only went by that name these days, even to the extent that his official documents also showed the same. A feat achieved by formally changing his name early in his adult life essentially as a result of going by that reduced name throughout his school life, a version which he preferred to the original. Nobody knew that name, or so he thought.

Falcon froze whilst thoughts were spinning around his mind at seemingly light speed, bouncing from one side of the brain to the other. Who the hell can this be? Puzzled, he remained in silence and after almost ten seconds it came at him again.

"Mr. Falconer, my associates and I would like to meet with yourself and discuss a consultancy contract we would like you to consider."

Falcon regained his composure somewhat.

"I am sorry but I think you may have the wrong number." He didn't really expect this to get his new stalker off his case but just in case it was a million to one unfortunate incident, denial is always a good place to start, even when you seem banged to rights. The Englishman began to lose his composure. His mystery caller was invariably calling from a pay phone due to the traffic noise in the background, a cell phone user could easily have found somewhere quieter to discuss business. The accent was part French but he could not place outright the origins of the caller, although no doubt if he was as skilled as Falconer himself, then he could mislead people easily in that regard with being multi lingual. He began to feel beads of sweat build up on his forehead and his hands felt somewhat clammy. This was unusual for the assassin as his planning and prediction of what might happen had generally saved him from being under such pressure. The last time he felt this way was several years ago back in Africa and that was an experience he did not wish to repeat.

"Mr. Falconer, we simply wish to discuss a transaction that may be of interest to you, my associates are most insistent that they speak with you in person, your reputation precedes you."

Falcon replied, this time with greater emphasis and purpose, "I am sorry but you appear to have the wrong number, good day." He then replaced the receiver and stared at the phone for a short while as though anticipating it bursting back into life. Some animate object leering across the room after him! Now he was on edge which was not the start to the day he had planned.

Maria came out of the bathroom, a trail of hot steam escaped from the room she had just exited as the door opened and she glided into the living room sporting a heavy white towel that was just big enough to retain her dignity, but only just. Yet she enjoyed parading around in front of her man in such a glamorous and seductive manner, though today he never flinched. He looked at Maria and stood rigidly still near to the telephone.

"Something wrong darling?" she asked, somewhat surprised at his unusual lack of immediate attention.

"No, just some crazy kid with the wrong number," was the best he could come up with when put under the spotlight.

He lifted the telephone receiver and placed it back down on the table just in case the crazy caller decided to have another go. He decided to go and get himself ready for the day away from the villa, especially now as he wanted to get away from the telephone as quickly as he could. He brushed past Maria towards the bathroom and gave her a playful squeeze and quick peck on the cheek as he passed; she knew there was something on his mind. This was his world, he had many things that preyed upon his mind he never divulged to Maria but she always could tell when he was troubled, although today would not need the input of a rocket scientist to help with that diagnosis. For now skiing was on the menu, this is one area where she knew he could relax and perhaps as the day unfolded he would let her into his world and recount whatever had happened that morning to put him on edge so much.

He stood in the shower for what seemed an eternity, hot water cascading down his face yet he was motionless. As though he were cleansing his mind of evil spirits with the shower head pounds water constantly against the top of his skull, water exploding into a fine mist. What the hell has just happened here, he just couldn't get his mind around it? He decided that he must act as if nothing has happened and see if they tried to contact him again. Now what better way to cleanse the soul than some fresh mountain powder, pondered the bemused Englishman?

He snapped out of his trance and swiftly set about getting on with the day's skiing. Very quickly he was donned in multi layers of thermal wear to keep out the chill and retrieved his favourite blue and white Spyder ski jacket from the closet. Although not officially together, Maria also had a fairly extensive wardrobe at the villa including her own ski wear, or at least most of it. They both possessed multiple pairs of skis, one for every occasion an onlooker would say. Today would be off piste so no good for carvers so they took the Rossignol skis they each owned for powder skiing although Falcon's were a little longer than Maria's and set off to the mountain.

The mountain of Watles was chosen as the day's destination, simply because it was the closest of his preferred haunts to the villa and Falcon was keen to get stuck in as soon as possible. As the season was not officially started, the cable cars would not go all the way to the top of the piste but only to the first staging post. This was still at two thousand three hundred metres, so sufficiently high to afford a substantial length of powder down to the snowline, if they could get that far down.

They stacked their equipment into the Alfa with the skis needing to be placed in the ski rack on the roof and were very quickly off. Down and across the valley they trekked in their vehicle ready for the ascent on the opposite side. There was not much traffic going up the hill today which was in a way a good sign, the hills should be peaceful but hopefully still accessible. The road took them past the near nine hundred year old Benedictine Monastery, Marienberg Abbey, the highest such building in Europe, as they bore a sharp left and continued up the hill before eventually arriving at the foot of the ski runs after a twisting and turning ascent.

They were in luck as the cable car was running up to the first level. The joy and relief at seeing the cars in motion and the chance to indulge in one of his favourite passions took Falcon's mind momentarily away from his morning mystery caller which had most definitely unnerved him, placing him in unfamiliar territory. Maria grabbed his arm and pulled him towards the cable cars. There was no need to buy lift passes as the couple were two of the many regular users of these slopes who annually purchased their season tickets. They stood in front of the four seat ski lift car, only the two of them, so they both took centre seats for balance. The chair scooped them up like children in their mother's arms and whisked their feet off the ground in one sweeping movement. Soon their legs were dangling free and the fresh snow was beneath them just beckoning Falcon to try his luck today. Maria hugged her beau once again showing her affection for the man she dearly loved, but something was still not boding well with him, which to her was very evident. Ever since the morning he had hardly spoken yet despite asking for a second time on the chair lift, he assured her that all was fine and it was probably just work sub consciously playing on his mind. She was assured he was in need of a rest and there was nothing else to worry about. She squeezed his hand and he playfully returned the compliment reassuring Maria that at least he was still attentive to her presence, which helped ease the concerns a little.

On reaching the top Maria pushed away from the lift and teasingly squealed, "Come on Englishman, see if you can keep up with me."

At which point she veered left down a short slope then a long run towards the main mountain piste, although not yet fully groomed they were still appealing. Nothing like a challenge thought Falcon and he set of in pursuit of his quarry, albeit a very experienced one. She was a better skier than he although he was no slouch. Yet Maria was born skiing and taught it as a secondary profession so he would struggle to surpass her in technique, although he did have the advantage in the fearless department. Where Falcon excelled was speed, this he never feared. Problem was speed without technique could be dangerous and Maria was repeatedly telling him to slow down and work more on technique, but the lure of speed was still too great. He loved Maria and enjoyed the chase down the mountain. The unfinished snows meant that it was sometimes hard work and very quickly perspiration was forming all over the body to the extent of it being uncomfortable; yet the exhilaration of chasing Maria down the slopes overcame the discomfort for the Englishman. Powder was brushing past their faces as they turned and twisted in snows which at times came up to their knees, jumping and twisting all the time. Stopping would mean very hard work to get started again so onwards they went. Falcon just could not catch Maria and she regularly turned and teased her pursuer shouting words of ridicule at his lame attempt to catch up. As much as he considered himself a speed skier, powder skiing did not lend itself to such pursuits, he just had to work hard at staying upright. Soon he would be on the groomed slopes of the piste as the season really kicked in; then he would be able to more readily satisfy his adrenalin addiction.

At the bottom Maria was already removing her skis when Falcon arrived.

"So, where have you been sugar?" she quizzed.

"Oh you're so funny. You got a head start on me what do you expect?" The pair embraced and laughed just like young lovers without a care in the world.

"Shall we go again or have you had enough already?" she again teased sporting a wide grin which revealed her perfectly formed and glistening teeth.

"I need to get some clothes off first"

"Is that all you think about? Try and clear your mind just for a few hours," she retorted; only further teasing the Englishman as she knew full well what he was intimating, but she enjoyed the playful banter.

"Oh we're in fine form today. Let's take the chair back up and get a coffee . . . or brandy."

Again they jumped on the ski lift and headed to the restaurant at the top of the run. Once inside, the heat impact was akin to opening an oven door. Not that it was that hot but with the differential from outside as well as being wrapped in numerous thermal layers of protection, it was like being the traditional Christmas Turkey on its last ever journey before being consumed by a higher order of the food chain. They chose a table and started to loosen some clothing. Maria purchased a couple of cappuccinos and they sat opposite one another in silence warming their hands around the cups.

They quietly gazed at one another for a few seconds when Maria asked, "Are you sure you're okay to continue today? Maybe we should go home and rest, you must be quite tired from the last few weeks, I'm sure you don't look after yourself properly when I am not around. You need to recharge and chill out. Maybe I can assist you with a massage in front of the fire when we get back."

"Now you're talking girl," he replied, revealing just how wide he could smile.

"No, really I am fine, all charged up and ready to spend some quality time with you; business can wait a few days. So if I am fine . . ." he paused for a couple of seconds as she waited with anticipation for him to finish, ". . . is the offer of the massage still on?"

He was caught a playful glancing blow to the side of the head with the back of a ski glove and they both burst into quiet chuckles and again their hands met across the table.

The pair were still giggling like school children when Flavio, one of Maria's colleagues from the Ski School, approached their table.

"Guten tag Maria, Tony, how are you both today?"

Flavio was another local boy born in the valley who lived for skiing in the winter. Summer times were as with most young men in the valley, spent helping the family with their farms and small holdings. It was a way of life and accepted by the majority, summer was a means of survival until the tourists hit town. Flavio was a little different, he was saving to push himself through medical school so had been a ski teacher in one form or another since he was around fourteen years of age and was saving as much as he could from his earnings for his college career. He was nineteen now and figured one more season would provide him sufficient cash flow to make the leap, topped up with vacation teaching back on the mountain. He was over one hundred and eighty centimetres in height and athletically built as would be expected with farming and skiing, although his complexion was somewhat paler than many of his contemporaries within the valley. For some reason he just did not tan as much as the others and when over exposed to the UV rays on the snowy slopes had to take additional precautions not to turn red rather than golden brown. This never bothered him though.

"Some guy brought this to the ski school office. Said it was a bit of a joke for you both. He asked if any of us knew Tony which of course we all do, so he asked us to give you this envelope. Seemed a bit strange but he assured us you would see the funny side then away he went. Sorry I did not bring it across earlier but we were making preparations for this year's classes. We believe the pistes will be open for business next week so I have scheduled you in as usual Maria for the weekends for now, hope that is okay?"

Maria politely nodded her approval as Flavio handed a small brown envelope to Tony, no larger than an A5 size.

Falcon reached out and gingerly accepted the envelope from the Italian instructor. He was somewhat reticent about accepting the package, however he knew he had to, even though he feared it would invariably only generate further personal unrest. This was again adding further anguish to the uncomfortable start already experienced earlier in the day. This was no ordinary day and certainly not the restful break he was looking for.

"Come on Tony, what is it? Get it opened," she begged.

Falcon's insides were turning over and he hoped he was hiding his inner panic as he slowly opened the manila envelope. As he opened it he peered inside, a single sheet only. He reticently slid his hand inside the envelope and pulled out the paper. It appeared blank as it slid from its housing.

"It's a photograph Tony!" exclaimed Maria.

Falcon turned over the paper to reveal a picture of him and Maria taken only the day before showing the pair entering Falcon's villa arm in arm, clearly very happy. Now he was really internally panicking. There was another message here, this combined with the call that morning meant that someone was stalking him . . . but for what purpose . . . surely not a job? This was not the way he did business. Was it an old client catching up with him, maybe to tie up some loose ends? Could it be associates of one of his former marks finally catching up with him with revenge in mind? Falcon's mind was racing yet he had done nothing out of the ordinary that he was aware of. He followed a strict regime of covering his backside wherever he went, or so he thought. His work was secured through very select channels only so there should be no seepage of information from those sources, they were very few and to date had been very efficient and discrete. All missions had gone as planned so surely a client could not be dissatisfied. After all, they had all paid their dues as agreed; some even donated additional unplanned bonuses showing their satisfaction at the services rendered. A million thoughts bounced about his head but none could make sense. Who . . . Why? It was a mystery that he felt sure would reveal itself in the not too distant future. A prospect he was not savouring as he felt his stomach tighten. How could he explain this? He looked again in the envelope, nothing else in there. No note, no writing on the envelope save for the words, *A Falconer*. There was nothing scribed on the photograph itself. "Hey Tony, that's us. That is a lovely picture, how did you get that taken? How sweet, you are always full of surprises."

She lunged across the table and pecked him on the cheek but he never flinched. Now he was showing clear concern just by his lack of response. Maria took the picture from his clenched hand and slumped back in the wooden benches around the restaurant tables, cushioning her movements with several layers of clothing and coats spread across the seats. She just looked in admiration at the inopportune photo and was convinced it was a gesture on her man's part, blissfully unaware of the reality behind the sinister implications of the picture.

Falcon would have to play on this innocence for a little while whilst he planned his way out of this predicament, the problem being that at this time he had no idea what his predicament actually was.

"So who has done this Tony?" she playfully asked.

"I was about to ask you the same question," he replied. "I never thought you could be this sneaky!" Falcon decided that he would adopt a playful strategy and string Maria along for a while. He knew she would be convinced he'd arranged the picture, so for now this could work to his advantage.

She laughed at the suggestion and wagged her index finger at him shaking her head and laughing aloud. "You crazy, crazy Englishman. I need to keep an eye on you."

Falcon, half relieved that at least the immediate pressure was off him, could divert his inner thoughts to getting to the head of this problem. He was in a zone of his own as Maria and Flavio discussed the forthcoming ski season somewhere in the background. Falcon joined in their conversation quizzing the pair on what they thought of the forthcoming season, anything to get them focused on something other than the photograph he thought. Hopefully Maria could be kept at bay.

Flavio said his farewells to the couple as he needed to get back to organising the staff cover for the ski school, as he would have a busy schedule for the next week himself getting his own house in order. As he left the table, Falcon jumped up and called after him but rather than let Flavio return to the table he pursued him across the restaurant. He did not want this discussion in front of Maria.

"Who left the picture, do you know?"

"I had never seen the guy before Tony, why?"

"Oh, just wondering who would play such a joke, maybe one of my army pals. I am expecting to meet up with a couple of them in the next few weeks but hadn't expected them so soon. No worries, I think I know who it must have been, just could have done with a description so maybe I could turn it around on them. You know, let him know I knew all along; describe his movements and what he was wearing. Never mind, just a joke. Some guys never grow up . . . do we?" Falcon clearly trying his best to play down the importance of the picture

"Sorry Tony, the guy was well wrapped up in his ski gear, nothing out of the ordinary. Even kept his glasses on when he was in the office. I didn't see it as important. I will ask the guys whether they saw him anywhere else but he did shoot out of the office, said he didn't want you to see him just yet. He did have an Italian accent though, if that helps."

"Ah well, not to worry. Don't tell Maria about this discussion, I want it to be a surprise if they turn up. She's never met any of my old army buddies."

"Secret's safe with me. See you later Tony, enjoy the snow before the crowds get here. Today it's still your mountain, next week you will have to share," laughed the instructor as he walked away with a casual wave back to his office.

Falcon returned to the table where Maria was sitting, still puzzled at his sudden shooting up from the table.

"So what are you boys plotting?"

"Nothing really, I was just wondering whether you would be working every weekend or if we can arrange for some time off for you so we can maybe take a trip away for a couple of days some time soon."

Maria smiled lovingly across the table and said nothing; she knew it wasn't necessary to let her feelings be shown. Knowing that her man was always on the look out for her welfare was a comforting feeling for sure.

"Are you ready to ski back down?" asked Maria keenly, after all it was her first skiing experience of the season also.

"One more trip, then I would like to get you home I think," replied Falcon slowly and deliberately.

His reasons were different to what Maria expected, although he never let on. Why should he, the important factor was to get her off the mountain, at least he could feel more secure in his villa. There was no telling who was out there . . . still watching.

They donned their gear and set off down the mountain. This time together for reasons Falcon kept to himself but Maria enjoyed the close company for the descent. They followed a very similar route to their last run although tried for long runs of virgin snow wherever possible. Once at the bottom they quickly extracted themselves from skis and boots. The sudden surge of freedom of foot after the unwieldy and unnaturally fitting ski boots were removed was as good as jumping into a hot soap filled steaming bath tub. Ski boots were very practical for the purpose, ergonomically designed

and great feats of engineering, but even for the more seasoned skier they were cumbersome and unnatural. Walking
in them, whilst maintaining dignity and verticality, was an
achievement in itself. So now, freedom of the limbs once
again and they packed the vehicle and returned to the villa.

Once home the skiing equipment was swiftly despatched
to the warm rear vestibule where they could all thaw at room
temperature and be ready for the next session at short notice.
Falcon cleared the vehicle on his own and insisted Maria
went inside and prepared coffee. This gave him the opportunity to scan the surroundings without question for anything
out of the ordinary. Left and right he scoured from behind
the car, nothing unusual. He peered into the woods behind
the villa. They were fairly dense and should provide cover to
even the most inept surveillance operation, so without actually venturing up there, which would in itself raise questions
from the house, there was little else he could do. At least
the fact that the villa was approachable by road by one way
only afforded an element of seclusion and with it improved
safety, although there was always the option to come cross
country.

He was sure somebody somewhere was watching. The
photograph bore testament to that, but why? This was plagu-
ing Falcon's mind like nothing else had ever done so. Impli-
cating Maria now was a grave concern; nothing must happen to her, at any cost. This was something he could never
anticipate recovering from and he would be prepared to die
to ensure her safety. Such was his love for the Italian goddess. After repeated scans revealed nothing, he walked tenta-
tively to his post box to see whether any deliveries had been
made. He rarely received mail at this address as he often had
correspondence stored or even sent to the bank in Zurich.
However, today something urged him to check his mail box.
Something he could not explain.

He opened the box to reveal another envelope and a card.
The envelope was another brown manila one similar to that
received on the mountain a couple of hours earlier but this

one was a little larger. The card was a simple one as issued by the Italian post office. They had tried to deliver a package to his address earlier that afternoon but of course nobody was there to sign for it. The card simply stated that it could be collected from the local post office in the village but he would need a form of identity. A parcel, how strange he thought. He was not expecting one but at the same time it could be anything. Maybe something as banal as junk mail samples, whatever it was he could not imagine. However the concern right now was the envelope, two in one day. Again, he threw a swift glance all around. Who is watching? What the hell is happening here?

When he thought he was alone, he tore open the envelope whilst still outside in the open. Oh no, more photographs. He couldn't dare to think what these could show now. No thinking or planning could have prepared him for what he saw. No amount of thinking outside the box. This was a nightmare unfolding before his very eyes, and he was starring in it. He laid out four different photographs recently taken of him in the UK. These were no ordinary run of the mill pictures, they were not portraits. No, these were pictures of Falcon at work.

One picture showed him leaving the farm house he had rented, the date stamp on the bottom right hand side of the picture clearly confirming that. The hire car was also clearly visible along with its registration. The second picture showed him tampering with the crash barrier on the morning of the accident. The third showed him sat in the woods above the crash site only a couple of minutes prior to the impact and the fourth clearly showed him clearing away debris from the roadside and kicking it over the edge of the precipice behind the smashed up Daimler and its two deceased occupants. Someone had betrayed him. Events had now taken a turn for the worse. Now the English stalwart knew he had a fight on his hands, but did not know with whom. The package at the post office could not now be a coincidence and as much as he regretted pursuing it, he knew he needed to see what its contents were, sooner rather than later.

He folded the photographs back into the envelope and returned the envelope to the mailbox. He didn't really need them for now and certainly didn't want Maria to be exposed to them. That would only lead to inevitable further questioning and an irretrievable situation for sure. She would never check the mail box so they were secure there for now. He needed to get to the post office before it closed, but he needed to go alone.

Falcon ventured into the house. It felt strange to act as though everything was in order knowing what he did. Yet for her sake, he couldn't drag Maria into this. Maria suggested that she would prepare dinner; a perfectly good and unused casserole from the previous evening was still waiting to be devoured. Falcon suggested she organise dinner whilst he quickly called to the village for fresh bread. Not an essential today, but the best excuse he could find for getting away right now.

Off he shot on foot to the village, walking briskly, very quickly creating cool beads of sweat on his forehead. The result of a little exertion mixed more with a substantial amount of stress. He never liked loose ends and always satisfied his clients, but somebody had something in store for him. Why not simply send the pictures to the authorities, why the charade? Would this be a prolonged campaign against him, wanting him to suffer rather than simply wipe him out? There were far too many questions without a hint of the answers to any of them. It will be one step at a time until his foe revealed himself, only then could he formulate any sort of defence, or if necessary . . . counter attack.

The late afternoon sun was setting behind the Alps and the far side of the valley was already in darkness and street lights clearly visible in the distant villages. The coolness in the air was being exaggerated as the sun lowered only compounding his generation of perspiration. Briskly he walked on to the post office, arriving only about ten minutes before it was due to close. The shop was hardly occupied with only a couple of local villagers there, not really purchasing anything, the place being more of a social meeting place for many of the village elders than anything else. As he entered the counter clerks attention was immediately diverted to Falcon. The local conversation stopped as the English alien arrived. The old adage of the piano player ceasing playing his tune in the old time western movies sprang to mind as the stranger entered the saloon. Yet he was no new comer to the village but his life of semi seclusion and privacy still leant itself to having him cast as the outsider. This was a small problem as far as he was concerned; his money was as good as anybody's and all trades were welcome of it. He was always befriended at the restaurants and cafés and was well respected with his selected circle of local courtiers, which was sufficient for him to get by comfortably.

He presented his card to the clerk who studied it just as a forensic scientist would examine a clue at a crime scene. There must be finger prints on here somewhere . . . In truth, the card represented only one thing, a parcel which could not be delivered. How many parcels was the post office holding awaiting collection . . . only one: The one for Mr. Anthony Falconer of Villa *Giardino Rosa*. Everybody in the post office knew the Englishman at least by sight if not in person, but Falcon still took the liberty of presenting his Italian driving licence which showed his address, to avoid lengthy conversation and get out of the establishment as soon as possible.

The clerk handed over the package he was due. It was a neatly wrapped cardboard box with dimensions approximately twenty centimetres square and not more than ten high. No great weight to it and Falcon's name and address printed on the box; no hand writing, merely a crisp and clean computer printed label, untraceable. He took the package outside looking un-interested although internally very anxious to discover the contents. As the door was still closing behind him, the conversations inside were clearly heard recommencing. God knows what the topic of discussion was, but he never cared. What was in the package? That was the burning question now.

Should he open it back at home? Not really the best idea when he had no clue to the contents. If it was explosive . . . that sudden thought flashed across his tiring and aching brain, but he quickly erased this option. There would be plenty of opportunity to eliminate him, the stalking alone had shown that, so why go to the trouble of tracking his home down and sending a parcel bomb. No, it was something else and not likely to kill him . . . at least not yet.

He started unravelling the brown tape that sealed the edges of the box releasing one flap of the box sufficiently to allow him to peer into the box. It was a cell phone. A cell phone! He wasn't expecting one, he had not requested one and was quite happy with the one he had. There was no documentation with the phone whatsoever. He stumbled along the cobbled streets, passing local pedestrians without even a glance; they were not really there in Falcon's world at this moment. He just stared at the phone in the box, not removing it from its cocoon as there was so much mystery still surrounding its existence. He ambled back towards his home still in a distant world; puzzled, confused and apprehensive beyond his wildest nightmares. Once again thoughts of his escape from Africa flashed across his mind. He had hoped that was his last real nightmare but a new one was unravelling again many years on.

Suddenly the cell phone burst into life. Falcon was clearly not expecting this as he threw the box out of shear fright as the shrill ring tone came bounding out of the cardboard tomb that encased it. His heart was racing like never before and visibly shaking from head to toe as he scampered on the ground to gather up the box, still ringing from within. The colour drained from his features and he felt the chill of death upon him. He gathered himself and still shuddering took the phone from the box with his trembling hands. The luminescent LCD display was flashing with the message *visitatore sconosciuto* (unknown caller). The phone kept on ringing for what seemed an eternity; eventually Falcon depressed the green answer key and slowly raised the phone to his ear.

A short pause ensued from both caller and receiver, however both parties were aware of the other as breathing could clearly be heard by each. Eventually the silence was broken by the caller:

"Buona sera, Signore Falconer." Falcon recognised immediately the voice from earlier in the day.

"We have found it very difficult to retain your attention, can I take it we have now done so, or do we need to move to the next level of attention seeking? She is very pretty isn't she, Maria?"

"You bastards, don't you even think about going anywhere near her or I swear I will kill you. You have no idea . . . ."

"Anthony, please calm down," interrupted the caller. "We have no desire to involve Maria or anybody else into this matter. We simply want to talk to you but you don't want to listen. So we had to find a way to get you to listen. And here you are . . . listening."

"So what do you want?" growled the Englishman. Falcon was now regaining some of his composure and at least starting to think with a little more clarity. He was still slowly walking towards the house as the conversation went on.

"My associates and I would like to meet with you to discuss a proposition. We have a project that requires your special services, and of course you will be handsomely rewarded."

"What makes you think I am the man you are looking for?"

It suddenly dawned on Falcon that somebody was watching him even now. Either they were the ones calling him or, somebody had tipped off the caller that he now had the phone; it surely couldn't be coincidence that it rang right now. He glanced around himself in all directions but could see nothing out of the ordinary. Who could he trust anyway? If anybody was on a mobile phone or even a pay phone would that be the caller? He just had no idea, everybody was under suspicion. This was a more daunting prospect than the fact that he had been betrayed.

"Mr. Falconer, the time for games has passed. I trust the photographs tell you that. So let's get on with business so we can all go our separate ways sooner rather than later."

The English assassin was used to negotiating from a position of strength; he could usually pick and chose contracts. This was unfamiliar territory, somebody else was calling the shots and he didn't like it. For now he could do nothing about it. He had to play the game out to a conclusion, despite knowing the path would be fraught with dangers.

"Alright; where and when? And the where needs to be away from here."

"No problem Mr. Falconer, you keep the phone handy, we will be in touch later this evening. Now you get home to that girl of yours . . . and give her a hug from me."

The line went dead. The low life had cut off Falcon before he could even reply. He was enraged at the prospect of Maria being involved in this but for now could not keep her out until he met with the hunters. He quickened his pace to get home.

He entered the villa, a freshly brewed coffee aroma lingered along with the casserole he had prepared the night before, and still seemingly as fresh as when it was first made.

"Hey Tony, no bread?" commented Maria as he entered the kitchen.

Christ he thought, he had to be thinking on the run every time he opened his mouth from now on and he told her that the baker had very little left that he was interested in so would go back out in the morning for fresh supplies.

"What's that, a new telephone? Where is your usual Nokia?"

"Oh no, this is just the old one I use for work calls, rather than clutter up my personal phone. You know me, try and keep work and social apart don't really want our time interrupting do we. I had a bit of a problem on the last job so gave them this number just in case, big client so can't really leave them in the lurch if they get any problems over the next few days, then I'll switch it off and the times all ours. I know you youngsters won't see it as much of a fashion statement but at least it makes and takes calls, which is all I want for work."

Maria returned to the stove and began serving dinner. They again sat in the orangery and gazed out over the valley now swathed in total darkness as they ate. The luminosity from the different villages lighting danced around the darkened valley like fireflies or distant twinkling stars. The conversation was limited until finally Maria spoke.

"Tony, I can see you have a problem somewhere, can I help you with anything . . . anything at all? I don't like to see you this way. Is it that work problem; is it worse than you are telling me?"

"Sadly honey, I may need to go back to work very shortly, I'm just waiting for a call to see what needs to be done. I am sorry to have to bale out so soon but I'll be as quick as possible, promise. Do not want to waste all that good snow do we and let the foreigners get the best out of it before we do. I was trying to sort it out on the phone and not interfere with you."

"Don't worry about me. I know you have to work Tony; I am back at school tomorrow so really there's no problem. Please tell me everything is alright though, I do worry when I see you like this. You're not my Tony when you are like this. Please give me a call though if you have to go away, just let me know everything is fine. I'm sure you will sort everything out and be back before you know it."

Falcon smiled at the innocence sat across the small table from him, little did she know what a mess he was potentially in, and moreover what danger he worried he had placed her in, simply by association. He was sure he needed to take the problem out of Mals, which was the only aspect of any plan he had contrived so far.

The couple were laying in each others arms gazing out across the valley, lights dimly lit inside their villa in a reclusive world of their own. This was the sort of relaxation he enjoyed and regularly longed for with Maria, but he could not enjoy it at the moment although he tried not to let it show. It was just before eight o'clock in the evening when the old mobile again burst into life. Falcon shot bolt upright jarring Maria's neck as he did so. She yelped as he apologised profusely, rubbing her neck as he left her for the cell phone. His heart once again racing, he picked up the phone. Unknown caller again displayed on the screen. Of course this was them, who else could it be.

He quietly answered the cell phone, without manners—well why should he, as he walked towards the rear of the property, hoping to keep the entire conversation out of earshot of Maria.

"Hello" he grunted in a hushed voice.

"Mr. Falconer, I trust we have not disturbed you."

"Strangely enough you have, but I guess you already know that. So let's just get on with this shit and I can get you out of my life"

"Ah, a straight talking man of action. We like that. However Mr. Falconer, rashness and boldness are not necessarily the traits we need to employ in the circumstances, so please just remain composed and we can make this as painless as possible for everybody."

"Your call, when do we meet?" he sighed, trying to hide his frustration and disgust at the intrusion.

"My associates would like to meet you tomorrow, let's say in Venice around midday."

"Venice? Anywhere in particular, I mean it's a big place, unless of course you want your man to pick me up on his way and we can go together."

"Nice try, no just get the centre of Venice and make sure you take the phone. We shall call you again nearer the time. Get yourself a coffee somewhere near the Piazza San Marco. Take the tourist trail until we call, relax and chill out a little, don't worry we shall meet in a public place."

"I take it that's for your security rather than mine," Falcon rallied back.

"Oh come on Tony, if we wanted you dead we would not be having this conversation would we? Think about it. Now, let's just get down to business and we can all profit from it, then you get back on with your life, we shall never cross paths again. You never know, you may even like working with us . . ."

"Don't hold your breath on that one my friend."

"See we are already friends, so until tomorrow Mr. Falconer, I suggest you get yourself a good night's sleep."

Once again the mystery caller cut the conversation and the line went dead.

He ambled back into the main body of the house where Maria was still lounging where he had left her. She never quizzed him on anything on his return except to say, "I guess that was the call you were expecting. So when are you off?"

"Tomorrow morning", he replied. "I am just not sure yet for how long I shall be gone."

Maria shrugged her shoulders and gave Falcon a gentle comforting smile. Maria climbed up from her sofa and slowly headed towards the Englishman.

"I guess we'd better get an early night then," she said, as she passed him with a playful slap on the behind as she burst into a trot for the bedroom.

Chapter 4

The following morning the two lovers rose early. She needed to get back to the family home to get ready the coming week's classes. When they had both finished breakfast and dressed, Falcon insisted that he take Maria home in the Alfa rather than let her walk. It was only two minutes in the car or twenty on foot, but he didn't really want her alone at this time. He still had no idea who was watching. They kissed one another farewell and hugged for several minutes outside Maria's family home. He promised he would be in touch during the week and again that he would be back as soon as possible.

Once she was safely within the home, he jumped back into the car and threw it back down the narrow Italian lanes to his villa. Now he could prepare himself for the day's task, or at least the best he could, as he was about to venture into the unknown. He hurried back into the villa and immediately descended the cellar steps. This was not an overly large cellar for a villa but did comprise a couple of separate rooms. This is where the quality wines were kept, not by the barrel but there were a couple of hundred bottles of quality wines, many expensive vintages which were primarily an investment but also some nice wines for drinking now, even if a trifle more expensive than the run of the mill table wines. He made no secret of his passion for wines and Maria never questioned him on their cost or value. In fact Maria never questioned him about anything much, he was lucky that way.

He was not in the cellar today for wine; that pleasure would have to wait. He went to one corner of the cellar where he had storage boxes, wooden crates and even a couple of bicycles and other sporting equipment. The cellar was a clean room, not a dusty dank and damp room, allowing many things including clothing could be stored securely. But he was here now for something in particular. There was a large cupboard in the cellar where many miscellaneous items were stored, predominantly older skiing equipment. Adjacent to it was a gun cabinet where he legally had, under lock and key, a couple of shot guns and a hunting rifle, all of which were certified and registered with the authorities. However, it was what lay behind the cabinet that was of more interest. He levered the free standing cabinet away from the wall to reveal a small wall safe built into the hefty stonework of the basement. He keyed in his six digit code number to open the safe and yanked open the door. This was a safe no bigger than a typical microwave oven but its contents opened up another life for Falcon. This is where he stored some additional identities, ready cash, keys for safety deposit boxes at various depositories around Europe and most importantly right now, a couple of hand guns with no serial numbers and virtually untraceable. Usually weapons were either disposed of after a job or returned to other boxes for safe keeping, but these were for personal protection should an eventuality such as this arise. This would be the first time he has had to remove the hardware from the safe for any purpose other than routine maintenance.

His military days had given him a liking for the Colt 45 automatic handgun. This always proved a reliable weapon, plenty of punch and very handy for close quarter combat with rapid reload abilities and it had stood the test of time through various upgrades. However it didn't really lend itself to discrete placement within the person if sporting everyday clothes. For discretion yet still retaining reliability and firepower there were suitable alternatives.

The favoured weapon for concealment was the Glock 19. A superb weapon favoured by many militia forces personnel the world over, especially combat pilots. It is compact, lightweight as even fully loaded it weighs in at a mere eight hundred and fifty grammes, the added benefit of it being capable of chambering a magazine of fifteen rounds, extendable to thirty three if required but negating the compact traits for which the weapon was favoured, but importantly utilising a

9 x 19 calibre which provided good stopping power at close
quarters. It has ability to punch which makes it good for
shooting at targets within vehicles but could, at very close
quarters even penetrate through human targets without causing great damage if missing vital organs. Obviously though,
for a head shot this mattered very little. Whatever the result,
with a muzzle velocity of around three hundred and fifty metres per second, the unlucky recipient would know he had
been hit.

The second tool in the private arsenal was a sub machine
gun, the P90 manufactured by the Belgian firearms specialists FN Herstal. Hardly a standard weapon of choice for
most as it looks nothing like a traditional weapon, in fact
quite ugly by any standard. The overall length of the weapon
is only around five hundred millimetres and at a push could
be concealed under a bulky coat but it has stopping power,
rapid fire and ideal for close to middle distance fire fights.
The main aspect of this equipment was virtually all of its
kinetic energy is transferred to the target on impact, minimising collateral damage as well as being able to penetrate
the majority of commercially available sets of body armour.
This tool has the ability to discharge at nine hundred rounds
per second, which if unchecked, would very quickly empty
the standard fifty round magazine. However the big plus is
the weapon is still effective at a range of two hundred metres
and can be fitted with optical and laser sights. This weapon
is easily concealed within a vehicle so would be put in the
trunk of the Alfa as a fall back position. It was a good all
round combat tool in the field.

Falcon removed both weapons, checked them over and
loaded both magazines into the respective weapons. He returned the P90 fully loaded to the safe and felt that today the
Glock would suffice. He also took a couple of spare clips
as these would drop nicely into his jacket inside pocket. He
took the shoulder holster for the Glock and pulled it over
his torso. It fit as though it had been made to measure, never

worn before in anger although tried for comfort and fit on a regular basis, ready for a quick start that he hoped would never come.

As he did not feel he would need to be travelling incognito imminently, he thought that he would simply travel as Tony Falcon himself today. After all, his car was registered in that name and there was not sufficient time to arrange another vehicle. So he left the new identities where they lay and picked up two cellophane bags of cash from the well stocked money tin, each containing one thousand Euros. This should suffice he thought, even in Venice, not renowned for being a cheap get away. He closed the safe and returned the gun cabinet to the wall so it looked undisturbed, ascended the stairway from the cellar and back into the main house. Time for a quick change into suitable clothing for Venice, he thought he would go in his casuals rather than formal attire as he could drift into the throngs of tourist should there be a need for getaway. He had no idea of whom, or how many of his foes he would come face to face with today so every little helps.

Soon he was back behind the wheel of the Alfa heading for Venice, setting off at around seven fifteen. He drove with his jacket on so he could keep the hand gun under wraps and the newly received gift of the cell phone was on the passenger seat next to him as he drove. No map reading necessary these days with the advent of publicly available satellite navigation systems, this made journey planning so much easier. The computer calculated the route as taking around three and a half hours, however, he felt that allowing four would be more prudent, as he would probably stop just outside Venice and compose himself. The journey would take him west initially away from the mountains and towards Merano then south-west to Bolzano. Here he would pick up the A22 Motorway and its obligatory toll charges and take it south for around one hundred and forty kilometres, running parallel in the latter stages to the glorious Lake Garda. Once at Verona, the journey would then head East on the A4 for around an hour to the outskirts of Venice. Here he would make his choice of whether he drove into Venice or perhaps took a tourist bus or train.

It was almost impossible for Falcon to focus on the journey and he was thankful for the navigation system. His mind was still racing as to the perceived threat to his beloved as well as the threat of exposure to himself. Neither could be tolerated. Never mind what they wanted, would he get the chance to erase these treacherous bastards who were suddenly the tormentors of his life in one fell swoop? The answer was probably not, or at least probably not today. Would they look to wipe him out? The answer to that question was unknown but unlikely, as he took comfort from the previous evening's discussion with the mystery caller. They could have wiped him out any time it seemed as they had apparently been stalking him for some time. The scenery drifted past him totally unaware. He had never been a frequent visitor of Venice and hoped for a romantic holiday there someday with Maria, but to date it hadn't happened. Today he would be there on his own, hardly perfect in such a renowned city for romantics he thought.

The motorway traversed through Padua before arriving at Mestre and mainland Venice. Falcon decided he would park his vehicle here and take alternative transport across the waterway, either a train across the Ponte Della Liberta or even a vaporetto (water taxi). The Ponte Della Liberta was the only fixed access link between Venice and the mainland and was just less than four kilometres in length. As only two lanes wide it would not lend itself to speeding cars as overtaking would be limited at best and probably impossible. It would be easier to park at Mestre station rather than try and drive off the island in a hurry. There was very little scope for motor vehicles in any case across the water with the roads effectively stopping just after the bridge. There were plenty of streets to walk down of course as well as the infinite number of waterways . . . but no vehicles. This would give a couple of possible escape routes, satisfying one of Falcon's golden rules, even though there was still only one place to go when leaving the island and that was back to the mainland. The other way was out into the Adriatic if not careful. At least on the mainland he would have the option of car or train as an immediate exit route.

Falcon followed the A4 motorway into Mestre. He decided he would not park exactly at the station in case he was being tailed but would take an alternative parking house just off the main drag if at all possible. He came off the motorway opposite the Parco Piraghetto and headed westward in the general direction of the train station. He meandered through the smaller but busy side streets dodging and weaving other road users milling around like colonies of ants, oblivious to other traffic on the road, until he came across a suitable facility on Via Cappuccina. This would leave him with around a ten minute walk or a one kilometre run if the need arose, from Stazione di Venezia Mestre. One good thing about this location was the number of people around, perhaps that was some form of security. Maybe this is why such a place was chosen, this would give both parties the opportunity to safely assess one another.

For a winter's day it was pleasantly warm. No need for him to wear a heavy overcoat, the light sports jacket would suffice he thought. This would invariably require fastening throughout his stay to keep his Glock protector hidden from general view, but would leave it more immediately accessible than under a bulky coat. He parked the vehicle after purchasing his ticket. He had no idea how long he'd be there for and indeed wondered whether he would ever be coming back for this vehicle, but purchased a day ticket in any case, the extra few Euros far outweighed the need for discord with the parking officers later in the day.

"What shit have I wandered into here?" he muttered to himself as he removed the Glock pistol from its holster. One last time he looked it over, again checked it was fully loaded and ready to go. No need to worry about the safety catch as one feature of these guns was that the safety was inherent within the design, no accidental firing and shooting off something in your pocket that you were hoping to keep. Despite its extensive use of composite and non metal parts, the gun still had a good balance and feel to it. A common misperception was that these could not be detected in an x-ray machine at border controls or airports due to their plastic content; however Falcon knew better and would not have relished the thought of trying to smuggle one. He knew the machine would light up like a Christmas tree if anybody was ever stupid enough to try. Plastic or not, it was still an enemy stopper when needed. He put the weapon back into the shoulder holster and for the first time in the journey, his frustration was turning to apprehension. He sensed the sweat in his arm pits, something he was not familiar with, but then again he was not familiar with this situation. Another bad omen he thought. He re-fastened the navy blue striped sports jacket and grabbed the newly donated cell phone before locking up the vehicle.

He felt he was dressed as a typical Italian alpha male. Dark blue chino trousers with white heavy cotton T shirt now covered with the jacket, very chic and complemented by the dark socks and leather blue deck shoes with brown leather laces. Yep, he could be on the catwalk, ready to turn on any prospective fashion writer who slated him, but he was not. He was certainly on a tightrope though and needed to get off it as soon as possible. He couldn't help but feel that today would be the start of a chapter in his life he would rather omit.

Chapter 5

Falcon strolled out of the car park walking at a steady pace towards the railway station. Ten minutes would see him there comfortably. He patted his firearm for comfort one last time as he left the car park and headed south making sure once again he had the cell phone in his jacket pocket. He had plenty of time on his hands, it was now only around eleven a.m. so he still had an hour or so to spare, and in any case they could always call if he failed to show up where they planned. Besides, he was sure he would be followed, if he was not being so at this very moment. He just didn't know.

The train from Mestre ran several times an hour across to the island to its only station, Santa Lucia, so there should be no problem in Falcon finding timely passage. He purchased a return ticket from the station counter and set down to the platform to await the very next arrival. Falcon only waited a few minutes before the double deck regional train pulled into the station. On boarding he was surprised just how quiet the carriages were, obviously he had not hit peak tourist times, winter of course helping this but he was convinced there were still plenty of tourists in the city this time of year. He decided to take an upper deck seat despite the journey being only very brief. Moreover he attempted to establish whether any obvious or inexperienced trackers were on his tail.

The commuter train trundled out of the station towards the island. Very soon it was crossing the stone and brick constructed arched causeway, the Ponta Della Liberte. Not long after the train began slowing as it ambled into Santa Lucia station, the end of the line for the trains. From here it was a turn around and back to the mainland. With all the phenomenal architecture Venice has to offer, hundreds of years of history, Santa Lucia station was itself a bland white building resembling something of a modernist and even communist cube type façade. There are two platforms in Santa Lucia station and Falcon's train utilised the one to the right. On stopping, he waited for the other passengers to disembark until he could wait no longer without standing out. There were only a couple of passengers remaining to disembark when he made his move and these were generally elderly and required assistance. He exited the platform and turned left into the main station hall. There were more people here thronging about and from the looks of it many more outside. Barrow traders and stalls were selling coffees, flowers, souvenirs and other peripherals you would expect to find in a European railway station. The Englishman took the opportunity to purchase a tourist map, he was sure it would be handy at some stage during the day, besides he was not sure how to get to St Mark's Square and didn't want to rely solely on finding the tourist signs if he found himself in a hurry. If he adopted a back route it would make any following more obvious than within the tourist swarm.

Once outside the station hall, passing through the main exit, he found himself alongside the Grand Canal. The water was buzzing with vaporettos and water taxis as well as several larger vessels obviously capitalising on the over charged and unsuspecting tourists that were visiting this unique city. There was a cooler breeze rolling off the water than he had experienced in Mestre, but still not sufficient to warrant a heavier coat; probably ideal temperatures in reality for the travelling hordes. He thought how nice it would be to be here with Maria and knew one day he would return with her, in fact he made it a promise to himself that once this escapade was concluded he would come back at the first chance they got. Such thoughts of himself and Maria easily detracted him from his imminent problems so he quickly placed them in storage at the back of his mind and set about looking for the Piazza San Marco. He unfolded the tourist map and found that he still had a few kilometres of walking even if he got through the foot traffic almost unhindered. He would no doubt be late and whilst he knew his assailants would call, he would prefer to be facing them on the front foot rather than be playing catch up before they even got down to business.

He turned back towards the Grand Canal and hailed a water taxi, he knew this would be expensive and he did not even wish to get into a haggle with the operator, time was more precious than money. Money can be replaced but time cannot. He wasn't even choosy over which taxi he got, simply the first available would suffice. He could have taken a vaporetto but these had a habit at stopping on several locations although he noted that the Number eighty two only stopped at three, one of which was St Mark's Square, but he opted for solitude so a personal taxi was the answer.

He secured his deal with a boat owner and clambered aboard the highly polished wooden craft, Very soon he was heading down the Grand Canal towards Piazza San Marco. Unfortunately his craft, despite its splendour and speed capabilities did not have the right of way on the canal so was still regularly interrupted. Right of way always went to the traghettos, the cheaper gondolas that ferried passengers only across the Grand Canal rather than on romantic journeys along it, a need in Venice due to the surprisingly few bridges across the main arterial waterway. In the past there had been fifty or so such Gondola crossings although this number has been reduced now to around only six. Still, despite their numbers, they managed to interrupt Falcon's flow on an uncanny number of occasions. He marvelled at the splendour of the pavement free structures rising from the water, leviathans of history and splendour. What a place this must have been in its trading heyday, what wealth and opulence he admired. The taxi worked its way around the snake like Grand Canal until reaching the Piazza San Marco. Falcon made land from the taxi, thanked his chauffeur who quickly set off back to the station as there were no obvious fares to be collected just now from the square.

Falcon started into the square and there before him rose the immense tower of the Campanile. A generally brick constructed structure but housing a bell tower at a level of around fifty metres. The structure housed five bells, historically each of which had different significance including the announcing of executions as well as the start and end of the working day. In its day, it was the Venetian residents' timepiece. At just under one hundred metres in height, the Englishman's initial thoughts were about the benefits of such a vantage point for observation, or even a sniper. This was the bell tower of the St Mark's Basilica, (*Basilica di San Marco*—the city of Venice Cathedral), which itself was a mean feat of architectural design and construction. The building's opulence had earned it the nickname throughout history of *Chiesa d"Oro,* (Church of Gold), and it was clear why. You could not fail to be impressed in Venice.

Falcon recounted his thoughts and decided to wander into the square and do as his tormentors had asked, become a tourist. He looked around the Piazza at the magnificence, yet he was anticipating the cell phone to burst into life at any moment. He was sure they knew he was here but what could he do? Today he was the prey so he simply had to wait it out. The copious amount of pigeon's reminded him of Trafalgar Square in London, haunting and pursuing tourists for tit bits of food, but the main difference he thought was no traffic. There were no vehicles polluting the environment here other than the motorised vehicles on the water. No traffic noise to contend with. He put his map into his pocket and decided a coffee would be the order of the day.

He decided to try the most auspicious and highly renowned Caffe Florian. This was allegedly the oldest coffee house in Italy and has been operating for almost three hundred years. Another popular jaunt with tourists and on arrival it was clear why. The aroma alone was enticing but quality of service was evident all around. He took a table and waited for service. No sooner had he done so than his cell phone began vibrating in his jacket pocket, trembling against his thigh as he sat. He jumped up from his seat catching the attention of other coffee house dwellers. Fumbling into his pocket to catch the cell phone as soon as possible, Falcon hurriedly removed it from its hiding place and pressed it firmly against his ear.

"Yes," he shouted yet in an almost hushed voice.

"Good afternoon Mr. Falconer, I trust we are well today?" came back the reply.

This was the same mystery voice that had spoken with him only the day before, instantly recognisable by Falcon whilst at the same time causing the hairs on the back of his neck to stand proud.

"I'm coping," snapped back the Englishman, "so what now?"

"Patience Tony, please be patient. We would like you to take another water taxi and we would like you to do it straight away. You've not ordered any coffee yet so there's no waste there. We shall have a good coffee very soon."

Where the hell are these people he thought? They must be watching every damned move. He scoured the restaurant as he engaged his caller but again thought his stalker was blending in extremely well. Nothing at all seemed out of place. In fact there was not a sole he could see that was on the telephone, this place was quite civilised.

"So I guess I get back to the Grand Canal?"

"Yes, when you get there you will see a taxi waiting for you already. There's only one there at the minute so it should not be too difficult to spot. Please just get on board. He knows where to bring you. Just a small precaution on our part, I am sure you don't mind really. See you very soon . . . my friend."

The line again went dead. Falcon returned the phone to his pocket and walked out of the coffee house back into the main square leaving behind him the fantastic aroma that had tantalised his senses since entering the establishment.

The square was just as busy as he made his way back to the waterway. The pigeons were just as boisterous as when he was there last with tourists still milling about in all directions. He looked around as he walked back to the canal, left and right but nothing out of the ordinary was evident. They were there for sure, but where? These guys were good he thought, or at least better than he was. He decided not to move too quickly as that could attract attention, but it also gave him time for his own surveillance, for what little good it would do him right now. Today he was on the receiving end and it was not a good feeling. Back at the water's edge Falcon could see the highly polished brown chariot that awaited him. The small wooden jetty that strutted out from the steps was littered with gondolas, adorned with either bright blue covers for those that were not working, of which there were many. Some were in use today also and they were patiently parked awaiting custom. Several gondoliers dressed in their customary striped jerseys called to Falcon to see if he sought transport as he walked along the wooden jetty, but he was focused solely on his awaiting ride. The engine was already running in the taxi in anticipation of his arrival. He reached the taxi at the end of the jetty, the driver nodded and Falcon nodded back as if this was expected. He clambered aboard without a word being exchanged by either party. He sat at the rear of the taxi as the driver reversed out of his position and back into the main traffic flow on the water.

He admired the beauty once more of the surrounding architecture, now seeing in all its glory the Basilica Di Santa Maria Della Salute across the water on the opposite bank of the Grand Canal. This four hundred year structure rose above anything else around with majestic grace. This was another fabulous Venetian landmark, a huge octagonal building which was supposedly built upon a hundred thousand wooden piles. The building is topped by a vast dome which in itself has become a potent symbol of Venice. Its beauty in the flesh was unparalleled to anything he had seen so far today, and he had been very impressed already. Again the splendour detracted him momentarily from his true reason for being there today, but it was difficult not to be taken in by the aura of the city.

To Falcon's surprise the boat never turned back up the Grand Canal but instead headed south then West up the larger waterway separating this island from another, the island of Giudecca in the Venetian Lagoon. Oh well he thought, more mystery. It was out of his hands now, he again touched his breast pocket through which he sought comfort from his 9 mm protector safely strapped away under his jacket. As the boat sped up the watery highway, it was evident there was much less traffic on this route and soon he could see the main port of Venice ahead. The winter sun had already started its decent from its meridian as the time was now approaching one o'clock. The boat took it's passenger around the port and then for some reason back into the Grand Canal at the northern entrance. Now they were back in traffic and had to once again abide by the speed limits and rights of passage of other canal users.

A further ten minutes passed before the boat came to a halt at the very place it had departed from not too much earlier. A bemused look came across the Englishman's face, to which came a wry smile as a response from the boatman. He passed Falcon a piece of paper, on which was simply the words *Caffe Florian*. The boatman nodded again after Falcon had read the script and signalled for him to get out. He clambered ashore and made his way back up the stone steps away from the water's edge. Not a lot had changed since he was last in the square. The pigeons and tourists were still there, but at least he now knew where he was heading.

He decided not to rush, half expecting at any moment a tap on the shoulder. It never came. He walked into the café, still the same as half an hour or so ago! He stood there bemused for a few seconds when a very smartly dressed waiter politely asked,

"Excuse me sir, but are you Mr. Falconer?"

Falcon gazed at the waiter for a few seconds assessing him. Is he an assassin? Doesn't look much like a trained killer he thought; he's only a boy, surely not him. He scanned the surroundings again quickly before answering.

"I am."

"Excellent sir, if you would follow me please, your friends are expecting you."

Falcon followed the waiter obediently around the myriad of closely spaced tables where people were expending unusual amounts of hard earned Euros on food and drink. He led him to the far corner of the room where a table was awaiting with three occupants already seated and one spare chair.

One of the men tipped the waiter with a ten Euro note as he thanked him for his assistance. Falcon stood there in silence for a few seconds eyeing up each one around the table. They in turn returned the compliment assessing the legend that stood before them.

"Mr. Falconer," one of the group broke the eerie, unnerving silence.

"At last we get to meet you in the flesh. I trust your journey has not been too unpleasant under the circumstances. Please don't be offended but I would like one of my colleagues to search you, you know . . . just in case there is anything untoward on your person."

Falcon was impressed at the command of the English language possessed by the apparent leader of the trio. Before he could object, he was being patted down by the largest of the three men as he remained seated in his chair. They touched the gun, and it was obvious that he was carrying one, but this did not seem to bother the frisker.

He spoke something swiftly in Italian which Falcon could not fully make out but he sensed they were happy, which worried him as they had obviously found the weapon.

"Tony, may I call you Tony?" started the leader once again.

"If you wish, you appear to be in the driving seat today after all."

"There are certain things we need to check. You know, we, like you, are in what some may class a high risk business. We need to search you for our security. What weapon are you carrying?"

Falcon attempted to remain un-phased by the question although somewhat amazed at such a casual approach by his tormentors.

"Glock nine millimetre, why?" he replied in a blasé manner.

"Only curious what a man like you would carry, nothing more."

"Why does it not concern you. I mean I am sat here with a loaded gun in my pocket, you know all about it, you search me yet no problem. Why?"

"Tony, if you had come here today unarmed you would have disappointed me. We expect you to be armed. I would be if in your position, you had no idea what you were coming in to. Don't worry; you can keep your gun. Besides, you attempt to pull a gun on us and you will be dead before you get a finger on the trigger. We too take precautions. So if it makes you feel more secure, you keep it close by. No, we are more interested in any special listening devices you may have hidden inside your person, nothing else. This is a private meeting after all."

"So why the mystery tour with the charmless taxi driver?"

"More precautions on our part I'm afraid. We just want to make sure you were not being followed, nothing more."

"But I was already here, an hour ago."

"Yes, ironic isn't it, but we didn't mind the wait. The coffee is superb here. We've taken the liberty of ordering you one, hope you don't mind. We needed to be sure you were alone."

The same waiter arrived once again, this time carrying the four espresso coffee's as ordered. He placed the tray in the middle of the table as the leader of the group stated "*molti ringraziamenti*" and nodded, signalling the gatecrasher to leave the quartet, which he promptly did.

The natural light in this area of the cafe was limited so there were a number of electric lamps of intricate and ornate design around the establishment to provide the necessary yet pleasantly subdued lighting. Falcon reviewed his companions: three men, one of which remained the apparent leader. He was a slightly built man, probably mid forties he guessed, although experience had shown the Englishman could under estimate a well groomed Italian male's age, and clearly well educated. He wore stylish clothes and could have easily passed as a successful businessman, in fact for all Falcon knew, he could have been. His hair was short, black and brushed back in a slick style which bode well with trendy Italian's. His skin didn't look as though it had endured a hard life so Falcon knew he was no manual worker. It appeared that he was the brains behind the gathering, and maybe even the money. The second man was the one who had searched him earlier. This was a total contrast to the leader. Aged probably late thirties, Falcon assumed he had either had some form of military or police training as he looked the sort. Outwardly well regimented, responds to authority and understands the protocol of listening to the leader. He was dressed casually although not scruffy, clothes were all still of good quality. He had no hair on his head whatsoever and the scalp was well polished, so clearly shaven on a very regular basis. He had a rather large neck which was a good indication the guy was also muscle bound underneath that baggy coat, Falcon thought he wouldn't wish to get caught up in fisticuffs with this chump whom he assumed to be the muscle in the squad. The third interviewer, was somewhere in between. Certainly better built than the leader but for some reason his casual attire did not seem to be of a similar quality. This guy had less care about his personal appearance and Falcon assumed that he had not had sufficient if any military background where such disciplines are instilled from an early stage. He was older than the others, certainly approaching fifty and had clearly not shaven today. He hadn't bothered with the oil on the greying hair which simply rested where the prevailing breeze had decided to allow it to. He sported an over coat which Falcon thought probably too long for the weather as although winter was approaching, it wasn't that cold, clearly this guy felt the cold a bit more than the others. The jury was out on any assessment for this one.

"Allow me to introduce ourselves Tony. I am Marco, this is Francesco, who you have already met," as he pointed out with an outstretched palm to the bulldog which had searched him earlier.

"And I am Gunther," grunted the third man in guttural tones just as Marco was about to introduce him.

Gunther was clearly not an Italian. The name itself an obvious give away but the accent was most definitely German or Austrian. Marco slouched back in his chair as Gunther had interrupted his flow. Marco enjoyed acting out the part of the spokesman of the group but unfortunately Gunther never took kindly to people thinking he was just a follower.

"Well gentlemen, it's a real pleasure to meet you, but what game is this you're playing with me?" asked the Englishman, displaying little respect in his voice.

"We need your talents Tony," Marco replied instantly.

Falcon glared at the Italian, "What talents? What makes me so special? You guys seem resourceful, why me in particular?"

"It's all down to trust. We feel that we can trust you. You have come here today on trust so that's a good start to our relationship," said Marco as he nodded politely, acting as if trying to convince a jury already with his opening statements.

"I come here today because of the implied threats against my friends, nothing to do with trust."

"Then we understand one another," Gunther quickly shot in, again showing his insecurity as not being seen as a player.

"Our approach and your response shows that we can trust one another. We trust you to perform a small task for us, in return you trust us that once completed we shall never see or contact you again. You have our word."

"What about Maria?"

"Does she know you're a hired killer?" asked Marco directing his gaze squarely at Falcon. "If not, then why tell her, we won't? It serves no future purpose for us."

"And the photographs?" asked Falcon quizzically

"They're yours if you want them, but consider them an insurance policy for now. We have no real need for them, the purpose was to get you to the table and here you are. Would we benefit now from handing them to the authorities? Only if you were dead, but what benefit would that give us? If you were alive then you could possibly identify us, again no benefit, even if you tried to do a deal with the authorities. You would be a marked man, as would we. We all have benefit in mutual silence Mr. Falconer, so let's keep it that way. We would rather have you on our side than looking over our shoulders for the rest of our lives wondering where you would come at us from . . . and vice versa. We know your capabilities and background. We've done our homework. We promise, one job then we all go our separate ways." Marco sounded very convincing, after a small pause allowing the information to sink in with Falcon he went on.

"By the way, now that we have met, don't get any ideas about turning on us. You need to understand there may be more of us in this very room right now. I assure you, our organisation will terminate you and your lovely lady if you cross us. Unfortunately Tony, we are now bonded together, like in marriage; even if you don't like it. "

Marco's words sunk deep into Falcon's head. He was right. Where could he go now? Not the authorities, otherwise at the very least the pictures would put him either in jail or face down in an unmarked grave somewhere. Even if he survived, could he protect Maria? Not indefinitely that was for sure. He realised that he was to some extent, as Marco put it, in an unhappy marriage with this crew. Perhaps his reputation was keeping him alive at the moment but he wondered what would happen after the job was complete. They wouldn't really need him then, and if he was dead he couldn't identify the gang. That was a problem for another day, but one which he knew would need serious consideration before the job was completed. He needed some counter insurance, but as yet had no angle at all on what that could be.

The quartet drank their espressos in silence for a minute or so as Marco's words continued to echo around Falcon's mind.

"By the way Tony," added Marco, "please don't think we want you to work for nothing. We know to get the best you need to pay. So we have this morning authorised a transfer to your account of Apollo Holdings two hundred thousand Euros. This is a down payment only; a further one point eight million will be deposited on completion. When you get a chance, check your accounts, it should at least have flagged up by now even if not authorised as fully cleared just yet. Our banking associates are usually very efficient in such matters"

"You're confident I will take the job?"

"We are."

"You are prepared to pay two million for a job, there's hundred's of guys out there who would give their right arm for such a pay day."

"Our motives are our business Mr. Falconer," Gunther grunted sternly. "As already told to you, we want quality but most importantly we need trust. With you we have both and we do not wish to fall foul of you, hence the payment. It's a business deal, we pay you for a service, and you perform it. Basic contract principles really, there will be no redress by either side if all obligations are fulfilled. The payments just close the loop, everybody knows what they do and can expect from the outset."

"Usually contracted parties have a choice, do I or don't I?"

"Oh, you do have a choice Mr. Falconer. Does she live . . . or does she die?" retorted Gunther with sombre fervour.

Falcon jumped up and sent his chair spiralling backwards into another diner's, causing unwanted attention from other restaurant dwellers. Marco quickly ushered Gunther and Falcon to calm and be seated.

"Gunther," he said, "I think Tony understands the situation so let's not get off to a bad start. Let's take the discussions outside; I feel we may not be welcome here much longer."

He turned to the Englishman and apologised about his associate's behaviour, explaining that tact was not necessarily his strong point. Falcon was burning with rage internally but he knew he couldn't take on these guys right now. Maria would be in even more danger if he even contemplated such a move. Fresh air would do him good he thought as he turned and made his way out of the restaurant, followed closely by the over sized Italian, Francesco. He was sure these wouldn't turn out to be their real names, but so what. In truth he wanted to know as little about them as possible as this would make his separation from them much easier when the time came. The bright winter sun greeted him once again as he exited the subdued lighting of the cafe onto St Mark's Square.

Chapter 6

Detective Inspector Francoise Duval was awakened by the sharp ringing of his mobile telephone. The Nokia was obviously set to vibrate as it danced around his bedside table bursting into song with some dreadful in built polyphonic ring tone. It was four in the afternoon yet he had only been in his bed for a little over three hours after working through the night on some recently obtained information.

Francoise Duval was a workaholic. The price he paid for his devotion to his profession was two failed marriages, no children and a life for the most part devoid of company with the exception of his work colleagues; hardly an impeccable personal track record for a man of only thirty five years of age. These were the only real friends he had these days so he never managed to really escape from the daily grind. He had little time for hobbies, simply work and sleep when he had to was what his basic routine amounted to. He rarely took holidays but did travel with his job, which was a small benefit although he rarely got the opportunity of experiencing distant shores due to the dedication to the profession.

He was around one metre seventy tall, a slender man weighing in at around eighty kilograms. He was always clean shaven and smartly dressed, even in a suit worn daily for work whether office bound or not. He had a good covering of oily black hair although quite fine and sported a well groomed moustache. He was proud of his appearance and rarely allowed himself to appear less than presentable.

His bad habits included excessive smoking, however in French society this was not yet seen as distasteful or anti social, although it did cause some issues when operating in international operations and some of his colleagues were not too keen on this pastime. His vices, if they could be called such, included enjoying French wines, in fact anything in a bottle that could be called French from fine Napoleonic brandies to Ricard. He also enjoyed the occasional visit to the Parisian red light district whenever time and location permitted, but again this was also seen as an expected pastime in many quarters for a red blooded Frenchman.

He had an apartment, which he called home when in Paris although the job often meant he was away from it for long periods of time, but at least it was a bolt hole when he needed that bit of extra time off to recharge the batteries or when he was working from the offices in or near to Paris.

Francois Duval had been transferred to Interpol several years earlier, seen as a shining light by his superiors with a true nose for detective work and attention to detail. His dogged and tenacious character meant that once he had developed a lead, he could never let go. He was highly intelligent and physically fit although not what one would call an athlete, yet his aptitude fit the bill for Interpol perfectly. Within his debut year he secured his first promotion and was now a section leader with numerous officers working for him, both on intelligence analysis and office work, as well as agents all over Europe in the field, some of which were under-cover.

He rubbed his eyes profusely until he was able to focus on the telephone, initially feeling for a split second as though he was in some form of state of stupor. As his sight cleared so did his mind enabling him to focus and pick up the vibrating nuisance clattering away against his porcelain bedside lamp.

He looked at the fluorescent screen and all that was displayed were the letters JPR. Duval of course knew who this was, one of his oldest colleagues in the force Jean Paul Reynard, an agent currently assigned to surveillance operations in Italy. Duval had not heard from him directly for several weeks so this was a surprise.

"Good morning Jean Paul," Duval croaked, "this better be good." He cleared his throat and took a quick drink of mineral water from the bottle he kept beside the bed, a ritual he has followed for many years due to his regular bouts of dehydration as a consequence of excessive consumption of his beloved red wines.

"It's the afternoon sir!" retorted Reynard ". . . and it is."

"Its still morning to me . . . and what is?" asked a bemused and now more coherent Duval.

"Had a long night sir?"

"We have had two long nights, now if this is a social chat, just send me a bloody email. If it's important then spit it out man," gnarled Duval to his distant intruder.

"They have met with a mystery man today in Venice. They have been quiet for some time but we were assured from information received that something was coming up and an outsider was to be called in. For what we don't know yet; but we are digging," came back the excited report from Reynard, finding it difficult to get all his words out in a single breath.

"Who has met with the stranger, who are we talking about?"

"Gunther Menzies, the German, suspected of having links to the PLO, but nothing ever came of it. Now he has been associating himself with old known members of the Red Brigade in Italy although as yet not apparently active, but there are many meetings and there's a lot of general activity in their presence."

"I thought Gunther had dropped from our radar years ago and was no longer a real target. He's been on the inactive list for years."

"He was until a couple of weeks ago when he showed up here. We were given a tip off that some German heavy hitter would be coming to town to see the brigade but never knew who it was. We knew who he was meeting so started there and were pleasantly surprised or probably unpleasantly surprised to see who turned up. So we need to resurrect his status until we know what is really going on. It's no coincidence that he meets some known members of the Brigade," explained Reynard. "We've been keeping tabs on several members since he showed, including Gunther, and it seemed just the same old faces meeting in usually fairly public places; that was until today when the stranger showed up."

Duval paused for a moment trying to recite Gunther's details from his memory bank. "So we now need to know who the stranger is. How do we do that? Has your informant any idea?"

"None whatsoever, we certainly don't recognise him. We have his picture though and a set of fingerprints?"

"How the hell did you get those?" requested Duval.

He knew that there were European procedures to follow in terms of respecting the human rights of individuals, whether suspected criminals or not. Duval though was happy to be flexible of the interpretation of such stupidity and would cross that technical bridge when and if it ever came to it. As far as he was concerned, if he could stop a terrorist atrocity and save innocent lives, the end certainly justifies the means, irrespective of what liberal policy makers decide upon in Brussels, whose only real goal in life is satisfying every possible minority group going in order to preserve their own position. In most cases, the premature tracking down of a terrorist suspect would lead to a shoot out with hopefully the bad guys ending the day lying in a body bag, so there would be no complaints as to how the fingerprints were taken.

"Well, there seemed to be a little discord at the table in the café where they were having a meeting in Venice and they all suddenly left. One of our officers decided to follow whilst the other protected the table where they were all sitting until the waitress appeared to clear it. He then offered her a sizeable tip and asked if he could take a couple of the souvenir espresso cups from the table. He pocketed one belonging to the stranger and also that of Gunther so we can see if his prints match those on file and confirm his presence here. I am sure it will be listed on expenses sir . . ."

Duval sat upright in his bed. He once again had his blood hound nose on and could sense a chase coming. "So where are the prints, have you any feedback yet?"

"No sir, we have the cups and they're on the way back to our offices in Milan where they'll have the prints taken off and analysed. I'll get them emailed through to you and you run them internationally and see what comes back."

"Improvising in the field . . . I like it. Keep me posted on their moves Reynard, good work, good work by the whole team. Anything you need, let me know, if additional resources needed just ask and we'll see what can be done. If Gunther is active we need to find out what he's up to and soon. Send me those prints the minute you get them, okay? Oh and send the picture of your mystery man, we'll focus on him at this end as well."

"Okay sir, speak to you later." Reynard hung up his phone satisfied that his boss saw the fruits of their labours in the field, maybe they have hit on something big. He hoped that they would be able to put a stop to it in time.

Duval was wide awake now. Excitement was circulating his body, adrenalin fuelled thoughts were abound of nailing another active terrorist, hopefully permanently. He decided there was no point remaining in bed now, there would be no chance of sleep; he had to get ready for work. What does one have for breakfast at four p.m. in France? He strolled to his refrigerator which resembled a typical bachelor's cold store. Some cooked meats, cheese and beer; looks like bread and cheese again he thought. Not one for much home cooking, he tended to stock the simpler items, sandwiches and the occasional ready meal were about as far as he would go in his own kitchen. He much preferred to dine out whenever possible. He had little else on which to spend his salary after all, other than personal indulgences. He snacked on what he could forage from his meagre provisions then set about preening himself in readiness to return to the office in downtown Paris.

It was a suite of small offices with a central more open plan area that was utilised by Interpol in the main Parisian police headquarters situated in the Place Louis Lépine on rue de Lutèce. Plenty of artificial light adorned the work space with the constant and clinical luminescence generated by the over head incandescent lighting. There were few windows to the outside world in this quarter of the building, with that luxury generally reserved for the smaller office suites in this section. The furnishings were not plush but there was no shortage of it nor of communications equipment, essential utensils for this aspect of detection work. Duval of course, had his own office being the section head looking after anti terrorism activities, but many facilities were also shared with the French Police who also occupied this building. Still, the system worked.

Duval entered the office with the customary cigarette in hand. Some of his colleagues who had started the day whilst he was on duty were somewhat surprised to see him back so soon, however it wasn't long before they realised why. The blood hound was back on the scent . . .

He beckoned Nicole to his office as he made his way past the rest of the team. Nicole was a relatively new addition to this section but showed great promise, and was always very eager to learn and get stuck in. To date she had been involved with fairly mundane tasks but perhaps now that was all about to change.

"Can you get me everything we have on Gunther Menzies as soon as possible," he barked at the newcomer. Everybody was used to his brash attitude and his direct and seemingly impolite approach rarely offended his staff. He was admired by those who knew him well, due to his success, yet revered by those who didn't know him that well due to his attitude. As far as Duval was concerned he was not entering a popularity contest, so for him the attitude was *take me as you find me*.

"I am also waiting for some information from Reynard so if it comes in to the pool let me see it immediately. If I am not here find me!"

"Sounds like something important may be about to land, sir?" she asked timidly

"Could be very important and it could turn out to be nothing. Until we get the low down on the intel we won't know will we?" he replied, whilst looking down at his desk and glancing through recent paper deposits that had materialised since he left earlier in the day, without ever looking up at the shapely dark haired debutant.

Nicole made a hasty retreat from the boss's office and set back to the team inquiring how to get the dossier together on one Gunther Menzies. The old hands who worked the data bases and archives were more than keen to help young Nicole achieve her goal, almost fighting like lions over a kill to win her attention. Suddenly there were several screens around the central open plan office that burst into life, shadows dancing on the ceiling as screen after screen came on line. It was always a good feeling for everybody when something new came in rather than simply trawling through reams of potential intelligence, written, video and audio. Almost one hundred percent of what the team trudged through looking for valuable information was useless, but sometimes in the myriad was a shard of knowledge that could track down a ruthless killer or expose some odious plot. It was, for the main, a mundane job; which required special dedicated people who could remain sharp and focused ready for that moment when the slither of intelligence materialised. But when a specific project kicked into life, the whole place developed an intense buzz as though all were given a holiday from their daily grind, which effectively they were.

M E N Z I E S was methodically and hastily spelt out on the keyboard of the main database as the office members, six in all excluding Duval, peered at the screens to see what would be thrown out. Surprisingly the screen spewed a whole list of MENZIES hits out and it was down to the operator to scroll through and find the appropriate catch. It didn't take long; there was only a single entry under the name Gunther Menzies. The mouse was positioned over the relevant search result and again the screen changed whilst the internal workings of the system shot runners off to the main databases of Interpol at supersonic speeds to retrieve any information which had been archived as tabbed or connected to this hit.

As they watched the dossier load the team knew there must have been a lot as the file size grew and grew.

After about five minutes, the download was flagged as complete, and was there a lot of it. The archive contained video footage, transcripts of interviews and court appearances, informants' testimonies and much more as well as the known personal details of the new object of Duval's enquiries. The usual: date of birth; height; weight; eyes; hair; schools; education; history etc, all the personal stuff. It also showed known associates and the same data for them. Telephone and banking records were accessible as well as meticulously kept diaries taken by officers tracking these people, often more detailed than they could have probably written about themselves. Nicole had of course seen various elements of such files before but this was the first time she had witnessed the generation of this dossier first hand and on a live case. Hopefully she would get a chance to prove herself on this one she thought. The photographs were somewhat dated and surely he had changed a little in later life. The file shots were over fifteen years old now. The dossier was compiled and saved to a central server so all team members could access it. They were all emailed a hyperlink for that purpose, including Duval. Once it was deemed necessary to probe the file further, it would be broken into individual sections allocated to each member to generate key information from. These would then be compiled into a dossier which was more manageable and should contain the salient information. Unfortunately the intelligence computers still relied on some police work to achieve the pertinent information. Meanwhile, whilst they waited for the next instruction from Duval, who was in turn waiting for further news from Reynard, the team each began briskly reviewing their next target.

The silence in the room was ear splitting. Not long earlier there was the usual hive of activity with the usual to and fro between the Interpol detectives as they each trawled through their various deposits of intelligence. Calling to each other like stockbrokers on the trading floor exchanging information, but now all was at peace. This was not routine, now there could be a real case at hand, these were always the more exciting times. For young Nicole this would be her first major, so she was a little more excited than the others. Time dragged as they waited for further news to be received from Reynard, but they knew it would come. Preparation now could only help. Nicole was especially intense in her analysis of the cavernous data file she had just been given access to.

"Nicole," barked the catarrh ridden voice of the heavy smoking detective inspector Duval from his office, "grab Patrice and both of you get in here."

She scurried into the leader's office like the ever obedient class favourite at school after accosting Patrice at the coffee maker, a favourite office meeting point. It was not the best coffee in the world, but since Patrice had recently given up the pastime of smoking, he had to find another legal method for getting pollutants into his system, and caffeine was a good substitute for nicotine. They both stood attentive in front of Duval's desk. The boss himself was rocking back and forth apparently reading from a script furled up in his hand. It was a photograph, of someone he did not recognise, although he knew himself that even with his experience it would be unlikely that he would be immediately able to identify the unfamiliar stranger from St Mark's Square.

"I've got some advance info from Reynard. I think this is a newcomer!" he said, as he handed the document over to Patrice.

"Let's run it through the system and see if anything comes out but Reynard thought the guy had an English accent. If we come up with nothing bang it across to the FBI and the British and see if they have any data on this guy. I'll send you the data I just received from Italy. There's also a set of finger prints of the new guy and they don't flag up in our system. Gunther's do though, so at least we have a positive ID on one of them. Nicole, you work with Patrice on this but keep me informed as you find anything. I don't like the thought of this guy back on the streets and becoming active."

The two dutiful servants Okayed the chief and backed out of the office. Quickly they set about at Patrice's desk in assembling data to pass on to the security services of fellow crime fighting states. Within minutes the mixture of whorls and swirls were travelling across the electronic superhighway on a secure network to counterparts in the American Federal Bureau of Investigations and Scotland Yard. Patrice would follow up both requests immediately with the courtesy of a telephone call explaining the potential importance of the lead. The French systems clearly had no familiarity with the stranger either by face or prints, so the hunch that he was an Englishman as suggested by Reynard, was going to be favourite. As such, Patrice placed greater emphasis on the needs for a quick response to his Scotland Yard counterparts.

The minutes ticked by in the Paris office and the coffee consumption increased accordingly. Duval preferred to continue putrefying the atmosphere of his office with cigarette smoke than the caffeine buzz chosen by his colleagues. The minutes eventually became an hour and still nothing came back. There was little point in adding to the delays with further calls. They just had to wait, sit and wait. At least nothing negative had come back. It was now approaching eleven in the evening. So much had happened suddenly this afternoon, Duval had managed to work through his fatigue, but now it was catching up with him. He decided that today there was nothing more he could do.

He suggested his staff get some rest also, leaving half of those currently in the office to take care of business over night. He asked that should they not hear back from the British or Americans then feel free to make follow up calls. Nicole clearly didn't want to leave now but she too had been on duty with Duval from early in the day. As was customary, Duval asked he be contacted should any significant developments occur. He walked Nicole to her car and said he would see her back in the morning refreshed and ready for action. He knew the follow up was in good hands as Patrice would remain in the office overnight, he was due a long shift thought Duval.

Duval awoke the following morning feeling revitalized, but was somewhat surprised he hadn't heard anything from his office over night. This was most unusual he thought. In this day and age of super computers, searching even the most comprehensive data bases should be completed by now. However, he decided not to call the office but to see what awaited him on his arrival. He fought his customary route through the Parisian randomised traffic management system back to the rue de Lutèce and police headquarters. He loved this city but loathed the traffic. On entering the office he found Nicole had already arrived and the gang was huddled around Patrice's desk. Something had come in . . . but what?

The buzz in the gathering ceased as Duval approached and his staff all turned to face him as though he were an approaching movie star.

"Well, what's happened, or not happened?" he quizzed in a very sedate manner, much to the surprise of the incumbent staff.

A bedraggled looking Patrice, now shirt open and tie hanging more like a medallion chose to take the lead. "We had a simple no record on file from the UK and we're still waiting for the FBI to come back. We've called and chased but still waiting."

"It's probably way too early for me to lean on anybody in the FBI right now, give it until later this afternoon, if we've not heard anything I'll make some calls. We need a push on this one way or the other. So what do the men at the Yard say?" asked Duval.

"That's the strangest thing. They just said no record. No usual back up information even offering near misses, just nothing. No suggestions on where else to chase, no 'can we help you in any other way', just cut us off dead."

"Do you think there is more? Are we sure he's not just a newcomer?"

"All I can say chief is this is not the format of the usual re-sponse from the British," replied Patrice, not wishing for his own beliefs to be translated into fact. He preferred that his boss play the politics, he would rather act the foot soldier.

"Send me their reply and I'll see what I make of it. What about trying MI5 and MI6?" asked Duval.

"Never tried that, I thought we would just stick with Scot-land Yard. If he was on the radar of the British surely the anti terrorist squad would have his details. Shall we try the other channels?"

"Not for the time being. Let's see how the day unfolds, I may push British Intelligence later but will need a higher authority to play that card if things aren't quite black and white. We may need to call in a favour. Any further news from Reynard?" asked the chief.

"His report is on your system, they tailed the group for over an hour then they went their separate ways. The stranger left Venice, we know that, and it seems that Gunther and the others are staying in a local hotel. They've not really done anything out of the ordinary. Not been examining any spe-cific targets that we are aware of, just seem to be moving around a bit during the day, like tourists, however the three of them are nearly always together."

"Keep on Gunther, let's try and see what the agenda may be. Any political rallies or visits of diplomats or VIPs to Ven-ice scheduled in the near future. Check with local police and see if there are any plans. Right, let me get at Scotland Yard." The boss seemed to have the bit between the teeth now, he had a focus and didn't like being shafted, and he sensed that today he was being so.

Duval returned to his desk and lit the customary Marl-boro as he entered his office. He sat at the desk and began rocking as he pondered over the curt response they had ob-tained from Scotland Yard. He could see why Patrice thought it odd. They had a good working relationship with one an-other and information flow was usually pretty good, both ways. Yet, this was definitely out of character. He wondered whether this had come from a newcomer to the team perhaps in whom the protocol had not yet been ingrained. But even so, this surely would still not be the way to issue formal communications on a matter so delicate and important. He looked for the details of the sender but there was nothing. No name other than that of Scotland Yard Fingerprint Section, no individual he could reply to and berate.

After musing through the response and playing out the scenarios in his head of possibilities as to who and why this had come through the system, Duval decided that he needed to take the bull by the horns and do the digging himself. He moved the mouse of his computer to bring the pc screen back into life from its suspended animation. He wasn't really a computing expert and saw them as a necessary evil, but he could manage the basics, one of which was his contact directory where many details were stored for individuals who could be contacted through less official channels. These were generally direct lines to individuals who he had worked with over the years, and he too appeared on similar direct contact lists of theirs he was sure. Many times unofficial information had been relayed in this manner, the old boy's network. Duval preferred this approach as he hated red tape getting in the way of progress.

Duval scrolled through his contact directory and stopped at one DI John Duggan. He was a senior officer in the Anti Terrorist squad and a long time acquaintance of Duval's. They had worked together on a couple of occasions and with great success at intercepting arms bound for Northern Ireland organised through a French organisation. They fed off each other and both received their dutiful accolades for their successes. He knew he could speak with John off the record. Duval keyed the number into his desk phone which was on the speaker setting and waited for an answer at the other end.

"DI Duggan," came back the speaker in a fading Scottish accent.

Duval picked up the receiver of his phone so the conversation was not fully relayed around the offices.

"John, Francoise Duval speaking from Paris, long time, yes?"

"Hell Francoise, what a surprise. Not heard from you in a couple of years. How are you keeping?"

"We are fine here, and you?"

"Always busy at the yard, always busy."

"I bet. Still throwing down English ale for lunch with some other gastronomical disaster, what is it . . . fish and chips? Ah yes that was it, fish and chips . . . in a newspaper!"

"You lot still eating garden slugs and amphibian's feet or whatever you call them?"

Both officers laughed a little at the apparent discord between them, but both knew that their cultural differences were only an opening gambit and ice breaker.

"John, seriously old friend, I am in need of a bit of information. We sent across some prints yesterday for analysis and your guys have come back and said no information available."

"Well then there can't be any. What's the problem? Surely you don't want something making up? You know those days are long gone . . ."

"No, nothing like that. The reply was . . . well it was just not right. I feel there is something else to add but we are being kept out of this one. It could be important. He has been seen with known targets and we're worried something is being set up and we don't have a bloody clue what it could be."

"I saw the response an hour or so ago and never thought anything of it. Maybe it was a bit short, but we're all cutting back somewhere," Duggan joked.

"Is there nothing else you can tell me. Is this guy a total new comer?"

"From our records we have to assume that. We have run his picture and prints as you asked but nothing I'm afraid. Maybe he is just having a meeting about something totally different, an old friend. Surely not everyone the terrorist speaks to is a terrorist themselves. What if they speak with a waiter or a hotel porter, would you tag them as terrorists as well? No Francoise, maybe this is nothing more than a coincidence, an unrelated meeting to your case. If you find otherwise let us know of course, as we will need to get him on the system if he's a villain."

"Oh well. I thought it was worth a try. I just have this hunch that this guy is up to something and we can't get a lead yet."

"If there's not one there don't waste time looking for it. There are plenty of villains out there to get behind bars. Hey old friend, I'm getting buzzed to another meeting, damned management systems and all that crap you know. I've got to dash, but good talking to you again. Keep us posted if any developments. Good luck with it but as I say, don't rely on Le Hunch, work with facts instead of chasing rainbows. Know what I mean buddy?"

"I most certainly do. Alright old friend, maybe I will see you sometime soon. If you do drag anything up on this guy you will let us know?"

"You bet; no worries there."

Both men put down their telephones and the conversation was terminated. Duval rocked back in his chair replaying the conversation over and over in his head. This case was now beginning to concern him. The loose ends were increasing in number as were the dead ends. He thought Duggan was not as he expected after not having spoken for a couple of years, but was he now being paranoid and starting to mis-read the situation? He continued his rocking and contempla-tion, again reviewing the response from Scotland Yard and proceeded to light up another cigarette and putrefy the atmo-sphere of his working domain.

Chapter 7

DI John Duggan replaced the receiver on his desk phone knowing that his colleagues had heard and understood the conversation that had just taken place with the Frenchman. Only a select few were privy as to the reason why, as the majority simply thought that there was no information on this guy, it was just another lead gone cold. Yet another small piece of the myriad of intelligence gathered that leads to nothing after analysis, yet still has to be checked. No, for the majority in Duggan's office there was nothing unusual in this conversation at all.

Duggan's superior officer was sat opposite him during this conversation. On completion of the call he smiled at Duggan as he rose from the chair, nodded nonchalantly and said, "There's a good lad John. You know it makes sense. We have our own interests at heart here also you know."

"Yes sir."

"I need you to keep tabs on this guy. Keep in touch with the Frenchie and see how much he spills."

Duggan was not happy to play the conversation the way he did, but orders were orders. There was no way he could reveal information on Anthony Falconer, he was a national asset. Duggan didn't have all of Falcon's details to hand but had been briefed by his superiors. They in turn had already had their briefing from the security services, as to his role in our society and his importance. His own feed back on Scotland Yard's systems showed no information other than classified status. However the attempted search had flagged up at the British Secret Service, hence their sudden involvement on the top floor. Falcon's association with terrorists was not foreseen by his handlers in the UK or the USA so they had their own interest in his movements now. This was not any operation they had instigated, or at least they were not aware of it, although both British and American agencies are notorious for not communicating with one another. They always considered Falcon a closely kept secret and not part of the inventory available for all the agencies to draw from.

DI Duggan now pondered how best he played this issue. Did he send his own recon team out after Falcon, in which case he would surely fall foul of Interpol and get in the way of their investigation, or did he rely on Duval. Maybe he should pull in Falcon himself and see what he had to say. That would be easier, although, again it would spark off a spat between Britain and France, although not for the first time. He too was not one for too many rules. He had a job to do and it seemed that there was a protocol way and a right way for everyone to win. But what was it?

Duggan clambered from his comfortable desk chair, a bit of a couch potato these days being tied to the desk for too long. He had lost the youthful athleticism he once had although was still reasonably fit for his age and size. Yet as Duval had reminded him, he did have a weakness for British ale and fast foods. It was back to business as usual. He joined his team for an update on the day's activities and the issue with the stranger in Venice had now passed and was resigned to a distant memory for the team as they trawled on with the other tasks of the day.

Finally it was after five p.m. and Duggan had had enough for one day. He looked for volunteers to share a beer with on the way home as was customary. As was often the case there was regularly two or three more than happy to share a scoop with the boss, although it was as though they had some rota going as to whose turn it would be on any particular night. He didn't care. He enjoyed the beer and enjoyed company with it. He was not of a mind to drink alone in a pub.

The gathering headed to the favourite haunt of the Dog and Partridge, not an untidy establishment but certainly not up market. It was fairly near to Scotland Yard offices so had a captive market, and never really put anybody off route on their way home. Here the ale was well kept and there was rarely any trouble. People knew that there was a good chance the yard men would be in there so those who wanted trouble tended to err on the side of caution. It was rarely a heavy drinking session, couple of beers to wind down after yet another day of nothing startling and away to their individual kingdoms. They would all return home to join wives and families, through the rat race that was London traffic, all just to get ready to start it again tomorrow. It was once again normal, except for Duggan. He knew what his colleagues did not, and even that snippet of information he had was troubling him. He had nothing against Falcon, even perceiving him as some James Bond style character which added to the appeal and intrigue. However if he had gone bad then that was a big issue and maybe the boys upstairs with their approaches would not be able to get to the bottom of the mystery in time. He laughed and joked with his colleagues for an hour before they all decided that was enough. There was no way the police would drink over the limit in this pub.

Duggan jumped in his car and headed home. He passed a large supermarket as he neared his home and often nipped in there for a bottle of wine, tonight was no exception. However he had another reason for calling in. On entering the supermarket, which was thronging with early evening shoppers, some like him on the way home from work, others out looking for end of the day bargains; he took a sharp left and headed for the toilets . . . and pay phones. He enjoyed the quick trips in the evening to the stores as he always amused himself in looking in shopping baskets to work out who lived alone, who could cook and who could only work a microwave and relied on the *ding* meals, so called as the chef knew their ready meal was cooked on hearing the customary chime of the microwave timer. He couldn't criticise too much though as he only ever bought alcohol and he was mindful he wouldn't be the only person in the supermarket playing such games.

Tonight however, there was a greater purpose.

It was just after eight in the evening when the telephone rang in Duval's pocket.

"Francoise, it's John here."

"Ah, why are you calling so late, should you not be at home now, nine till five isn't it?"

"No, just listen. Don't ask anything I have to be quick. Just listen. Your guy did come up on the systems . . . but not ours. He was black flagged; only those with the highest level of security clearance can get into his files. I don't know what he is or really who he is but it stirred something up big style at the ministry that's for sure. His name on our records is shown as Anthony Falconer. I have no more than that that I can tell you, but he seems to be one of ours. If he has gone rogue I need to know. Maybe you can get assistance at the top to find out more, I can't and I've been told not to try. I hope this helps you but I can't be any more specific."

"Many thanks John, Le Hunch seems to have been right. I owe you a fine cognac when we meet, one you will remember for ever I am sure."

"Any drink you buy me I will remember for ever. Right I must go. Bye." He put the telephone down. That call cost him best part of four pounds out of his own pocket, damned pay-phones. He had done his good deed for the day he thought. He believed he hadn't breached any real security; he had merely saved Interpol a lot of running around and hopefully his own people also. It was still in everybody's interest to discover what was going on, and now they owed him something. Now, for the wine he thought. He headed back into the supermarket for his usual provisions but today he decided that a bottle of scotch was the order of the day. It had turned out to be a strange day after all, even though nothing seemed to have happened.

Duval was again rocking in his chair when Nicole entered to say she was leaving for the evening, the rest of the day team had already left.

"You look happy sir," she said quizzically, hoping that he would share his thoughts.

"Only thinking Nicole, always thinking," he paused for dramatic effect knowing the protégée was hanging on his every word.

"I know the name of our mystery Englishman. Well I know a name he goes by at least."

"How did you find that?" she asked genuinely startled as the teams efforts had drawn a blank all day "Did you get something back from the FBI?"

"No. I haven't tried them yet and maybe won't for now. This is from a trusted source so it's what we shall start running with tomorrow. Now the chase can begin."

She could see the legendary bull dog spirit stirring up in her boss whom she admired greatly, although she hoped that it was never too obvious.

"So where did you get the info from sir?" she again asked, although this time with a little more emphasis.

"Ah, Nicole, let's just say from a trusted source. That's all anybody ever needs to know and that's how it will stay. That knowledge comes with the territory I'm afraid. One day when you are sitting in this chair you will have similar dilemmas to contemplate."

The young detective blushed and chuckled nervously under her breath. "Good night sir," she said as she turned and left the offices.

"Good night Nicole," he shouted after her as she had already left his doorway. The office was silent now except for the creaking of Duval's constant rocking back and forth in his aged chair.

ANTHONY FALCONER, he wrote in capital letters on his desk jotter, and he stared at it for several minutes muttering the name over and over again. He took the black and white photograph he had of Falcon taken in St Mark's square and wrote the name in biro on the bottom. Now he had a name and a face . . . all he needed to do now was find out who he really was.

Chapter 8

Major Peter Henry Falconer was a proven military man. He was a highly decorated member of the specialist American combat unit the 7th Cavalry. He underwent several tours in Vietnam, with a focus on the La Drang Valley, where some of the bloodiest conflicts of the war were fought. Unfortunately, due to mortality levels on the American side, promotions were readily available for the right candidates. Peter Falconer had demonstrated his ability with the troops to act as a leader, inciting team spirit in one of the most hostile fighting environments the American military had ever entered. This was a theatre of war where military might alone was not sufficient for success. He had shown courage under fire, selflessness and consideration for his fellow men, but most of all he had shown the top brass he was a thinker. A strategist of rare talent, hence the need to have him lead a good number of troops in the hostile war zone.

Peter Falconer was a true patriot and never complained about his lot. He had chosen the military for his start in life even though his own academic prowess would have opened many alternative career opportunities. But this was a war they should have won easily but constantly struggled with. The Cavalry was one of the elite fighting units of the American military with an enviable pedigree. Highly trained specialists, who had traded in their horses for helicopters and heavy armour many years ago, yet retained the cavalry status, fearless chargers. Sadly, this often meant front line work or even behind enemy lines, but still there were no regrets. The Major's prominence emerged when seniors realised he suffered very few casualties within his troop. Not that there were none but his numbers were vastly lower than virtually all his counterparts. He was earning a reputation. It turned out that the Major's greatest asset was his ability to think under pressure; none of this *gung ho* attitude and hope for the best. Consequently, he earned his promotions which got him more and more involved in operational planning, those whose finer details were established on the ground, not the full blown offensives whose details were addressed back in Washington by guys who had never seen a live battle before let alone actively taken part in one. Most of the military strategists had never even seen military service before, politicians and mathematicians, dressed in their civvies each day for work, yet playing chess with the lives of American families' sons and daughters. Major Falconer deserved higher office, but unfortunately his fighting career was cut short when he took another bullet in the leg on one rescue mission too many. This time the damage was too severe such that even after recovery, he would no longer be fit for active service.

He had received two purple hearts for injuries he had sustained as well as the Congressional Medal of Honour, for the bravery he had shown in assisting in the rescue of another platoon which had become surrounded by Vietcong forces, on what was meant to be a relatively straight forward mission of seeking out hidden armaments in a local village. However, he had his life which was more than could be said for many of his comrades in arms. Peter's pride at the receipt of such accolades was entirely internal; he never allowed his honour to be displayed publicly knowing that so many of his fellow combatants had given their lives virtuously anonymously, something he always felt guilty of. His parents would not mourn, as so many others would have to. He was retained to assist in some military security once he was mobile with an unofficial attachment to the CIA, at the American embassy in Saigon but this was a short lived post, as the upper echelons felt this strategist would himself best serve his country outside the war zone and he was returned to Washington early in 1970. Despite being away from the action, the cause was never away from his mind, irrespective of what project he was involved with in the years following his departure from active duty. It was a sad day in Peter's life as it was for many when the flag was lowered for the last time over the embassy in Saigon and the mighty American war machine had to suffer the indignity of retreat. Despite overwhelming odds, the VC's resilience and familiarity with their own environment ultimately won through.

Many soldiers were demobbed from the military on the return to the USA as there was no longer such a need for as great a force, but Peter Falconer had opened up a new avenue of employment for himself. His planning and calculated thinking had led him to the security position for the American embassy in Vietnam, and this specialism was to be pursued back in the USA. His services were retained and he moved in to the diplomatic services where, over time, he became the chief of security responsible for safety and security of American overseas installations. These were essentially classed as *non military* installations such as embassies, although it is common knowledge that even the embassies contained their own small army of Marines and MPs. This was an extremely interesting job for the Major and a role he relished. His reputation opened many a door for him, even before his arrival at any new location. He was well respected by people he had never met. Clearly, even within the secretive corridors of power, the whispers about him were ostensibly good.

The position also afforded the Major the opportunity to be on the ground operating the latest technology in surveillance, intelligence and security long before it was rolled out to other departments, and well before anything similar was commercially available. He enjoyed the cutting edge of it all as it still allowed him to use his brain. He was always focused and remained thorough in his approach to work. The other benefit it provided was the need to travel. He needed to visit many locations around the world, basically wherever the US had a diplomatic presence, he would need to oversee in some capacity their security. Obviously, he couldn't personally take charge of all locations, but he had assembled a good team around him to assist with the whole picture. However, he did get the opportunity to visit many of them, albeit briefly, as well as take personal ownership of the larger and more important facilities.

Being the American security specialist in Russia always meant that when he travelled there he always had a tail from the KGB. But this was known and expected, his Russian counterparts were offered the same courtesy when in the USA. It went with the turf and as long as the local rules were obeyed there was never an issue. Of course, as the security chief, he was always suspected of being the number one American spy, so surveillance in Moscow was always very close, but they had nothing to fear in truth. He was interested in security, that's all, he was no James Bond! Yet it amused him that the Russian's, and other nations, thought differently. Hell he thought, with that damaged leg he would find it difficult to outrun most people these days, but the attention was on the whole, good fun.

It was the travelling to the embassy in London that provided his greatest thrill. It was here that he met his future wife Katie Pearce. Katie was a typical English Lady, just as portrayed by Americans everywhere. She was well spoken, well mannered and well educated. Although she was only an assistant to the American Ambassador, looking after his diary and press releases, she had a university degree in Economics and Politics, attained at Durham University in the UK, an old and well respected establishment. Such was the skill requirements set by the American Embassy to even be considered for posts within the so called inner circle. Even posts in administration and typing were not easy to come by but Katie had done well in her role so had earned the ear of the ambassador. She never travelled from the embassy, these roles were reserved for her American colleagues, but this didn't bother her. She was happy doing what she did, but also enjoyed her return home each evening to her own space, an apartment in Notting Hill occupied solely by her and her pet cat, Cleo. She was happy following this relatively simple but fully occupied lifestyle. She had a few friends with whom she would occasionally party but nothing outrageous, all very civilised and usually reserved for the weekends. Katie's family offered a strong military history spanning back through several generations, which of course helped in her success and security checks within the embassy prior to being employed. It was one such security check where she first met Peter Falconer . . .

The two of them instantly hit it off despite an instinctive show of resistance at first from Katie, but she couldn't resist the American's charms for too long. Within two years of their first meeting in London, they were married. Katie Pearce became Katie Falconer. The Major managed to shift his assignments so that he could do a lot more work from a base in the American Embassy in Grosvenor Square in London rather than be based almost full time in Washington. He still had to travel frequently to the USA but at least he could now call London home. Katie had no desire to leave her post at the embassy so it all worked together nicely. Peter Falconer still needed to travel with his work, but it didn't really matter whether that journey started in London or Washington. The couple set up their home also in Notting Hill. Katie relinquished her apartment for a larger terraced property but at least one where they could develop a family; long term planning but plans which were called into play sooner than originally envisaged with the arrival of their son Anthony only eighteen months after their marriage. He was a healthy boy, entering the world on the 15th June 1974 and weighing in at seven pounds eight ounces. Despite the early arrival, he was still a much welcome addition which provided closure to the family unit. Now they were complete. Katie's position at the embassy would remain available for her when the time came to return to work, either part time or full time, and child care assistance was also available. There were plenty of options for the future. Although not wealthy, the family was fairly comfortable financially so there was no panic on the employment front. They could easily survive on Peter's income alone so the choice of future working would be down to Katie, and her alone.

Anthony was only eight years old when he suffered his father's premature death. A routine overseas visit to what was seen as a friendly state, yet he was gunned down in his car whilst parked at traffic lights. Whether it was Peter or his travelling companions from the local embassy who were the target was not clear. The fact remains that all occupants of the vehicle were mercilessly slaughtered that fateful summer's day in 1982. Of course details were sketchy, the full facts about the incident would never be revealed as his father's business was inexorably shrouded in secrecy. Katie was never sure what he really did as a career, only what she saw at the embassy. She also knew not to probe too deeply as she would only get the official line in any case, so why bother. The day she was told of his death would without doubt be no exception. Only what the public would be told is what she would be told.

Katie's life was shattered. She had of course support from her family and friends, as well as from the embassy itself, but she had lost her rock. There was still Anthony to remember her husband by, in whom his memory would live on, but she couldn't bear going on without Peter. She became very reclusive, never alienating Anthony but instead taking the loss out on herself. Anthony was always looked after, but her self destruction was going on when he was not around. She thought he had no idea. The self annihilation led to drinking, vodka being the favoured choice. Clear liquid and more difficult to detect than other spirits on the breath, but even this couldn't numb the pain of her loss. All the sympathy, all the well wishers and offers of help could not bridge the gap left behind by the sudden departure of her dear Peter. No goodbyes, no plans for the future. She needed to be with him so badly. The depressions sank deeper and deeper resulting in her drinking to excess day by day. Soon it was needed just to get by. The drinking was no longer an anaesthetic for the pain she constantly felt; it was in reality now her life support machine. She was an alcoholic and getting even deeper into the murky depths of that lifestyle.

Fortunately, throughout this turbulent time, Anthony also had the guiding hand of his mother's brother Paul, who lived outside the city in a more rural environment. He was a regular feature in Anthony's adolescent life almost taking over the role vacated by his father. Most of Anthony's schooling was on a weekly boarding basis so he never really saw the depths of depression his mother often sunk to during the week when she was alone. Yet, as he matured he could clearly see her decline and inevitable failing health. Despite the best efforts from his Uncle Paul, his mother could not quit the drink and Anthony could no longer be shielded from her illness. Unfortunately shortly after he had turned sixteen, Anthony's mother's health finally failed her. A failure of her internal organs pre-cursed by her alcoholic dependency led to her collapse, slipping into a coma and passing away peacefully in hospital within twenty four hours of collapsing. At last she could be at peace and with her beloved, but Anthony was now alone. He had now been cheated of both parents and was instantly taken into the care of his Uncle Paul. At least this was familiarity in his life which could now take on some form of normality. He had a lot of catching up to do; after all, the boy had effectively been robbed of a normal childhood. Yet, at his age, he was already well on the way to adulthood, albeit prematurely.

Uncle Paul couldn't give back Anthony his lost years, but he could help steer his future. There was still an opportunity to shape the future for this bright young man. After much soul searching, both agreed, although a little reluctantly on Paul's part, that Anthony would himself enter military service and once his schooling was completed he enlisted for service with the Royal Marines. Of course this was not essentially cut and dried, he still had to pass selection and basic training, however he was fit and healthy and more importantly had the desire to succeed in this area. They discussed the option of pursuing a graduate entry into the Marines and taking further studies; however he would rather he started as soon as possible and chose to start at the bottom and work his way up. He was ambitious and wanted to earn respect, just like his father had; rather than expect it simply due to the insignia on his shoulders due to a higher education. This was, in reality, his own way of coming to terms with his internal anger of losing his family, a way of venting his own aggression without simply turning into an aggressive wayward youth with attitude. At least he had the common sense to be able to see how he would best serve his own purposes, even if this was only looking ahead for now to the short term. He would still give it a go. He was sure his father would have approved.

Anthony sailed through his training and passed out almost top of his class into the British Royal Marines as he had hoped. Basic training was tough and as much a shock to Anthony as it was to the rest of the crew. Attrition rates were high but he could live with this, even when some very good friends were thrown out. This was after all, an elite fighting unit, so it needed every member to be able and worthy to wear the highly prized dagger insignia on their uniform. He had made it to being a commando. His father would have surely been proud. Anthony passed into 45 Commando, based at Arbroath in Scotland. Hardly close to home for weekend visits to Uncle Paul but it was not his choice, and it also afforded a greater variety of specialist training. Of particular interest to Anthony was the chance to indulge in the winter activities and training this unit specialised in. This is where his love for skiing was developed. Skiing turned out to be something Anthony took to very well, as well as marksmanship. Discipline never proved to be his strong point though and despite his abilities in certain quarters, it was clear from early days in the corps that he could not develop into a real team player. He was certainly more akin to being a loner than being a cog in a larger gearbox.

He had missed the units greatest success in the Falkland Islands back in 1982 but saw his first overseas duty following training, in Northern Iraq, offering safe haven to the Kurdish population, followed by overseas protectorate duties in Kuwait in 1994. But this was not enough for Anthony, it was not his bag and this had not gone unnoticed by his superiors.

His talents were well recognised as were his weaknesses. This led to more individual tasks being undertaken by the young soldier, away from his unit. Many of these operations were not publicised and often his works were in advance of other operations, yet his success here did bring him to the attention of others and on occasion some extremely untoward operations came his way. On two occasions he had been called upon to operate behind enemy lines, both in Bosnia, where he used his marksmanship skills to eradicate military personnel who were responsible for atrocities and war crimes but were not getting brought to account for their sins. The bureaucracy that ran the United Nations prevented such things happening swiftly, yet many in the West knew they required solving swiftly. Senior civil servants within Europe and the USA knew action needed taking, and Anthony was chosen as the special one. However, with his aversion to discipline, despite his abilities, his continued run ins with senior NCOs meant that he did not really enjoy his career as much as he thought he would, as such he left the corps after completing his twelve years service as required by his original commitment, at the tender age of twenty eight.

Chapter 9

Now, Falcon was in the big wide world. He no longer had the protection of the Corps and needed to find a career himself. He ambled through a number of jobs as a security guard, sometimes roaming on patrol looking after construction sites and office buildings then moving on to being a doorman on several nightspots in London's club-land but the prospect of fighting hand to hand on a regular basis with stoned drunks, who may at any instance produce a lethal weapon, was hardly fulfilling. Despite the training in hand to hand combat, karate versus a shooter was definitely a mismatch . . . whoever the players. It was whilst working at a gentleman's club in Mayfair where Falcon was first approached about a job that would change his career direction.

There was no trouble at these clubs. They were frequented by captains of industry, government ministers and civil servants as well as peers of the realm. No, his duty here was solely to provide assurance to the patrons, who had paid a hefty price for membership and the exclusivity it brought, that they would not be troubled by any undesirables, this included the paparazzi. Members were escorted wherever they wanted and this even included all the way home if desired. Sometimes he'd be called upon to act as driver to some of these members if needed. Of course this was not a complimentary service, but the members never needed to ask the price. They wouldn't be there if they had to ask the price. In most cases they probably never knew how much they actually spent there, this would have no doubt been taken care of by a lowly employee or accountant. One evening in the summer of 2003, a seemingly routine lift home for a couple of patrons back to the Home Counties, changed his life forever.

As he drove his passengers home, the guests simply chatted in the rear of the dark blue Bentley Arnage, one of the most sought after taxi carriages owned by the club and reserved for very special members, enjoying more complimentary quality brandies from the vehicles exquisite mini bar. These were certainly the upper echelons of membership as this vehicle was not openly available to all members. He couldn't hear their discussions, neither was it his place to try to. There were often indiscretions that took place in the club's vehicles and premises but discretion was always assured; whatever happened at the club, stayed at the club. Falcon drove for over forty minutes out to the leafy stockbroker suburbs that surround London, a good distance could be covered that time of the morning when all decent folk were asleep in their beds. On reaching the desired destination, the Bentley serenely glided into a sweeping leafy driveway from which the main house could not be seen for over one hundred yards. This was certainly a private retreat. He pulled the vehicle to a steady halt near to the pillared double front door of the graceful residence and jumped out to assist his occupants from the vehicle. After all, he was there to attend to their needs; it was expected with the territory. However as he jumped to the rear off side door, his passenger was already alighting, as was his colleague from the opposite door. This was most unusual as these guys often enjoyed the pandering from these services; nonetheless, what was stranger was yet to come.

"Many thanks Tony," said the elder of the two gentlemen.

This was a great surprise to Falcon, as it was unusual for many of the guests to even acknowledge the hired help in such a way, and even stranger for them to know his name. He wasn't the only driver assigned to such duties at the club, there were at least half a dozen others and it could have been any of them on this run. However, it was him and not somebody else; and not by chance. This meeting had been engineered with one purpose in mind, and that was a face to face discussion with Anthony Falconer; away from any prying eyes or ears.

Falcon remained his usual composed self and acknowledged the thanks.

"Now Tony," started the elder again, "my colleague and I would like a word with you if you please . . . in private".

"I trust there were no problems gentlemen," replied Falcon, a little surprised. He had never had any issues with clients previously, and in fact was often commended on his manner with the patrons. He had an ability to deal with people at all levels and it was appreciated.

"None whatsoever young man. We simply have a proposition for you that could be of interest."

Falcon appeared uneasy and shuffled his feet a little whilst looking away from the patrons and tried to make his excuses that he needed to get back to the club.

The second dinner jacket donning guest began to chuckle.

"He thinks we're a couple of faggots Henry. Better nip this in the bud PDQ I think. Don't want that sort of crap circulating the club do we?"

Still laughing, the first who Falcon now knew as Henry, assured Falcon "We're not Faggots as my esteemed colleague has so eloquently put it," chuckling to himself at the thought. He continued, "Tony, we have a real job which we think is well suited to your credentials. Don't worry. We've squared it with the club that we may be taking a detour for a couple of hours so you're covered on that score. Come inside, we can discuss it over a large Napoleon, or whatever may take your fancy. It's too bloody cold to be standing out here gassing."

Despite it being English Summer time, his breath formed ghostly clouds in the still cool early morning air, spookily back lit from the low level ground lighting emanating from the house.

Falcon hesitated for a moment glancing from one to the other of his seemingly friendly passengers. Both were gently nodding their approval to him when Henry beckoned them both indoors more with an instruction than a request.

"Come on now the pair of you," he snapped and went up the stone steps towards the main doors, where a faithful butler opened it just as Henry reached the top most step.

Falcon wondered just how long this guy had been standing there waiting for his employer to finally ascend the steps.

Surely he doesn't wait up all night for his employer to return home. When does he get his sleep if he attends to people like this all the time he wondered? The other man followed Henry up the steps, followed just behind by Falcon. What did he have to lose? He already had a pass out for a couple of hours so this would mean probably no more taxi service tonight as when he got back to Mayfair, the patrons should have all gone home. Maybe an early finish for a change, although finishing at four a.m. can hardly be classed as early but at least whilst he is here he is not getting saddled with some shit detail left to be cleaned up at the club. Falcon was greeted by the obedient Butler just as was Henry; he was for a change on the receiving end of some pampering. It felt good. The doors were closed behind them almost rhythmically as the last man entered.

"Hamilton, we shall take some brandies in the study, then you may retire, we have some business to discuss so won't need you any more this evening," said Henry.

"Very good Sir Henry," retorted the obedient servant to his master and made off to the study to prepare drinks for the three guests. Falcon never saw the butler again that evening.

On entering the well furnished study, as directed, there were three crystal tumblers and the matching decanter containing brandy on the coffee table. This was nice, Falcon thought. Hard deep red leather chesterfield style sofas and high backed chairs surrounded the central coffee table and traditional mahogany desk with red inlaid leather surface took pride of place at what would be perceived as the helm of the study. The oak panelled walls were adorned with paintings, none of which Falcon could recognise but he was sure they weren't just mass produced prints. There was money here without doubt and lots of it.

"Gentlemen, please make yourselves comfortable," requested the host. "No need to stand on ceremony here, after all, we are all friends now."

Henry unloosened his black tie and threw it across his study without a care as to where it landed. No doubt some under paid minion would collect it later and return it to its rightful place.

"Now Mr. Falconer, or can I call you Tony. Your choice, you're effectively off duty so you don't owe us any airs and graces," continued Sir Henry.

"Tony would be fine Sir Henry."

"Now now lad, Henry is quite good enough here. The Sir only comes in handy for opening doors you know, queue jumping at restaurants, that sort of thing. In here, good old Henry will do nicely. Now, do you know my colleague?"

"I'm afraid I don't . . . Henry"

"Tony, let me introduce you to a very dear friend of mine, James Fairfax."

The two leant across the brandy table and shook hands, although a little warily on Falcon's part. "Pleased to meet you Mr. Fairfax."

"Likewise Tony, I've been looking forward to this opportunity for several weeks now, so at last we can put a face to the name".

Falcon seemed puzzled and Sir Henry quickly jumped in to the conversation.

"James, slow down a bit will you. Give the guy room to breathe for God's sake. You're like a sex maniac just released from prison, your brains aren't where they should be."

James Fairfax knew he now needed to take a back seat for a little while.

Clearly, whatever was transpiring, Sir Henry was to take the lead in the negotiations. "Now let me start at the beginning and shed some light on the situation. I am sure you are a little confused at the moment Tony."

"You could say that."

"Well, as you may or may not know I'm a member of the House of Lords and as such have access to some rather special information, if you know what I mean. Well, in truth I do not have direct access but have access to the right people who do. Is this making any sense so far?"

"Go on, I am after all still here and am fascinated to see what I, a mere club doorman, can possibly do for either of you that you can't get done anywhere else."

"Well Tony, it's easier to come straight to the point. We are looking for a man of your calibre and mentality, take that in the right way please and let me finish before you have any thoughts of tearing my head off, to undertake a rather delicate operation for us. We need someone with specialist military training for this role but also do not really want to advertise the fact. I called in some favours within the MoD and your name popped out of the hat. You're an excellent soldier, skilled in many forms of combat, specialist jungle and arctic training so well used to hostile environments; but above all, an excellent sharp shooter who prefers by far to work alone. You fit the bill for what we are looking for."

"Gentlemen, I think you may be mistaken. I'm no longer in the military. That life is all behind me now, several years behind in fact. I think somebody has sold you a wild goose Sir Henry. I hope you didn't pay for the information." Falcon threw the brandy down his throat; a lovely warm sensation overcame him as he quickly arose to leave. "I guess I must say goodnight to you gentlemen, and thanks for the drink, very nice."

"Tony," stated Sir Henry. "Is it your intention to be a bouncer all your life? You're destined for better things and this is the start of it. You are not the wrong man!" he said forcefully. "Have you any idea how much trouble we have gone to, to arrive at these findings. Do you think you were randomly selected out of a fucking hat? For God's sake man, sit down and hear me out. This is no joke; this is very important and will also be very rewarding for you. Just listen to the whole story before jumping to conclusions about it not being for you. Then, if when we are done, you still decide it's not your bag then you will prove us all wrong, you can then go on with your little life with the smug satisfaction of getting one over on me."

Falcon was surprised at the sudden forcefulness of the honourable knight, although it didn't intimidate him as he could easily have taken out both of the elderly guys in unarmed combat very swiftly. He was, however, more intrigued by what they had to offer. Falcon sat back down and lifted his empty tumbler and again pointed to the crystal decanter sat on the table.

"Please, feel free to help yourself. In fact pour three more out James would you. Well, I guess we have your attention for now."

"For now you do, yes," replied Falcon in a slower manner than usual, showing still some hesitation.

"Right then, James Fairfax, do you know who he is?"

"Unfortunately not, Henry."

"He is the Chairman of Coltex Mining, you no doubt have heard of them."

"Indeed, who hasn't?"

"Well, Coltex have a major problem in Zambia. They own and operate several of the world's largest copper mines down there but there is some local unrest. If this gets out of hand then it is possible they'll be stripped of their rights there and the operations all shut down. But it is not only Zambia where the concern is. Once this type of thing starts, then it just spreads and their operations all over Africa could be in jeopardy. Not only Coltex but there are several other British interests down in Africa on various mining and mineral activities that we need to ensure remain operable. They are a great source of income to this nation as well as the host nations. We know that if the European expertise is lost then so would be the efficiency in the mines, they would become unsafe, un-maintained in virtually no time and effectively be shut down in a very short space of time. Everybody loses. The last thing we want is the government nationalising the mines again."

"Especially Coltex," replied Falcon.

"Including Coltex!" replied Sir Henry sternly. "We are here to represent the interests primarily of Coltex, however, there are numerous other players who will also benefit, and ultimately the crown benefits from the revenue streams."

"Please, spare me the propaganda Sir Henry. I may just be a doorman but I'm not stupid. I am very much aware how much these major corporations make in dealing in Africa, raping the landscape of its resources and returning very little back to the people, dealing in the conflict diamonds fuelling further bloodshed in pursuit of riches at somebody else's expense. So please do not insult my intelligence."

James Fairfax finally spoke. "Mr. Falcon, for your information and it can be easily verified, Coltex actually do return a significant amount of revenue back to the state as well as additional funding locally to the employees and their villages. We are not totally heartless. Yes it is a great earner for us and if it was not us it would be somebody else who would no doubt not be as caring as we are. We're no angels, but we are the best of a bad bunch if you want to put it that way. If the uprising that is growing gets out of hand, then probably most of western Europe's operators will be closed down in Africa within months."

"Okay then, what can I do, a doorman, an ex soldier?" Falcon asked quizzically.

Sir Henry returned to the discussion, "The whole uprising is headed by one individual. A tribal leader, Kapwepwe Mizinga, from one of the smaller tribes in the area, which is too far away from the operations to reap any real benefits. He is riding his popularity by stirring up hatred against our operation. He's intimidating locals who are starting to stay away from the mines and production is steadily falling away. His popularity is growing and he is uniting the many tribes into a single force, which if he does so will be a very sizeable party to deal with. He is now seen as an idol in some of the towns there with the support from the countryside sweeping him higher up the popularity trail. But it's not just politics; it is starting to turn violent. Several tribesmen have been murdered including village elders, who have previously declined to join Mizinga's masquerade as a man of the people. He is claiming immortality and that he has been sent from the Gods to unite the land and its people and take back what is theirs from the foreign oppressors. He walks on hot coals, eats fire and undergoes various other ritualistic ceremonies with snakes and such like to prove his immortality . . . and the people are buying in to it. He is promising them a better way of life; I guess he is the Chairman Mao of Zambia. More likely he will be another Idi Amin."

"But what can I do about this? Where do I possibly fit in?"

Now it was Fairfax's turn. "Mizinga is no man of the people. He is a crook, just like a lot of the politicians over there. He is out to line his own pockets, we know that for sure. He just needs a vehicle and the people are becoming that vehicle. If he can achieve unity then they will see him as their saviour, but Africa is steeped in such events that have tragically unfolded into nothing but utter chaos. Just look at the mess in Zimbabwe, all down to one man . . . a man of the people. A prize nation now reduced to nothing, the people are starving and the resources remain un-tapped; greed by an individual, killing an entire nation. We do not want that to happen here. It's not just our money, its lives, lots of people's lives."

"I go back to my last question . . . where do I fit in?"

"We want you to take out Mizinga?"

Falcon almost choked on his own saliva. Did he hear right? Neither of the proposers flinched a muscle when they made the request.

"You want me to kill somebody I've never met to save your company from a bad financial year, are you guys in sane? I am not a merc or a hit man. I told you, you have the wrong guy."

"On the contrary," replied Sir Henry, "you are the right man as we said before, you just don't know it yet . . . but you will."

"You really think so do you?"

"Tony, this is not just a killing. It's not a mindless murder or even just for the money. It's for more than that. Stability in the region helps us all. The last thing we need is to send more troops overseas to keep the peace in a foreign land. A war we can't win fighting people who believe they have nothing to lose anyway. At least with the mines still working they have a future. Granted, as you say perhaps not as rich as they ought to with all that wealth in the ground, but without the likes of the British, the French and others, they would have nothing. If it gets in the wrong hands there will be anarchy across the continent. The economic effects alone will impact Europe widely let alone the humanitarian problems it will then create. There'll be tribal wars over the spoils, African versus African when one cheats the other out of what he feels he's been promised. At least this way we keep stability. Yes, Coltex keeps its mineral rights but so does the government. Even that is full of corruption as you can imagine down there but at least some of the money gets through to the people. Tony, whatever your cynical views, let me assure you this is more than just private enterprise."

Falcon sat dumbstruck at the passion with which this case was being fought. Sir Henry continued, "What I am about to tell you is highly classified. You have of course signed the OSA and you are aware you are still bound by its terms until your death."

"I am aware of the implications of spouting my mouth off which is why I have never done so. Let me tell you gentlemen, I have done a few things myself which you won't find any official records of and I've never told a soul. I can keep quiet when I need to," replied Falcon assuringly. Without realising it, he was slowly becoming interested in their proposition. The challenge was starting to bite at him and he was slowly being hooked.

Sir Henry and Fairfax cast a fleeting glance at one another. They sensed he was being lured, it was just a matter of keeping up the momentum and he would be theirs.

"This is not just something dreamt up by myself and James. Of course, we analysed the problem and arrived at suitable scenarios based on information received from our own government departments, but we would simply not be in a position to sanction such a task. We proposed it though and the intelligence service has given its seal of approval. The snag is they will never admit to it. This is off the record totally. They will not interfere with it and will supply any intelligence we may need to assist, strictly under the carpet. However they cannot be seen to participate in political assassinations, it's not good for the good old British image you know. They are fully supportive though due to the benefits it will bring to the region as well as to European interests down there."

"Well why not send in the SAS under cover or somebody like that."

"Quite simple really, there can be no official involvement at any level. Can you imagine the ramifications if a serving British Soldier was captured down there, our operations would be wiped out in an instant. We would be lucky if our people even got out alive never mind if at all."

"Right, but why not use a professional, a hit man or a mercenary? There's no shortage of them surely."

"Mercenaries are just that. They sell their souls to the highest bidder and it is such a small environment there would be too much gossip. We can't afford the risk. As for a hit man, when did you last see one advertised in the yellow pages?" said Fairfax sarcastically, whilst finishing off his latest shot of his friend's fine brandy.

Sir Henry took over the reigns; "See why you fit the bill Tony. You are skilled in solo combat, a loner, a marksman, used to the environment. You are perfect for this. Your country needs you and we think you need some sort of challenge. You're not cut out for the nine to five market, you are a soldier and by all accounts a damned good one. It's a pity about the authority issue you had but that's not really a factor in this line of work. Oh, and by the way you will be paid, handsomely. So in a nutshell, you will be doing something you like and getting rewarded, and a whole new career will open up for you."

"Oh so I can advertise now in the yellow pages!"

"No, there may be other delicate projects that the government may need some assistance with if you get my drift. It can be arranged you know. People have no idea what really goes on behind the closed doors of power. Forget the figurehead in number ten, that's the face the people want to see. Who do you think makes the day to day policy decisions that keep the nation running? These people will be in their jobs irrespective of who sits in the P.M.'s chair. These are the people who can help shape your future."

Falcon was now in the zone with these guys, consequently up popped the big question.

"So what is it worth to me then?"

"Apart from a career move you mean?" asked Sir Henry

"You know exactly what I mean," replied Falcon with great haste.

"Well, Coltex will foot the bill; after all this is a purely private venture. They will meet all of your expenses between now and the time of the contract and pay an additional one thousand pounds per week living money for now. When the job is complete there will be a payment of fifty thousand pounds, paid in any currency you like into any bank of your choice anywhere in the world. I would recommend the Cayman Islands personally but the choice is fully yours."

"What about timing, planning, security and the likes? How do I get there, how do I get out more importantly? What about the gear?"

"Tony . . . Tony." said Fairfax, "Too many questions for one night. Let's just have an understanding that we are going ahead, and then we can get to the detail. At the end of the day it's your ass down there, so we give you the info you need and you tell us how it's to be done. We will get you in and out and get whatever gear you need, that's the easy part."

Sir Henry then spoke, but in a sudden change of tone from the previous exchanges. "Of course Tony, if you do get caught, which I am sure you won't, but if you do . . . then we have never heard of you. That will be the deal. Even if you talk, all knowledge of your very existence will be denied. Your records will be scrubbed from the database and you won't even exist as far as this country is concerned. I trust you fully understand the consequences of this undertaking?"

Falcon slowly nodded showing his understanding, then slowly but purposely spoke "One hundred thousand and I'll do it, but my way."

"A negotiator, how nice, at least we've established principal. I guess it's now just quantum we're arguing over," mused Fairfax. "Okay," he continued, "on the understanding that Mizinga is dead within two months. I guess you start tomorrow working for me. I'll square it away with the club and make sure you get a good reference, but I don't think you'll be going back to that line of work, do you?"

Sir Henry reached across his desk for the inlaid mahogany cigar box. Clearly another expensive object thought Falcon, yet inside were the finest quality cigars money could buy.

"Gentlemen, I think this calls for a celebratory cigar on this momentous occasion," said Sir Henry triumphantly as he passed around the opened case.

"Make the most of this Tony, this doesn't get opened for us guests very often," chuckled Fairfax as he keenly took his own from the box.

"I shall send a car for you tomorrow evening and we can start the planning. You can work from my flat in Belgravia for the time being. It's handy for us to call in as required but also nobody will find you there. The staff will take care of your day to day needs; you just concentrate on the job. Meanwhile I shall get the files sent over there with any relevant info we have on this guy. Looks like you better work sharpish dear boy, completing in such a short time frame will be no easy feat."

"As long as there is the opportunity for a shot then it will be easy. If he drives around in a bullet proof pope mobile, then it's not so easy. Let me decide on how easy it will be. How do you know this will work anyway? Even if Mizinga dies, surely someone will just take his place."

"Ah yes. That is so. But we know who. A greedy little bugger in his own right, but just not as greedy as Mizinga. He knows they need us all down there to keep the operations going; he's not after glory or immortality with his people. He just wants money, in a Swiss bank account. He is more than happy to unite his people in alignment with our wishes. This is where most of the intelligence will come from."

"So you are taking out Mizinga for his number two who just wants his hands on the money pot."

"I suppose, in a nutshell you could see it that way. That's the way the world runs I am afraid, at least this way we keep control and more importantly stability. We know Mizinga is already being financed by the Cuban's and it would not be great for us if they moved in with the Russians after we were kicked out. There really is a lot at stake here Tony and if Mizinga's trusted aide gets rich out of it then it's just a sad indictment of commerce, but it is unavoidable. The greed always corrupts them in the end anyway."

Falcon was shaken by the hand as he was shown to the front door by his two hosts. "Until tomorrow Tony, we shall collect you from your apartment early evening," said Sir Henry as he closed the door on Falcon as he got back into the Bentley.

It was a strange drive back to the club. Falcon of course needed to return the Bentley as he could hardly take it home. The roads were incredibly quiet; this time of the morning was always pleasant to drive around London. There were the very late revellers just going home, the early starters just go-ing to work; all as the darkness was getting ready to lift its black cloak and bring the city back to life for another day of hustle and bustle. Falcon took a steady drive, there was no rush. He needed to contemplate what had just happened. He had mixed emotions, what the hell was he doing . . . him an assassin. Yet at the same time he regained the buzz of his specialist military days, the thrill of helping mankind in Bosnia on his last special op. This would really change his life forever. Once he was a hired gun there would be no going back. He knew that. He had no real friends to speak of so that wouldn't be any great loss and he hardly ever kept in touch with his Uncle so it would be easy to fabricate some story about his existence to keep that side of his domestic life intact. But what about him, what could he do after this, would he ever get a life, would he spend the rest of his days looking over his shoulder? The thoughts spiralled around his head as he weaved the car through the desolate streets of London town watching the dancing traffic lights spout out their discotheque aurora of red yellow and green. It was fascinating to see just how much light there was in London when there were no other distractions.

After the keys were deposited with night security for the Bentley, Falcon grabbed the first available taxi and headed home, he really needed his bed tonight but he knew it would be difficult to sleep.

Right on cue the following day, as planned, the limousine collected Falcon from his apartment and drove him to Sir Henry's apartment in Central London. It was just as he expected; several floors of accommodation, six bedrooms, domestic staff and even more demonstrations of opulence. Some flat he thought. He wondered why do these people wanted more money, as he surveyed his surroundings.

Sir Henry was there as expected and showed Falcon to the guest room. "You can stay here for as long as you wish. My car is at your disposal should you need anything and I shall be here regularly, in fact most days I am afraid. Let me know what info you're short of and I shall see what I can do. There's beer in the fridge and better tell cook what you do and don't eat. We can use the office as the planning HQ if you like; have no fear, the staff are restricted from there with one exception, and I can assure you that their discretion is guaranteed, I will put my life on it."

"Glad to hear it," replied Falcon. "Let's see what we've got then."

He was shown to the study where there were a couple of mahogany desks and a rather large rectangular dining table on which were sat the box of documents Falcon was to start analysing.

"There it is Tony, all over to you now. Well, better get to the club for an appointment you know? See you later perhaps. I think I should be back in time. If not eat without me, no ceremony required here."

"How do I contact you if I need to?"

"You don't. See Jenkins, he can always get hold of me and I'll get in touch when I can." With that Sir Henry left the study and Falcon was left alone with his destiny. No time like the present he thought, and set about emptying the box of its documents to see what he had got himself into . . .

Chapter 10

The first thing that struck Tony Falconer as he got out of the Hercules converted transport plane that brought him from the capital Lusaka to the nearest airstrip to the Coltex operation, was the arid atmosphere. This was not tropical Africa where the humidity could be felt all day long, this was very dry. The heat was sweltering and the landscape scorched. It was akin to pictures that were advertised portraying what the surface of Mars must look like. This whole place looked inhospitable, yet there was no shortage of people around. Clearly they had found a way to survive in these conditions but he wondered how. There were no major townships near the airstrip but more small villages dotted around sporadically, although by car modern life was only a few hours away. His equatorial training had really only been in jungle type environments, although a brief spell in Oman on joint exercise with their military did offer a small insight into what he was about to enter. However, it was not as great an insight as he had hoped. Still, this was his choice so he had better acclimatise as quickly as possible and get on with the job at hand. Falcon wondered what had happened to all the greenery he had seen when flying over the country. Where were the forests? The truth was that in the mining areas they had been cleared away and devastated by the onset of uncontrolled expansion and industrial pollution creating ecological damage, often irreparable, in pursuit of short term financial gains.

It was only four weeks ago that he had first met with Fairfax and Johnson, yet how quickly things had moved. Falcon liked it this way, as long as planning was done correctly he failed to see why anything should be dragged out unnecessarily. He had arrived in Zambia as a mining geologist working for Coltex, nothing unusual in that. There were regular shift changes from all sorts of personnel working for Coltex and the other operators in the area so it fitted in quite nicely. The only problem would be if Falcon was ever asked any technical questions on geology, but what's the chance of that, he thought? What was unusual was that he travelled under the name of Robert Vaughan. Falcon was surprised at how quickly his patrons had arranged false identity papers and passport bearing this name, all with the Queen's seal. They surely must have been well connected. He was collected from the airstrip by a local driver, also an employee of the mine, driving one of their logo emblazoned Toyota pick up trucks, a must for the terrain. The driver was sporting a placard bearing the name Robert Vaughan, so there was little mistake over where he was due to head.

Falcon ambled across the red dusty terrain to his waiting driver and threw his carry bag into the back of the dusty pick up.

"Welcome to Coltex, Mr. Vaughan, very nice to have you here sir," said the driver in almost faultless English.

"Thanks, so where do we go now?" asked Falcon.

"First we need to get you to the camp and get your bedroom allocated. Then we need to do the safety inductions, everybody has to do the inductions, Company policy I'm afraid. Then I guess we see the boss and see where you are to go. I believe you're surveying possible new sites? Your truck has arrived from South Africa still in the container with the rest of the equipment."

"No secrets here then?"

"No sir, a close knit family you could say. I also spend a lot of time in the office so I see who is coming and going. It helps keep me abreast of things."

"You're a nosey bugger then?" replied Falcon dryly, without even breaking into a grin. The thought of smiling in this place made him cringe, the sooner he was away the better.

The driver broke out into an infectious laugh showing his set of yellow tarnished off white teeth; almost complete although a few gaps visible towards the rear of his cavernous mouth when it opened wide.

"Yes sir, I am a nosey bugger as you say. You English have some funny words. I am Kato; I am your driver whenever you need me. Just ask for me if you need anything on camp. I have been instructed to make your stay as welcoming as possible. You ask and I am to get . . . if I can get of course," the driver quickly added.

Falcon could see that he could get to like Kato, he seemed genuine enough, although he realised he was not here to form friendships. He needed a low profile and to be able to slip away virtually unnoticed so it was probably best he only had the one point of contact with the rest of the operation. It was certainly going to be interesting.

It was only a relatively short drive back to the mining camp but despite the lack of comfort on the plane down to the site, the truck journey was even less so. He could see why there was a need for such vehicles here. The vehicle could not seem to go in a straight line as it followed the snaking, dusty, graded roads across the scrub land. Why they could not build them straight was a wonder to Falcon as he sat admiring the view and wondering what awaited him at the camp, whilst all the while Kato seemed to enter into an incessantly long conversation answering his own questions as he went. Falcon said very little on the journey back, even if he had wanted to Kato seemed to be worried that if ever he stopped speaking his jaw would seize up. Still, at least Kato was a jolly guy regularly breaking out onto what appeared to be forced fits of laughter but that was just the way he was. The clouds of red dust propelled into the still fiery air adding further to the impression that this was an oversized furnace into which Falcon had entered. The inside of the truck was covered with the stuff and Tony knew that within minutes he himself would be.

"I hope there are showers at the camp Kato," he said whilst drawing with his finger through the red dust which had settled over a period of time along the black dash board of the pick up. Kato simply nodded whilst continuing with his laughter.

"I see you valet the truck regularly," he said with a dry wit that Kato was probably not used to. Perhaps this was the wrong thing to say as Kato turned serious for a moment.

"Oh no sir, I clean the truck every couple of days. It does not take long here to get dirty. I always do the air strip runs you see so I need to keep the truck clean. Mr. Striker would not be happy with me if I didn't sir." Kato seemed somewhat concerned at the comments from Falcon who had to reassure him that he was only kidding and not to worry.

"So who is Mr. Striker?" asked Falcon, now taking the conversation to another level.

"You will meet him shortly sir. I've been told to take you to his office when we arrive. He's the manager here, we call him God."

"And the reason for that is . . .?"

"Mr. Striker is the law out here. Whatever he says goes. He is very protective about the mine and will not let anything get in the way of stopping production. Even when we have an accident we lose very little time. Anybody hurt or killed seems to get forgotten about very quickly. Their families are paid off and the matter gets closed and mine back at full production. Not good sir, not good at all but we all need the work. Without the mine many people around here would starve."

"I take it the union doesn't help?" asked Falcon sarcastically.

"UNION!" exclaimed Kato in almost disbelief at hearing such an expression. "There is no way any workers' union would ever be allowed within the mine. Mr. Striker would probably eat anybody who dared suggest it. Anyway Mr Robert, no more of this discussion, we're nearly there now. See, over there the mine and nearby the workers and staff camps."

The vehicle approached the mine but pulled off to the right down another track about a mile away from the main entrance to the offices and camp areas. The whole area was surrounded by chain link and barbed wire fences around nine feet high. Heavy duty double gates were manned by armed guards and were swung open as the Coltex truck approached. They of course knew Kato so he had no problem with gaining access but did have to explain who his passengers were each time.

"Security sir, every time."

"I fully understand," said Falcon as he glanced around at the surreal surroundings. "This place is well guarded, looks more like a prison than a camp."

"Well here we have the office area sir on the left with the main camp on the right hand side. The whole complex is fenced in for security purposes."

"Are they afraid that people will run away?" Falcon said again with sarcasm in his voice.

"Oh no sir. It keeps out the wild animals and things. At least we can walk around in the dark without fear of being attacked by a hungry leopard."

"I suppose it keeps out Mizinga as well then."

Kato's head spun around so quickly that the vertebrae in his neck clicked as he did so. "What do you know of Mizinga?" he asked startled.

"Not a lot really; I just heard that I need to be careful out in the bush as there was a local stirring up a little trouble, just avoid him I was told."

Kato for once was speechless and glared straight ahead, afraid to turn again to his passenger. He was not sure where to take the conversation now. He was utterly surprised that the intruder to this baron world even knew about Mizinga let alone dared to ask about him. He quickly decided to change the tone.

"First, I take you to your quarters, then to see Mr. Striker and you can set out your programme. Of course, if you need my assistance then I'll be happy to drive you around the bush."

"We shall see. It depends whether they have sent me up all the gear I requested. Not sure if I will need a hand or not yet. Rest assured though, if I need a driver I will ask for you personally. Right, where's my bed?"

Shortly after throwing his holdall into his quarters and quickly washing down, Falcon was standing in the office of Gerald Striker. He was an arrogant man of sizeable proportions. When he spoke Falcon knew at once he was of South

African origin and clearly at ease working in the African environment, which explained his attitude towards his black employees. Typical arrogance of white supremacists who believed their right to dominate simply due to their skin colour was Falcon's first impression. He was approaching two metres in height when he stood from behind his desk to greet Falcon. Blond hair and weighing in well on the wrong side of a hundred kilograms, Striker was aged around fifty but looked somewhat groomed considering the profession he was in. He had been involved in mining all his life and had from an early age, demonstrated to various employers, his ability to supervise and push the work force on the African continent to extremes and work his mines efficiently and productively.

"Gerald Striker," he balled out as his outstretched hand the size of a small shovel was thrust across the desk in the direction of Falcon.

"Welcome to my humble establishment, I hope the accommodation is within your expectations. I'd like to say it's good to have you on board," said Striker with some obvious reticence.

"Robert Vaughan," replied Falcon. "Likewise, although I'm not sure for quite how long I'll be here. Accommodation will be fine for now but I guess I'll spend a lot of time in the field."

"Well Bob, I'll get straight to the point. This is my operation and I run it my way. Rarely do I get any interference from head office because I deliver. However, I've been told to assist you as required and not question you on your being here. I don't like it but have no real choice. The top brass has spoken. So, as far as I am concerned we get you sorted out with your business and get you the hell out of here. I have enough issues to deal with rather than nurse maid somebody's stooge, or whatever you are. Any questions?"

"I guess not, other than where's my gear? Oh, by the way, you can trust me to be as quick as possible. I don't wish to have you extend your hospitality any more than you need to," retorted Falcon, showing no fear for the oversized and loud mouthed bully who was to be his temporary landlord.

"A container arrived for you, it's at the stores. We were told not to touch it and keep it out of the way of everything else. Whatever secrets you got in there I don't want to know. Just get on with it and get out. The damn thing's causing too many questions already in the yard and it's only been here a couple of days."

"Let's get started then, take me there and I'll get on with my business."

"Kato will take you wherever you need to go. There are already all sorts of rumours about your visit. Some say you're here to give a valuation on the mine for a take over, some say you are a looking at expansion. Me, I know you're doing neither and frankly I don't give a toss. I just want the mystery gone away so I can get back on with running my mine."

"Well, pleasure to meet you once again. No doubt I shall see you later." Falcon turned and went out of Striker's office into the reception where Kato was still sitting waiting for further instruction.

"Charming man isn't he?" stated Falcon in a satirical voice, raising smiles from the receptionists and Kato who were meant to hear the comment. "I see why they call him God!"

"Where to now boss?" asked Kato, hoping he was still to be of use to the new arrival.

"To the store yard, I need to check my gear."

The pair returned to the pick up outside the main office and set off to the store yard which was near to the mine operation itself. A ten minute or so ride around twisting meandering roads which encircled future expansion areas of the mine venturing around the back of the operation into the industrial facilities and workshops. Through the industrial area could be found the main stores. Kato was expected with his visitor, so there was little questioning when he requested to be in the so called restricted zone. This was an area specifically set aside within the stores area which was off limits to most visitors, due to the value of equipment, and more so, small tools and consumables that could be pilfered by opportunists, and there was no shortage of them around here. All usual visitors went to a service counter with a requisition slip and everything else was out back and brought through for them whenever possible. Where size dictated, trucks were allowed in but under close escort to make sure only the requested goods were taken. In the front of the stores was the fuel depot and plant work shops. Construction equipment was also stored out front as this was not the sort of stuff that the passing thief would likely take, after all he was miles from anywhere at the mine so could hardly hide a Caterpillar Dozer unnoticed.

The gates to the restricted zone were opened by one of the store assistants who enquired as to whether Kato knew where he was going. Of course he did, he knew everything.

As they drove around the well laid out stock yard Falcon asked, "What brings you here then Kato? Where are you really from?"

"Oh, I've been here many years Mr. Robert sir, several years before even Mr. Striker came."

"And you stayed on after that . . .?"

"I have little choice, I need the money. Well, my family needs the money. For an African labourer this is good money here. I want my boys to have a good education and not have to work in places like these. The world is opening up for people their age and I want them to have a chance. Maybe in this country or perhaps South Africa these days; who knows, maybe even London. But wherever, I want them to have the chance to not work like I have to."

"So where's your family?"

"My wife and two boys are back in Lusaka, well a small town just outside actually. My mother also lives with us so I need to support them all as well as school fees. I don't want my boys working too early or they will get no education. I cut short my education for my family and you never get out of the trap."

"How often do you get to see them? It's not as though you just pop home when you feel like it, is it?"

"I can usually get home every couple of months. It depends whether there is a slot on any of the supply aircraft at the time going back that way. It's too far to drive out here. Mr. Striker is okay like that, he knows I am loyal so tries to look after me a little better than many of the others, for what that's worth. There are many here who never see their families for months and months. It is a big price to pay, but I'm sure I will get my reward in heaven if not in this life. Besides, my reward is the safety and comfort for my family. They are quite well off really compared to many people in this country, although you may not think so."

"I'm sure you will get your rewards soon enough. So you were here before Striker eh? I bet you have a few stories to tell?"

Kato could not help himself but to continue talking. He rarely got the opportunity to speak with someone who was actually listening.

"When Mr. Striker came, we had many troubles here. There were lots of breakdowns with machinery, production stopped for one problem after another. We even had people striking for better conditions and pay. Many people here are desperate. They need to work whatever the conditions but some big trouble makers wanted to bring change, big change. There were a few people killed, beaten to death, simply because they wanted to work and they would not let them. When Mr. Striker came, all that changed. He came in with a lot of new people, some big people. They were armed and equally ruthless themselves. He soon got the place working again and the trouble makers were out. He has made this a better place for many of the workers. If you think the conditions are bad now you should have seen it ten years ago. We have good production now and very few breakdowns, all that has changed. We get better pay than most workers in other mines but in return Mr. Striker expects everybody to work to death almost. Still very few people would leave for another job if they got the chance. Money is everything here for people with nothing."

"You seem to admire Striker. Is he that good?"

"Well he may seem strange sir, but all I can say really is that he gets the job done. For the company he makes money and I know he is well rewarded personally. I'm not sure how well but we know it is well. But so are we in our own way so why complain. I have my own vision for my family and that's why I stick here."

Kato paused for breath, thinking he had probably inadvertently said too much already. After all he had no real idea who Robert Vaughan was other than believed to be a mining engineer sent down by head office.

"Ah, here we are, your container. I understood you brought keys with you for the locks?"

"I have yes," replied Falcon, still amazed at how quickly his employers can get such obviously tricky things done out here in this baron out back. His papers were done quickly, he had no problems entering customs so his papers were in order, and now his equipment was here.

Falcon jumped out of the dusty pickup, clouds of the interminable red dust still swirling around in the heat haze from their braking. It was an old container, brought to the site from its origin in South Africa through Durban, then by boat up to Dar Es Salaam in Tanzania then by road to Coltex's operation. Falcon thought it incredible that this had been organised and shipped in such a short space of time. Why had it not been held up at the customs in Tanzania or even Zambia itself? Clearly Coltex's connections were very strong with the authorities in one way or another, even if not via the front door. The fading red painted container had obviously seen better days but that did not matter. The doors were still sealed, as per the instructions given to Falcon prior to his leaving London for the assignment. The shipping documents hung in a plastic wallet attached to the container hinges. Falcon opened them to see that the package had cleared customs and was now officially in country. He read the manifest, *assorted equipment spares.* How original he thought.

"This is yours Mr. Vaughan?" asked Kato, rather interested to see what lay inside the mystery container.

Falcon nodded and grunted his acknowledgement. "Well, lets get it open," he said.

Falcon took the keys he had been given back in the UK and began to open the outer lock. The pair then swung open the heavy door on the container. The stale air that had been cooking inside the sealed container for a couple of weeks spewed out just as if an oven door had been opened. The heat blast drew their breath away for several seconds. Allowing their eyes to focus on the darkened interior, it was a couple of seconds or so before the contents were revealed.

"It's a Land Rover!" exclaimed Kato, rather disappointed.

"Why, what were you expecting?"

"Not sure really, just seems like a lot of trouble to get you a truck. We have pick ups here at the mine you could use."

"I doubt it," said Falcon. "This one is geared out for me and my work."

Falcon squeezed himself into the door on the driver's side and used his keys again to start the engine. First time it kicked into life.

"It sounds good anyway," said Kato, "better than ours here at least!"

Falcon drove the vehicle carefully out of the container.

"Well, I better get the kit checked out," he said turning to Kato. "I guess I don't need a taxi any more. I'll see you at dinner later."

Kato knew exactly what he was being told. "If you are sure Mr. Robert; I mean, you sure you don't need any help?"

"I'll be fine, just want to check out the gear here, make sure it's what I ordered then I can get on with my work. Won't trouble you any longer . . ."

Kato simply nodded and trudged back to his pick up, somewhat disappointed that he could not take part in the mysterious stranger's activities. Probably more concerned that something was going on he did not know about, rather than the indignity of just being sent away, but he knew when to follow orders, and this was one such time.

As he left, Falcon set about checking out the truck. It was a long wheel base Land Rover Defender, built for functionality rather than luxury. Such vehicles were common sights out in the bush so should not attract any unnecessary attention. However this one had no Coltex markings anywhere whatsoever. In fact, although Falcon did not know it, there were no distinguishing serial numbers or markings on any of the main vehicle components that could lead to future identification. The chassis and engine numbers had been ground down and were now untraceable. There was nothing that would tie this truck to Coltex or anybody else for that matter. It was time to check out the cargo bay. He unlocked the rear door to reveal a number of jerry cans neatly strapped to the inside cabin for additional fuel loads if necessary. There was also a roof top tent available for camping out in the bush, safer up on high than on the ground out here he thought. Then there was the long wooden chest; that was the main item he wanted to check. Hopefully that would be the key tool for his operation.

He opened the chest, making sure first there were no prying eyes looking over his shoulder, to reveal the American made M24A2 Sniper Rifle, as manufactured by the renowned firearms specialists, Remington. Falcon was familiar with the weapon having used its predecessor, the M24 on joint exercise with US Special Forces during the earlier stages of his military career. He was advised that this would be the weapon to be delivered and due to his familiarity with it, gave it the okay, especially as he would be getting the upgraded version. He knew it was a capable and rugged machine, well suited to the terrain he would be employed in. The rifle was capable of a reasonably accurate hit from eight hundred metres so should suffice. As requested, the documents he needed were also in the chest and the satellite phone. Most importantly, there was also the sum of ten thousand US dollars, not especially for Falcon's use, but, just to buy himself out of any trouble he may encounter along the way. He had a contact with Mizinga's aide, who was to advise of the best place for a shot at the self proclaimed people's champion. Unfortunately, an exact itinerary for Mizinga was difficult to schedule too far in advance so Falcon would need to be prepared to be in the locale, so to speak, at any required time, then move, on getting the tip off to the scheduled hit site. He knew he could be in for a few uncomfortable days and nights.

Chapter 11

The information was that Mizinga would never be more than a few hundred kilometres away from the mine as this was his main target and object of the people's planned uprising. He also did not want to stray too far away from the border country with the Congo where despite their ongoing civil war, he had allies and further support for his quest. This was in truth to be the starting point of his country wide rebellion to over throw the foreign investors and take back for the people what was rightfully theirs. This was the political agenda despite the government itself being a shareholder in the venture, although everybody knew there were those in the government that were making themselves rich at the same time as representing the supposed best interests of the people. In truth, he was merely going to switch sides with the Cubans and Russians. So, in time the people would see little difference, but a few locals would get rich, once again at the expense of their fellow man. Falcon needed to arrange rations and water for around a week away as well as fuel. Then it was simply drive off into the scrub to the locale where he anticipated Mizinga would be, based on the latest conversations with their contact, and simply await confirmation.

The efficiency of Sir Henry Johnson and Mr. James Fairfax still amazed the assassin. This trip could be shorter than he thought. It was just like clockwork. He put the slim portable satellite phone back in its waterproof wallet after ensuring it was fully charged. It would be charged during travelling from the cigarette lighter in the truck, but he knew from experience that these little beasts for communication could devour up their juice very quickly when being used. It would be essential to keep it fully charged whenever possible. The basic plan would be to drive back to Lusaka once the target was eliminated, dispose of the vehicle then catch the first available plane out of the country; preferably to South Africa, from where he would be able to make arrangements to get home. A steady drive out of there would not be so easy. The distance from the copper mining area in the North West territory of the country back to Lusaka would be around five hundred kilometres, no easy feat if he had to go off the main roads and would certainly take several days. Despite it being outside of the copper belt territory, the mine at around one hundred kilometres west of the prestigious operations at Kitwe was still highly productive.

Falcon was happy with what he had been given, just what the doctor ordered he thought. The sun set quickly in the African continent and the September evenings were very pleasantly warm with the only problem being the very persistent mosquitoes. A daily dose of garlic seemed to do the trick though, an old lesson learned from camping in his childhood, far better than any prescription drugs available. It seemed the blood thirsty mosquito could smell garlic circulating within an individual's veins and wouldn't go near it. He had better get back to the camp and make himself ready for tomorrow and put old Kato at ease. He locked the trunk and the back of the vehicle and set off to the base camp. He kept some of the paperwork including maps of the country in his rucksack along with the satellite phone for some bed time revision on his subject. Planning always makes perfect. Tomorrow he would depart from the camp and probably never see any of these people again. He wondered whether they would bother sending out a search party if he simply didn't come back or whether Mr. Fairfax will advise them he had left the country.

Falcon was awake early the following morning and took his shower whilst it was still dark outside. This could be the last one for a few days so he thought he might as well go out clean. He had stocked himself with all the essential food and water he could justify. He had told Kato the previous evening he could be away for around a week so by mid morning everybody on the site would inevitably know the stranger had left town, albeit temporarily. The early morning would be a much more comfortable period in which to drive this terrain and Falcon knew he needed to head west for around a hundred kilometres or so towards the small town of Chibwika. He understood that his prey was scheduled to be there sometime soon as his audiences increased in size with his popularity. This took him even closer to another alien border with Angola. This town was a mere thirty kilometres away from the border itself. Falcon had no intention of going to Angola, never been there but had no desire to do so. The plan should be straight forward and as long as he could get away it should be plain sailing.

He plugged the satellite phone into the car charger simply as a habit, it didn't really need any charge but at least he knew it would be fully charged when needed. He admired the splendour of the unspoilt areas of the country as he drove along its tracks, with occasional interspersions of metalled roads, quite a luxury in reality. The greenery he once again admired along with the wildlife that was surfacing with the rising sun was splendid; he wonder just how could the rapists of the countryside come to these places and just decimate them without a care for the surroundings. They would all disappear once the resources were depleted, but the environment wouldn't recover so quickly he thought to himself as he drove. There was no chance of music in the vehicle to help pass the time, such luxuries were not on order but the peace itself was soothing enough at that time of the day.

As he neared the town of Chibwika, Falcon decided to have a closer look at his maps and see where he needed to go even more off road to find somewhere he could hold up for a few days, whilst he was waiting for his subject to arrive. He had left the best quality roads some time earlier and already his teeth were aching at the constant bouncing up and down they were subjected to, dancing in unison with the interaction between rain forged pot holes and his vehicle. The Land Rover was certainly not quiet inside but he knew it was a rugged enough vehicle for the job at hand. He found a suitable spot around ten kilometres away from the town, the outskirts of a large green belt with substantial tree coverage and certainly off the beaten track. There were no indications of population centres in the area from the map although he knew he would most likely encounter people who lived in isolated pockets in the bush areas, or possibly loggers, or worse still the illegal poachers. These were probably the worst threat as they would be armed themselves and would rather kill him than run the risk of Falcon turning them in to the authorities. They would likely assume that he was the authorities in any case, so there would be no debate between the two factions, simply a matter of who shoots first.

He took the vehicle off the main tracks and surged up the hilly terrain towards the covering as best he could. The tracks were virtually disappearing beneath his wheels, he must certainly now be travelling on roads that had not been used for years, which in one respect was very good. It did the trick and he managed to get the vehicle into the forest camouflage, but he didn't want to venture too deep as he would need to keep the signal available for the telephone. He parked the truck up and was glad to switch off the constant droning of the hard working diesel engine. The chatter in the forest was captivating when the mechanical beast had ceased its roar, wildlife teaming all around. It could be heard but rarely seen. Tree branches often jumped violently, usually higher up in the canopy as monkeys of various types jumped around. Birds were heard calling one another but not seen. It was eerie but also spectacular in an audible sort of way.

The profuse perspiration was already showing through Falcon's shirt. The humidity was immense now in the forest, more than he was used to historically, but the sudden change experienced when jumping out of the vehicle into the open was overwhelming. He needed a drink so took his first slurp from his supplies, boy was it welcome. It was still only around ten in the morning, he had made good time due to his early start allowing him to use a lot of the better roads almost unnoticed. However he knew that now it could be a long and slow process. He had to sit and wait. Falcon took

the satellite phone from the Land Rover, picked up his rucksack and walked back to the edge of the forest, a distance of
merely thirty feet or so. He could still see his truck but more
importantly could now get a signal on the phone. He decided
to clear a little area of foliage debris with his feet and sat
down to make himself as comfortable as he could.

He surveyed the surroundings to the west from his elevated position. He could just make out in the distance, what
was in essence, the main road he had been using a short
while earlier as it headed towards the town. Green grass-
lands meandered down to the road side where the once lush
green grass had turned red with the road dust deposited by
selfish vehicles. He took the compact binoculars from his
bag and decided on a closer look. He had no idea what he
was looking for or at. He just wanted something to do. There
was little point in setting out a strategy as he had no idea yet
where his target was to be. No, this surveillance was more in
the hope of wildlife spotting than anything else, but it was
a method of killing time and remaining alert. As he scoured
the road into the town, he saw that there were a couple of
establishments along its route, one clearly a filling station,
the other some sort of road side eatery just as the outskirts of
the town were reached.

"Wonder what they're serving today?" he mused out loud
to himself. "Maybe I'll stroll down after a nap and grab a
beer and a steak?" The harsh reality was he would be living
mainly on cold foods for the foreseeable future with his only
warmth being a small military type folding stove, sufficient
to heat a mess tin for a cup of tea or bit of soup. Hardly Mi-
chelin star cuisine but that was the case. There was always
the fruit of course, that would probably last a couple of days
in the heat, and then it's down to the dry rations. So, the
sooner the job's done the better in that regard, but he knew it
was not his call.

He chose to lie down for a while on his back using his
bag as his pillow. He pulled down the brim of his bush hat to
cover his eyes as he looked skywards at the azure blue that

greeted him. He could have been on holiday it was so peaceful, just the monkey chatter in the back ground.

The shrill artificial ring tone of the satellite phone startled Falcon and roused him from a light sleep. It was almost three in the afternoon. He temporarily lost focus of where he was but soon realised the phone was belting out the din. He looked on the display and all that was displayed was *CALL*. He depressed the green key and held the telephone to his ear whilst casting a glance around. He pressed himself down to the ground and spoke softly into the mouthpiece.

"Yes."

"Mr. Vaughan?" asked an equally unexcited voice from the other end.

"It is, who is this?"

"That's not your concern. Are you anywhere near the town as advised?"

"I'm near to it but out of sight, why?"

"We shall be there tomorrow."

"That's earlier than thought isn't it?"

"It is but the rising is gaining strength, the popularity of Mizinga increases day by day. He has the people believing he is some form of higher being and a lot of elders are adding weight to the claim which is bringing the people on board quicker and quicker, and not just those in the villages. We need to move very soon, are you ready?"

"I'm waiting for the call. Just tell me where and when and I am on the case."

"There is a small restaurant about three miles outside the town, have you seen it?"

"I have noticed one right on the edge of town, the only other thing I can see from here is the filling station."

"That's the one. The restaurant is behind it." The voice said excitedly. "If you go down the road you can't miss it, I assure you."

There was haste in the callers voice, Falcon was not sure whether that was fear on his part at being over heard and exposed for the traitor he effectively was, or whether he saw his own goals in sight and couldn't contain his excitement.

"So you think the restaurant is the best place. I can't get inside the building . . . you know that?" Falcon enquired.

"No we don't even want to know you are there, but we will stop there. Mizinga will like to look his best before entering the town on another one of his carnival shows to address his children, as he calls them."

"Right then, what time do you plan to be there?"

"The town rally is set for two in the afternoon so we will have lunch there probably, that is the usual routine while he gets dressed up, but it's not totally up to me you understand. You just be ready as he will be exposed there. It will be a lot more difficult in the town itself."

"That's all I need to know," said Falcon, still showing no emotion in his voice or even daring to speak any louder. "Hopefully we will not need to speak again."

Falcon disconnected the call. His hands were sweaty after the call. Not from the heat or humidity but this was something else. This would be his first killing for money and not for his country, although they had justified his actions as being for the benefit of the nation to help him over the psychological boundary he was about to tread. Nevertheless he would become a killer, a lot different from being a soldier who killed. Still, this was a bad man, responsible for murder himself; this would be justice, not murder. And of course, he was still a soldier, the government wanted this doing but needed to sub contract it. That was it, Falcon told himself that he was a specialist sub contractor to the state, hence the handsome rewards.

He jumped up from his position and thought he would go and take a look from a distance at the restaurant. He went back to the Land Rover in the forest, took another drink from one of his water bottles and put it in his bag. He locked the vehicle again out of habit and set off across the slopes of the hillside to get a closer look at his shooting gallery.

He stayed high on the hill hugging the tree line as he went to avoid standing out to anyone who happened to be looking around. The number of cars using the road in and out of town had been steadily increasing during the day, but no one had dared come up the hill to his area, it was way off limits.

He reached a suitable high point after around twenty minutes where he could effectively see straight across the valley and look down directly into the restaurant behind the filling station. A good site for a turkey shoot he thought. Plenty of opportunity presented itself if his target was out in the open,, but if his vehicle blocked the line of sight to the quarry then Mizinga could easily make it inside to the restaurant without even realising he was under threat. Falcon knew that an element of luck went with this project. The sun was already starting its decent in the sky and the light was changing dramatically. Falcon decided he would wander down the hill a little to see if he could find a suitable vantage point. With such frontage to the restaurant, this would be a great opportunity.

Falcon had previously taken out a target at distance travelling within a moving vehicle; as such, the challenge itself did not present a real worry to the assassin. However he needed to make his escape so this needed to be quick and easy. He found a small hillock which rose up again as he was making his way down the slopes. This would be perfect he thought, it offered a good view along the road in both directions and full on to the shooting gallery. Yep, tomorrow morning he would set up his base here. He was pleased with the little bit of the day's reconnaissance and looked forward in a perverse sort of way to completing his first job in a new career the following day. The climb back to the Land Rover took a little over twenty minutes, although the majority of the walk was along the hill line, there was a bit which went up hill also. He needed to make sure he could get back to the Land Rover as quickly as possible and unnoticed. There were no other spots to park the vehicle he could find as he made his way back, so this return may well prove to be the most difficult aspect of the mission.

He decided it would be best if he slept inside the vehicle for one evening only, avoiding the need to set up the roof tent, convinced that it would only serve as an added item of curio to the inhabitants of the forest. He would do another equipment check and make sure the rifle was in a full state of preparedness for the impending activity.

Chapter 12

Dinner was fairly modest comprising a good old cup of tea was always well received in the field, military training saw to that when alcohol was definitely not on the menu. The boiling water was also used to make up a dehydrated ready meal that had been supplied as part of the field rations in the wooden treasure trove from Coltex's owners. Tony spent the evening listening to the incessant chatter from the tree tops. He was sure he was under close surveillance yet none of his primate stalkers could be seen. They were better at this than he was. He cleaned down the sniper rifle several times even though it was already pristine. It was stripped, checked, re-greased and cleaned again. Falcon could not afford any equipment failure here. He fitted the scope which also had an infra red feature allowing him to survey the surroundings in the dark. What a pity he could not take the shot at night he thought with all this cover, but he wasn't making the plays on this. His planning was virtually done for him, not quite as it was behind the lines in his military days where he was more of a free agent with an objective. How it was done was his business, the result was what mattered. The truth was, that the hierarchy that sent him on these missions didn't really want the details, as little information as possible was the agenda as far as government or military officials were concerned. Here, he was in an alley with only the one straight forward way out. Back down the same road that Mizinga would have just travelled minutes before being sent to meet his maker.

The African nights were very dark and there was little light emanating from the town that could assist his vision so far away. He passed the time scanning with the night vision scope hoping to spot the wildlife. The occasional bright green pair of shiny emeralds peered back at him from up in the trees, then they were gone and another on a different tree would take its place. They seemed to be guarding him or maybe he was being stalked for a change! There was nothing else to be done and Falcon knew that as early a night as possible was essential in order to be at his optimum for the following day. He already foresaw that lying in a sleeping bag in the back of the Land Rover was not going to be all that comfortable, and he was right. He tossed and turned throughout the night unable to placate his body, furling as much of his wrap beneath his frame as possible to provide the most meagre of cushioning. Despite a lack of sleep, he was thankful when he decided to rise at around four a.m. He quickly threw back on his shirt and pants from the previous day, relieved himself outside into adjacent bushes and set about scouring around for whatever seemed palatable at that time of the day to satisfy the cravings of his stomach. He had a pain in his stomach, neither cramp nor a result of the night's discomfort. This was nerves . . . anxiety. Today was the day his life was to change for ever. After today there would be no going back . . . Tony Falcon would be a gun for hire. Or at least he would be if he got out alive he thought.

He half heartedly chewed his way through an apple, gnawing at it more like a rodent than actually sinking his teeth into it. He was not really hungry but he knew he needed to eat. He filled his rucksack with the provisions for the day including water, biscuits and additional fruit. The rifle sound suppressor was placed on the barrel of the Remington rifle, the magazine clip was again checked to ensure that it was fully loaded with the 10 rounds of standard NATO issue 7.62 mm ammunition. He also packed the handgun that had been left in the trunk. Hopefully it would not be needed but if he did get into a close quarters battle with someone then it was far more suitable than the rifle.

Daylight had not yet broken but Falcon thought now would be the best time to get along the tree line with his gear, set up and simply wait. The forest chorus was increasing in volume as his fellow campers arose from their sleep and the invisible athletics that were taking place in the tree canopy started to warm up again. Falcon took almost half an hour to get to his spot this time, not that it was any more difficult but he made sure of his footing in the dark, after all there was no real rush. The spot itself was still easy to find, there was really nowhere else suitable around that he could see so the place was really unmistakeable. He settled down behind the furrow, took a small towel from his bag and placed it on the brow of the furrow. This was to be the resting place for the rifle so it was massaged until Falcon felt it had a comfortable resting position which correlated to his own. He knew he needed to make sure he was comfortable if he was to make such a long range shot. The forest line was merely a hundred yards or so behind him from his watch tower yet the noise it generated as the sun rose was tremendous.

The town was starting to come to life and it was merely six o'clock. The first cars started venturing out of the town, not many though; even yesterday he had noticed that the highway did not carry a great deal of traffic for its quality. He sat in the shooting position scanning through the scope at the road along which the object of his mission would travel; then at the restaurant and then at the town. There was no way he could even contemplate going into town after the assassination, he would be the immediate suspect; white stranger, black victim. Oh no, he knew one way out only.

He concentrated more on the restaurant. Watching the sporadic cars and vans pull into the filling station and examining possible shooting zones. Would it be possible that the entourage's vehicles block his line of sight? He did not know. It was a waiting game but not one where he could relax. He ranged the distance to the restaurant and made it at around nine hundred metres. Luckily, it was a still day so little allowance would need to be made for wind, but certainly elevation and range needed to be taken into account. He adjusted the scope accordingly and felt that it was about right.

"Time for a marker Tony," he said aloud to himself from his little cubby hole.

He looked for a suitable target over the roof top of the restaurant through the scope. He found a tree where a branch had fallen off leaving a torn stub where the limb once proudly hung. Not ideal but at least it was a marker he could measure against, and if all went astray the rogue lead projectile would be lost forever in the depths of the forestry behind it.

He took the safety catch off the rifle and cocked it ready for action. He once again checked the settings that he had made and settled himself down into the shooting position. Again adjusting the towel constantly until he felt it was the best comfort he could attain from here. Then it was zero time. He pressed his eye to the rubber shade that surrounded the scope and honed in on his target. He had it in the cross hairs as he held his breath. It must have been ten seconds before he released the first round. The shrill whisper as the bullet left the barrel spiralling its way invisibly across the valley into the safe keeping beyond the restaurant. His eye was still stuck to the scope when he saw shards of timber erupt from the forlorn woodland giant. He missed the mark by around a foot and slightly right but not a great deal. Clearly wind was not a great problem across the great distance but he still needed a slight adjustment for both though. Experience taught him how much he would need, or at least how to be somewhere near. The tree would be around thirty metres further behind the objective later in the day so that also needed to feature in the equation although not significantly.

The adjustments were made and the second shot was allowed to whisperingly ring out. This time, the line was good. As long as the wind did not pick up he would be fine with that setting, but the elevation still proved a problem. Elevation was a lot easier to compensate for when source and objective were at the same level, but shooting downhill over long range required extra refinement. The third shot however was right on the money. This would suffice for the Mizinga shot; the slight divergence in distance would not make a great deal of difference. He was pleased that he had managed such a feat in broad daylight and unnoticed, although he knew there was not really an audience out to catch him. Still, the silencer played its part with no real detriment to the equipment. From pulling the trigger, it could take a second or two before reaching the goal so the more stationary the objective the easier the shot. A swiftly moving target from this range could prove unpredictable. A millimetre out and the prey could be missed altogether.

There was nothing more he could do. He replaced the three rounds of spent ammunition in the rifle's magazine and picked up the used brass shell casings and put them back in his rucksack. No point in leaving calling cards he thought. He was then on surveillance duty checking out every vehicle he heard coming down the road towards the town, switching back any time a vehicle pulled into the filling station. The daytime heat was building up and he was starting to feel un-settled. He was sweaty and longed for a brief walk around to stretch the legs. Unfortunately, he was in hiding and that was that, so any stretching and massaging of cramping up mus-cles had to be done on the ground. From this position there was no chance of risking any form of compromise, no mat-ter how uncomfortable. He allowed the perspiration to build up under his arms until it started to clearly show through his shirt then it was rubbed at irritatingly to wipe it all away. This simply increased the visible leakage and did nothing to alleviate the discomfort. Now the flies were bothering him also. They loved the attraction of human sweat. He dove back into the bag, he needed water to try and keep his cool. He ate another apple to help pass the time but that only lasted five minutes and the tetchiness again started. After a further ten minutes or so of constantly wiping his brow, there was a penetrating single beep escaping from the rucksack. It was the satellite phone. He wasn't expecting any more commu-nication from that today. He picked up the phone and there already displayed was a text message, clearly from the inside man in Mizinga's party.

'1 hour' is all it said. That though was sufficient. Now Fal-con was pumped up, he knew the time was fast approaching. This could easily prove to be the biggest test of his life so far. He could feel his heart now pounding against the inner

walls of his rib cage. His core temperature rose as he felt the warming sensation all over his body, which did nothing to quell the secretion of sweat which was now running down his face almost at will. This was it. No time for bottling it now he told himself. He wiped his brow with the back of his hand and tried to dry his damp hands on the front of his shirt. He checked his watch, they were earlier than planned, but maybe that was a good thing. Now he focused solely on the road, on the traffic coming towards him. Every time a vehicle slowed down as though it was going to stop at the filling station he would go back to the rifle and scope . . . just in case.

Although he had no idea how Mizinga would be dressed, he was sure from the photographs and profile of the man that he would easily stand out within his group. Besides, if he was perceived as some messiah, his disciples would unwittingly highlight the target simply through their loyalty and demeanour around him. It would be around mid day when they arrived, which would leave him five hours to affect his departure in daylight.

He watched and watched the horizon where the road disappeared out of sight, just awaiting his quarry to come into view. The occasional vehicle drew into sight but he just knew it was not his mark. Then it happened. Falcon looked at the entourage of three vehicles, the centre one being a distasteful stretched white limousine. This was so out of character with the area, in fact with the entire country it could only mean one thing; Mizinga. Research had shown Falcon that this guy was a showman but this just demonstrated that he had no class whatsoever. He was already showing his people an opulence they would never enjoy in their lifetimes, yet he was here to win them over. Falcon wondered how on earth anyone could be taken in by such garish front, how could they be convinced that a sloth of such character could change their lives. That was not his concern today as he had another problem to deal with.

The binoculars were put down and the rifle picked up. The lens caps were flipped off and the shoulder strap wrapped around his arm for stability. He then tracked the entourage for several minutes, its size increasing in the scope as it made its way towards Chibwika. It was not travelling exceptionally fast, probably because they were ahead of schedule and, for a man seeking an audience, being too early may mean a vastly reduced one. This was good; this should make it necessary to stop before the town he thought. His cheek was pressed hard against the stock of the rifle and eyes glued to the rim of the scope. The time was upon him. He stared at the cavalcade as it slowed, just as planned, and drew gracefully into the filling station. They went straight through the forecourt and around to the restaurant before coming to a halt in what cannot be described as an orderly fashion.

He was taking short deep breaths now and he could again sense his internal organs bursting and ready to explode, but he needed calm right now. He slowed down his breathing and still took deep breaths. Two men alighted from the limousine in quite a formal manner and both went to open the rear doors to allow the occupants to enter the real world outside. Occupants from the other vehicles already seemed in party mode. No order, no apparent discipline or purpose. Seemingly they were nothing more than hangers on, just along for the ride. One thing was for sure, they were certainly not politicians.

Falcon concentrated on the rear doors of the limousine. Which side will it be he wondered?

"Come on . . . come on," he whispered; suddenly it was clear. From the driver's side, a set of shapely brown legs that could only belong to a female started to materialize from within the vehicle. Falcon quickly switched attention to the opposite side of the vehicle. This was not the time for stalking beauty. He waited and waited and it seemed an eternity before the other passenger decided to make a move. In truth it was more likely four or five seconds but clearly this one needed to be centre stage at all times. His other followers were a boisterous and shabbily dressed bunch but Mizinga was quite the opposite.

His legs came out of the car first as he was helped out by the occupant from the front seat. Falcon assessed his prey momentarily, clearly a giant of a man looking at those around him. Well built and well dressed for Africa. The intended victim was sporting a full tailored western style suit, not African dress of any sort and very western style sun glasses. Yes, this was the showman. He seemed in no hurry to get inside and stood nonchalantly adjacent to the open door smiling and looking all around him. He was nodding his head and swivelling it as he checked out the surroundings when the first shot whistled from Falcon's silencer and across the valley.

Unbeknown to Mizinga, within a moment he would be impacted by several ounces of lead. The bullet cut through the air like a knife and spiralled into Mizinga's neck on the left side, causing a fountain of bright red blood to spurt outwards over his assistant. He slumped against the open door with his arm draped over the top of it for support as the second shot found its mark. It catapulted into the back of Mizinga's skull shattering bone fragments in all directions and leaving again at the front of his head. This was the killer blow and death was instant. The girl screamed and brought her hands up to her face but remained glued mystically to the spot with sheer blind panic. She was pulled by the driver behind her still open door and dragged to the ground as Mizinga's aide pulled him off the door and onto the ground. The white limousine had undergone an infusion of colour and nobody seemed to know what to do. There was panic amongst the rowdy bunch, most of them running towards their crest fallen leader, now lying motionless on the ground. The floor was changing colour as life drained from Mizinga but it was clear to all that he was not immortal after all. A good portion of his cranium was missing from where the second shot had exited.

There were screams and telephones seemed to appear from nowhere, but who could they call. What could be done? Falcon watched the commotion but he knew the job was done.

Mizinga was clearly dead so time to depart. He felt his entire body tense up and a sudden nausea overcame him causing him to vomit in his fox hole. Fortunately there was not a great deal of content in his stomach making the taste of the escaping fluid even more foul. He grabbed for his water to try and clear the dreadful feeling as he stared across the valley at the ceaseless pandemonium. There was no assistance, no one came. They were a few miles out of town, what could be done now anyway?

Despite all the screeching and crying, a couple of the entourage produced guns from their belts. Falcon was sure they couldn't see him but they were looking across at the forestry as that was the obvious place for the shooter. They waved pistols and fired aimlessly into the tree line. They would be hard pressed to get any sort of killing power from that range thought Falcon but still he needed to keep his head down. At almost a kilometre away he would be difficult to spot but it was not worth the chance.

After ten minutes of commotion a siren could be heard and an ambulance and police car arrived at the scene. The whole squad was still ranting and the lady was kneeling on the floor beside Mizinga, whose head had been covered with a jacket which was itself turning red as the blood diffused through its fibres. The two gun wavers were still shouting and shooting recklessly but Falcon thought it was time he got back to the Land Rover. He gathered his belongings and made his way straight back up the hill to get into the tree line for additional cover. His legs were like jelly, he never felt like this in Bosnia, then again this was not really the same as Bosnia. He hugged the tree line getting within the deep foliage whenever he could to assist the camouflage and regularly looked over his shoulder at the commotion below. His pace quickened, not intentionally as he had always planned a steady escape, but the nervous energy in him seemed unstoppable. He walked briskly and more upright than he intended to the Land Rover, but couldn't help himself. He got back into the under growth and put his equipment back in the vehicle. He removed the silencer and put it in the wooden chest alongside the rifle.

The incessant sweat just kept on coming. His eyes were stinging from its constant appearance on his face but he had no time to worry about that now. He took a much needed drink from the water bottle, took the binoculars from the bag and went back to the edge of the forest. He crouched down and once again cast his eye around the chaos below. There were now three police cars and they were loading the body into the ambulance. He watched as one of the police cars took the lead and escorted the ambulance back into town. The female was still being consoled by the driver of the Limousine. Unbeknown to Falcon, this was Mizinga's wife, being consoled by his aide, the inside man. How ironic!

Falcon watched intently for several minutes, the eternal arm waving and obvious, yet seemingly pointless, shouting from the crew. As he was now a couple of kilometres away there was no chance of hearing the shouts, but there was a lot of arm waving and pointing towards the forest. The two men with hand guns still had them drawn and were shaking them in the air with their wild arm swings. Then it happened. One of the men with a gun who was talking to a policeman, with his back to Falcon at the time, became extremely excited and started pointing directly at Falcon. There was more movement in the mouth but the crowd seemed to turn from disorganised ranting into an organised frenzy. He was still pointing directly down the binoculars of Falcon, and now the others were also joining in on the spectacle. He couldn't believe his bad luck; surely they couldn't see him from there! Then it hit, the sun was setting opposite and he must have been caught a reflection in the lenses at an inopportune moment. This was not in the plan.

"Oh shit," screamed the assassin aloud, clearly showing instant distress in his tone.

The commotion at the filling station changed into a mad dash for vehicles. Falcon knew he had to move and move fast. He jumped back into the Land Rover and fired it up.

The rucksack was beside him but the rifle was still in the back. No time to get it now, he had to get away and put some distance between himself and the pursuers. Now the hunter was becoming the hunted. He still had a couple of kilometres between himself and the pursuers but they would have faster cars he was sure of that. He started back down the track as fast as he could and headed down towards the main road. He would never make it in time, they had the better carriageway and he couldn't match their speed. He shot off along another track which ran parallel to the main highway for a couple of kilometres, but this road was certainly better suited to his vehicle than theirs.

He was being buffeted around in the cockpit of the off road vehicle as though he was in a badly designed fair ground ride, yet he knew if he slowed he would be caught. He had no idea what other resources, if any, the police would have in the area; neither did he have any idea where he was heading. He just knew he needed to stay ahead of his chasers. If he would be caught, he knew only too well that his killing would not be as swift or painless as it was for Mizinga. His back jarred and teeth smacked together relentlessly as he bounced along the track. He constantly checked his mirrors and could see traffic in the distance but on the main highway, yet gaining ground on him all the time.

He had no choice but to continue off the main drag, knowing his pursuers would have to turn off and follow him shortly. He was right. The chasing saloon cars were no match for the off road vehicle but they still gave chase. They were not designed for such use but as they steamed up the mountain on the progressively worsening terrain for them, they still gained ground. One of Mizinga's convoy cars was ahead of the police vehicle which was probably to Falcon's advantage as there was no real area for overtaking and the police car would surely have been the more powerful of the two. Onwards and upwards they came, still gaining ground. Falcon was heading back up the hill and as the twists and turns became more prevalent, he could clearly see his pur-

suers gaining on him. He was probably less than five minutes ahead as he rounded a sharp bend on the brow of a hill.
There was a fairly steep incline on the other side but it was a
long stretch of very open country. He knew that he would be
in plain sight for some time if he went on and they were still
able to keep chase.

Falcon thought it was time to make a stand. He had to stop
the chase. He rounded the bend and parked up his vehicle
on the downward side of the hill, hopefully below the line
of sight of the chasing pack. He left the engine running and
jumped out and retrieved the rifle from the rear of the truck.
He threw himself to the ground and searched for the hunters.
The Mizinga vehicle came into view first, he didn't want to
kill anybody else but if he was cornered he knew he would
have to. He fired a shot which was loud and the flash visible.
Falcon had decided that there would be no silencer required
any more as discretion was no longer the order of the day.
The extra power the gun had without the silencer may just
come in handy. The chasers saw the flash of the bullet as it
was fired but it didn't seem to cause them any damage. It
missed but did enough to make them aware they were now in
danger. They pressed on though, weaving the car as best they
could on the limited space available when the second shot
ripped through a front tyre of the leading car. It swerved out
of control and off the road, down a rocky embankment for a
few feet but effectively immobile.

The police car continued the pursuit. It too took a shot
from Falcon. One in the windscreen not intended to kill, but
to act hopefully as a deterrent with another volley of shots
fired in quick succession at the front of the car. Bullets pep-
pered the engine housing and front of the vehicle as it sped
towards Falcon. Headlights were smashing and steam started
spewing from under the bonnet. On and on the car came,
although labouring heavily now, until it finally died. Too
much damage under the bonnet and the tired vehicle just
could not cope. By car they would have been up to Falcon in
one or two minutes but on foot they had no chance. He fired

another shot into the police car to warn its occupants then darted back to the Land Rover and hurtled it down the hill. He didn't bother worrying about what was behind him now; he had a pressing need to create a void between him and his new hunters as quickly as possible. He knew they were still there but did not know what else they had available to pursue him. Undoubtedly the police radios would have been communicating, but Falcon had no idea where he really was, where he was going or what lay ahead. Every turn could be another problem.

He continued driving for several hours as darkness started to fall. Once again he sought overnight refuge. The tracks regularly took him through lush vegetation and forestry, not as dense as where he was the previous evening yet still able to offer some protection. He knew he needed to pull off into the forestry wherever he could and needed to get off any made tracks. He found what he considered a suitable spot. Falcon got out of the vehicle to test it under foot first before attempting to pull the truck in, just in case it was marshy as that would leave him completely exposed and quite possibly dead by morning if he lost his truck. It was solid enough so he pulled off the track and savoured yet another night in the now well worked Land Rover.

He looked at the satellite phone which was jumping in and out of signal reception due to the overhead shrubbery. When working it would display your GPS co-ordinates but needed a good signal to do that. He took the phone out of the vehicle and stood in the centre of the track where signal reception should have been best. After a minute or so, the signal was picked up and he could get some co-ordinates. The power levels were very low as he had not bothered recharging the phone during his travels; then again it was not top priority in his mind that afternoon. This place was different to last night's camp. The silence was extremely unnatural, to the point of being deafening and somewhat disconcerting. Nothing could be heard. This was very strange, he wondered if he started his engine again how far the sound would carry. He couldn't risk that in all this stillness. He had to stay holed up again and could not risk driving the forest at night, even if he had dared put any lights on, it would still be dangerous.

Once again, Falcon, now thoroughly stinking clambered into the back of the truck for the evening. He could sense his own stench and found it repulsive, so was thankful he was not in company, especially female company. It was extremely humid in the forest and the air temperature was well into the high thirties. Out came the trusty camping stove again and he proceeded to cook inside the vehicle for the second night.

The following morning he awoke and daylight was already sending shafts of light through the forest's leafy canopy.

"Christ what time is it now?" he moaned, rubbing his eyes and mouth opening to let out yet another yawn. "Half bloody eight," he yelled at himself, "shit!"

He was extremely annoyed at having missed a couple of hours of daylight, not setting him up for the appropriate mood for the day's challenges ahead. Still, he wasn't surrounded so nobody was quite on his trail just yet. There were many turns and side tracks through the forest, many of which were used by the loggers in their trade, so it would not be that easy to follow him after some time. He had the advantage of being lost although just how much of an advantage this really was, remained to be revealed.

Chapter 13

Falcon examined the map that he had been given by his hirers and tried to ascertain from the coordinates he retrieved from the satellite fix last evening where he actually was. The daylight revealed the stark reality of his plight. In the commotion of yesterday's escape, ducking and diving left then right, covering the trail and turning back on himself, Falcon had lost track of his own whereabouts. The map he had in his hand, and the coordinates he took from the GPS signal, revealed that he had crossed the border and was now in the war torn state of Angola.

He couldn't believe what he was looking at. He checked and double checked his coordinates. It was not the best map in the world and not a great scale, but there was sufficient information for him to know he was the wrong side of the line. He checked the phone again in the clearing in the centre of the track. There was no mistake. Not only that, he was also lost. It couldn't have been much worse. The map detailed several towns, although Falcon had no idea of their size and in truth, had never heard of any with the exception of Luanda, and even if he was next door to it, he certainly did not want to go there. There was a lot of trouble in Angola, not only the fighting but the discarded unmarked land mines were a constant threat to its people, let alone a fugitive on the run effectively running blind.

There was also a lot of industry, especially mining. Despite its problems, Angola was a mineral rich nation with very extensive resources of metals and precious stones. The sad fact was that due to its wealth it has been ravaged by civil war for years and the people saw no benefit from their assets. Perhaps he could find supplies or even help, to get himself out of this hole. Now he was scared. He had never felt this feeling before. Previously working under orders, alone for days on end, staking out a target, behind it all there was always a good chance the military could come to his aid. On this trip there was no back up. He was on his own.

He paced up and down the desolate jungle track, still in awe at the relative silence. It seemed so unnatural for such a location which should be teeming with wild life. He wondered if this was the result of the battle scarred nation, destroying itself from within.

"Focus man, focus," he snapped at himself as he paced up and down whilst smacking his head with the map. "Where the hell can you go? Think . . . think!"

He looked at the satellite phone he was holding in his greasy hands. He decided, much against his better judgement, to call Striker and see if he could help navigate him out of his predicament. It was a possibility even though they never hit it off. He was still effectively a Coltex employee lost on his watch. The number was easily remembered by Falcon as it was emblazoned on every company vehicle he saw. Not a long number, no need as there were not that many fixed line phones in the country, but more importantly, easily memorable.

Falcon keyed in the digits and pressed the small green telephone key bringing the luminous screen into life.

"Mr. Striker please," said Falcon, when the receptionist answered.

"Yes sir, may I say who is trying to reach him?" came back the sultry female voice in perfect English.

"Yes, it's . . . Robert Vaughan."

"Very good sir, please hold the line."

He was put on hold for what seemed an age, and was in fact a good thirty seconds. He wondered whether Striker would even take the call. He began to think that maybe this was a bad idea after all.

"Bobby, where the hell are you?" Striker barked down the phone. "Hope you're having better luck than we are boy."

"Not really. I seem to be lost and think I have crossed the border into Angola."

"Well just turn around and get the hell out of there. We can't just go there when we want; they'll bloody shoot you if they catch you. Don't you know there's a bloody war on? Are you on a suicide mission or something or just trying to destroy this company's name? What in God's name are you doing out there man? Shit, as if I haven't got enough problems today and now this crap. What are you hoping I can do for you then?"

"Well I'm not sure really. I wondered whether you could send someone to help guide me out or something . . . I don't know, I just don't know," repeated Falcon, the fear in his voice starting to show.

"You must be kidding me. I can't get people in or out of the mine. No equipment no supplies, its all gone crazy here. The police and army are everywhere, the airport is locked down. Somebody shot a local chief and the mines are under suspicion so I have enough shit to deal with right now. Of course, this only helps stir up the natives so to cap it all I am looking at a possible strike. What the hell else can get fucked up today? Then you call. Jesus!" Striker was really on a roll with his problems, walking around the desk, spitting as he spoke on the phone, showing signs of tremendous stress.

"I'm sorry Bobby chum. There's nothing I can do right now. My hands are tied. I suggest you get back across the border wherever you can. You've got GPS so it can't be too hard, you're supposed to be an engineer after all so work it out. If you can't, then stay low and give me a call in a couple of days and I'll see if the situation has calmed down and see if we can do anything then. okay. I've got to go; it's all hitting the fan here. Hey Vaughan . . . stay lucky yeah," said Striker, then the line went dead. Falcon felt Striker enjoyed that conversation a lot more than he did. Clearly the shooting of Mizinga has had an impact, whether it was what Fairfax and Sir Henry were after was something else.

The frustration was starting to show even more now. Falcon paced rapidly around in small circles shaking the phone.

He couldn't believe Striker just dumped him like that. He knew there would be no help from that quarter, even in a couple of days. No, he was being hung out to dry.

"Henry!" he said under his breath.

"Why not, there's nothing else to lose. Maybe he can persuade Striker to help me out. Surely they won't want the dirty washing in public. Yes, Sir Henry."

Falcon felt a sudden sense of relief as he thought this could be a possible solution even though in his nervousness he realised he was actually having a conversation with himself. Henry obviously had contacts in this part of the world, and a lot of influence. Why did he not try that avenue first? Stupid, stupid, bloody stupid he thought to himself. He knew Sir Henry's number in London having stayed at the house, hopefully he would be there. Again the satellite phone kicked into life and as if by magic, he was talking from the middle of a jungle in Africa to Jenkins in London.

"Good morning Jenkins." Falcon spoke excitedly at hearing a familiar voice, "Tony Falcon here. I need to speak with Sir Henry urgently."

"I shall just see if Sir Henry is available sir, I am not sure whether he is in residence this morning or not. Please hold the line Mr Falcon." Jenkins demeanour was exactly as portrayed in Hollywood movies, like the stereotypical English butler utilising proper Queen's English and the plum in mouth. Falcon knew Sir Henry was there otherwise Jenkins would have said so straight away.

"Tony, how are you?" came back the unmistakable voice of Sir Henry. His tone was as though they were good friends more likely to be arranging a golf game than overthrowing politicians.

"Sir Henry, I need help. I need an out. The job is done and I am in a spot of bother. I've had the police chase me and Mizinga's guards and somehow I've ended up in Angola. I need you to pull a few strings and get me out. I tried Striker but he won't come. He said maybe in a couple of days he can help, but I need help now."

Falcon was almost pleading for assistance. He spoke quickly and struggled for breath panting as he spoke, inhaling more air than he needed.

"Who's Striker?" asked Sir Henry

"He works for Coltex, the mine manager and seemingly he's all powerful down there."

"Thus he works for Fairfax, nothing to do with me. Still, if Fairfax gave you his details he must be the best man for access down there. If he can't help you then I don't know what we can do." Sir Henry paused and he could hear Falcon breathing heavily into the phone. He could sense the panic in the silence.

"Tony, there's nothing I can do for you from here. We have no access in Angola. I suggest you get back to Zambia ASAP and get back to the mine. I'm sure they will be able to get you out if you get back there. It's certainly not good for you where you are."

"Sir Henry, I can't. Striker said the police and army are everywhere. I don't even know which way to turn to get back."

"You knew the rules when you took on the job. It's your job and your responsibility to plan it. It sounds to me like you simply fucked up. Always remember the three P's, Piss Poor Planning Tony. Your job and you make the rules as you go, that's what we pay you for; you plan the job, we only try to make it as easy as possible for you. Get that right and you are almost there. There's nothing more I can do. If Striker can't help then I certainly can't. Now I've got to get ready for a luncheon appointment so need to go. You look after yourself now, oh . . . and by the way, don't ever call this fucking number again. We've never met." The barrow boy in Sir Henry came to prominence yet again; he would never be able to master that trait, especially when he got riled, despite the wealth and the social trappings that went with it.

Sir Henry put the phone down on Falcon. It was then that he realised they didn't want him to get back. That was never part of their plan. This was probably a suicide mission for anybody down here. Falcon's fear started to turn into anger. He had been shafted and that was not good, certainly not good for those doing the shafting. There was a new resolve forming in his mind. Now he was going to get out by himself, it would not be the first time he had ever had to go off limits and improvise. No, now he had an objective to live for, he too now had an appointment in London to keep. It suddenly became personal.

He stopped at the Land Rover and put the map on the bonnet.

"Well, I guess I would be less welcome across the border right now than here so it looks like we're going in," he said loudly to the imaginary audience.

He figured there was no easy way to navigate his route through Zambia for quite a while yet. The only alternative was to stay low and find a way of getting down to South Africa. It was a long shot but his only one. At least he could get a flight from there. No Zambia just yet and to leave Angola for the Democratic Republic of the Congo was just jumping out of the frying pan into the fire. He again scoured the map looking for a general heading but he wanted to stay away from major conurbations. There would be too many police, and even worse, militia with itchy trigger fingers. The smaller towns may be easier pickings for the scavenger that he may need to become. If he was killed down here nobody would ever know. That was a terrifying prospect.

He targeted the town of Lucusse. He figured it was somewhere between one hundred and two hundred kilometres away subject to how twisting these roads become and whether he could ever get out of the jungle onto the main highway. He had no real idea of its size but it was represented by smaller dots than others on the map so he hoped this was some indication. It was very tempting to head for Luena, a hundred and fifty kilometres further on, as it had an airport. But an airport right now would probably not be a good idea here. He had no visa and would be thrown in some stinking hole of a jail never to see daylight again. Lucusse was the objective; he might get supplies there and be able to see how his escape could develop.

It was a few days since he had left the camp and now the un-cleanliness was taking its psychological toll. A warm shower and a shave would be very nice right now he thought; however instead it was time to fill up the jeep and get on the way. He emptied three of the six jerry cans he had of additional fuel into the truck which almost brought her back up to full capacity. It was now after nine and it was time to make some headway. Another apple for breakfast, washed down with some rather tepid water again, then he was off.

He revved the truck as fast as he dared along the narrow dusty roads, leaving the dust cloud behind himself but feeling relatively safe in the knowledge that there was little chance of him actually being seen in the bush. Every time he came upon a possible turning, the vehicle was halted and the GPS compass checked to see if it would perhaps take him in the general direction of Lucusse. Of course, he knew none of these jungle tracks would be straight but hoped that their general direction would be somewhere near. He had been driving the trails for three hours and had hoped that by this time he would have made it to Lucusse itself when he finally came upon a metalled road.

"Thank Christ for that," he shouted to himself inside the now somewhat quieter cockpit, overjoyed at getting away from the constant buffeting of his bones and organs. At least the driving will be easier and perhaps less sweaty. He could open the windows now on the bigger road without fear of being slashed in the face by low lying tree branches that had been bouncing off the bonnet most of the morning. It was not a major road and no other traffic was visible, but as it was in this condition, chances were it would lead to a major road not too far away.

Falcon decided on another drink of water and a stretch of the legs before he got out into the open country. He also took the hand gun from the wooden chest in the rear of the truck and placed it under his seat in the front of the car. The package containing the ten thousand dollars would also now be called into play. Fortunately there was quite a bit in smaller notes. Falcon removed the bigger notes, around nine thousand dollars, and carefully split it and hid half in each of his socks. An old trick he developed when on overseas duty and on recreation days, just in case the local muggers and hard boys wanted a crack at a soldier. At least if he was mugged by an opportunist he would still have some reserves.

He looked at the compass heading on the GPS and again at the map. He hoped that at the end of this road, wherever it may be, a left turn would send him in his general direction. It came quicker than he was expecting but it was there. He was now on the road to Lucusse, and as he past a road sign realised that he should be upon it within the hour. There was more traffic on this road than he had seen so far. More of it was commercial than cars as such. There were lots of local trucks, the type that looked as though they were hanging on to life by the merest of threads. Heavily overloaded invariably, leaning one way or another and running on what most would consider dangerous and illegal tyres. Then there was the other end of the spectrum with the newer and more modern trucks that were owned by the bigger international companies. There was not nearly as many of these but there were enough, Plant and Equipment manufactures from America and Japan with heavy equipment on board. Then there were military vehicles, a lot of short wheel base army Land Rovers transporting what looked to be bunches of simply ill disciplined soldiers, clearly with no real objectives in mind. There were a surprising number of children in military uniform, albeit shabby, in open trucks travelling with the smaller jeeps, who Falcon knew were the intolerable child victims of this troubled nation. It was well documented about the number of children who had been robbed of their childhood and drafted into one of the warring factions.

He stuck to a steady speed, not wanting to draw any attention to himself and continued towards his first stop. It was now early afternoon and soon he would need to start thinking about the evening's respite. There was a bit of a rest stop looming up in the distance. Falcon thought he would drive up to it or maybe even past it first and see if he could assess the type of patrons. It was only a form of roadside bush café made from bamboo and corrugated sheeting with assorted local foods cooked on open coals. However, there were seemingly plenty of customers looking at the number of trucks outside but he needed to avoid the militia. If there was any such presence there then he needed to press on. He drove past the eatery and could see no reason why not to stop. There were a few people there and the trucks were no different to what he had seen on the road so far. Mostly local trucks with a vast array of assorted goods in transit but there was a new rig carrying a Caterpillar bulldozer on which the paint could well have still been wet. It was immaculate and clearly destined for a profitable location somewhere. Inevitably such gear will be for one of the mines either diamond or copper, maybe Uranium or Cobalt. All were present here in Angola and all were the subject of much corruption.

He pulled in and parked near to the tractor unit carrying the dozer; the logic being the owner of this rig would probably be more receptive towards him than any of the locals. The company name and address on the doors of the truck showed it was from a CAT dealer in Durban. Probably no CAT dealer down here thought Falcon. He got out of his truck and sauntered across to the eatery. There were about half a dozen shanty tables made of anything from old wooden pallets to pieces of un-sawn tree branches. At least they were functional. Somebody was sat at each table and there seemed little interaction between most of the diners. There was only one white guy and Falcon assumed this was the South African. It was a reasonable bet and worth a punt. He approached that table,

"Mind if I sit here?" he asked.

"No bother mate, help yourself," came back the reply. "Not very often I get company on these trips."

Falcon could sense straight away that this was a South African, but had a twang about his accent that indicated he was not a native.

"Thanks, could do with a bit of company myself," he paused a little while, "I guess that's your fancy rig out there with the CAT on the back."

"Sure is, be glad to get rid of it and head back home. She's a good runner and comfy too, but hell, nothing beats your own bed and your own women eh?"

"I guess not," replied Falcon. "So, where are you from originally, you're obviously not South African through and through?"

"Christ, can you tell. Most people can't you know. The family moved from Scotland when I was a nipper and been in SA ever since. It's a great place, better than these shit holes. You want to eat? There's not a great choice unless you like monkey done in a variety of ways. I reckon go for the fish and plantain, safe and reasonably palatable."

"Yea, that would be good." The thought of warm real food seemed very appealing to Falcon, whatever it's constituency.

The South African beckoned over the large black lady who was obviously the owner, and asked for Falcon's fish. She was dressed in very bright colours, not whom one would expect to see working in such a place. The place looked disgusting and would never get a European hygiene certificate, but the fish looked fresh and it was getting barbecued, so he figured it should be virus free. Even if not, he would take the risk. A few of the guests were obviously regulars and chatted with the owner and they started to drift away and get back to their trucks and their drudge of a lifestyle.

"Robert Vaughan," said Falcon, as he passed his hand across the table to his new South African buddy.

"Ryan Koetze, good to meet you Robert. Like I said, don't get to meet many folk when I do these runs. Well, many white folk that is. No shortage of locals who wouldn't think twice about robbing and even killing you. So what brings you to Hell's Kitchen?"

Falcon could see where the name came from. The heat could be hell but the surroundings were certainly surreal. A beautiful landscape ravaged by war and corruption. The widespread lawlessness he had heard about and was seemingly being warned about by Ryan. The people didn't look as though they knew how to smile. They had probably never experienced happiness as he had. They had certainly suffered. Yep, Hell's Kitchen was apt.

"I'm prospecting for exploration sites for new mining enterprises," he replied. That was the best he could come up with on the spot and didn't feel as though he was really convincing.

"Really, that sounds as though it could have its interesting moments," decried Ryan. "So you're a rock collector or something."

"Well something like that. A geologist we call it but yep I do collect a few rocks if I need to."

The fish arrived and was slapped on the table for Falcon on a wooden plate. The fish was complete, lying there all crisp and brown looking back at him.

"No knives and forks here son. Fingers or go without I'm afraid."

Falcon started to tear at the fish, despite its appearance, it was heaven sent as far as his stomach was concerned. It could easily have been steak at the Ritz at that moment for Falcon as he allowed the beautiful tasting grey white fish to crumble in his mouth. There were bones in there but he had no time to dig them out before it made its way to his mouth. The stomach was calling the shots on this one; the teeth would have to sort out the bones, at least for now.

"Christ son, you not eaten for a week?" asked Ryan, as he admired Falcon's attack on the former meal.

"Not much decent that's for sure. I've had a few days in that old thing, eating pre packed food and biscuits. This is great. You have no idea how good this is." He nodded his head towards his Land Rover which had been home these last few days.

They were alone by now in the café and the lady had returned to the inside, sitting on her wooden stool just waiting hopefully that more people would come. A one roomed shanty shack, home and work. What an existence he thought.

"Did you find any good prospects then on your travels?" asked Ryan as he sat back on the bench and threw a cigarette into his mouth. "You smoke?" he said as he offered the packet to Falcon.

"Afraid not," he replied, "managed to stay away from that vice."

"You've got some then?"

"Hasn't everybody?" He was trying to steer the conversation away from work but Ryan still showed interest. Unfortunately Falcon was feeling as though he was under interrogation from Ryan. He was sure his cover was in doubt.

"Anyway, back to you stranger. Was it a successful trip?"

"Possibly, I just identify possible locations. Then we assess them back at the office and see what info we have on the areas that are potential sites and see if there are any indicators that lead us to spend a bit of cash on further investigation."

Falcon was certainly winging this conversation. He could feel the perspiration start to build up even though the sun was going down well now and the light starting to fade quite quickly, as was the air temperature. Still not cold, it rarely was in these parts, but cooler than the rest of the day. How he longed for the rains of England . . .

"So where's the local hotel?" asked Falcon in a serious tone.

Ryan spluttered as he choked on smoke, his eyes started to water and stream down his rugged face. It sported a few days beard growth and he certainly could have done with a shower, but he was no worse than Falcon in that regard.

"I take it this is your first time here Rob?" exclaimed Ryan with the wide grin appearing across his face. "No hotels around here mate; well nothing you would stay in as a white man for sure. Your throat would be cut before you hit the pillow."

"Well where do you kip then?"

"In the rig, and usually somewhere secure if I can. Tonight I will stop at the local dealer and he'll unload this beast in the morning, then I'm off."

"Back to Durban?"

"Yep, homeward bound."

There was a silence and Ryan could see the boy was troubled. "Where you really headed now son?" He asked with genuine concern.

Falcon paused before replying. He remained looking at the table and said "I'm not really sure," in a low toneless voice.

"Are you in trouble son?" asked Ryan. "You look as though you are. You're not a bloody merc are you? I don't want to be caught with a bloody merc down here."

"No, nothing like that," he quickly replied. "It's delicate really but I'm not a merc, guaranteed."

Ryan breathed a big sigh of relief. He eyed Falcon and could see he was in need of rest for sure. He could not work out what he was looking at but knew there was a good guy somewhere in there.

"How about you sleep in my rig tonight, there's bunks. Be a bit cramped but got to be better than dossing in your Landie. Only tonight mind you, then I am away early morning and you can be on your way. I've got a few beers in the truck and you look like you could do with a drink. By the way, a word of warning . . . I'm no queer and if you try anything you'll end up like that monkey up there." He pointed his nicotine stained finger, holding the remnants of the cigarette, at the bush meat that was hanging from the café roof near the grill.

"You're okay, there's no need to worry on that score. It's been a while, but not even that would turn me over to the dark side," replied Falcon as a wry smile was swiftly born across his face. "And a beer, what luxury. Thanks Ryan, you've no idea just how much this means."

"Ah, no worries, we've all been on hard times or been out on a limb at some stage. It's better than having your death on my conscience, it's a long drive back and I'll need to concentrate."

They both chuckled and got up from the table to go. Instantly the lady owner surfaced gracefully without saying a word. Ryan took out his bank notes of Angolan Kwanza and threw two hundred on the table and nodded at the restaurant owner. She looked at the cash and nodded back. He looked up at Falcon who was still staring at the cash. "I guess you've not got any funds either?" Ryan said knowingly and threw another note on the table, pointing his finger at himself and Falcon. Once again the female nodded back. "We've probably paid over the odds there."

"Thanks, I'll pay you back, promise."

"Well don't leave the country, between us both that cost me a couple of dollars. I've got to get rid of the few notes I have before I get home, they're no damn use anywhere else."

Falcon turned and smiled at Ryan, he could get along with this humour. Ryan climbed up into his rig.

"Just follow me." He said. "It's about twenty minutes and we can park up for the night. I'll tell them you're with me, service engineer or something, don't worry. Come on, let's get the beers in."

Chapter 14

The prospect of a mattress was unthinkable for Falcon. What comfort. He felt security with Ryan but needed to work on a story, the subject would surely come up. He wondered how he could use the guy to get him back into South Africa, at least once there he would be almost home free. He would need to make sure he locked the vehicle up and the tools of his trade were out of sight. Comfort, that would help him think and resolve his situation. He could fall asleep thinking about catching up with his employers, now that would be a spectacle worth watching. They were giving him up for dead, what a surprise they had coming, that was the focus now . . . London. He was sure Ryan could be part of the strategy, just how.

He followed the CAT transporter steadily down the highway to the CAT dealer which was in, what Falcon assumed to be, an industrial area on the outskirts of a town. He wasn't sure where but it was a town. No planning and poverty all around was evident. Industrial facilities, workshops, open factories, interspersed with people's ramshackle homes made from assorted industrial waste. They pulled into the fenced compound of the CAT dealer and the heavy duty gates were dutifully closed behind them, encasing the expensive equipment and its human companions within the dealership.

There's very little equipment in here thought Falcon. What was there was clearly broken and would be lucky if diesel ever flowed through their veins again. It was not the sort of workshops or dealerships he had seen in the UK. No stock, not pushing the brand anywhere. The workshop was nothing more than an open fronted shelter. He later found out from Ryan that the company had no money, typical of the region. They simply had the CAT franchise but could never afford stock. They sold equipment to industry, mainly the mines, more as a middle man, country politics really but CAT would not supply them direct. So Ryan's company were the nearest supplier they could rely on and they only brought up the equipment after payment was received.

Ryan parked his truck and beckoned Falcon to pull up alongside.

"You'll be able to keep an eye on your gear if it's close by," he shouted, from the open window of the lofty truck.

"I thought you said it was safe."

"I meant safer. Only messing with you son; it'll be fine in here. Look at the barbed wire for God's sake. Anyone climbing through that will bleed to death before they get to your truck, I promise."

Ryan jumped down from the rig and went into the office. Falcon could see that hand shakes were being exchanged along with some finger pointing from Ryan towards the rig, and even more talking. After five or so minutes he came back out to the truck.

"Well, better make yourself comfortable," said Ryan. "This is home tonight. We can get into the office there when they go in a few minutes. There's a shower and more importantly there's a kettle. Bet you want a cup of tea. I bloody do for sure. Mind you, I bet you want a damned shower looking at you. You're in a worse state than me."

Again Falcon grinned and nodded in acceptance. He wanted both and couldn't decide which should take precedence. The truth was that the shower would probably edge it if he got the choice. Darkness was now fully upon them but they were going nowhere. They were safely tucked away in the compound and alone. Ryan put on the tea but Falcon insisted that Ryan also take the first shower whilst he went and sorted out his gear. He of course had alternative motives than simply being polite, his priority being to ensure that everything incriminating was locked away and out of sight. He put anything that could indicate his true purpose in the wooden chest and placed his meagre toiletries and small towel in the rucksack. He also put the hand gun in there just in case, but at the bottom where it would be out of sight.

Everything securely locked, he scoured the compound and felt a slight relief come over him, maybe things were improving, although he knew for sure tonight would be interesting.

The shower and shave made Falcon feel like a new man. When Ryan saw him he commented that he was an attractive man when cleaned up but this was just his way of joking and putting Falcon on the spot.

"Well Robert, shall we retire to the bar?" he said nodding at the truck. "Mind you, the toilet's over here so I wouldn't come out barefoot if I was you."

"I'll take that advice on board," he replied, as they both headed off to the monster rig. Examining the state of their surroundings, this was really seen as good advice. Unmade ground was the basis of the depot, oil spills every where and where there were none the ground was nothing more than mud pools more suited to hippo wallowing grounds than workshops. Still, as far as he could tell, Falcon was still better off than he had been for the last few days.

The guys settled in the cramped conditions of the truck, which although reminiscent of prison conditions, afforded two separate bunks complete with mattress and bedding. Enough room for the guys to have a beer and chill out until morning. Idle chit chat took place for most of the evening jumping from family to career to girls and travel and inevitably back to the start again. Falcon felt unease for most of the time in so far as he needed to be careful what he said to Ryan, obviously not wanting to give his real position away. He extended his tales on mining exploration and talked around that and edged the conversation to South Africa and what it could offer him. Of course, this was Ryan's field, so he could sell the virtues of his homeland all night long, and enjoyed doing so. Falcon listened and could sense that his temporary host, whilst happy to work with the natives, certainly felt that the loss of apartheid was a blow for his country. This at least gave Falcon an angle to start from.

"I wouldn't mind spending a bit of time there," he said. "Sounds like a land of opportunities!"

"It's certainly that for the guy that wants to make them. Look at me, my family run a successful business and we employ blacks and whites. No problems there at all. I don't mind working along side the natives; they're only people just like we are after all, bloody sight cheaper too. We employ only those willing to help themselves; you can usually weed out the wrong ones in a very short period of time and we quickly get rid. But a guy wanting to move on up we don't mind giving a chance. We have too many now that just rely on the colour to give them a living. I mean, all these damned liberals chasing the ethnic vote, 'give 'em what they want' whatever the consequences to the country. The country's gone to rat shit. Only a small minority are happy to work on equal footing and go and better themselves and I've got no problem with that. Just the same is happening in Oz with the Abbo's. Only the old school sees what's happening but like I say, for the right fellow, there are still opportunities."

Ryan's accent was a little slurred, despite his size he seemed to start taking the effects of the beer after only a couple of bottles, not drunk, not by a long way, but certainly less coherent.

Falcon thought there was no time like the present to fire a shot across Ryan's bow.

"So . . ." he began, after pausing for a second and seemingly getting Ryan's attention, "what's the chance of me coming back down there with you, maybe have a look around the place?"

Ryan may have slurred a little over the last couple of hours but he still had his faculties about him. His brow furled and eyes opened wide as he turned and stared at Falcon for a few moments analysing his companion. He knew there was more to this guy than he was being told.

"Look son, I think it's time for a little more honesty here. What shit are you really in? I mean, out here alone, in bandit territory. No money, a dodgy story. You're not dressed like a merc but I guess that's no definite proof you're not one. You're running from something and it looks to me like you're in the need of a bit of help. But, if I don't know what the problem is, then there's no way I'm going to get mixed up in it. I just met you a few hours ago and I kind of like you."

He paused momentarily and looked Falcon straight in the eyes, "but I'm not planning to die for you. That's not in my game plan. So it's down to you now."

He took another swig from his beer whilst waiting for Falcon's response. It was a long time in coming. Falcon just held his beer, not drinking just staring at the bottle top. His mind was racing; he wanted to tell Ryan but knew he couldn't. He was sure Ryan would embrace him for what he did rather than throw him out, but nobody must know what he did . . . nobody. No matter what lies he had to tell to make himself seem even more despised, whatever story splurges out of his mouth in the next few seconds, the truth remained buried. That was a must.

Eventually the piercing silence was broken. Falcon started in a broken and almost apologetic voice.

"Either you're a clever man Ryan or I'm a piss poor liar," he started.

"I'm not that clever son so you make your own mind up," was the quick witted reply, clearly intent on dragging this conversation on. He sat intently, waiting for Falcon's next instalment.

"You're on the money," replied Falcon.

He paused again before the succeeding sentence was started. This fraction of time allowed Falcon to try and think ahead of the need to speak, playing dumb and apologetic, almost pathetic, afforded him this luxury of extra thinking time. There was little noise around save for the occasional car that passed by on the main road, the industry was all closed down for the night and the air was still so little noise carried out from the town. The only noise Ryan was interested in was that emanating from Falcon.

"I figured that son, but how much money. What's the score?"

"Well . . . here goes. In a nut shell, I'm scared. More scared than you can imagine."

Ryan sat upright and ever more intent, he too could not drink as he hung on Falcon's words as they meandered from his mouth. A further pause only served to make Ryan shuffle himself around the bunk on which they were both sitting whilst waiting for the details to emerge.

Falcon raised his head slowly and stared at Ryan and blurted out methodically and in a serious monotone.

"I'm scared that I might have killed someone, at least injured them and they're probably dead now anyway. I didn't mean to but things just got out of hand and I flipped. It's not my nature, I promise you."

His pace of speech accelerated as he was talking and defending himself almost before Ryan had had the chance to digest the words he was hearing.

"Go on, what really happened to get you in this state?"

He could sense Ryan was now hooked and he had to make this credible, yet appealing in some perverse way.

"There was this guy, a coloured guy from the mine I was working for. He was with me on the field trip. We were exploring across the border in Zambia, not here. It was only the second night away, you know, looking for new exploration sites like I told you before."

"Yep, I remember. You're some sort of geologist or engineer type."

"Yea, that's me. Well, we were camping and it was the end of the day. We sat around a fire we had lit you know, just chatting. Cooking a bit of soup over the fire and looking forward to the old cup of tea. Well, he suddenly put his arm around me. I didn't know what to do. I'd never been in a situation like that before. I just threw it off and thought he was horsing around. But it seems he wasn't. He put it back and tried to push me down. He was a biggish guy you know, used to manual work in the mines. I never knew he was a queer, honest. I never led him on. But he was my guide and the son of one of the managers in the mine so they though it would be good experience for him."

Falcon's speech and explanation was becoming disjointed and the fear started to show in his mannerisms as well as his voice. This act was getting better and he sensed Ryan was buying into it, at least for now.

He continued, "As daft as it sounds, you know what was going through my mind. I was fighting for my life, at least that's how I saw it. Who's to say I wasn't really? You never know what he would have done to me afterwards. It was just a reaction. It was an accident. I never meant to kill him, it just happened to be there."

"What did?"

Falcon again paused then replied, "My shovel. My fold up shovel. I had used it for digging a small pit for the fire so it was there."

"And you whacked him with it."

"Yeah, I can't remember how many times, honestly. I don't know if once or ten, I just can't remember. It's all a blur; I just know that when I stopped, he stopped. There was no more forcing from him. But you see, they'll be looking for us in a couple of days. We were planned to be out for about a week and that's soon upon us. I just left him there, maybe dead, maybe dying. I don't know and got to live with it now. But I was defending myself."

He stressed his defence stance as he started to show emotion, even Falcon could have believed his own performance. He also managed to show tearful eyes which he duly wiped for Ryan's benefit. It was a beautiful performance.

Again the cabin was silent. Ryan seemed to show as though he believed the story and he too was thinking. Falcon was on a roll, so he continued,

"I can't go back there, do you see the problem. There's no way I can go back there. Who would believe me, this guy had contacts, and his family is high up in the business. Well respected and everything. They'd throw me in a rat hole of a jail with no rights. Who would look after me then? I'm not ready for that. I was only protecting myself for Christ's sake."

Ryan sat dumbfounded, never taking his eyes away from Falcon as he poured out his woes.

"Shit son, you are in a hell of a mess. A black guy tried it on with you, didn't you see it coming?" No indications of what he was like?"

"No," Falcon replied as he still stared at the floor speaking softly now, "not a hint. I just want to get out of here. Can you help?"

Ryan sat and stared out of the front window of the truck into the abyss beyond the windscreen. There was just a black hole, nothing in sight. Anything could be out there but there was no way he would go out to check. He shook his head lightly from side to side, clearly disturbed by what he had heard.

He turned quickly to his guest and grabbed Falcon by the chin and lifted it so he could see into his eyes. Falcon's eyes were clearly bloodshot now with the tears that had been welling up as he told his story.

"We'll get you home son, just got to do a bit of thinking." It's getting you across the border that's the problem. Depends on the day really and who is on duty, whether they want to give us a hard time or not."

Falcon's face showed clear delight and stretched a smile showing genuine happiness for the benefit of his temporary landlord. His story had seemingly been believed, but whatever, he was going to get help from someone familiar with the territory and customs. What a relief. The thought of seeing messrs Johnson and Fairfax back in London after they had left him for dead was the aphrodisiac that spurred him on, and it was getting closer to reality. Falcon realised it would not be easy but at least he had a start.

"I don't know how I shall ever repay you Ryan, I really don't."

"Don't worry son, can't leave you down on your luck now can I? What sort of guy would I be then? Huh? No we'll get you home, let me sleep on it."

Ryan paused before continuing "Then you can worry about paying me . . ." he said in a joking manner, hoping to put the Englishman at ease.

That was the cue to retire for the evening. Nothing else to do and they had both done talking. The seeds were planted for both men, now they had to germinate overnight and their plan should blossom tomorrow. Falcon needed to get rid of his equipment but that would have to get dumped along the way. Tomorrow should be a fruitful day.

Chapter 15

Falcon awoke to the sound of engines roaring and steel clanking and banging. The whole trailer was bouncing up and down on a wave of activity, as Ryan was at the rear of the truck off loading the new bulldozer. A mammoth beast to most operations but out on the big mines of Africa, the bigger the beast the better, and Caterpillar was usually seen as the Rolls Royce of heavy equipment, hence the need to purchase from so far away. It's what the customer wanted so that's what the local dealer had to get.

He rubbed his eyes to see, that despite the arrival of the big dozer, there was still very little activity elsewhere in the yard, there was nothing else really to speak of in the place. Bits of broken rusting equipment and a tatty workshop seemed out of place with the brand spanking new Caterpillar. The few workers there were concentrating on watching the new equipment arrive like a child on Christmas morning.

It was yet another humid day and Falcon was relieved that at least yesterday he had managed the luxury of a shower. A bed to sleep in only served as the icing on the cake for what had been so far, as he saw it, quite a difficult week. The sky was blue although the clouds were forming and the traffic on the road outside was building up again, in contrast to the eerie silence from the previous night. He decided to throw his trousers and shirt back on and get to the front seat and monitor the activity at closer range. His appearance brought a fleeting glance from the watching audience but they had no real interest in him, they all wanted to have a play on the new plaything.

After about ten minutes, the machine was off loaded and parked in pride of place in front of the office block, a trophy for all around to witness, at least for the time being. Inevitably this kit had been paid for and at over quarter of a million dollars would surely be collected before too long. Ryan threw open the driver's door to find Falcon awake and alert in the other seat. He threw his leather clad rigger gloves behind the driver's seat and nodded at his guest.

"Morning dozy. You feeling good today Bob?" he asked.

"Much better now, egg and bacon would be nice though."

"I think that's a few days away yet, don't push your luck," replied Ryan with a chuckle in his voice. "Give me your keys and I'll throw your truck on the back. No need in running two rigs; it's a long way and a hell of a waste of juice."

Falcon sat bolt upright. He didn't want anybody climbing through his stuff in the Land Rover. "I'll put it on, need to stretch the legs a bit anyway. You just tell me if I'm going off the rails."

"Have you never done this before?"

"Of course I have, only kidding."

Falcon jumped from the rig and opened his Land Rover. The engine burst into life with little opposition, like a finely tuned race car. It would be a shame to lose her he thought, but it had to go, along with any trace of his very existence. He revved the engine a few times, throwing plumes of purple haze out of the exhaust. The audience didn't even glance over at the racket. They were all too preoccupied pawing over the new machine, much to Falcon's benefit. He edged his vehicle forward and perfectly up onto the bed of the low loader and killed the engine. Ryan promptly jumped up and started to strap her down.

"Well Ryan, do we have a plan?" he asked quizzically, squinting as he looked into the ever ascending sun.

"Kind of a plan, but let's get out of here first I think."

"Good idea, certainly with you on that one."

When the truck was seen to be secure, Falcon again checked it was all locked up and that nothing untoward could be seen within the interior of the vehicle. Ryan raised the hydraulic tail gate of his rig and pumped up the suspension once more and they were ready to hit the road. He had handed over all the necessary documentation for the dozer and had his receipt signed so they could be on their way.

The journey home began for both of them. The monster rig burst into life. You could almost sense the relief felt by the truck at having lost its heavy cargo of sixty or so tonnes to be replaced by a baby load by comparison, the rig was full of life. The engine purred as Ryan threw the big rig into gear, waved at his customers and swung the truck back out towards the main highway.

"Where are we headed now?" asked Falcon, eager to learn the plan of his exit strategy from this place he now regarded as the end of the world.

"Well, the best route is to stick to the main roads and believe me even the main roads won't be like you're used to back home. There's no way I can get this baby through the dirt tracks and that means a border crossing. We've got about seven hundred and fifty miles to go yet on tarmac so a couple of days driving while we figure it out. We've got to go back up to Luena and across country a bit. Try and enjoy it, the scenery is fantastic in places, pity the country's so fucked up. There's so much here you know, just not looked after at all. Only the chosen few see any benefit. That's life, well that's Africa really. It's a pity you didn't have an entry visa so we could have put you on a plane at Luena, but without one there's no way you would get sorted there. We need to drive across, that's the best chance to get out."

"Can't I walk through in the bush or a river somewhere and meet you on the other side?"

"Oh, if it was that simple," sighed Ryan. He continued slowly in a monotone and almost patronising manner, "You need to get your passport stamped into Namibia so you can get out the other side into South Africa. We've got to get a cross border permit to leave Angola for Namibia, so unfortunately you're just going to have to stay cool while I do some explaining on your part. I'm working on a plan, but there will need to be some liquidity in it for the guards. Do you have any cash at all?"

"I have some US Dollars, around five thousand I think, will that be enough?" Falcon thought it would be best if he saved a little in reserve for himself, he knew there would be costs in South Africa, not least his plane ticket.

"Hell, I would have thought so. It depends on how many are there at the time really as they share it out. They're not well paid; in fact they're lucky if they get paid. That's why they fight to get jobs like the border crossings or even the police. It's well known they can top up their salaries, just as long as they don't get caught."

There was silence in the cab for several minutes before it was broken again by Ryan.

"You know we're going to have to lose your truck. There's no papers for it being in Angola so they won't let you take it out, and if we turn up with it it'll only attract further attention. You okay with that?"

Falcon was very relieved to hear that and let out a big sigh as demonstration of the lifting of the burden. He wanted nothing to remain to tie him to the Coltex organisation. He knew they would stitch him up if he was caught here; he had been left to die after all. Distancing himself from his current employers was uppermost in his mind right now.

"I figured it would have to go, but I need to get my personal stuff out of it first before we dump it. How do we get rid, it's not like we take it to a crusher or anything is it?"

"Almost, they've got the next best thing."

"Really!" Falcon was astounded by the statement. "Where's that then?"

"It's all around you Bob," laughed Ryan. "All around you and you can't see it for looking."

"Where?" He glanced across at Ryan who was laughing and curling his lips as he did so. "Come on then . . . where?" Falcon asked, his impatience starting to show.

"If we park it up in the middle of nowhere and make it look as though it has broken down and been temporarily abandoned, I guarantee you that within twenty four hours it will have been stripped by the locals better than a river full of angry piranha could do to a stray cow. There would be no trace of it at all, there would be different bits everywhere, some used for spares, others used for the most curious of objects. The seats would be in someone's house and maybe even the doors. The radio would even go for what good it would be."

Ryan knew the way of life in this land, the fact is that it would be stolen not for a purpose, other than the fact it was there. They would not even know what they were taking as it was systematically stripped, but they would eventually find a use for it. It would just disappear with so little trace of its previous presence that even the finest forensic scientist would be dumbfounded.

Falcon mused over the relative simplicity. The best way to make something disappear was to leave it out in the open. What a parody. He had never condoned thieves but in this case they were angels from above.

"So where do we do it then?" being keener than ever to dispose of his connections and develop new ones.

"There's plenty of time yet," replied Ryan. The best place is where the towns thin out and get smaller as we head south. Get past Menongue and there'll be plenty of opportunities."

"I'll need to empty the back out first."

"Leave it all if you like, it'll all go. They won't know what they've got, trust me."

Falcon would feel more assured if he had some control over the goods in the back. "Just the same, there's some stuff I'd like to see go personally."

"Suit yourself Bob, your energy you're wasting. There's no shortage of rivers you can dump stuff in where it'll never be found."

"That sounds good to me Ryan. Now, what's my story?"

"I was thinking the best bet is that you work for me. There's a spare set of coveralls behind your chair. They're lived in so it'll help the story. Pity you haven't swelled up around the middle like I have because I think they'll hang on you but it's the best I've got."

"Hey, no problem," replied Falcon. "I'll make them fit."
He paused before daring to ask the next stage, "but what
about my passport?"

Ryan concentrated on the road ahead and went quiet
again. His brow furled revealing the lived in features across
his face as the sun came through the side window. Falcon realised this was a big stumbling block so decided not to push
him too hard just yet. He could see Ryan was thinking and
after all, he was trying to help him. Right now this was his
only friend on the planet. The pair sat quietly as Ryan continued driving his hauler along the reasonable quality roads
that he had sought. Falcon just gazed out of his window and
as suggested, admired the views, although it was impossible
to pretend he had nothing else on his mind. They had been
driving for over three hours and were just passing through
Luena when Ryan decided to pull in at a filling station to top
up the tanks.

"Need some gas Bob, may as well get it here, it's as cheap
as anywhere. We can grab a bite to eat here as well if you
like. Bet you'd like some breakfast or maybe even lunch?"

"Yeah, good idea. I could sure eat something and a bathroom break wouldn't be unwelcome."

"They've got one of those here as well, you'll be glad to
know, although it's not quite the Ritz."

The truck came to a halt and the local attendant ambled
out without a care in the world to tend to his customer.
Not that he was overwhelmed with business and didn't really need Ryan's money; it's just the way it was. There's no
rush in life down here, Ryan told the boy to fill up the rig
and both he and Falcon climbed out. Falcon stood by his
guardian, unsure of what to do or where to go. He thought it
better he shadowed his protector and not let him out of his
sight. They both entered the station where they could also be
served some local foods.

"I'd recommend you don't ask for a steak, unless you think
your guts will handle it," Ryan advised.

"I take it the steaks aren't their best then?"

"It's a case of not knowing what it's a steak of . . . if you get my drift. Like I told you before, at least with fish you know its origin, to some extent at least."

"Yea, fish again sounds good."

They both ate the fish with rice and ever present plantains. At least it was edible and nourishing. Washed down with sweet seven ups and water, they finished and Ryan settled the bill for the dining and fuel and away they went. As they climbed back into the rig, Ryan turned to his new friend.

"I've got an idea!" he piped up, "and unless you've got anything better, you need to buy into it, and quickly."

Excitedly Falcon turned to his friend as he was manoeuvring the truck out of the garage and back onto the main highway.

"I'm all ears," he said.

He sat and listened as Ryan explained that the best way to cross would be as his work colleague. They would tell the story that the passport was stolen when Falcon got mugged in Luanda. They would say they managed to retrieve it as the robbers threw it away but did make off with his wallet. Perhaps that way they would be able to get the necessary exit visa from Angola which would make things very easy getting into Namibia.

"Namibia's no problem," Ryan said. "Once across that border you're home free. A few days away but no more worries for sure."

"But do you think they will go with the passport story, I mean fighting off some robbers and getting it back?" he quizzed.

"Like I said son, if you have any better idea let me know. You've got a couple of days to come up with something and if you can't and you don't like what's on the table, then I'm not taking the chance with you at the border. They'll end up throwing my sorry ass in jail with you."

"No," replied Falcon, even before Ryan had finished his response. "I'm bloody grateful, you'd better believe it. I'm just nervous I guess. We'll get the story straight. We have a couple of days before the border? We'll work on it for sure." Falcon couldn't help but show his nerves at the prospect of facing an underpaid, over zealous Angolan Soldier who would probably have his finger on the trigger ready for trouble.

"We come back into bush areas in an hour or so, we may as well dump the Landie sooner rather than later, agreed?"

Falcon nodded as he stared straight ahead at the brown landscape spattered with patches of grass and shrubbery. He could see the hills in the distance and clearly they were fertile lands. He regurgitated the plan over and over in his head, silently thinking how best to explain to the officials about the passport. What would seem credible? Would he crack? The questions came and went but at least he felt comfortable in Ryan's presence. This guy was a hardened veteran of these parts and knew how to deal with the locals. He had a lifetime's experience. He would have to go with his mentor and simply do as he was told if he was to have any chance.

The truck pulled into the side of the road at the foot of the hills. The occupants got out of the air conditioned cab into the midday sun, and it took Falcon by surprise and sent him dizzy for a few seconds.

"It's getting hotter I'm sure," he said. "What's the idea now?"

"Well I figured we may as well unload your truck down here and you follow me up the hills into the bush. It'll be a damn site easier to unload down here. When we find a suitable turning we can then just dive off the main track with the Landie and go and dump it."

"Sounds like a plan," replied Falcon.

He was now sporting his partner's overalls. They were clean at least but had certainly seen some action in their time, and made to measure they were not. At least Falcon thought this would give him an opportunity to tidy up the stuff inside the Land Rover before leaving it. He was not sure how to get rid of the firearms though, that could be a problem. Still, he had to think on his feet now and see what unfolded.

Hopefully, Ryan would continue believing the story and this would all turn out right in the end. Falcon jumped into the Land Rover and fired it up. It was running just as sweet as ever, what a shame to lose it. He reversed it off the trailer and then got out and helped Ryan reset his loader ready for the long journey home.

Off they set as a convoy of two being led by the big Mercedes truck. Slowly it climbed as the roads elevated from the horizontal and started to gain height. The forest gradually encroached up to the roadside as they went but there was still plenty of light. Falcon drove with the window down and although he could not hear much outside except his and Ryan's diesel engines banging away, this was the first time he had not felt uneasy since his escapade across the border had started. He was buying into the concept of the stolen and retrieved passport; after all he had little choice.

Ryan's great orange indicators kicked into life signalling that he was about to pull in. This must be the place, thought Falcon. It was. There was a turning into the bush on the left to where Ryan pointed.

"Just take it up there. Pull it off the road a bit but still visible. It'll be gone before you leave the country. I'll stay here otherwise the rig will disappear instead."

Falcon looked hesitant at this point and Ryan reassured him that there were no big cats stalking the jungle just waiting to feed on him.

"Don't be a bloody girl," he said. "Come on, daylight's burning. You don't need to take it far. I'll hear you scream if you start to get eaten," he mocked his wary stooge, as he sent Falcon on his way.

". . . and don't forget your passport," he shouted, as the Land Rover turned up the narrower pot holed track.

Falcon drove slowly up the narrow track watching intently for any movement in the trees. The light was getting darker as he rode further in. He had not gone a hundred yards before Ryan was out of sight. Then he looked for a bit of a clearing where he could pull in as directed rather than just leave it in the road. He would prefer it to stay hidden away for ever but he could see the benefits of the body shop workers stripping it back to its skeleton and dispersing the corpse to all four corners of the country.

He soon found a small level area adjacent to the road which suited his purpose. He could pull off the road some ten yards quite easily and afford an element of covering for the truck whilst it still being visible. At least he now had an opportunity to try and eliminate anything incriminating inside the truck. He delved straight into the wooden chest for the sniper rifle and hand gun. This was a war ravaged country; Falcon could not leave such items for these people to find. They already had a life of bloodshed and he didn't want to contribute to it further. He stripped the sidearm into various pieces and set about tossing the three main components in differing directions into the bush. Then the same process with the rifle but that would be harder. He took the rifle by the muzzle and smashed the stock against an adjacent tree. The wooden stock came away without much resistance and a few more bashes against the tree also served to at least damage a little the remainder of the weapon. He removed the clip and ammunition and scattered the individual bullets like a seasoned gardener feeding his prized lawns. Then a mighty heave and he threw the rifle as far as he possibly could. It probably went a few feet only before becoming entangled in the web of vines and shrubs that were growing thickly there, but he was sure that in time the forest would consume these little monsters before they were found, and they would be lost to the world forever.

This was a big load off his mind, although it was not an easy thing to do. After all, he now had no defence but he could not risk Ryan finding any of the weapons. That would be the cover blown away totally. There was the issue of the paperwork detailing Mizinga, Falcon put a match to this and burned it in the back of the Land Rover. It scorched the paintwork on the deck which started bubbling around his little camp fire but that was of little consequence. He made sure that among the ashes there was nothing at all that was readable or incriminating. Now he was Robert Vaughan, a mechanic for Caterpillar, and there was nothing which could disprove that any more.

He shut up the vehicle and locked it. Why he was not sure, just habit. Then he launched the key way into the forest, he was sure that would never be discovered. As he walked back to the main track and Ryan, his sense of ease allowed him to take in the surroundings. There was life in this forest clearly audible in the trees. Moving branches caused him to quicken his pace although he was fairly sure it was only monkeys, but Ryan's parting comment about being eaten still registered. He heaved a bit of a sigh as he rounded a bend and could see the back end of the truck maternally waiting for one of its offspring to return.

Ryan was standing by the door of the rig as he came Falcon emerged from the darkened lane. "Job done," he said as he flashed a smile to his driver and waved his maroon coloured passport.

"Good," replied the driver, "let's go home. Oh, first I need your passport!"

Ryan dutifully handed it to his requestor. Ryan looked through it, "Not got many stamps in here yet," he said as he leafed from page to page. "Ah well . . . here goes."

He dropped the passport to the floor and started to drag it around with his foot.

"What the bloody hell do you think you're doing?" screamed Falcon.

"Have a bit of faith Bob. It's been stolen remember. It may as well look like it's been in a fight. Maybe you should too; now there's something to think about."

After a bit of a grubbing in the damp stony soil, the passport looked well and truly bedraggled, just as required. Pages were crinkled and most had dirt on. He wiped it on his coveralls to get the excess filth off the document but it did the trick. It now looked as though it had been plucked out of a garbage can. Then he proceeded to tear out several pages of the booklet and those that were left he strategically tore across the pages themselves, but leaving them still attached to the books spine. He made sure that the data page with Vaughan's information on was not damaged and still easily readable but also showing signs of dirt.

"There you are, now it looks like it's been in a fight wouldn't you say?" as he handed it back to Falcon who looked through it amazed at the way this man was thinking. He had an answer to most things.

They both jumped into the truck and Ryan honked the horn in celebration three or four times as the rig started to work through the gear box and head back towards South Africa and shouted, "Homeward bound, yee ha."

It was two more days of uneventful travelling in similar territory before they reached the border crossing at Santa Clara. As the border was only open during the day time, Ryan's experience was such that he knew when to stop for the evening so they did not end up sleeping at the crossing itself. They reached the area around ten o'clock in the morning. The streets were already teeming with people all trying to cross from Angola into Northern Namibia. A few cars were making the crossing but the main modes of transport were the bicycle and the feet. He marvelled at the multitude of colours worn by the people and the obvious differences in wealth between individuals.

"Is it like this all the time?" he asked Ryan.

"Yep, every day hundreds of them cross the border, some for work but most go for shopping. A lot of stuff is a damn site cheaper on the other side than here in Angola, even everyday essentials. A lot of Angolan traders get their stock from Namibia. There's a thriving trade centre just on the other side, even an area called China Town due to the number of Chinese Traders there. You'll be pleasantly surprised at just how different it is through those gates. Fuel's cheaper here though so they cross to Angola for that."

The rig pulled into a truck parking area up from the crossing.

"Why are we stopping here?" asked the bemused English-man with the border crossing and safe haven clearly in sight, creating more anxiety and apprehension.

"We go on foot now and get the paperwork sorted out. It's not usually that involved for individuals but we do have our own issues to sort out. The truck will be easy; I've got paperwork coming in so I won't have any real bother. Now, are you up for this?"

"As ready as I'll ever be I guess," replied Falcon tenta-tively.

"Well, just look a little worried but don't show scared. You have a valid reason for the problem, just remember it. You were robbed. Led astray in Luanda by hookers but it was a set up for some muggers. You got that. You came here with me in the truck okay, just like we rehearsed, and now we want to get back home to Durban."

"Hookers! Why hookers?"

"Because it works with the story. I mean, we can always go with queers if you'd much prefer but I figured that would be a little close to the truth for comfort right now. Just let me do the talking unless they ask you anything direct. I wouldn't worry about them thinking you're a dirty little bug-ger, if that's what it costs so be it. Speaking of costs, let me have your dollars."

Falcon handed over a bundle of screwed and folded notes, he still had another roll in his sock but that was his emer-gency fund if needed. Ryan screwed the notes into no appar-ent order and squeezed them into a couple of his pockets.

"Right kid, let's go for it," he said with an air of confi-dence as they got out of the truck.

It looked just like disorganised chaos to Falcon, people weaving here and there. There were pedestrians trying to avoid colliding with carefree trucks and cars. Pick up trucks loaded with people in the back like crammed cattle trucks, salesmen and women beckoning at strangers to purchase their wares. The pair walked casually down to the checkpoint through the bedlam where they joined in the commotion.

After a few minutes Ryan presented his trade documents for inspection and as expected they were rubber stamped without hesitation. The border guard never even looked at the document. Then he handed in the two passports. The battered one of Falcon's obviously got his attention. He held it up and showed to his friend with whom he had been talking all the while, more interested in socialising than working. However this was a little different. The guard raised his large head and looked at the pair in front of him. His eyes were showing signs of yellow staining and bursting blood vessels. There's something seriously wrong with this guy's health Falcon thought, or he had a good night last night and hasn't yet recovered. Even the jet black skin could not disguise the brightness of his yellow stained teeth as he opened his mouth.

"This passport no good," he shouted. "You need a new one to cross."

"No it's still okay, look the picture and everything still there. You can see who it is," replied Ryan, maintaining calmness at all times. He knew that losing his temper with these guys, no matter how irrational they're being, would have only one result.

The guard threw it on to a desk to his side where his colleague was sitting. This was obviously the senior official at the site; he had the sergeant's stripes on his jacket sleeve, albeit a steel badge. He studied Falcon's passport and thumbed through what remained of it page by page, just as if he was studying a new text book. It was blank but it was still being read. This was the intimidation phase. They both knew they would be scrutinised so it was not unexpected.

"Mr. Vaughan," said the sergeant sullenly. "Can you come here please?" he beckoned. Both he and Ryan went to the sergeant's desk as he motioned for them both to take a seat. It was not a desk that was being heavily used, not for clerical duties in any case, despite its ragged appearance.

"What's the meaning of this?" he said, as he waved the torn passport in their faces.

Falcon tried not to spurt out so thought he would take a deep breath before speaking. Fortunately for him, Ryan took up the reigns.

"The lad was robbed in Luanda a few days ago. He lost all his money and bank cards but they seemed not to want the passport so threw it away as we chased them. When we got it back it was like this. We managed to clean it up though."

"How can I let you cross with this document, it's not legal is it? What was he doing in Luanda to get in this predicament?"

"Well, you know some blokes. They can't keep their fly zipped up for very long. I warned him about the local girls but it seems he wouldn't take my advice and look where it got him."

Falcon was feeling the fear well up inside and hoped he would not be called on to speak in the immediate future as he was so unprepared. He could sense this was not going well. Ryan and the sergeant went to and fro repeating the same argumentative points for several minutes then Ryan threw in a curve ball.

"The police in Luanda said we would be alright to travel with this passport. It was still legible and would do for my colleague to get home. Why don't you give them a call, they should have all the details on file. That way we can clear this up straight away. My friend wants to get home, he has things to collect from Durban then he'll be away to the UK. This hasn't been a good trip for him as you can imagine."

The sergeant turned to Ryan finally. "So you thought you would entertain some of our girls did you?"

"It seems that way sir, yes."

"Looks to me like you got properly screwed wouldn't you say? I bet you didn't even get that far," he said, whilst laughing aloud for the benefit of his colleagues.

"Can we please call Luanda and straighten this out, we would be very grateful to be on our way?" asked Ryan politely cutting short the officer's jibes.

The sergeant turned his attention back to the South African. He sat back in his chair and started to rock it backwards leaning against the wall. He placed his hefty standard issue black boots on the desk getting comfortable before asking,

"Just how grateful would you be?"

Ryan knew instantly he was gaining the upper hand. The principle had been established as expected and they were entering the famous barter phase.

"How grateful do we need to be?" he asked politely.

The sergeant's smile broadened as he nodded his head, glancing across at his colleague who was still dealing with the hordes of daily travellers.

"There are four of us here. You know we're a poor nation, we all have families that need feeding and there is a certain amount of administration required for such a crossing."

Ryan nodded sympathetically seeming to understand the guards' plight.

"I know how it works Sergeant, let's just cut out the crap and get the deal done."

"Well Mr . . .," he paused as he reviewed Ryan's passport and opened at the photograph page, ". . . Koetze. Let's say fifty thousand dollars US . . . should suffice."

Ryan knew this was just an opening gambit and they never expected in their wildest dreams to get anywhere near that amount.

"Let's not," replied the South African totally un-phased by the whole process. "I would suggest more like fifty dollars. I too have a family that needs feeding, and they're much cheaper to keep than yours!"

The sergeant let out a raucous false laugh and bellowed something to his colleague at the desk who also started to laugh. He turned back to Ryan and Falcon now with a serious look on his face. He removed his feet from the desk and leaned towards the pair of negotiators.

"Fifty dollars is an insult Mr. Koetze. What can we do with Fifty dollars? How about we get serious now, let's say ten thousand dollars for both of you."

"That makes it five thousand each does it, because my paperwork is fault free? So we're looking at five now. Some climb down. How about we say five hundred dollars for my friend and nothing for me?"

"Mr. Koetze, you're playing with me now. Let's agree on five thousand and you are free to go."

Falcon could feel the relief inside ready to burst out. The way he saw it the deal was just about done and on budget, yet Ryan did not want to let go.

"I have a better idea," he said. "Let's agree on one thousand and you don't need to call Luanda and take up any of your precious time, I see you are very busy."

Ryan took out a handful of dollars and started to count it out in front of the border guard. He grabbed Ryan's hand and slammed it into the desk. He prised the cash out of his hand and grasped it, pulling the wad close to his chest as if he was doing it surreptitiously yet everybody in the office knew the system.

"There's only fifteen hundred dollars here Mr. Koetze. How do you think we can do this transaction with that amount? What else have we on offer?"

"I would offer that if you need any more for the administration charges you give me a receipt and we check out the prices with Luanda, just to make sure you're not over charging me 'cause I'm white."

It was rare for the border guards to be met with such resilience, but they knew this was probably as far as they could push Ryan if they wanted anything from him at all.

"You drive a hard bargain Mr. Koetze. I think today you are lucky; I have many other things to be doing. I will take the fifteen hundred and no receipt. We all need to keep administration costs down, understood?"

Ryan nodded his understanding as the sergeant threw the passports back to the desk and told the clerk to make the appropriate passport entries. Falcon was still reeling from the performance he had just witnessed, such steely determination as though it was a recital for a well rehearsed play. Never did Ryan give an inch, nor show any fear. He knew how to play this system for sure. Falcon knew that he would

never have achieved anything like that. The two men retrieved their passports and strolled out of the office back the
couple of hundred yards to the truck park.

"Just stay calm, wait till we get back to the truck," Ryan
said feeling the furore that was imminently to spew forth
from his associate. "They'll be watching for sure."

"How the hell did you keep your calm in there? I was
crapping myself, you didn't flinch."

"It's knowing just how to deal with these people. I know
what they want, its all just cash and fifty thousand dollars
makes you very wealthy here, its way too much and they
knew it. We still paid plenty; they'll be drunk for weeks.
Now let's get across the other side, we've got to go through
it again soon, then we're on our way."

Once again the rig burst into life and started the slow roll
jostling for position with the foot traffic as they all crossed
the border. Falcon was perspiring as his body exuded eu-
phoria and relief, his delight at overcoming the greatest hur-
dle envisaged on this epic journey was difficult to hide. He
rocked in his seat as the truck crawled towards the crossing
point. Falcon was not unhappy at leaving Angola. The bullet spattered border crossing bearing testament to the areas
volatility, the building quite in contrast to its counterpart in
Namibia. Ryan had to undergo the same explanation as to
the state of the passport to the Namibian officials. However
they were less abrasive and satisfied at the explanation. After
all they had cleared Angola with official documentation, a
British subject and Ryan having been a regular visitor over
the years all added to the ease of passage.

The roads improved almost instantly as the official border
was crossed. Namibia had a far better quality of highway
with the majority being metalled. By comparison it was a
pleasure to drive here. The remainder of the journey back
to Durban was in fact quite a pleasure for Falcon. It was so
relaxing after the tensions from the previous week it was almost recreational. He never lost focus of his plans for when
he got back to the UK, but could at last unwind and lose

all that nervous tension. Ryan was a good guide highlighting the beauty of the nation they were travelling through. It was breathtaking scenery of immense contrasts as they travelled the length of the African nation. There was the beautiful wildlife in its natural habitat where it belonged. People of differing characters throughout ranging from city dwellers in their smart suits and dresses to indigenous tribesmen dressed just as smartly in traditional costume, their daily dress. Even hotels were something else again and far better than the truck and immeasurably superior to the Land Rover floor.

Ryan persuaded his guest that he needed to stay with him a couple of days in Durban where Ryan's wife never stopped fussing over him from the moment he landed. She was obviously pre warned by her husband of the impending house guest. It turned out he was roughly the same age as their own son who had left home several years before and his mother often seemed lost with the emptiness that remained in her home. This was even worse of course when Ryan was travelling; fortunately he was rarely away for more than one or two nights. The Angolan trip was something far less frequent, but a blessing to Mr. Robert Vaughan aka Anthony Falconer.

Falcon was escorted shopping to be kitted out for suitable attire for the journey home. Luckily he had a bit of cash so had no need to impose himself on his host any more than he had to. He managed to secure a single ticket back to the UK for around one thousand dollars at short notice which still left a good two thousand out of his five that Ryan was aware of. A friendship forged in a little over a week would take a lifetime for Falcon to repay. He secretly hoped he would get the chance to reimburse these people at some time in the future, but he knew the reality. After he left South Africa, Robert Vaughan would cease to exist. He would disappear into the ether and Tony Falcon would be back on the scene.

As he departed from his newly adopted parents at Durban Airport, he slipped an envelope to Ryan. This contained a note of thanks that he knew he would never be able to express in person, and also the additional cash he had left over for the couple, as a gift. He knew no other way that he could show his appreciation, either now or at some future date.

"I will never be able to repay you for what you have done. You saved my life, and there's no price I can give for that. I hope we meet again some time, and I'll buy the fish," he joked. "There's a little note in there from me, please don't open it until I have gone. This is hard enough now."

He was in reality choking up with emotion as he said his goodbyes. It was as if they were his own family and he was going away for a long time. He was and they felt like they were. He knew this would be their last meeting and he was guilty at having used them. At the same time though, he was happy they believed him and nobody got hurt. So everybody felt good for doing the right thing. He hugged Mrs Koetze for several seconds, reminding her of the hugs she missed so regularly from her own offspring.

The two men shook hands vigorously and Ryan slapped the boy on his back. "Get back to a normal life now son," he said, offering what seemed fatherly advice. "You can put all this crap behind you, go and get a decent job and get yourself a wife. You've got plenty of years left in you yet; don't let this experience drag you down."

Falcon simply nodded as tears welled in his eyes. He needed to go but couldn't let go of his new friend. But he had to, the plane was checking in and he needed to go.

"Goodbye my friend. You take care of that good lady there," Falcon advised trying to act as though there was nothing wrong, but all three knew this was an emotional scene, at least for one of them.

"Go on, be gone with you, the bloody plane's waiting," Ryan urged him on waving him towards the departure gates.

It was time; he knew he had to go. He nodded profusely to the Koetze family as he turned and mimed the words 'thank you' to them as he went. Soon he was gone. Family life could return to normal for Ryan and his wife. Falcon breezed through passport control, helped by his note from the Brit-

ish Consulate validating his passport stating he would organise a replacement on returning to the UK. Very soon he was
on a British Airways Boeing 747, three hundred tonnes of
metal hurtling down the runway at Durban. The behemoth
lumbered into the air with a slovenly push as the last of its
wheels sprung the mighty jet off the ground and then just as
quickly packed them neatly away into the belly of the plane.
He was going home. Not too long ago, he thought he would
never see London again, tonight though, he realised such a
thought had been premature.

He eased back his chair and settled himself down for the
long flight. It would still be relaxing and he could now focus
on what to do when he got home. He would need a job for a
start although he had his down payment from Coltex to fall
back on initially. But the priority would be catching up with
his current employers who left him for dead. That would be
the sweet dream that would send him to sleep for the best
part of the duration of the flight.

Chapter 16

It was a typical damp, overcast, October morning when Falcon's plane hit the tarmac at Heathrow. The pilot threw the four vast Rolls Royce engines into reverse thrust to bring the flying beast to a manageable speed suitable for parking up. Now he was awake! Even at just after six in the morning, the flight traffic was already creating log jams at Heathrow, just like most days. He knew there would be further chaos inside the terminal as he joined the crowds of tired holidaymakers struggling with irritable children suffering from lack of sleep, all trying to get to the front of the baggage carousel. Falcon was lucky in that regard. As he had no luggage except the little rucksack he still had on his person, once through the snake line at immigration he was away.

Twenty minutes later, he was in the arrivals hall, the eager crowds readily assembled to welcome back loved ones. There was no-one for him. Just as well as nobody should know where he was. He changed his last five hundred dollars into sterling at the Bureau De Change and set off for the train to take him back to London, the Heathrow Express, which ran into Paddington Station on a regular basis, so irrespective of time, he would not have long to wait before he was once again homeward bound. Once back in Central London it was easy to jump on the Circle or District Line tube and get back to his home district. He needed to get back to his flat and his bed. Any other business would keep another day at least.

Falcon had himself a modest flat, also in the Notting Hill area, not far from where he spent the best part of his childhood. Although he grew up in the area, he didn't wish to keep his parents' house after their death. However, he did buy as an investment, the apartment, which when he was not able to live there was rented out to provide a growing but modest investment fund. Once he knew he was nearing completion of his military services, he decided he would like the place back for himself. Free from being saddled with the debt burden of a mortgage for London property, Falcon never really needed a significant income to sustain a reasonable, although never flamboyant, lifestyle. The investment fund was dwindling, albeit slowly, but his property asset was rising sharply in value. If needed, he was not so emotionally attached to the place that he could not sell it.

He was feeling the cold long before reaching home. Dressed only with a thin pullover, he had already acclimatised to the African heat and humidity. He retrieved his door key from his neighbour who had been keeping it safe for him whilst he was away and set off upstairs to his own apartment. It was all alarmed so he knew the neighbour would not bother with his place. She was a kindly old soul who Falcon often ran errands for when she needed. He could smell the stale air in the apartment as he entered and immediately set about opening windows throughout the place. Next was to grab a heavy duty rugby shirt from his wardrobe and swapping out the South African pullover he was sporting, for something more in keeping with British weather. Then it was time to lie on his old comfortable bed. Moulded over recent years to his body profile, this was now heaven and he could feel himself sink through the aerated quilted coverings. He pulled the large duvet over himself as he lay there fully clothed, shoes and all, staring blankly at the ceiling. He pulled the covers up around his chin as the thoughts of the past few weeks raced across his mind, along with the infinitely valuable assistance received from his new friend Ryan, who would unfortunately never know the full extent of what he had actually done.

Falcon lay there for fifteen minutes recounting his last few weeks when he decided it was time to close most of the windows, take a shower in his own bathroom and sleep off the fatigue that had once again enveloped him. When he was refreshed he would decide upon his future. He slept very unsettled for the best part of the day and, although he knew he had benefited from the rest, there was no point in staying in bed any longer. He was actually rejuvenated, despite the restlessness and thought he had almost immediately adjusted his body clock back to the days of night shift work down at the club. Maybe he had. Maybe that was where his future lay, although right now, the club was holding mixed emotions for him.

Still, he had to do something. He was revitalized and raring to go, but at what? He knew he would need to track down Sir Henry and his cohort but was not anticipating doing so, so soon. He wanted to get back into the London life again before doing so such that he could plan his strategy. But what strategy could he plan? He had no real idea how he would react if he ever caught up with the pair again, although he knew that at some stage he would catch up with them. Maybe together or maybe as individuals but he would make sure he caught up with them eventually. Then he decided, he was fit enough to do so, why put off till tomorrow what he could do today. It would only gnaw at him the longer he left the issue unfinished. That was it; he would start at the club this evening and see if they were there. He knew Sir Henry was a frequent visitor from his working there in the past, so it was a good place to start, besides why would he need to change habits now? After all, all those in the know believed Falcon would no longer exist.

It was back out of the wardrobe for the evening suit, the glad rags once again happy to see the outside world. There was no way he would get across the door inappropriately dressed, but he could still pass off as working there and not be out of place, as such dress was expected from the staff. He had lost a little weight on his African venture but was sure nothing too drastic, the suit still fit well enough to allow it to be seen in public. That weight would soon come back.

It was soon seven o'clock in the evening and time to hit the town. He now had his own identity back along with his own credit and debit cards. Once again he could be Anthony Falconer and enjoy whatever came along with it. He restocked his wallet with sterling from the bank cash machine not more than five minutes away from his house, and hailed a taxi. No point in jumping a bus in the evening dressed like a penguin, it could get him into even more trouble than he was planning. What would it be like seeing his employer again he wondered, who would be the more surprised? They had unfinished business together. Even more important to Falcon was the fact they had an unpaid debt to settle up. No small debt either, this was one hundred thousand pounds . . . cash. They would surely be hoping he wouldn't be around to collect it.

Falcon entered the main door of the Mayfair club where he was immediately greeted by one of his old colleagues.

"Hey Tony, we thought you'd done a runner my old China," he said, allowing his working accent to drift back to his London roots for the benefit of his old mate.

"No way Pete, you know me. Live a little, love a little. Just had to get away for a little while you know. But I'm back now. Looking for a bit of work really, I may even try Andre later, see if there's space for me to come back sometime."

"You know Andre would take you back like a shot. Do you want me to give him a bell, he's upstairs now?"

"No, I'm not desperate just yet. I may call in and see him later."

Falcon paused a few seconds as his friend, looking just as equally debonair in his own dinner jacket, was trying to retain some decorum at the front desk, despite the delight at his old friend calling in. Everybody got on well with him at the club and was sorry to see him not return.

"I'm actually due to meet someone, here actually, an old regular. Thing is I'm not sure of the night. Too much ale you know but I'm fairly certain it's tonight. If not I'll just have to keep on trying."

"Oh, lording it with the knobs now are we. You have gone up in the world. Good for you."

"Nothing like that, just watch your mouth matey. No, there may be a bit of personal driving in it for me for a few weeks. I gave him a lift home not long before I left and we seemed to get on okay. He left me a message a few days back on the answer phone but I cleared it out and now, well let's just say I can't remember."

"A wild few days was it?"

"Not worthy of discussion, you'll only get jealous and we'll fall out," Falcon teased.

"Go on then. I'll risk my job. Who is it?"

"Thanks Pete, I owe you one. It's Sir Henry Johnson, you know him?" Tony asked.

"Aye, I know that tight git. Loaded you know but tighter than a ducks arse. Miserable old sod if you ask me. What do you want to work for him for?" asked the doorman somewhat astonished at Tony's choice of employer.

"It's just an opportunity Pete, got to take these things when they come along. So anyway, is he in tonight?"

"Na, not yet in any case. He was last night and well leathered, as ever. I expect he'll be back tonight as well. He was saying to some of his old cronies in the library he'd see them today, so we'll see. Do you want to come in and wait, I'm sure the guys would like to see you?"

"Not just yet Pete. Tell you what, give us a ring will you if he turns up, but discretely. Don't tell him I'm here or have been asking for him."

"Hey no problem bro'. You going far; is it the same old number?"

"Yep, same number and no I won't be far. Just have a walk around the block and take in a bit of winter air. Maybe grab a beer and something to eat. No matter what time he turns up yeah, discrete. I'll see you right for it, don't worry." Falcon started to walk away back into the damp evening.

"Okay mate, see you later, yeah."

Falcon raised his hand for his friends benefit as a gesture of a wave and sauntered off down the quiet streets. This area of Mayfair had very little traffic at night but once out onto Park Lane the streets were once again bouncing. The dampness and misery associated with dull English winters never stopped the folks of the capital or visitors from venturing forth onto her streets at all times of the day and night. Black

cabs were honking horns as lanes were randomly being selected whilst they circled around the park; homeless folks
sat not too far away from the five star hotels of the city, waving mercilessly their paper cup from McDonald's, stinking
of stale beer and cheap spirits. Immigrants stood with plac-
ards around their necks pleading their plight, but you never
knew who the real causes were and who the fraudsters were
out to prey on your conscience. Falcon ignored it all and
weaved through the tide of people coming against him not
really knowing where he wanted to go.

He made his way to Oxford Street and decided he would
stroll along there. There was lots of light with the shops remaining open until late, ensnaring the unsuspecting tourist
with a bargain. Yet he found something quite comforting in
the civility of the mass crowds. He was anonymous within
it yet not alone. He had company and that was reassuring,
these people were not hunting him, they didn't even see
him in person. He was just another obstacle in everybody's
path. He stopped to explore the occasional shop window
yet he wanted for nothing. He had no one really to buy
for. He was killing time. A small but rather busy Italian
Restaurant caught his eye so he decided it was time to get
out from the chill for a little while and see how the evening
developed.

It was a little after ten in the evening when the mobile
phone he was carrying provided him with his first call since
returning to the UK. It was Pete from the club, no one else
knew he was available and very few people even had the
number. Not a trendy phone by any standard but functional.
He had managed to get some pasta inside him and a bottle of
what seemed to be defined as designer continental beer. Still,
he was glad for the call so sprung into it whilst it spewed
forth its dreadful artificial ring tone.

"Hey Pete, what do you know?" he asked.

"Your guy has landed, already half cut. He has a guest
and they both seem in good form. Are you coming down
tonight?"

"I'm on my way. I'm about ten minutes away and I'm coming right now. See you shortly. You haven't told them I'm on my way I take it?"

"No way man, what do you think I am?"

"Good on you, see you in a minute, ciao."

He put the small cell phone back into his pocket, left cash on the plate which held his receipt which had inconspicuously been dropped at his table by the waitress, and left. The warmth of the restaurant soon drained from his body as he stepped back into the chill, the demonic air biting through his protective layers. The air temperature had dropped several degrees since he went inside and again he sensed the change, Africa had softened up his temperature resilience, at least in the short term. This sped him up in his quest to get back to the club, his breath easily visible in the night air, hauntingly lingering ahead of his face as he walked. He moved off Oxford Street and decided to go down the back roads of Mayfair and avoid the crowds. This would quicken the journey by a few valuable minutes.

His heart was pounding as he strode towards the club. He could feel his chest tightening, a combination of the deeper breaths he was taking due to the increasing anxiety and the icy air he was now inhaling at a quicker than normal rate. He rounded another corner and there, one hundred yards away he could see the entrance to the club.

As he entered for the second time that night, his buddy Pete was still acting as concierge.

"They're in the library again," he said to Falcon, as his friend strode in. "Want me to call them down to sign you in?"

"Come on Pete. Don't tell me I need signing in after all these years?"

"Years!" exclaimed Pete. "Maybe weeks or at a push months, but not years sunshine."

"Pete; can I go in or not?"

"Go on then. You know where you're going. Don't forget mind you . . ."

"What?" asked Falcon with trepidation in his voice.

His friend chuckled and struggled to keep a straight face. "You don't have an account with us so be careful what you order . . ."

Falcon walked on through the club. He knew where he was headed and needed to get there as soon as possible before bumping in to other colleagues. This was a surprise that Sir Henry would not be expecting. Now he could not wait to see that look of surprise. He hoped Henry wouldn't have a heart attack at the surprise, at least not until he'd paid up. He stepped up the wide stone steps to the first floor past the numerous works of art that adorned the walls. The air of affluence was all around and clearly the club had a very select membership, usually measured by wealth rather than austerity. He saw the door to the library ahead and paused. A couple of deep breaths more then he was on his way. It was showdown time.

He entered the library, a room he was very familiar with and scanned the surroundings for his foe. There were several esteemed members enjoying the solitude of the club. The air carried the scent of expensive cigars and all patrons invariably had their cut glass tumblers filled with over priced brandy and whiskey. There were several valets milling around attending to the whims of the patrons. Cleaning ashtrays which were still clean, folding newspapers and gathering them up. Every time somebody shuffled on their chair there would be someone in attendance. There were a few small groups, maximum usually two or three people, but conversation was very limited. There were few conversations actually taking place. However one was a little louder than others and very distinguishable. The hairs on Falcon's neck stood to attention. He knew that voice, Sir Henry Johnson no less. He was not visible but eminently noticeable; his party was in one of the more private corners of the room. Falcon needed to go in a little further before he could turn and meet once again the catalyst that sent him to Africa, then turned him over and left him for dead.

Falcon had no pre conceived idea of who his quarry would have as his guest at the club, but was blown away when he turned on the esteemed member's table to see Sir Henry in dialogue with none other than Gerald Striker. The main man had his back to Falcon so he never stopped spouting off on the intruder's arrival but Striker was not so oblivious. His jaw dropped as Falcon turned on them showing absolute astonishment at the apparition before him.

"Holy mother of Christ!" he exclaimed. "What the fuck are you doing here?" he blurted out as he lurched across the table at Falcon, clearly suffering from an over indulgent evening.

Sir Henry was a bit slow on the uptake and turned around to see his intruder, just as he landed a swift but firm blow onto Striker's chin sending the big guy back from where he came. The table rocked and glasses were strewn with contents to the floor. The sudden commotion brought the attention of the whole room. Striker started to climb back up from his slump with blood already emerging as a crimson trickle from the corner of his mouth, and made an attempt to get back at Falcon.

"Try again shit head and you'll be eating through a straw for the rest of your life. Your choice," explained Falcon menacingly, and he meant it. More importantly Striker knew he did, but credibility wouldn't permit him to take such a whack without redress.

Sir Henry was still trying to grasp the situation but managed to raise his arm in time across Striker's chest as he was preparing for a second assault, to save him from a further beating and inevitable dentistry.

Striker clearly wanted another crack at his assailant, his pride was hurting now, but he knew Henry had the shout. He still had sufficient wit about him to obey his master. The blood was now running from Striker's mouth profusely and his eyes filled with rage. He really wanted Henry Johnson to give him the chance.

"He's bust my bloody lip, probably knocked out my bloody teeth."

"Let it go Gerald," said Sir Henry. "We'll straighten this out like gentlemen."

Henry Johnson started to realise the gravity of the situation. He was now dumb founded at the arrival of Falcon. He was clearly not expecting this tonight . . . or ever. Striker was still smarting and stood coiled, ready to pounce like the rattle snake he was, once given the authority; but it never came. A number of stewards came rushing to the area and began immediately setting the table to rights. The manager was also called to the commotion, it was Andre. He was more surprised than most at the disturbance when he saw Falcon at the scene.

"Sir Henry, please accept my apologies for this intrusion. I shall have the authorities deal with it right away. Please can I move you to another room whilst we straighten all this out?" Andre couldn't sound more apologetic. He was grovelling repulsively to appease his clientele.

"It's fine Andre. Just leave us will you. This is my guest this evening, right Tony? We're old friends. Everything's under control. Better get the members a drink though eh, on my tab if you would, my apologies. We'll keep it down from now on, you have my word."

Falcon mused at just how money could solve most problems. The whole affair would be forgotten in a few minutes after the complimentary brandies were circulated around the library. The members had gone from the shaking of their heads and tutting at the intrusion back to their newspapers and cosy little gatherings. The table was reset and the place looked as though there had been no incident within seconds, that was save for the blood still leaving Striker's mouth, the cherry colour blending well with the ox blood leather chairs that adorned the room.

"Well my boy, this is somewhat of a surprise. Glad you could make it. I knew you would," started Sir Henry trying to retain his dignity. The whole affair had managed to sober him up extremely quickly as he suddenly seemed to be in control of his faculties.

He turned to the Andre and requested another round of drinks for the trio, insisting on rather fine whisky. Whether this was to impress Falcon or whether it was an appease-ment was not clear. One thing was for certain, it did neither. Speaking with clarity and without slurring, "So what hap-pens now?"

Striker sat staring at Falcon like a tethered hound to a wandering fox. Falcon could sense this and advised his as-sailant ,"I suggest you sit back Mr. Striker and chill a little. Whatever's going through that tiny mind of yours I suggest you send it to the back . . . for your own safety."

Sir Henry once more waved at Striker nonchalantly and suggested he relax in the high backed comfy chair. He mo-tioned to his mouth advising Striker that he still had blood running down on his chin, as he passed the bleeding victim a white napkin from the table to dispel the trickling red flow. He turned his attention back to Falcon as Andre returned with the drinks.

The conversation ceased whilst the club manager was present, his experience taught him over the years when he needed to make himself scarce, so he promptly did so.

"Now Mr. Falcon, what happens next?" asked Sir Henry

Falcon raised his tumbler and threw the whiskey down his throat as though it was cheap mass produced sour mash as opposed to the refined aged single malt that it really was.

"I think I'll have another of those, Sir Henry," he said lick-ing his lips savouring the last elements of the liquor, "That is if you don't mind of course?" he added with an air of sar-casm, quite sure that his affluent associate would not object. He signalled the waiter who immediately rushed over to the gathering and took away the empty receptacle, raising his finger indicating only one more drink was required for now.

As the refreshed crystal tumbler was returned refilled with the pretentiously over priced drink, it was time for the dis-cussions to begin.

"I don't want to be in your presence any longer than you wish to be in mine, so I'll make it easy. You left me for dead down there, all of you. A piece of meat for you bastards to play God with."

"No one forced you to go dear boy," replied Sir Henry rapidly.

"You're missing the point old man. You fucked me and that's not advisable. You could have helped, but why should you. It was best for you that I never came back. Right?" he said forcefully.

"It would certainly have had its advantages."

"Financial I am sure."

"Tony, the financial rewards are immense. Beyond whatever you could imagine."

"My money?"

"No way; your money is negligible. You'll still get paid. Removing Mizinga opened the door for another concession. Coltex have found emeralds there, not far from the copper mine; the first find in that part of the country for the little green gems. The geology was never seen right for them you see so nobody ever thought of exploring for them, Why throw good money after bad, but Coltex, they found a strike accidentally and been doing some more trial works, and it looked promising."

"So what, what's that got to do with the stability of Africa?"

"You may be good at your job son, but I guess politics and business is out of your league."

"I told you before Henry, don't patronise me."

"It's like this. Mizinga wanted to throw the conglomerates out, he knew about the emeralds. We could not afford him to get into power and raise the people against us. The profits will be significant, a better strike than most of the mines up in the emerald belt. Can you imagine that in the wrong hands?"

"You mean in the hands of the people who own it."

"Keep your righteous head on Tony, its only business."

"What about Mizinga's successor. Does he know about the new mining operation?"

"Of course he does. But he doesn't want to be a politician, he just wants looking after. We'll help keep him in relative authority, increase the wages for the locals who work the mines, which in turn supports the local economy. We supply the local schools with books and stationary, and all claimed to be a victory by the new man. Why would he want to throw Coltex out when he has bettered the lives of his people? That's what he's in power to do, not to wage war."

"So you've bought him off," Falcon sneered.

"We certainly have, and for more money than we pay you, and it's still value for money. So now Mr. Falcon, what do you think of your new career? We could help you find work if you want," Sir Henry scoffed.

Falcon leaned across to his former employer and grabbed his shirt at the throat.

"I don't want any further part in your dirty little games. It wasn't politics, it was just money. The greed has corrupted you far more than any of those tin pot dictators down in Africa. You're no better that they are; you'd sell your own family for a profit. No, all I want from you now is my money. One hundred thousand pounds as agreed in the original deal, and another fifty for let's say discomfort money. Call it the additional costs you suffer for shafting me. Consider yourself lucky that's all I'm taking from you. I have my account in Switzerland, you know the details. You transfer there tonight."

Sir Henry seemed very calm throughout the lecture as Falcon pressed his face close to his own. "Don't think you're frightening me son, I've seen it all."

Falcon let him go but stayed close "You haven't seen me yet, I assure you," replied Falcon purposely.

"Look Tony, I'll speak to Fairfax and sort your money. Not sure if he'll swallow the extra fifty thou' but you never know. It'll get transferred tomorrow. Now, is there anything else you'd like to discuss?"

Falcon sat back down in his chair, still staring at Henry. In a lower tone he urged, "Don't try and screw me this time . . . once is enough."

"Don't threaten me lad, it's so unbecoming. You're a little fish in a big pond and you have no idea who you are really dealing with. I'll sort your cash and we can part ways, but don't even think about threatening me."

Falcon remained unmoved. "You have my word Sir Henry . . . I'm not afraid and I'm not going into hiding. Money tomorrow then!"

He rose from his seat, finished his whiskey and nodded at his two companions. "Don't get up," he said wistfully, as he turned his back on the two and left the club.

That was the last time he ever set eyes on Sir Henry Johnson or Gerald Striker in the flesh, and true to his word, there was the sum of one hundred and fifty thousand pounds deposited into his account in Switzerland the following day by the Coltex consortia. Sir Henry was a major stock holder in Coltex and a senior executive of the board Falcon was later to discover, purely by chance in a newspaper article, hence his own personal interest despite the political stability front also portrayed.

He thought he could just return to a normal life after that but within a week he was picked up by what transpired to be the British Secret Service and essentially coerced into this new lifestyle. Hardly a choice of profession but at least in keeping with the military background that he enjoyed, except for the discipline, so immensely in his earlier life. He was essentially a sub contractor to the service, a hired hand needed when there was dirty work to be done. Just like Zambia when somebody else's finger prints needed to be on the trigger. All nations have their so called black ops guys, but Falcon was a little different. He was chosen for the more refined jobs and always afforded the luxury of assessing a project and fixing a price before hand. He was not just a hired gun or an outlet for some pathological crazed killer who needed a semi legal route to vent his fantasies. He was not the stereotypical loner or psycho usually associated with these positions. What he was though, was a thinker and a planner, but he was still on call to the services of the allied nations. Luckily this service was not over stretched and only special assignments were offered, he could even decline if he felt there was no moral justification for the killing. They knew that, so whilst they were special jobs, the marks were chosen especially for their lack of moral fibre and ability to avoid justice. That attribute always made it easier to get Falcon to accept the assignments. How much of the intelligence that he was given was actually true, he was never sure, yet as the missions rolled on, the job became easier with practice. The fact was that he had found his niche . . .

Chapter 17

Gunther was heading the group back into St Mark's Square, followed by Falcon and Marko, with Francesco dutifully undertaking his role as the rear guard. Gunther walked ten yards ahead of the rest of them as though he had no interest whatsoever. The crowds were still plentiful.

"Do you know what that is?" asked Marko, as he pointed to the Campanile in the Square.

"Unfortunately not," replied Falcon, showing very little interest whatsoever.

"Tony, relax a little will you. Everything's going to be fine. Trust me. Enjoy the moment; you never know when you'll get the chance to be back here. You know the expression about when in Rome I take it?"

"Of course, but we're not in Rome are we?" he replied.

"Not yet, but you never know. However we are in Venice and Venetians, real Venetians that is, are never in a hurry; with the exception of course to the chasing of tourists."

"Okay then, humour me."

Marko raised his hand and proudly pointed to the tall brick structure in the Square

"That tower there is the Campanile, a bell tower through the ages and a look out tower for Venice. It's the highest structure in the city. Even Galileo used it for his science demonstrations. It's one of Venice's finest structures, you must admit to that. It collapsed earlier last century and had to be rebuilt, but it's as good as new. You know, they used to hang cages with criminals in them from high up so they could be mocked and taunted by the gathering and jeering crowds. Humility was a form of punishment, like your stocks were. Do you know what the prisoners would do to the crowds below?"

"I have no idea," he replied, feigning interest whilst they still walked through the square.

"In Italian, they used to call it Pissarli Adosso. I bet you can guess."

"It has a ring to it," replied Falcon seeing the amusement of the description.

"Piss on them from above," exclaimed Marco with some pride. "That's what they would do to get back at the crowds. A big tourist attraction it was. I couldn't see it catching on much these days myself, but I guess there are a lot of strange people in this world."

"Gentlemen, thanks for the tour guide stuff, but can you say what you have to and I can be on my way," barked Falcon now somewhat irritated at the apparent lack of progress.

"Tony, are you keen to get started?" asked Marco, as they stopped at the foot of the tall structure.

"No I'm bloody not, I just want to get this over with so we can part our ways."

Gunther came to a halt ahead of them; he was now only a couple of yards distant. He turned to join the trio.

"Alright Mr. Tony Falcon or whatever your real name is, or may soon be. Let's all stop the pissing around. I'm already tired of the softly softly crap."

The German paused for a moment and looked over his shoulder, left and right. There was nobody around, at least within earshot, so he continued, but in a voice noticeably lower in volume.

"We would like you to kill an individual, only one person, for a two million Euro pay day. Hell, you can retire if you want, but I think people like you and me never really retire . . . do we?"

"I wouldn't go so far as to liken myself to you. We may play in the same pond in your opinion but I at least follow a good cause."

Gunther snapped and again threw his face right into Falcon's, he was furious and started spitting as he snarled back at his foe.

". . . and you don't think I have a good cause. What gives you the damned right to tell me my cause is any worse than yours. You British are so far up your own arses."

Gunther's eyes seemed to be growing ever larger as the rage swelled up inside him. Clearly he was an individual of little self restraint. This is why he needed Marco who prised the two warring warriors apart, not for the first time in a very short space of time.

"You're attracting unnecessary attention you ass holes, now just drop it."

Gunther reluctantly let go of Falcon's shirt and sarcastically tried to neaten up his ruffled appearance. "You tell him how it is and get the fuck on with it," he growled to his Italian mentor, as he turned away and stormed off across the Square.

Falcon regained his composure as he joked, "I see he never finished charm school."

"Tony, I want to be nice to you . . . but you've got to let me. Whether you like it or not you're in a puddle of shit and getting deeper. Only you can get yourself out. Now go with the programme or drown. Your call but you'd better make it bloody quick. Even I have limited patience."

There was a noticeable change in Marco's attitude and Falcon could clearly see that although he may have been the calming influence in the firm, there was a definite fear of Gunther himself.

"Well, are you playing the game or not?" asked Marco.

Falcon paused. A deep sigh came out of his body as his chest heaved in and out. He started to look at the innocent tourists surrounding the piazza, none with a hint of what was going on. They were there with the cameras and feeding the birds, unwittingly passing by a conspiracy of murder. He observed Gunther across the Square with steely eyes looking back at him. He turned to Marco and in a dulled voice eventually responded to the Italian peace keeper, "I guess at this stage I have little choice . . . do I? However, you will need to tell me what the actual job is. For two million, it sounds like it'll need a bit of planning."

"Oh it will, but we know you will cope. You have around three weeks but we'll firm that up with you over the next few days." Marco stretched out his hand, "Good to have you on board."

Falcon nodded only once before responding, "For clarity, I'm not on board. I am not part of your cause. I am merely a tool you are using for your own ends. As long as I do the job you don't care about me being part of the team; and for your information, I don't care about your cause."

"At least we have our lines in the sand Tony, everybody knows where they stand. So, I guess you will want to check with your bank?" quizzed Marco.

"Let's just say, if you made these promises and haven't delivered at this stage, then this arrangement has got off to a rocky start."

"Glad to see the trust there Tony, but just in case you want to check we won't be offended."

"Oh I'll check, but in my own time."

Marco raised a hand to Gunther across the Square, signalling that the negotiations had been completed. Gunther threw another cigarette in his mouth and walked back across to the trio. This time he was smiling, grinning to be more precise. He sensed a little victory, but in reality Falcon had no option. He could not and would not put Maria in unnecessary danger and was quite prepared to die for her if it came to that. That was his weakness, probably not a good trait for a man in his profession, but it was not planned and he now had to work with it.

"Sorry about the little misunderstanding earlier," said Gunther, as he threw out his hand towards Falcon, who gave it a customary albeit unfeeling shake in return.

"Okay, so what's the real deal, when do I find out?" asked Falcon.

"Very soon. We've just got a few details to sort out then we'll be in touch and give you the plan," replied Marco.

Gunther just remained silent now, gently puffing away on his cancer stick, rejoicing in the victory at having secured the services of one of the best long range shooters in the world, at least out of those who were for hire. He now left the nitty gritty details to his Italian colleague.

"I don't need a plan. I work alone, I work out the plan. You give me the mark and the pieces of the puzzle, and I'll do the rest," insisted Falcon.

"A bit of a loner Tony, we heard that. However, there are constraints. There will only be one chance we could get this guy so there's no room for changing the dates, do you understand."

"I do Marco, fully. Like I said, give me the info and I'll do the planning of the how and where, at least within the guidelines you give me."

"Right then, we'll be in touch, like I said, in a couple of days. Where does Maria think you have gone?"

"England."

"Then I suggest you go to England, maybe give her a call from there."

"But what about you contacting me? Surely I need to be here?"

"Go to London Tony. You still live at Holland Park?" asked Marco

Falcon couldn't believe what he was hearing. "How long have you been tailing me?"

"Long enough, as I said, we too do our planning. Go back to your London apartment and we'll contact you soon, very soon."

"So, where will the job be? Here, Venice?"

"Venice was just convenient for all of us today, so don't get any ideas. It'll be Italy though, so be prepared to get back here probably in a week's time, but . . ."

"Yeah yeah I know, you'll let me know," jumped in Falcon realising he wasn't going to get any further information from the crew at this stage. "Can I take it we're done now?" he asked.

"We are. I advise you to go down to the water's edge; your boat is waiting to get you back to the railway station. Then I suggest you head for the airport."

It was not clear whether that was advice or whether it was a veiled threat, but Tony knew he had no option but to get back to London and watch this drama unfold. He could not afford seeing Maria again so soon. After all, she was expecting him to be away, so London was as good a place as any, and it was only a couple of hours away.

Falcon crossed back across the square down to the waiting water taxis, his new colleagues though remained behind in the square waiting for his departure. They exercised caution to see whether there were any obvious people movements following Mr. Falconer that they needed to be aware of. Falcon stood on the steps at the waters edge, seemingly unsure about getting in the boat. He wondered what was going to happen next, was he in too deep? These seemed heavy players, they had the cash so were well financed. The target must be a big one, what additional pressure will that bring on him. These thoughts raced across his mind as he stood gazing across the water, straight past his waiting chariot, at the splendour of the Santa Maria Della Salute, probably one of if not the most famous of all Venetian land marks. His thoughts still rambled, how could such treachery be hatched in a place as beautiful as this? Yet history itself has shown treachery to have been abundant in this most splendid of cities and what of him when this was over? A heavy weight political target would bring the cavalry down on him, no place would be safe, his relationship with the allied agencies would be terminated. Would his employers allow him to live? That was probably an even greater risk. There was some real thinking to be done over the next few days, but for Maria he was ready.

Sure enough, the same emotionless boat driver was waiting for him patiently to return and as if by magic he already knew where Falcon was headed. As he clambered into the small craft, bobbing up and down on the gentle waves created by the constant flow of river traffic to this ever popular drop off zone, the driver spoke.

"Stazione Santa Lucia, Signore?"

Falcon just nodded and sat back to take in the ride. He was helpless; everything he had done since reaching Venice had been at the mercy of his new employers. What would be the point in trying to make decisions for himself? Get back to the station and get the hell out of Italy, that's the objective right now he thought. To his delight, Falcon was not afforded the full tourist route back to the station. The boat simply went around the South of the main island again, using the Giudecca Canal instead of the thoroughly crowded Grand Canal. It was a quicker, wider and considerably less populated stretch of water. Heading west it rounded the island and soon had him back at the railway station.

Falcon started to climb out of the boat and produced his wallet to pay the driver. Whether he was meant to or not was unclear but one thing he did not want was a public scene. The boatman on seeing what was happening assured Falcon that it was not necessary and he ushered him out of the boat. Maybe he had to go back for the others thought Falcon, or maybe he was one of the others, he just would not know.

Tony was soon back in his car and on the A4 heading North East away from Mestre, soon to pick up his exit along the A27 motorway and down into Marco Polo Airport. It was only around fifteen kilometres from his car park to Venice's airport but he drove steady as his mind meandered. He was extremely confused as to how this had happened. He was always so careful but could not imagine where the leak had come from. Where was his armour chinked for such a predicament to be caused, he had always considered himself thorough in clearing his tracks. Somebody had betrayed him, but whom? There were very few who really knew what he did and it seemed unlikely they would want him out of the way. He tried to clear his head of these thoughts for now, priority London and make ready for the next round. The treachery would have to be resolved later, that is, unless of course, the culprit revealed himself during the course of this contract. Maybe it was a set up from within; maybe the treachery was way beyond simply being aimed at Falcon. There were many questions that needed answers . . . later.

Chapter 18

The Englishman found himself a spot in the long stay car park at Marco Polo, tucked away his firearms in the spare wheel housing of the Alfa and removed his overnight bag. He put the cell phone that the Italians had delivered him back in Mals into the hand baggage, along with his own phone. He figured they would probably use their phone to call him. That was it for hand luggage; he felt more of a nomad than an international explorer, of sorts. He looked around the boot a final time to make sure nothing incriminating was on display and slammed it shut. He pressed the key fob remote to lock and alarm the vehicle and headed for the terminal.

The sun was now well down in the Italian sky, it was nearing four in the afternoon on a winter's day. The sky was dotted with patchy cloud but the air was becoming distinctly cooler. The sun provided light but certainly not heat. Falcon walked briskly to the terminal, paying little regard for other vehicles circling the car park trying to find that last elusive space, one row nearer to the terminal than simply taking the first one available.

It felt good to get into the relative warmth of the terminal. He checked the departure boards to see what was heading back to the UK. There was an Al-Italia flight out that evening but not for another few hours, after that it would be early next morning. So the choice was effectively made for him. He knew this could be expensive for what it was, but there was little alternative. Sure enough he was right, the girls at the Al Italia desk, although very attractive, still parted him from six hundred Euros plus for a single flight to London, the cost of last minute desperation. He paid for the ticket in cash, deciding it was best not to leave a trail behind himself just yet, he too was unsure of just how much he was being tracked. He was sure though somebody was watching. They must be, they knew too much. Yet still in all the mystery to date, he had no real idea of who they actually were. It was just another piece of the puzzle.

He decided that four hours was a long time to kill just window shopping, so a beer or two must be the order of the day to help calm the fuzzy feeling that was swirling around his insides. It wasn't nerves, he rarely got nervous with his work; after escaping Africa everything else in the civilised world always seemed less stressful. This feeling was different. Was it that Maria was involved, probably? Yet there was also the unknowing. In the past he had always known who he was working for, and whether morally right or wrong as far as the profession went, he always took comfort from the fact he felt he was working for the good guys. This time, although forced, he didn't feel that level of comfort. How could he? They clearly could not go through the normal channels so they by definition must have been the wrong side of the fence to his usual clients.

Two gaseous Italian beers slipped past his lips, spread out well over the course of an hour. No more he decided, otherwise he would spend the flight in the bathroom. He sat and watched the other travellers, what a cross section of people. There was plenty of sound all around yet the place didn't seem noisy. It was still civilised, even the public address system was comprehensible. He passed a little more time with a cappuccino, not the usual form of caffeine intake that time of the day for real Italian's, but what the heck! He was going back to the UK so tonight he was British. Besides, he wanted something to last not a quick espresso. The sitting only gave him more opportunity to regurgitate the concerned thoughts around his head again and again. Time for a walk around he thought, clear the head. Soon he was being ushered to his seat on the Boeing 737 by the smartly dressed Al Italia girls. He couldn't even draw himself into his usual flirtatious banter with them as he mused over his predicament.

It was late evening in the UK when he left Heathrow terminal two. No way was he going to use the tube this time of night, the frame of mind he was in, so Falcon jumped into the front taxi queuing dutifully at the taxi ranks outside the arrivals lounge.

"Where to guv'nor?" asked the driver as Falcon entered the vehicle. In the presence of such colloquialisms he knew at once that he was back in the home land.

"Holland Park, Notting Hill. You know it?"

"Sure do, no worries. Business trip was it sir, back a bit late, long day?"

"It has been a long few days," Falcon replied, trying to remain polite, although not in the mood for discussions with a nosey taxi driver, whose real intention was simply to humour his fare towards a better tip.

"Soon have you home sir. Back to your own bed."

Falcon simply nodded as he gazed out of the window into the black night sky. Central London was shining within a dome of neon glow on the horizon. That's where he was going and he wasn't looking forward to it. This was no longer home, it was just a house. He wished he was back in his home in Mals, wrapped up with Maria watching the snow fall on the mountains. He drifted away into happy thoughts of the pair, the tender moments they had shared together only the day before. His life had turned upside down in twenty four hours, he knew it would not be turned back again in the next twenty four.

The apartment was just as it had been left. It must have been a month since he was last there yet the place was clean. The air needed freshening up and a bit of warmth wouldn't go a miss but this was soon remedied. One thing about Tony was he didn't like unnecessary clutter. Everything was in its place, not even crockery was left for any length of time to be washed. He believed that once he used something in the kitchen it needed washing. Whether this would be translated by some psychiatrist as a form of possessive behaviour would be open to debate, but it was his place and he wanted it such that he could walk into it at any time and be right at home.

It was going to be a difficult night's sleep; he was already prepared for that. However, Falcon knew that he needed his faculties in good working order for the next few days while he tried to find a solution to his quandary. So whether he slept or not, he knew it was essential to relax.

As anticipated, sleep was difficult and Tony was awake and dressed by seven the following morning. Outside everywhere was shrouded in darkness but the city had certainly already come to life. Tony decided he needed to clear his head and that would be best done outside rather than looking at the four walls waiting for his phone to ring. He would go for a walk to his favourite London clearing. Less than a mile from his house was Hyde Park, a vast area of floral and rural feel yet in the heart of one of the biggest cities in the world. He could get lost there in its size, the solitude and relative tranquillity would give him focus. A good stroll around the park would be good for him and maybe he would catch breakfast in a hotel or restaurant around Oxford Street.

Although he didn't consider London his home any longer, he never failed to admire how fortunate he was to be housed in such a location being so close to so much. He waited for the night's darkened blanket to begin to be pulled back revealing shards of daylight, before venturing out. If he was being stalked, he certainly didn't want to be followed in the dark. At least this way he may get a chance to see any assailants.

He purchased himself a steaming cup of relatively tasteless coffee from McDonalds, near the tube station at Notting Hill Gate, to take away, before heading off along Bayswater Road to the park. The days were getting colder, Falcon thought that it never felt cold like this on top of the Alps and immediately, his mind traversed into thinking about Maria. He wondered what she was doing now. All that innocence looking after the children, not realising just how much danger she was in. This was unforgivable, totally unforgivable. He needed to fight this problem . . . but how? He turned into the park and headed for the Serpentine, continuously mulling over his problems.

Despite it being a weekday and cold, he was surprised at the number of other patrons visiting the park. He ambled towards the large lake, the centre piece of the park and admired the surroundings. Central London he mused as he shook his head, there was nowhere else like it in the world. He started a steady stroll around the borders of the lake nodding and passing general greetings to passers-by as they encountered one another. He had no idea who could be trusted but knew he could not do this on his own. He had no idea who Marco and Gunther were, how could he take them on single handed. Then there was Maria, at what stage does he protect her or arrange protection for her? That would lead to the questions of why? Why would she need protecting, she would have to know. Then he would inevitably lose her anyway. His head was spinning from the permutations, the dull headache compounded by the interminable thoughts, the lack of sleep and the chill air.

He decided the strategy must be to get help. Which of his past clients could possibly help him? Most of them he never actually knew and he could hardly go to MI5 and ask for help, as if it were that simple. After what seemed an age of soul searching and self questioning, he arrived at only one solution. There was only one person he could contemplate and ask for help. It was a long shot and most likely he would be unable to make contact but it was his best, and to date as far as he could see, his only hope.

"James Brown," he said aloud as he walked through the park. "Let's hope my friend that you're not the shit that's turned me over, otherwise I'm truly screwed."

Falcon did not believe that they had turned on him, after all he had served the agency well these past few years and they kept coming back for more. He was an asset and he believed he was far better value to them alive than dead. After all, if they really wanted him dead, they could always hire somebody from the same pool as Falcon himself to carry that out . . . and they hadn't. The problem was they usually contacted him, not the other way around.

He took his cell phone out of his pocket and scrolled through the names in the memory. He knew he would not have any number for a James Brown in there yet he still went through it several times. The James Brown number last used after the Draper contract would probably be no longer in use. That was the norm; although once contracts were completed he had never had cause to call them back, as contracts were always closed out by both parties just as agreed. He knew he had numbers for James on his pocket data bank back at the apartment. They were just numbers mingled in with others, nothing conspicuous if it ever fell into the wrong hands, but he knew which were which.

A sudden lease of life came over the Englishman. He returned his phone to the deep pocket of his grey overcoat and quickened his pace to get back home as soon as possible. Any thoughts or desires for breakfast quickly evaporated as he now had a quest to complete. All the while he knew it was still a long shot but he had to try something. Doing nothing was admitting defeat. He had been there before and knew he could beat it. This was no different. While there was a breath in his body, there was no way he would let his beloved down.

Back at the apartment he started rifling through his personal wares stashed in one of the wardrobes. These things were rarely touched but nevertheless remained in reasonable order. There it was, cheap but effective, an electronic telephone book. These days all important or at least regularly used numbers were stored directly in the cell phone. However, those that wanted keeping but not advertising were kept elsewhere. He pushed the Casio electronic organiser power button like it had never been pressed before, with some apparent inane belief that the harder it was depressed the quicker it would burst into life. It did come to life but no quicker or slower than normal. He frantically scrolled through the myriad of numbers stored there until he found the numbers for James Brown. Falcon knew he only had details for one Mr. James Brown; the fact that there were three entries did nothing to dampen his enthusiasm. These were the different numbers that he had used as contact for Brown on various contracts over the last few years. If nothing else it was a starting point.

It was still only morning time in Notting Hill which meant that unless James Brown was overseas it would still be sleeping time in the USA. Undeterred, Falcon thought that time was of the essence and if his contact was as resolute as he was then he would be contactable. The only worry was whether he was available on any of the three numbers Falcon had stored for him. No harm in trying he thought and he started to dial the first number he had stored for Mr. Brown.

On completion of the dialling operation, Falcon was met with the message that advised him the number was incorrect and he should check and redial. Obviously this had been disconnected as was the norm. Somewhat disheartened, the Englishman, now with adrenalin flowing full force throughout his body, dialled the second number from his mobile. This time it rang, unfortunately after hearing only four rings from the receivers end the line went dead. No message and no answer phone. Falcon was now frustrated at the lack of response yet remained resolute in his quest. At least it rang he thought. Maybe somebody would know. He was clutching at straws of course but that was where he was right now. He had one more number to try. This was his last point of contact with the only person he thought could be trusted. He rang the number in anticipation of it being the one. His excited fingers danced around the keypad of his mobile phone akin to a skilled pianist. His sweaty fingers left a trail over each key as he hammered away single handed. This one also rang. This was a good sign as this was the latest number he had for James Brown. It rang and rang. After nine or ten rings a sullen voice answered at the other end:

"Hello, who's that?" a dazed voice came back in a heavy American accent, clearly originating from the Deep South.

"Hi there, I'm very sorry to trouble you but it's very urgent. I'm calling from overseas."

"Yeah, and what the hell do you want this time of the night?"

Falcon hesitated a few seconds then went straight for it, "I'm looking for Mr. James Brown."

"Hell buddy, I reckon you got the wrong number, there ain't no James Brown here."

"Are you sure, I mean this is the number I was given?"

"Listen buddy, I need to be at work in a couple of hours so I'm not that happy right now. Believe me there's no James Brown here." The connection went lifeless.

Falcon was very frustrated as this was the only contact that had proven positive. Instinctively he called back. The now very irate voice at the other end hollered:

"WHAT! I've told you that there's no James Brown here."

"But it's Tony Falconer from England."

"I don't give a damn who you are buddy, for the last time check your damned number. There ain't no James Brown here." Once again the telephone line went dead.

Falcon flopped back on his bed in disbelief. How could he not get hold of his only contact he thought he was able to trust? This was getting bad. What was already a ghastly situation had just become worse. Now who could he turn to? He started pacing about the apartment, stopping each time he got to a window to peer past the curtains to check the streets outside. Was he being tailed, he didn't know? Still, he had to look. There was nothing obvious. He walked around and around eventually throwing the cell phone on to the sofa. Suddenly the stress induced hunger pangs started to kick in. Tony suddenly realised he had not eaten for the last twenty four hours. Events had taken over his gastronomic needs and only now, his nervous tension sought to remind him of his lack of body fuel.

He strolled across the apartment to the kitchen. He opened the refrigerator knowing full well that there would be nothing in it; after all he only got back there late the night before. The freezer was just as welcoming with appealing foodstuff.

There was nothing. It was only his lack of progress coupled with the anticipation of waiting that made him so hungry. That was it. He had to get back outside. Although against his better judgement of culinary delights, this was an emergency. He had no time for shopping around . . . A McDonald's breakfast may not satisfy his nutritional needs but it would put his stomach at rest.

He gathered up his mobile telephone and once more donned the grey over coat and headed down the road to the fast food joint he strived so hard to stay away from as much as he could. He purchased his instant nutrient free food and took up a seat in the window of the restaurant. More plastic coffee, which was not a patch on its Italian counterparts, coupled with a traditional cheese burger. As he trawled through his cordon bleu breakfast he simply stared at the passers by from the window. Not a single one actually registered within his memory as his mind was working furiously elsewhere. Why could his only avenue for help be closed? Why now? Again his mind drifted to Maria and he felt so helpless. If he could not start a defensive attack, he feared they would both be killed in any case.

The Englishman even picked up a current copy of the Daily Mail to help pass the time. It may as well have been written in Yiddish for all the good that it did. Tony looked at the pages but never absorbed a single entity from its contents. He flicked through the newspaper as though it were a glossy flyer full of useless information, often found within the free newspapers. It passed all of two minutes to go from cover to cover; then it was a return to people watching.

Suddenly the cell phone in his pocket jumped into life, vibrating profusely against his leg. His first thought was that it would be his latest Italian and German friends checking in. How could they want him back so soon he thought, he had just got off the plane. He looked at the screen, *unknown caller* was clearly displayed. He was sure it was them, his persecutors and pursuers of the love of his life. He waited a few seconds as he calmed himself, trying to quell the feelings of anguish and hatred he bottled up on the inside.

"Yep," was all he said as he answered the electronic communicator, showing zero emotion as he did so.

There was a long spell of silence on the line, neither party wishing to be the first to break it. Eventually Falcon decided he could wait no longer.

"This is Falcon, what's happening?"

Another pause for five or six seconds before the caller's voice came back.

"Who is this please?"

"Who's asking? You called me?"

"Please hold sir," said the female monotone voice whose origin he had no idea of.

"Is this Mr. Falconer?" came back the mystery dialogue but now the caller had a different voice, now a male tone was leading.

"It is, who wants to know?" replied Tony, somewhat frustrated at the games being played.

"That doesn't matter. You called this number earlier, why?"

"You seem to know me, who are you?"

"We don't know you. That's the point, but there are very few people with this number."

"Well I must have it," said Falcon, getting somewhat angry. Then the penny suddenly dropped.

"Are you in the US?" he asked excitedly. "Is that James . . . James Brown? It's Tony. Boy am I glad to get hold of you." He was cut short by his caller.

"Excuse me sir, who are you after?"

"James Brown, I worked for him recently."

"Don't know anybody of that name. What was it you were working on?"

"I'm not at liberty to say really," replied the Englishman apprehensively, knowing full well he was being tested. This had to be Brown, but protocol warranted an element of caution.

"Where was this work undertaken?"

"The UK," replied Falcon rapidly.

"We haven't had many projects in the UK recently, the last one being the Doper Project. Were you involved in that in any way?"

Falcon knew he was now in the ball park, "No, but I was involved in the Draper project if that helps?" he replied with an element of smugness. Not sure if that was because he had managed to make contact with one of his handlers or whether he subconsciously thought he may finally have sourced some help.

A few seconds passed before a different voice came back.

"This is a secure line, this is James Brown. How can I help you?"

"James, it's Falcon. I never thought I'd be able to get hold of you."

"You have, so I guess it's pretty important, you know this isn't the way we operate."

"It is. I'm in a jam, my position has been compromised and I'm not sure where from."

"Well, what's that got to do with me? You know it's not the agency. Hell, only a hand full of people know you actually exist, so this stunt is a bit of a risk in itself."

"I had no choice."

"So you're in the UK right now?" asked the American.

"I am."

"I guess we need to meet, even though this is way off the reservation. If we meet Tony, you know you only increase the danger you're in. Are you prepared to accept that?"

"James, I think there's something here for you as well as me. This is free, I need your help and I may be able to give you something in return."

"Well my boy, you've taken a hell of a gamble; I guess you must be spooked over something?"

"I did and I am," replied Falcon.

"Right then, I can't discuss now. I'll see you in London later tonight. Be at the Grosvenor House Hotel coffee shop, I should be there by nine."

"I'll be there!" exclaimed Falcon. "But how will I recognise you?"

"You won't. We'll recognise you. You know the pond you peddle in Tony, if it's a shafting for me then you've picked an adversary you wouldn't want to cross."

"I assure you James, there's no shafting, but bring whatever artillery you want. For the record I'll be unarmed."

"Glad to hear it. Until twenty one hundred then . . ." Once again the phone line was unceremoniously disconnected on the Englishman. This was becoming an annoying frustration; however he had achieved his first objective for the offence. It was a long wait until nine o'clock.

Eventually the day passed and night fell, yet another onset of a winter's evening for the English Capital. Falcon threw on his trusty overcoat and set off for the hotel. A steady walk would see him there in no time, far better than getting a cab when there was no need. At least he would enter with a clear head. He entered the coffee shop of the hotel using the Park Lane entrance and was surprised at just how many people were actually in there. He had been here previously during the day when it was full of businessmen but never this late in the evening, yet it was just as busy.

He stole himself to an unoccupied table and removed his outer garments and draped them across the chair opposite. Even before he had set himself down, a smartly dressed waiter adorning an ivory white jacket was at his side awaiting his order. Falcon decided on that most British of thirst quenchers . . . the pot of tea. He looked around the establishment and nothing at all was out of place. He was some fifteen minutes early in the hope of seeing his contact arrive. He may have been smart but they were smarter. Unknown to Falcon at the time, his counterpart was already in the hotel, complete with armed back up, all watching and stalking their quarry.

Falcon sat and sipped his tea for several minutes, edging around on the comfortable arm chair that didn't seem in keeping with the lower tables on which the tea was set. Again his cell phone jumped into life. He threw a glance around the hotel to see who else was on the phone, but saw nobody. Instead there were disapproving glances from several patrons who despised the interruption of their peace by the piercing tones of modern mobile technology.

He pressed the cell phone close to his head, "Yes."

"There's a John in the corridor opposite. Go take a leak." Yet again the call was abruptly terminated.

He looked around again, nothing untoward. As he was on the back foot yet again, he decided he had better visit the plush bathrooms the Grosvenor House Hotel afforded its clientele, on the ground floor at least. The toilet was one of the cleanest you would ever encounter, constantly perfumed complete with an attendant who would dutifully hand you a fresh towel, whatever your business. Falcon didn't need a leak so decided to wash his face so as to make a reason for at least being in there. It was the briefest of visits yet still cost him the princely sum of one pound for the attendant, as was expected. There was no one else in the bath room so Falcon decided it was time to return to his table. As he exited from the rest room, he saw that someone was already seated at his table despite it being obvious that he was still around. He was ready to burst into explanation at scattering the squatter as he didn't want any superfluous company whatsoever, when the intruder spoke.

"Tony, James Brown."

Falcon stopped in his tracks a pace or two away from his chair. He felt his legs weaken as he froze. This was what he was after yet he didn't know how to handle the situation. He stumbled forward and stretched out his right arm to his friend, the only friend he hoped he could trust right now. James Brown was not quite what Falcon had been expecting, not the ex marine hard nut, in fact quite the opposite. He was probably around forty years in age although didn't look as though he'd had a tough life. A good crop of dark hair well groomed, and dressed like a successful city trader. Nothing loud about the attire, a well made dark grey double breasted suit in keeping with most of the square mile.

"Pleasure to meet you James. I appreciate you taking the time out. You've done well to get here so soon, I'm . . . well I'm honoured."

"Tony, you're one of ours. We help each other if we can. Besides, we weren't too far away, only over in Germany so don't worry. Now, you've broken a cardinal rule Tony and it's not like you. That's why we're here. We know it's not a money issue; your profile doesn't lend you to selling out the hand that feeds you, so we figured it must have been pretty important. So here we are."

"We," said Falcon surprised at the constant use of the plural. "There's more than one of you?"

"You think I'd come here alone. Hell Tony, the computer tells me one thing about you but I still like the comfort of a few nine millimetres on my side rather than an inanimate programme written by a spotty college geek who has probably never seen a naked girl in his life. Know what I mean. Old school, and it keeps me alive."

"I thought you were a desk jock."

Somewhat affronted by the accusation, Mr. Brown sternly hit back,

"Tony, just for your info, you have no idea who I really am or what I do so let's keep it that way. Now, what's so damned important you drag my ass over here tonight?"

Falcon spent the next twenty minutes giving James Brown a précis of the events of the last few days of his life when he noticed the American was not taking any notes what so ever.

"You not writing any of this down?" he asked somewhat offended that he may be wasting his time.

"No need Tony. There are half a dozen agents listening to this conversation making whatever notes I need. Technology does have some advantages."

Falcon felt a little uneasy at having poured out his heart to total strangers but realised that people were listening to phone conversations all the time, it's just that this time he was consciously aware of it. Brown nodded his head throughout the story as though full of sympathy. When Falcon had finished he asked the American, "So what do you think?"

"Not sure. What do you want me to think? You've got lady trouble, somebody who talks a big story and as yet no mark. What can I do without a target? We have no idea who these people are or what they want. I guess we need to just wait and see what they offer up to you over the next couple of days. See if that gives us any insight. Meanwhile I'll stick a tail on you, see if we can identify any stalkers and see what the computer throws up about a Gunther and a Marco, but with nothing else, I wouldn't hold out a great deal of hope at this stage. Keep in contact and let me know when you know."

"Where's the tail?" he asked.

"Well that would hardly be effective now would it, you don't need to know. Just go home and wait, we'll be waiting as well. Trust me, we've done this before."

With that the American got up from the chair, shook Tony's hand and left. Nobody else seemed to leave as he did so. Falcon waited five minutes then decided to head home himself. He knew it would be pointless trying to find the NSA surveillance teams; they could be anywhere and everywhere. Back out into the chill London air and the fifteen minute walk home. He felt somewhat satisfied that he finally met James Brown but on the other hand felt as though he hadn't really made any progress. Little did he know, but Brown and the expensive assets of the NSA were already working on his problem.

It was going to be another restless night for Falcon. No news and no further on with finding his solution. At least he had the NSA on side, or at least their promise that they would help him if they could. The night was now very chill and he wrapped the collar of his over coat over his mouth as he walked, yet still he decided to avoid a taxi. After all, if he had protection effectively watching him there was little point in trying to lose them. He wandered through the oblivious hoards of people who still habited Park Lane after dark. How some of them could come out dressed in so little showing off their party attire was beyond him and he shook his head slightly as he remembered his own youth.

Falcon arose several times during the night. Habitually picking up his cell phone checking just in case he had missed any calls, knowing full well that he hadn't. Then it was to the window over looking the main street at the front of his house, examining the street below to see whether there was anybody outside who shouldn't be. But there wasn't. He tried to get back to sleep each time but there was no chance. How many days he could go without sleep he was unsure but he did not want to be flat out when it was time to act.

Chapter 19

The following morning started in much the same way as the previous. Still the Englishman had purchased no provisions on which to live so unpalatable instant black coffee was all that was available. He paced around the living room for several minutes holding his steaming brew, drinking as he walked. It was only seven a.m. and outside the world should have still been sleeping with such darkness and mist that had seemingly appeared over the last hour or so, encasing all that could be seen. Only the piercing halos from the street lights along the road could be seen. The anonymous distant morning chaos associated with the city could still be heard through the fog.

Falcon walked and walked in circles around the room, still wearing only a towel robe. There had been no urgency to dress today. He could do nothing. No point in chasing James Brown, they were waiting on him. No point in chasing Marco, they would come to him when they were ready. Not even the TV could detract Falcon from his recurring misery. Suddenly out of the swirling mist a thunderous roar was heard. A courier, dressed in full leathers on a powerful Suzuki GSX racing motorcycle stopped on the other side of the road opposite the apartment building. Such a machine was unusual for that sort of work on the cramped London streets; rarely would the rider get the opportunity to open the throttle. There was no despatch box on the bike and the courier carried his package in his back pack. Falcon peered around the curtains. The rider didn't remove his helmet as he dismounted the mechanical beast and strode purposefully across the road to his building, removing his parcel as he strode. The intercom buzzed into life in Falcon's apartment. The Englishman turned sharply to the door.

He paced across the floor towards his intercom panel near the entrance to the apartment. He was not expecting anything that he was aware of. That said he had not been expecting the events of the last forty eight hours either, so nothing should surprise him any more he thought. The intercom buzzed a second time, this time for several seconds.

He pressed his receiver. "Yes!" he shouted as though extremely annoyed at the intrusion.

The dulcet cockney tones of the courier replied, "I've got a package for Mr. A Falconer at this address. Is he in? I need a signature."

"I'll come down, wait a second."

Tony wrapped up his robe and walked barefoot out of his apartment into the communal stairwell, down to the lower floor and the main entrance. He opened the door to have a digital receipt PDA stuffed in his face. The courier didn't remove his helmet, "You need to sign this mate, anywhere will do, the machine will pick it up."

Falcon pushed on the well scratched face of the electronic receipt device and was handed the package from the despatch rider who turned and left with as much aplomb as he arrived, and just as noisy. He slowly climbed the stairs, all the while feeling around the padded envelope he had just received. No sender's details, very strange, yet it was clearly intended for him, and must have been urgent for a courier to deliver like that.

He closed his apartment door behind himself and sat down on the soft leather sofa that took pride of place, in the centre of the minimalistically furnished reception room. He slowly started to tear back the sticky seal that was on the puffed up envelope, the size of a typical magazine. Once the seal had been broken all the way across, he turned the envelope so he could see inside, before yanking everything out.

There were several written documents, some photographs, a map of Rome and a DVD disc. A strange collection at first glance but very soon the picture was clear to the Englishman. This was the mark. The target he had been waiting for. No doubt everything was explained in the package. A small note was the top piece; it simply read, '*play the DVD then call me on this number*'. There was no name, no signature, just a telephone number with the Italian international dial-ling prefix at the head. Even more mystery he thought, but if they were to give him the info so soon, why the hell send him back to the UK. Something was not standard with these guys, but all he could do now was play along. They were always playing him and he did not like not having any con-trol.

He didn't immediately play the DVD. Instead he looked at the little bundle of documents without reviewing them and decided he should dress first before jumping straight in. Once he was ready to start the days work, he walked around the sofa a couple of times, encircling it ready to pounce like a stalking puma, staring down at his document pile.

"May as well get started then Tony boy," he said aloud for his own instruction as he flopped down into the sofa.

He put the DVD into his player and switched on the flat screen TV hanging neatly from the wall opposite. It was showing footage of a dignitary of some sort. Clearly it was shot in Rome; there were plenty of distinguishing land marks appearing throughout the footage. He watched the poorly shot footage showing the official, obviously an important man, judging by the entourage that he travelled with. Falcon could not recognise the subject but that didn't make him any less important. He was never a fan of Italian politics. When in Italy he just wanted the quiet life, leave alone and be left alone. He, for sure, never imagined in his wildest nightmares that he would have a contract on his doorstep. The movie only lasted about five minutes and then it was down to look-ing at the documents. There were several large ten by eight size photographs of an individual he could clearly recognise from the dodgy home movie. A well presented individual, probably in his forties but Falcon knew Italian men, espe-cially affluent ones, aged very slowly. He could always add ten years to any he ever met. They dressed impeccably, not a stitch out of place and were always well groomed and mani-cured. The additional paperwork showed a series of press cuttings, which were in Italian but for his benefit had also been translated and retyped. And then there was the resume. A CV for a guy they want to take out, how ironic.

Falcon read the articles diligently and slowly, absorbing every syllable that presented itself to his hungry mind. Salvatore Ricci, no he had never come across the name before. The articles though soon made it clear as to who he was. He was public prosecutor for the Italian Government and he was on a mission. He had made great in roads into the Italian mafia as well as playing a major part in destroying the out lying factions of the former Red Brigade and their off shoots. Some of their top people had been put away by Ricci on his way to the top. He was good and ruthless. He was not susceptible to corruption, he just had a job to do, and it seems he did it with a passion. There had been several attempts on his life in the past twenty years as he was rapidly making his way to the corridors of power. His skills and tenacity were soon harnessed by the Italian legal system, which soon had him working the most difficult of cases. Importantly, he got results, and as he grew in stature, was not only becoming the Country's top prosecutor, but taking an active part in spear heading the anti terror and anti organised crime task forces. The people loved him, the villains loathed him; even though, he was always treated with respect.

There was often much talk of assassinating him but even seasoned crime bosses knew that if their family was ever found responsible, then no stone would be left unturned, until they were crushed into dust. The heat such an atrocity would attract would be unthinkable. As such, Ricci in his latter years was somewhat indirectly protected by those he was after. They simply hoped he would be out of office before it was their turn under the microscope. Despite the ruthlessness of organised crime, it also served a purpose of lawfulness and keeping the status quo.

However this was not mafia, these were essentially terrorists who had hired him. They didn't bow to any such unwritten code of conduct. Their purpose was one of revenge for the comrades of theirs he had imprisoned over the years, and in particular, those who were jailed only a year before, one of which was the girlfriend of Gunther Menzies at the time. He managed to evade capture and fled to North Africa for a little while, seeking refuge in the desert terror training camps spread throughout the region.

So far, all that Falcon could see was that this was a revenge killing with no real other purpose, but he was sure they had their reasons. Two million Euros was a big pay day, too big to really be paid he thought. He was sure he would be set up for this so was going to have to plan meticulously and ensure his American friends were on side at all times. Falcon flopped back gain and sank into the wrappings of his soft sofa. He let his head fall backwards and stared blankly at the ceiling for a short while. What to do next he thought?

He was digesting the alternatives of either calling the number given or calling James Brown. The peace was suddenly interrupted and the decision was made for him. The rucksack started emitting a shrill sound which could only mean that the mobile telephone he had been given by the Italians had burst into tune. He reached for the bag on an adjacent lounge chair and removed the phone. It was vibrating in his hands yet he seemed reluctant to answer straight away. He composed himself for a couple of seconds before pressing the green telephone key.

"Hello," he said, in a disinterested manner.

"You were supposed to call. You didn't! Why?" Falcon recognised this was Marco trying his best to sound stern but he was unable to carry off his anger as well as Gunther could. Gunther, Falcon perceived, was simply a cold blooded killer, no morals no scruples and probably no real purpose. He probably just liked killing.

"I've not long since had the package. I've been watching the movie. It's very good," he added sarcastically.

"Don't piss me about Mr. Falcon. This is not a joke. As you know there's a lot at stake, you can't afford to joke."

"Well what the hell else do you expect me to do?" screamed back the Englishman. "You invade my life, have me jump through bloody hoops and Christ knows for what."

Marco returned to his more civil approach that Falcon had endured in the café in St Mark's Square. "Have you read the dossier?" he asked.

"I've been through it but of course I will need a bit more time to study it. I guess it's now just a case of when and where."

Marco paused for a second then replied solemnly, "Those decisions will soon be made Mr. Tony. It's just how we get you to the car?"

"Sorry, I'm not following. Why would I need to get to the car?"

"This has to be public . . . a statement . . . a warning. The world must know we are not dead and buried and the organisation still exists. We want it to be spectacular and on TV. The cameras are always following him so that part should be easy. We need you to get a bomb in the car, we can do the rest."

Falcon was dumb founded. The silence was painful for both of them. "Are you still there?" asked Marco.

"I am," replied the Englishman with serious purpose in his voice. "I don't do bombs. I'm a shooter, long range shooter. That's why you came to me in the first place. I don't do car bombs."

"Tony, you don't understand. We're calling the shots. We want you to place the bomb."

"There are dozens of guys who could do that for you. It's not me. If you want me then there's no bomb."

It was Marco's turn to be quiet for a second. "Are you forgetting about Maria? Could you live with yourself if you let her die?"

"For all I know you will kill her and me anyway. So, like I said, no car bombs. I don't like collateral damage and most of those movie images show him travelling with his family and they are definitely not my target, and I won't have any part of that. No matter what hold you think you have over me. I'm probably already eternally damned, but that would do away with any chance of parole."

Tony was speaking from a position of strength now, he stood up to them. He showed that his own morals still existed to some extent despite his career. "If you want me then it's my way. I do the planning and the exit strategy. Me . . . my way . . . no one else. You'll still get your TV cameras I'm sure."

Marco laughed a little nervously at the other end of the phone.

"Fine Tony, I guessed as much but thought I would run you through the mill a little and give you the easier option, but the consequences will be on your head. But we will tell you where and when it is to be done."

"I'll take the advice under consideration and I'll tell you if it's possible," emphasised Tony with his reply.

"You really are a sole trader aren't you, a true maverick?"

"Well Marco, I guess I am in both senses."

"What do you mean both senses?" quizzed the Italian.

"I guess looking back on my life, when I leave this life for the next and I am up in front of the jury, do you think St. Peter would classify me as a sole trader in terms of a lone business man or rather as a Trader of Souls, after all I supply him with a few. Now do you understand?"

"Ah," replied the Italian, "this is English humour, I see the point. So I guess you really are then a soul trader. S O U L," the Italian emphasised aloud. "I shall remember that. I take it you are prepared to trade your soul for Maria's."

"I suspect I have no soul left to trade. I think that was indebted a long time ago. It's just a case of seeing who holds my marker now . . . well when the time comes. So, timing, what about it?"

"We are just getting the current schedules sorted out now from his office. We still have people on the inside you know."

"So what's the purpose in all this?" asked Falcon.

"To get your lady back of course."

"No, you know what I mean. Your purpose, Gunther's purpose; what's it to prove?"

"Are you suddenly interested in our plight Tony? How touching. Basically we want our brothers and sisters releasing from their hell holes of prisons. They are only freedom fighters in what was supposed to be a democratic society."

"In democracies the electorate don't generally use guns and bombs. I understand one of those freedom fighters is Gunther's girlfriend. Is that significant I wonder?"

"Gunther has financed this operation so whatever his personal motives we are not to question. It will all be clear when this first job is done. After that, when we have shown the government that we can even get to their best protected servant and they realise no one is safe, they will listen. The assassination would be followed up with threats of further killings of politicians and public officials until such time as our demands are met. You would be surprised just how quickly the government may come to heel."

Marco was speaking passionately about the cause, even though the cause had effectively been underground and in the main ineffective for many years.

"Well I guess we both have our different causes to fight for," replied the Englishman showing distain for the alleged causes of the Italian revolutionaries.

"We do," snapped Marco. "Now you make yourself familiar with your target and his habits. You read up on him and understand every aspect of that man's life. I want you to think like he does so you know how he will react when the time comes. That's what you need to do now. Stay local as well Mr. Tony, I would hate for you to go astray right now. I'll be in touch very soon."

Falcon paused a little while, "How soon? When will I be back in Italy?"

"I would guess two or three days and we can bring you back to set everything up as you want it. Goodbye Mr. Falcon."

Marco cleared the call before Falcon could make any further conversation, not that he had a great deal to say but he did enjoy playing the Italian a little, just to see how far he could be pushed. He was concerned now at what they might be scheming in Italy. This was a very public figure; it would bring with it a lot of unwanted heat from all sides. If he carried out this job he was as good as dead anyway whether that be from Gunther and Marco, from the Italian authorities or perhaps even from the associates of Mr. James Brown.

What a mess. He collapsed back onto his chair tapping his cell phone onto his chin as he pondered his position. Only a couple of days he thought. Not long to get any counter measures into place. May as well get hold of Brown, this was his only route.

He arranged to meet James Brown by the Serpentine on his semi casual walk around Hyde Park. Falcon could not be seen carrying photographs of his target. He had no idea if he was himself being stalked, how could he possibly explain such things away if he happened to be picked up? He decided to jot down the name of his target on a scrap of paper and threw it into his jacket pocket. Then it was out the door and off for his stroll.

Once again he followed his route of calling into the burger joint and collecting an unsavoury portion of take away coffee, which he pretended to enjoy from his paper cup, whilst heading towards the park. At least this blended in with the antics of many other Londoners on their travels. He could see no obvious tail on himself, but that never meant they were not there. For a start he knew Brown would have somebody watching him night and day, but the question was whether they were alone. Marco and Gunther might even be following him. He still needed to exercise caution and make his meeting with Brown as casual as possible.

He spotted his contact walking briskly by the lake. It was another cold day in London and although the mist had generally cleared, the day remained overcast. He approached Brown who saw him coming.

"Just walk by," Brown said, "I'll see you at the news stand opposite the Cumberland."

Falcon screwed his face showing some form of misunderstanding but knew Brown was better at this sort of thing than he was, so he did exactly as he was told. He allowed Falcon to get a hundred metres or so ahead of him before turning back and following his footsteps. Falcon decided not to turn back and see if anything was happening, believing himself to be in very good hands with the NSA. Surely there were a few of them out there somewhere. On exiting the park on Park Lane, Falcon decided he would cross the road on the surface rather than contemplate any sub way crossings, being visible was suddenly more appealing than literally going underground. A lot of things seem to happen in subways which nobody ever saw. He waited for the necessary gap in the traffic and crossed to the news stand. Rather than simply loiter he decided to purchase a copy of a daily rag and stood around pretending to read it, going straight for the horse racing pages, not knowing the first thing about the sport of Kings.

He had lost sight of Brown but felt they had not lost sight of him. Suddenly there was a gentle prod in the back; it was his old buddy from the NSA.

"You're being followed Tony my boy. Did you know?"

Somewhat startled at the sudden outburst out of the blue, Tony swiftly replied, "No, although it wouldn't surprise me. I figured you guys were following me but didn't consider that a threat."

"We're no threat Tony. We're your baby sitters, but we sure as hell need to know who this guy is?"

Tony suddenly blurted out, "What if it's Gunther's people. How do I explain it if their cover is blown? Gunther will suspect me and all bets could be off." He suddenly thought of how he could endanger Maria simply by Brown's men pulling in the tail. "You, can't pull him, you can't."

The man from the NSA sensed the concern with Falcon. "Tony, it's not like you to be a little edgy, but have no fear, we're on it, okay. Now let's walk."

Brown steered his man up towards Oxford Street. They then turned left into the shoppers' paradise and headed down the busy crowd filled concourse. Falcon was sure they would get lost down here so was at a little more ease. They strolled for three minutes or so before Brown tapped his ear, "Say again Sam," he said speaking aloud in the street. "Okay copy that."

"What's going on?" asked Falcon. "Who was that?"

"Don't worry, stick with the programme. It'll be fine. Come on, keep up."

Brown hurried his man along dancing through the throngs of pedestrians, shoppers and tourists. They crossed the road and turned off the main drag into a side street. There were no crowds here, with the occasional passers by being solely for the adjacent hotel; a little foot traffic but mostly delivery trucks and vehicles to service the hotel.

Suddenly there was a commotion behind them in the street. A white transit van came off Oxford Street and came to a screeching halt near a service access to the hotel. The side door was thrown open and a gang of three or four men bundled another individual into the truck and slammed shut the door. One of the men stayed behind on the street as the van turned around and headed back into the city traffic. Brown stopped with his man as he again spoke into the invisible communicator he appeared to be using. The pair then turned and went back towards the encounter and approached the man.

"Target secured sir, off for debrief," said the man in the street whom Falcon had never seen before, yet the guy acknowledged him as though they were acquainted.

"Very good John; let's see if he can sing." He turned to the Englishman, "This is one of your baby sitters. We'd better go and see who this guy is. Shall we?"

Falcon was now confused. They had just kidnapped a stranger off the streets of London in broad daylight and nobody saw a thing. Would the guy even be missed, did anybody know he was there? These and many questions were again circulating Falcon's head as he tried to come to terms with what had unfolded in front of his very eyes just moments before. What was an arranged meeting with Brown had suddenly escalated way beyond his previous fears. What if he was working for Gunther then there was no way he could be released . . . probably ever.

"What do we do now?" asked Falcon.

"Coffee, I think Tony, and we wait."

"Wait for what?"

Brown seemed so relaxed. "We wait and see what my guys sweat out of him. No point in you going off the radar just yet. Now, let's get somewhere civilised and you tell me just what you know. Then we'll take it to the next stage. Let's grab that coffee now and get started."

The two walked off back towards Oxford Street and the mêlée that came with it. This street never slept day or night, only the clientele changed. They rounded the corner onto the busy thoroughfare again and headed into the now familiar Cumberland Hotel, opposite Marble Arch. "This is as good a place as any," said Brown, "public yet discrete."

He steered them towards a small table in the main foyer of the hotel where he threw his over coat onto a spare chair and sat down. He beckoned Falcon to do the same, but he was looking around for the third man. "Where's the guy gone we were just with?" he quizzed.

"Oh he's around. He's probably watching you right now."

"I don't see him anywhere," replied Falcon putting up a defiant front.

"Good. That means I won't have to kick his ass later then. Come on Tony, sit down, you're gonna draw attention to yourself. Jesus man, we're trying to keep a low profile here. Just have a coffee with an old friend."

"A low profile," an exacerbated Tony Falcon exclaimed in a loud whisper. "You've just pulled a bloody stranger off the street in the middle of the day, that's a low profile."

"I guess it's a lower profile than having the coroner pull a blanket over your head in the same street when they found you lying there with a knife in your back."

Brown smiled with tremendous pleasure as his English associate turned violently around on hearing such an outburst.

"You really think that was on the cards?"

Falcon started to sink slowly into the chair opposite James Brown. Clearly he was drifting into deeper thoughts and Brown knew he needed to snap him out of it.

"Relax Tony. No I don't think that was gonna happen but we've got to know whose following you. If his cover's blown then we lock him up until its safe to let him go. You never know he may be wanted somewhere so we can hand him over, then he's out of the way any way; and you don't even get the blame for his disappearance."

Brown ordered coffees for them both as a waiter approached the small table. "Okay Tony, what have you got for me?"

"Here?" he replied, somewhat surprised at the openness of the situation.

"It's as good a place as any. There's no one watching you now. Trust me."

Falcon seemed reassured although still a little hesitant by his associates conviction. He nodded slowly and drawled, "Right," showing a little concern, although still somewhat feigned concern.

"I know the target. He's an Italian prosecutor by the name of Salvatore Ricci. Seems some time ago he put away Gunther's mob or at least some of it. He's also made holes in the Italian Mafia and Christ knows who else. He's upset a lot of people and it seems it's pay back time."

Falcon was rushing to explain as quickly and as hushed as he could, to get the revelations out as soon as possible and avoid any threat of being over heard.

"Wow, steady on tiger; one thing at a time. So he's a lawyer is he, this mark?" asked the American.

"No, he's a bit more than that," explained Falcon. "He's not just a lawyer. He's THE lawyer," he emphasised. "I think probably the equivalent of the Attorney General as we know it or at least a high powered DA in your world. This guy has protection around the clock; they know he's a marked man."

"Well, it's a start. So what do we wait for now?"

Falcon shrugged his shoulders. "I'm not sure really. They're going to call me back in a couple of days to give me his itinerary, and then I'm off to Rome to make the hit."

"Are you seriously going through with this crap Tony? You know I can't let you kill a friendly? You know that . . . right?"

The American was starting to show concern himself at the apparent determination of Falcon, surely he wasn't being serious.

"You give me a better plan. They've got me set up. I've been betrayed by the organisation, somewhere along the line. To make matters worse they've got Maria implicated and threatened to kill her if I don't do it."

Falcon's voice was starting to shake as he poured out his inner feelings; he was in unfamiliar emotional territory. Brown was dumbfounded that this hardened rock, which had carried out so many difficult operations on his behalf, had a vulnerable side as well.

"We'll work something out Tony, you can count on that."

He put a reassuring hand on the Englishman's shoulder which seemed to help a little as Falcon eased down in the padded leather arm chair.

Just as the coffees arrived, James Brown's cell phone began churning away in his jacket. He fumbled around the ruffled mess for a few seconds before locating the vibrating voice box and yanked it out of its linen prison. "Yep, go ahead," he snapped into the telephone.

Falcon couldn't hear the other end of the conversation but sat intently watching the man from the NSA as he indulged in the conversation. He could see elements of concern appear, a ruffled brow, eyes occasionally rolling back in the head of this covert representative from the world's only real super power. What on earth could be wrong? Brown terminated the call, paused a second and looked Falcon straight in the eye.

"We may have a small problem," he said

Falcon did not like the sound of that at all. "A small problem. Where on earth in all this shit am I going to find another small problem?" he asked.

"Come on, drink up. We need to get out of here, there's something I need to attend to." Brown hurried his man along.

"What about me? What do I do now?" asked Falcon, sure that this was all to do with the kidnapping. Was it all back firing now? He wondered, but knew he was never going to get an appropriate answer.

"You go home, or go shopping; whatever takes your fancy. We'll be watching you all the time, have no fear. We'll know if you're being followed, but truthfully, right now I don't think you are."

Brown stood up and put on his coat as he threw ten pounds on the table for the coffees, "That should cover it, even here. I'll call you later yeah. You just take it easy, I'll be in touch as soon as."

The NSA man then hurried out of the hotel but Falcon could not see anyone else leave. Hopefully, the other boys from the NSA or whoever they had in tow were still around and keeping an eye on him. He decided that he too would get out of there and it looked as though the best place for him right now was to go back to his apartment as suggested.

Chapter 20

Francoise Duval was, as ever, sat rocking backwards on his office chair, seemingly defying gravity yet managing to remain calm and suave looking, even with the socially unacceptable cigarette hanging between his fingers. He was staring at the ceiling, digesting the report he had received from Jean Paul Reynard detailing the exploits of the meeting between Gunther, Falcon and Marco in Venice. It was most unfortunate he had no idea what was being discussed, but at least he now knew all of the key players. Thanks in part, a big part, to an old colleague from Scotland Yard.

Duggan could not give Duval much information, but a name was a very good starting point. It was immeasurable to Duval just how much time this act of comradeship between officers supposedly on the same side, had saved his department. He mused over the apparent discord that spilled out from the café and into St Mark's Square, where it appeared to continue. It certainly did not seem a harmonious relationship, which was always a good avenue to exploit as a way to get on the inside in these situations.

Reynard was surprised when his boss advised him of the name of the stranger, but they had learned over the years to accept what Duval told them and not to bother questioning its origins or ethics. He got results which is what he was paid to do. On hearing the name, Reynard immediately got in touch with his local contacts to see what information they had on Mr. Falcon. Very soon they had learned of the vehicle registered in his name so the inevitable trace was put out for that. Within twenty four hours it was located at Marco Polo airport, just where Falcon had left it. They decided not to tamper with the vehicle but rather put it under constant surveillance. At least they knew now he had gone to the airport.

The next step in the puzzle was to delve into the airlines records and see where or if he had flown to; a logical assumption when considering the location of his vehicle, always assuming of course that he had travelled under the same name. Quickly, the advent of computers speeding up such processes, it was discovered he had taken a flight to London, and the net closed in. On hearing the news Reynard despatched two of his under cover officers to the United Kingdom to try and locate the mystery English man and keep tabs on him. They needed to find out what he was up to with such bad company. The two officers were to take surveillance duties in shifts when ever they could as this was to be round the clock surveillance, wherever their target went.

Armed with the data of a name and arrival airport, it was easy for Reynard's team to speak with the authorities in the UK at immigration to find out the last known address of Mr. Tony Falcon, after all, there was full cooperation between the European authorities for everything from murder and drug trafficking through to missing husbands and petty thieves. The request was nothing unusual. He had had a little intelligence back from his scouts, but nothing of substance to date that could help him solve the mystery so far.

The silence in the smog filled room was shattered by the shrill ring of his desk telephone. This was his superior, Chief Inspector Lombard requesting his immediate presence. This was a most unusual summons from the main man so Duval ensured he was well presented, adjusted his already immaculate tie and headed off up stairs.

"Good morning Francoise," the commissioner said, as he entered the Chief Inspector's office. This threw him totally off guard as he was not expecting the Chief of Police to be present.

"Ah, good morning sir," he replied, "I trust you are well?"

"I am, thank you, and yourself?"

"Oh, just fine sir, just fine." The small talk was killing Duval as he had his teeth into what could be a major coup here and wanted to get back to the nerve centre as soon as possible. He could take it no longer, even though he had been in the room merely a matter of seconds. "So, to what do I owe this pleasure, gentlemen?" he respectfully asked.

Chief Inspector Lombard had not spoken yet, he had been studying the notes scribbled on his desk jotter as Duval entered. He looked up at Duval, "I'll be blunt Francoise, I know you expect that."

Duval nodded his approval based on many years experience, and in reality he preferred that approach. He always had little time for beating around the bush.

"I have just had a rather embarrassing discussion with the Commissioner, who has had an equally embarrassing discussion with the British and American Secret Service. Do you have an operation going down in the UK that we were not informed of? One that we have not informed the British was taking place?"

The Chief Inspector's voice was climbing in decibels as he neared the end of his outburst. His face was changing colour to a luminous cerise from the previous normal complexion that greeted Duval as he entered. Duval shuffled about on his feet, twisting his feet sideways so he was standing in the edge of one shoe then the other. He needed to respond and do so quickly, they were expecting an answer.

"Well, we do have a couple of guys in the UK right now sir, but hardly on an operation?"

"Well what would you call it then?" barked Lombard, still seething with pent up rage, obviously trying to show the Chief of Police he could control his force.

"They're on surveillance sir."

"You know the rules; we're supposed to tell the British if we go there, just like they do when they come here. It could cause an embarrassing international diplomatic row. The bloody president could get involved here if we're not careful. You know how that could affect your pension if it all gets screwed up."

Lombard was starting to slow down a little as he realised the potential gravity of the situation for all concerned. They would all go down, not just Duval.

The Chief cut in, "Francoise, why are they there? If it's only surveillance, why not tell the British, maybe they could even have done it for you or at least help. I mean, why not even tell us in this office?"

Duval now turned his attention to the Chief, "Truth is sir, it all happened so quickly. I tried to get some help from the British on a suspect but they came back cold. They blanked us, sir. They didn't want us investigating this particular suspect."

"Why not?"

"I'm not sure sir, but he was certainly well connected. Then we got a lucky break and found out who he was, or at least one name we know he uses. So we tracked him back to an address in London and I sent over a couple of guys to keep an eye on him, nothing else." There was nothing else Duval could really say, that was it in a nutshell.

"So why the interest in this guy, what's his name?" asked the Chief.

"Anthony Falcon" blurted out Lombard, much to Duval's astonishment. Duval was speechless for several seconds, how the hell did Lombard know that, there had not been any reports issued on this case yet?

"Yes, this Falcon fellow, what's the interest?" asked the chief again.

Duval was still on the back foot and had little choice other than tell his superiors what he knew. "Well sir, he's been seen associating with known terrorists in Italy who we had under surveillance. So really we're just trying to find out what his role is with them, we've never come across him before." Duval felt sure he was explaining away the difficult position he had suddenly found himself in. Terrorism, the global fight was always emotive and found support amongst the voters as well as the politicians.

"What have you found out about this guy since you single handedly invaded Britain? Anything?" Lombard knew that there was nothing more to add from Duval. "Let me answer for you. You've found nothing."

"I haven't had a report back yet sir, the men are on constant surveillance. As soon as they check in I'll have their reports straight on your desk."

"I've a better idea Duval. Why don't you go to England and speak to this Falcon yourself."

"If it were that easy sir I would."

"Believe me," replied Lombard, "it is that easy. One of your men was picked up by the NSA in London a few hours ago and is currently being interrogated at a terrorist holding cell by the authorities. So you won't get a bloody report from him today, if you're lucky you may get him back, although I can't say when! You may get a report from the bloody British Prime Minister if you're not straight on this one." Lombard was again losing his cool and was starting to spray as he shouted.

The Chief again jumped into the conversation offering an element of composure, "Look Francoise, you've opened up a can of worms here. Now we've all got to play ball. So I suggest you get across to London and straighten this mess out, get everybody pulling together and get to the bottom of this, before we end up with our ships firing at each other again in the English Channel. Is that clear? I don't want the President calling me tonight asking for an explanation."

Lombard had sat back down behind his over sized desk, which was immaculately tidy and obviously more of a show piece than functional furniture. He was again calm as he wiped his brow with his white handkerchief, "You know what to do Francoise; I suggest you leave right away."

Less than six hours later, Francoise Duval was exiting the Heathrow Airport terminal, after stepping off an Air France flight, to an awaiting car. The driver never spoke which was fortunate, as Duval was not in the mood for conversation. He was seething at how his day had unfolded. He had thought everything was under control. He had solved the mystery man name game and was now closing in on the hyenas and in a matter of minutes had all his kudos stripped from him by his boss and his boss's boss. The situation was redeemable but that required results and that would depend a lot on how the game played out with his British and American colleagues. They may well be calling the shots in the UK but he still had tabs on the others back in Italy, although he didn't know whether or not the NSA had the same. No doubt all would be revealed in the not too distant future.

Duval was amazed at the traffic chaos that reminded him so much of Paris, all these vehicles in one small space. He marvelled at the more organised chaos than was experienced down the free for all Champs-Elysées. But the weather was still British, although France was not much better in that respect, when he had left earlier.

To his surprise, Duval was not taken to a detention centre or a police station, but instead was dropped at the Landmark hotel, where he was again an expected guest. This was a fabulous arena, a converted old railway station that had been made into an expansive and up market hotel. The huge central atrium extending the full height of the building was somewhat of a waste and would not be tolerated in modern construction in the capital, land being at such a premium; however this was historic and did not warrant being altered as such, and no doubt would not have been permitted either.

He was taken by a single escort to the elevator where they stepped out of the lift at the second floor. The two men then went into a room just down the corridor from the elevator, the door partially open awaiting his arrival, which was promptly shut on his entry.

Duval surveyed his surroundings, the pomp associated with the central atrium and the well dressed employees all seemed to have disappeared. This was not even a fine bedroom, just a meeting room, nothing at all exquisite. There were several tables put together which held a series of soft drinks, snacks and the obligatory tea and coffee as supplied in the thermos style tea pots to keep hot. There were already four other people in the room, two of which he recognised.

One was in handcuffs, a pitiful sight, and this was one of Duval's own men who had been on surveillance duty on

Falcon. The other he recognised from the photographs, was Falcon himself. The third stepped forward and made his introduction. "James Brown, good to meet you Mr. Duval. I think you know already some of the people here . . . Mr. Falcon." Brown raised his hand to point out the Englishman just in case Duval didn't know.

"This is Mr. White, one of my associates and of course, or at least I think, you know this gentleman." Brown sarcastically raised his finger to the cuffed prisoner who solemnly stared at the floor as he was singled out, not being able to bear looking back into the eyes of his superior.

"Well thank you for the introductions gentlemen, can we get my man out of the cuffs now please?" replied Duval almost apologetically, hoping to secure the freedom of his French associate.

Brown looked around the room at Falcon and White. "I guess we could, there's enough artillery in here I think to keep order. Oh, as you saw on the way in, there are also a couple of guys outside."

"We're not running anywhere Mr. Brown, just let my man go if you would and we can start to sort this affair out."

Brown acted as though he was thinking about the request for a little while, before acknowledging to Mr. White that he could release Duval's man, who was soon rubbing his wrists where the cuffs had been biting into him.

"Right, don't plan on leaving me now, you hear?" said James in a sarcastic tone. He then turned back to Duval and motioned that he takes a seat around the circular dining table that was also in the room. He signalled to Mr. White who promptly started to pour coffee for the ensemble.

Brown motioned Falcon to join him at the table and Mr. White brought coffees for all three. The newly released French associate of Duval's was permitted to remain seated and simply enjoy his freedom, whilst his superior tried to iron out the international debacle that was unfolding before his very eyes.

"Mr. Duval," commenced the man from the NSA acting more like a school lecturer to an attentive class, than the international man of mystery that he seemed to be.

"Francoise, please," interrupted Duval. "We may as well keep this as amicable as possible."

"Okay, Francoise. Let's see what we have here; it's certainly one hell of a situation you've carved out in the last couple of days. For a start, I know from my people that the British are rather pissed at your being here without their knowledge, but that's for the over paid and over fed men at the top to sort out over lunch somewhere. But as for me, I want to know why you're following our boy here," as he pointed to Falcon, who sat stony faced throughout the opening argument from lead council for the NSA.

"Your boy?" asked Duval. "I thought he was an Englishman."

"English , American, it's all the same to me. He works for me; his origins are of little concern, only his safety . . . and of course his anonymity."

"What exactly does he do for you then, Mr. Brown?"

"Francoise, don't try and turn the tables on me my friend. I can lock you away and lose the key for a very long time. You're paddling in my shit pond at the minute and right now you could use a paddle. You've over stepped the mark, otherwise you wouldn't even be here. So, let me ask the questions, you focus on the answers."

Duval was taken aback by the sternness of Brown's approach. He was not sure about the locking up bit but he sure as hell knew he had a diplomatic incident to diffuse. He realised that he needed to play ball, the rest of his career may depend on it.

Brown, seeing he now had the attention of his French guest, decided to proceed. "Alright Francoise, back to the original question. What's the big interest in OUR boy?"

Duval tilted his head as he listened to the question, buying a little time in his head before jumping into a response. "Our interest? Well since we're not pulling any punches Mr. Brown I'll get straight to it."

"Please do," hurried Brown as he slouched back on his chair awaiting the academic delivery from Duval.

"Your boy appeared in one of our ongoing operations, and judging from the surveillance he seemed a key player." Duval was enjoying his little fight back as he felt he could possibly turn this around to his advantage. Maybe Falcon was a double agent of sorts and perhaps his handlers at the agencies were not too aware of his terrorist links.

"An ongoing operation you say? What sort of op would that be then?"

"It's classified, I'm afraid. It's a matter of National Security and I'm not at liberty to divulge," Duval answered pompously, but the self satisfaction was to be short lived.

Brown shot across the table at the Frenchman, as Mr. White came from behind and in one fell swoop managed to grab the arm of the French police officer and heave it so far up his back he fell forward onto the coffee table at lightning speed. His face was pressed so hard against the wooden table Falcon was convinced he would end up with the grain pattern transferred to his cheek. Duval was clearly in pain and taken by great surprise and let out the corresponding yelp associated with such a move.

"Now, Mr. Duval," said James Brown now in a more menacing manner. "Let's do this the hard way shall we? There will be one more chance . . . and one only for you to answer my questions. If you fail this time, I suggest you call the wife and tell her you won't be back for dinner, for a long time. Understand!"

Duval knew these guys meant business. Even his colleague didn't flinch from the chair, the look given to him by Mr. White was sufficient to freeze him in situ. He had already had his own up close and personal encounters with the American specialists and wasn't keen on any more. Duval's face was sticking to the table top and saliva dribbled from the side of his mouth as he tried to breath. Mr. White was leaning down on him very hard now, yet Brown was still waiting for an answer before his colleague would release the Frenchman.

"DO YOU UNDERSTAND ME NOW DUVAL?" asked Brown again, albeit this time with a little more purpose.

Duval nodded his understanding the best he could from his unenviable position. Falcon just watched the drama unfold; he had never imagined his American associate could be in action like this before. He always considered him more of a desk man and nothing more, not involved at the sharp end. Maybe after all these years he was wrong about Mr. James Brown or whatever he was really called. Brown indicated to his associate that he could release the Frenchman from his temporary position of severe discomposure.

"Mr. Duval, I trust you will see I mean business. I neither have the time nor the patience to play diplomatic games; and frankly I couldn't give a toss whether you come out of this smelling of roses or horse shit. Now, I shall try once more, where did you come across Mr. Falcon?"

At this point, Brown withdrew his standard issue 357 magnum and menacingly slammed it down on the table, from which Duval had just been released. Duval was sure they meant business.

Shakily, he started on his involvement to date with Mr. Tony Falcon. "We have been keeping surveillance on several known terrorists in Italy. There has been a bit more activity than usual with this crew which was a bit of a concern so we stepped up the operation for a little while. Luckily it paid off. A few days ago, an old adversary of ours appeared on the radar, a German by the name of Gunther Menzies. We knew he was dirty but had never managed to catch him, as you say, with his pants down. There's been plenty to link him with various terror activities but we've never managed to bring him in. We thought he had disappeared altogether but when he surfaced recently after many years away, we just knew he must have something planned. That's why we didn't pick him up; we wanted to see where this was going. It must have been big to bring him back into the open. Then your boy turned up. We'd never seen him before but eventually we discovered his details. After that we found his car at the airport, which indicated he took a plane which then led us to the UK. British immigration was kind enough to give me his address and we started surveillance on him yesterday. That's it in a summary. I know nothing else."

"You're sure you know nothing else?" asked Brown.

"Absolutely sure. My interest is in finding out what they are up to. I want Gunther badly, as do several other countries, but I also want to stop him in whatever he is up to at this moment. There's little point in me grabbing him straight away as we need to grab as many of his associates as possible."

"I see . . ." said Brown in his slow southern twang, drawing out his expression as he slowly arose from the chair. He started to walk around the room, Falcon and the other Frenchman followed him with their eyes. White remained focused on the back of Francoise Duval. His only thoughts were on the gun still resting on the table. Duval would be dead before he even got to touch it he thought, but he knew he needed to remain focused just in case the Frenchman had a rush of blood to the heaad. Brown beckoned Tony to join him by the window, overlooking the frantic activity down in the city streets below. The daylight was fading now as dusk started to settle in.

He whispered to Falcon, "I think we may be able to use this guy to help us out. He'll have local knowledge and guys on the ground in Italy. Maybe we can all get a win-win here."

"How's that going to work then?" asked Falcon. "Don't forget my problem."

"Your biggest problem Tony in reality is making sure you don't get killed by the people that are hiring you. You'll be a danger to them if you carry this off, not that you ever will of course."

Falcon turned and faced his man again, "Like I said before, I will get Maria out of this hole."

Brown grinned, that big toothy smile said it all. "I know you will," he replied in a condescending manner, "and we're here to help. Okay."

"Francoise, do you want to eat, I could do with a bite myself," said Brown loudly, suddenly shattering the atmosphere of conflict.

"I guess so," he replied hesitantly.

"Good, I'll get room service sorted with something. Mr. White, could you see to that please?" he asked of his colleague. White immediately left the room and discussed the requirements with his colleagues outside the door. He was back within a minute, "Taken care of sir," he replied.

James Brown once again took his seat opposite Duval. "Francoise, we're on the same side here. We're all after bad guys, right?"

Duval nodded slowly in agreement.

"I think we can work together on this one and all get the brownie points."

"Really?" asked Duval with fake amazement. "What about the international incident that was going to lock me away just a few minutes ago."

"It can still be arranged if you want. I just thought that you may prefer we work together, you help me and I'll help you."

"And how can I be of service to your organisation Mr. Brown?"

"I've got to think on that one Francoise, but I'm sure you can be." Brown paused a moment, "Now, what I'm going to tell you is highly classified. The only people, or at least the only good guys, that know what I'm about to tell you are already in this room. Even my superiors don't know about it yet, that's how fresh and delicate the information is." Brown paused before menacingly adding, "I need not remind you that accidents can happen if any of this information is leaked."

"I know the value of discretion Mr. Brown, it's my business also you know. There are many things my superiors don't know either. It's often the way it has to be played."

"Right then," Brown again paused. He looked Duval in the eye and asked, "Have you ever heard the name Salvatore Ricci?"

Duval sat back in his chair and threw a glance at the ornate ceilings above his head. He started muttering the name aloud as he churned it through his memory banks, kicking the cranial data files into life. "Salvatore Ricci, I have heard that name. Yes. He's the Italian mafia buster that's been in the news again lately. The Italian State Prosecutor, that's him, why?"

Brown threw a glance at Falcon who was now sitting on the edge of his chair leaning forwards to wards the table, "Well, our Mr. Falcon, who you've been following, has been hired to assassinate him."

"What!" exclaimed Duval, "assassinate Ricci, are you insane. Who the hell dreamt that one up? There are many who have tried and failed. What the hell have you got to gain from killing Ricci?"

"Jesus Christ Duval, did we hit your head too hard?" asked Brown. "We don't want him dead. Falcon is working under cover as the assassin they hired to do the deed. We want to get inside this crew, just like you do. We're not sure what they're really after other than a public slaying of a prestige politician. But we're sure there's more. We need to know who the backers are, just like you. Then you stumbled into our boy and could have blown it wide open, hence the reason for picking your guy up in the street."

Brown thought it best he not explain Falcon's predicament in exact detail, he had told Duval sufficient to warrant his interest as well as his cooperation.

"It's certainly an interesting scenario we now have Mr. Brown, wouldn't you say?"

"It is that. Now, are you in or not?"

"What do you possibly need from me? Surely I can't bring anything that the Americans couldn't?" replied Duval, secretly hoping for a lead in the operation as well as the corresponding glory that went with it.

"You can bring people on the ground. You have access to the local forces, I am sure there will be a great deal you can bring. We can't do too much at the moment until they contact Tony again, but we know that will be soon. I'm talking days or even hours, so we need to move quickly."

Brown was speaking now as though the team was operating on a united front, and although this was no longer Duval's operation, he was still a major player. Events had forced him out of pole position but he was determined not to blow the work that had already been done on Gunther.

"Tony, we're waiting on you now," said Brown. "Mr. Duval, I take it your guys will go back to Paris now, leave the surveillance to us over here. No doubt you are still keeping tabs on Gunther and his crew."

"We are."

"Good, you can keep me updated with their movements. Meantime we'll baby sit Tony until he's called back to Italy. Then we need to look at how we play this out. We're going into action too soon for my liking since we have no idea what to expect when we get inside. It's a hell of a risk."

"My risk," piped up Falcon, who had sat silent for many minutes now whilst the two narwhals jockeyed for position, although there could only ever be one winner. In fairness to Duval he had showed his metal and earned a little respect from the Americans.

"Your risk Tony, you're right. That's why we need to keep close to you and work the plan. I guess that's the meeting over and we all go our separate ways now. I'll stay in touch with you, Francoise, as it unfolds here. I'll get my people to advise your chief we're working a joint international case together or something like that. It'll get sorted and I'm sure you'll get the slack you need."

"Merci," replied the Frenchman, whose English had been impeccable throughout the ordeal. The two French officers then made their good byes to the group, albeit somewhat muted, and departed, even before Duval had the opportunity to dine. Still, he could eat away from his new colleagues where he would feel a little more comfortable, but his priority now was to get back to base and get a start on the next phase of this operation.

Chapter 21

Falcon called into a local convenience store on his way back to his Notting Hill bolt hole. He realised he had been back a couple of days and the apartment was still lacking in even the most basic of provisions. A few sparse groceries and fresh produce would at least help him with minor comforts as he sat alone awaiting further instructions. He still didn't know whether there was another tail on him from the Italians, he just preyed there was not. If there was then it was too late now. What was sure was that the NSA operatives were still keeping an eye on him.

The evening dragged without incident. He tried to amuse himself with TV but he had never really been a television addict so even this activity helped little. He tried to watch the news which served to show additional misery and suffering around the world; hardly something to take his mind off his own plight. TV turned to coffee and some bland almost outdated biscuits to help the passage of time but nothing worked. Falcon was still of sufficiently sound mind to realise that despite his passion for wine and whiskey, tonight was not the time to indulge in any of those pleasures either. It was a restless night's sleep for the Englishman leading to an early rise the following day. Somewhat dishevelled and still tired, he knew remaining in bed would serve no purpose.

Showered and dressed, Falcon ventured out once more into the early morning darkness. At least a stroll in the crisp London air might revive him he thought. He gathered up the two cell phones he had become accustomed to over the last few days and left the apartment. The air was immobile but still freezing, surely there was nobody watching him in this climate. He enjoyed the relative calm of so early in the morning and although there was a little traffic on the main streets round about, there were no pedestrians. He decided on the usual walk towards the park although staying on the perimeter rather than entering it was probably safer in such light levels.

The city had started to come to life as he was on his return journey back to the apartment yet he still had received no calls and effectively remained in limbo. He again called into the fast food outlet to collect a cup of instant coffee and walk back to his abode. He didn't even know why he bought it. He didn't care much for cheap coffee when he had savoured much finer in Italy, and also had the benefit of being able to brew his own at home. Yet this was some sort of habit, nay ritual that he had developed over the past couple of days. More heel kicking as well as keeping him out of that interminable damnation of an apartment where he was imprisoned awaiting the next step in his quest. Eventually he decided enough was enough and time to go back, the streets were filling up again so best to get out of the way. As he ventured across the road back to his apartment, one of the cell phones in his pocket surged into life.

It was not the Italians' phone screeching away so the chances are that it would be Mr. Brown, and it was.

"Good morning sleepy head," was the greeting afforded to Falcon from his American friend. "How we all doing today?"

"Bloody awful, but thanks for asking," came back Falcon's response.

"Well you don't sound too good that's for sure. You need to get some rest."

"Rest is what I can't do. I want to get on with this crap and get my life back."

"Do you want your life back Tony? I mean really, is that what you want?"

Falcon paused in the street and occupied the middle of the footpath forcing other pedestrians to navigate around him. He wondered what was meant by the American's question. He wondered did he really want his life back as it was before all this. Maybe he would be content if he just had Maria back and a change of lifestyle, in fact he was sure that would be an all round better solution.

"You still there Tony?" the silence was broken.

"Yes, of course; just about to go back into the house."

"We've straightened everything out with the French and got agreement for back up from them on the ground. So it's over to your guys now, as soon as they call you need to let me know."

"You can count on that," replied the Englishman with an air of certainty in his voice. "Anything else to report?"

"No, afraid not. Just checking our boy's in good health."

"Fine, I'll hopefully call you soon. Bye." Falcon pressed the little red telephone symbol on the cell phone to terminate the call and preceded his apartment building. Everything was just as it was left a couple of hours earlier. There was nothing needed cleaning, the place was tidy, save for his coat thrown over an armchair. He flopped back into the couch with both telephones by his side. Watching . . . waiting, even replaying the DVD from Marco and reviewing the documentation they had sent could not quicken the passage of time. It was a few hours later and countless coffees when the call came. Finally, the Italians made contact. Again it was Marco acting as the front man for the renegades.

"Good afternoon Tony, are we well?" asked his Italian contact.

"As well as can be expected, I suppose. What have you got for me?"

"We are not very patient are we Mr. Falcon?" asked Marco dryly, as though toying with his catch on the end of a line.

"We are not; would you be in my position?"

"You have no idea how close I have been to your position Mr. Falcon," snarled back the Italian, "no idea. But that's for another day. For now we want you in Rome, tomorrow, alright! There's a flight leaves Heathrow for Rome and gets here mid afternoon, around three p.m. You be on it. I suggest you book your ticket pretty quickly. We'll be waiting at the airport, see you there."

Falcon threw the phone back on the sofa. Tomorrow, he thought, nothing like a little notice. Still, at least he could be active once more; every step of this journey would be a step nearer to retrieving his loved one. He had better call Brown and let him know what was happening.

Brown told him that he would see him later in the day; he would call and advise arrangements as soon as possible. Meanwhile Falcon set about ordering his ticket on line as that was seen as the quickest and most efficient solution to the last minute needs. The task was quickly completed, and once again he had nothing constructive to occupy his mind. He went through the documentation pack one more time before putting it in his rucksack and set about packing a few things for his journey. He decided he would travel light, and if he ran short of clothes whilst there then additional attire would have to be purchased wherever he was. After all it was no fashion show he was attending, perhaps his own funeral. With that thought, Falcon decided it didn't really matter how he actually dressed.

An unexpected knock at the door later that evening revealed one Mr. James Brown and his associate Mr. White. They had arrived incognito disguised of all things as domestic plumbers. Well, that's what their transit van livery read, although up close it could be seen neither were actually manual workers. Nevertheless, by Brown's own admission, there was no certainty that there was no one else keeping an eye on him, so, for appearances sake, they thought it necessary.

They entered the building after buzzing the Englishman's apartment so that he could open the entry system and allow them passage straight up stairs. Falcon drew the curtains to hide the visitors' activities prior to their arrival, he too knew of the necessary precautions required. The door was left ajar for the two Americans to enter as they reached the upper floor of the building whilst Falcon continued to ensure all visible apertures to the outside world were sealed. Mr. White even carried what appeared to be an authentic tool bag to add to the façade.

"Well gentlemen, I wasn't expecting this visit. The main problem seems to be in the bathroom," he joked.

"I'm happy we've managed to humour you Tony. We thought we would come to you for a change. At least this way we get a better chance to talk about what's going down. So, any more calls?"

"No, all quiet on the western front as they say."

"Good. You got your flight sorted I take it?" asked Brown, hoping that had Falcon found a problem in that regard he would have already contacted the NSA for assistance. In fact Brown already knew within seconds of Falcon confirming his flight that it had been booked but there was no point in letting on just how closely he was being monitored.

"Yes sir. All booked, bag packed just waiting to get started."

"Right, let's sit." The pair moved to the lounge area of the apartment and both sat on the sofa. White brought over the tool bag and laid it at Mr. Brown's feet then stepped back, acting as though he were a proud lion keeping an eye over his brood.

"You know Tony, you're taking one hell of a gamble getting into this; so am I. I haven't told my people yet what we're up against here and taking out a politician, especially a friendly, just ain't in my portfolio. Anything like that needs to go upstairs, know what I mean? It's way above my pay grade. I tell you now, they won't be keen."

Falcon stared Brown straight in the face. He hung on the words as they left the American's mouth and were fully absorbed by Falcon's receptors, but all he knew was he had to save Maria.

"You know I have no choice as far as I see it."

"Wrong," said Brown sharply. "We can take them out in one go if you want, I won't need a sanction for that. Hell, there's known terrorists in the cell. I'd probably get a bloody medal, never mind an inquisition."

"I can't take that chance. You know I can't." replied Falcon almost humbly apologising for his actions and the position he was placing his allies in.

"Hell, shit son. If you're gonna do it we may as well be behind you," came the American's slow drawl. "Now let's make one thing clear. You can go through the motions, but you don't take the lawyer out. Understand. That's a given and if you can't guarantee me that then you will end up on the wanted list. And that . . . there's nothing at all I will be able to do about that. There's a damned good chance I'll be on it too."

Falcon realised the gravity of what was being said. He was treading on dangerous ground now with both sides and could be assassinated just as easily by either of them. He simply nodded his approval to the American so they could continue with their discussions.

"Intel is telling us that Ricci has a big case opening next week in Rome, it's probably here where they will want to make an exhibition of their public slaying. It's another big case, more Mafia crime family stuff, but it'll be all over the Italian media. It seems that Signor Ricci is not too shy of the media either so he's unlikely to be keeping a low profile. Its part of the, *I'm not running scared image.*"

"Looks like you may be a step ahead James," said Falcon with a wry grin. "Maybe we can pull this off after all."

"Like I said, we go through the motions. There'll be no pulling anything off. Now, since we think we know where the action will take place, we'll get a few guys on the ground pretty soon as will the Frenchies. They can be reporters or something, but will be in the locality, we'll think of something. There'll also be cover from us and Duval's squads. These will be roaming and we'll be tracking you."

"So how are you going to do that then without giving me away?"

"This is the NSA dear boy, don't you worry." Brown reached into the tool bag and pulled out a small cloth bag with a draw cord in it. He opened the bag and produced a watch. Nothing too fancy, a simple watch. "Here, wear this at all times. Then we'll know exactly where you are."

"Is it a tracker?" asked Falcon, as he admired the time-piece

"It is, and also a microphone, so if you talk in your sleep you need to be careful. You'd better not reveal anything about yourself we don't already know, none of that kinky stuff."

"How very James Bond," replied the Englishman with sarcasm.

"Maybe more Mickey Mouse than James Bond, but just remember, it could save your life. So wear it."

Falcon switched his own chronometer for the new one, which surprisingly was almost a good fit without adjustment.

"Now, remember we'll never be too far away from you. At least this way, we may even be in front of you if we know where you're headed. And you can always contact me on the cell or just speak out loud into the watch, there'll always be somebody listening. If you want us to call just say so, but keep that for emergencies, just in case you're still under surveillance when you're out there. Which by the way, I'm sure you will be. But don't forget, you will also have our guys looking after you and we're better. So we will know who is watching you."

"Jesus, this is starting to sound more like a puzzle quest than anything else."

"In a way Tony it is. One big puzzle, but we ain't got all the pieces yet. So we're relying on you to feed us what you can."

"Ah I see, now you need me?"

"Mutual benefit I guess. If it wasn't for your lady friend they'd all be picked up by now; maybe even dead."

"It's Maria. Her name's Maria," the affronted Englishman replied.

"Hey Tony, keep cool. We're trying to help you out here, okay. But we need your help as well so that we can help you."

"Yeah, I know. Sorry, it's just pissing me off now, this lack of action, the waiting."

"Well, by the looks of it, the action starts tomorrow, so you get your sleep and the next time we meet will be in Rome. I assume they'll be supplying you with the necessary weaponry, but just for comfort, I'll arrange for a handgun in your hotel once we know where you'll be staying. Whether you take it or not is your call, you'll know best on the inside."

With that Brown stood up and the faithful sidekick stepped to the front of the sofa and picked up the tool bag.

"Thanks for a wonderful evening Tony," said the pompous American with a cheeky grin spreading across his face. "We must do it again some time soon . . . oh yeah, and sort out your own damned bathroom."

"Gee, thanks for coming around boys, it's been a wheeze."

He opened the door to let the two tradesmen leave the house. "So I guess I'll see you in Italy," he said as they crossed the threshold to the corridor of the upper floor.

"Actually, probably not, well not until it's all over in any case. Like I said before, if you do see us then we're not doing our jobs all that well, are we?"

With that modicum of humour, the Americans descended the stairs and entered back into the darkened swathe that again shrouded the city this time of the night. Then they were gone and he was alone again, alone with his thoughts.

The next morning was not much better than the last. Awake quite early although Falcon had managed a few more hours deep sleep than the previous evening. This was more a result of exhaustion catching up with him rather than him now getting familiar with his predicament. Either way, it was needed and certainly helped rejuvenate the body for the task that lay ahead.

He lost count of just how many times he checked and re checked the sparse belongings packed into the travel ruck-sack. Another day where he was trying his very best to kill time; effectively wishing his own life away in pursuit of possibly reaching his final destiny sooner than planned. Eventually the time came to leave for the airport, and the prospect of setting right the wrong that the Englishman felt he had suffered. Suddenly he felt a new surge of energy; once more he had a cause to champion.

Chapter 22

It was a fairly monotonous flight back to Italy, Falcon once more happy to satisfy the cash strapped Al-Italia with his custom. The mid day flight out of Heathrow was only around half full, so Falcon managed to get a seat by the window with the benefit of empty adjacent seats. Just as well really, he wasn't in the mood for conversation, so, being cooped up next to a stranger for two hours wouldn't fill him with joy. As the plane soared above the clouds he found it refreshing that above that fluffy white padding there could still be found the dazzling winter sunshine emblazoned across the endless azure sky. He hadn't really seen the sun at all these last few days and it brought back fond memories of being high up on the Alpine slopes near his Italian retreat, enjoying the winter snows and sunshine at the same time.

The flight landed at Leonardo Da Vinci Airport or Fiumicino Airport to the modernists, on the outskirts of Rome, losing around ten minutes of the planned flight time due to unscheduled turbulence. Even that could not detract Falcon from his trance like state, spending the majority of the flight simply staring out of the window into the blue beyond.

He had no baggage to collect as he chose to travel light. There was no need for return check in as this was a one way trip, for all the right reasons he hoped. So it was straight through the airport once the maroon European passport had been flashed at the immigrations office, attended by Italian police officers. He was very nearly first through the arrivals area but, as soon as he stepped into the arrivals lounge of the airport he was greeted by his old adversary Marco. No sign board welcoming him there, he was virtually in Falcon's face as soon as he exited into arrivals. Marco's smile was unavoidable even though both players knew this was no genuine beam of friendship or delight at one another's joyous meeting. No, Falcon knew this was more of a knowing smile, just like that offered from the hunter to its incarcerated prey. Nevertheless the Englishman was sure deep down inside, whatever happened, he was going down fighting.

"Hey Tony," shouted the casually dressed Marco, looking more like a tourist than tourists tend to. Such greeting returned rather forcibly by Falcon, "Marco, thanks for coming." There was no emotion in this exchange for sure.

Both men gingerly extended their hands to one another to avoid any un-pleasantries in public.

"I see you're travelling light Tony. You planning on a little shopping while you are here. It's a good place to shop."

"Well you see, I've no idea what to bring. How long I'm going to be here, and as for a gun I was hoping you would supply me in that department."

Marco grabbed Falcon sharply by the arm and twisted round to square him up in the face. "Keep your damned voice down man. Don't play your stupid games with me; you're already in a hole so I suggest you start looking at working your way out of it. Savvy?" Marco kept exhaling particles of spit in the direction of the Englishman, as his anger was showing through his little reprimand; clearly flustered, yet Falcon remained a stalwart and never flinched.

Marco had his hand released by Tony who proceeded to walk towards the airport exit. He walked with the Italian a pace or so behind him but trying to keep up. "For all I know I won't need many clothes, for all I know I may effectively be dead already," he said.

Once again Marco grabbed his arm and stopped the brisk walk.

"Tony, you have our word. This is a single contract for you for which you will be rewarded. That's all. We don't want you out of the way, hell we have no idea who else you work for. Do you think we want that extra hassle down on our heads? When this is over we'll have enough to deal with without your friends contributing to the chaos. That's it, that's the deal. Now come on, the car is outside; we'll get you to your hotel."

The two hurried across the remainder of the airport concourse out into the car park area and into the waiting vehicle, chauffeured by the just as large and well built Francesco. Falcon hoped he would not find himself in the position where he was taking this guy on single handed at some future date.

The air temperature in Rome was substantially better than that he had left behind in England. The car manoeuvred its way through the throngs of vehicles that were picking up and dropping off occupants, but was soon out onto the main autostrada heading for down town Rome. It was only about thirty kilometres to get into the heart of the city but as they neared, just like many major cities, the traffic speed often reached a snail's pace. Added to the volume was the erratic positioning on the road occupied by many frustrated drivers in the city who inadvertently through their own impatience actually increased the journey times for everybody immeasurably. The thirty minute journey was escalated into one of an hour. The car seemed, once within the built up areas, to be forever twisting and turning as though the driver knew all the short cuts of back alleys and side streets to avoid the chaos, but it wasn't the case. This was the thoroughfare. There were occasional breaks in the helter-skelter with the arrival of good stretches of road, well they would be if they had not been cramped, but at least they didn't involve bouncing around the occupants of the vehicle for a few minutes.

There was very little conversation between the occupants of the car on its increasingly slow journey. As they effectively entered the city and the overcrowding began, casual conversation was commenced by Marco.

"Have you ever been to Rome before Tony?" he asked.

"Only briefly, some years ago," he replied, hardly being bothered to look back at his conversational stooge.

"It's a wonderful place. Just like Venice for its magic . . . only different. If you know what I mean."

"Well actually no, I don't," replied Tony, his turn to display a tone of sarcasm. "Still, I'm hardly here as a tourist am I? As far as I'm concerned I just want to get finished and get the hell home. I take it that meets with your approval if I live up to my end?" The Englishman furled his lip a little as he finished showing a hint of arrogance towards his effective captors.

Marco simply nodded, then shook his head and turned back to face the front. Francesco never partook in the banter; his only contact with the Englishman was the regular glances into the rear view mirror. He was the typical oaf as often employed by the arch villains in most corny movies thought Falcon, the real loyal uneducated henchman but truly unloved by his employer.

The vehicle eventually started to come to a halt of its own accord. Marco chipped in, "Here we are. We've got you a nice hotel Tony. It's all paid for, whatever you want. I am sure you'll be comfortable here. We'll settle you in and then you can relax and we'll talk again tomorrow."

He and Falcon left the vehicle in the charge of Francesco, after the hotel concierge had opened the vehicle door for the passengers and they stepped out onto the well trodden red carpet that adorned the pavement outside the opulent building. The driver pulled the car away from the hotel's main entrance as the others went inside. After all, this was a five star hotel. He didn't really want to attract a parking ticket, not today, of all days. They had stopped the vehicle outside the Hotel Splendide Royal. The hotel was based on the Via di Porta Pinciana in what Falcon realised was probably the old town, so to speak. Although the light was starting to fade, he realised that from its hilltop position the views across the city must be spectacular all year round.

"Beautiful isn't it?" asked Marco, as he could see his guest was clearly taken in by the whole aurora of the place.

"It's certainly inspirational. Pity I'm not here to enjoy it," replied Falcon as he drew himself away from the distraction and set off inside the hotel. Even allowing for his reasons for being there at that very moment, it was impossible for the Englishman not to be awestruck at the splendour that awaited him inside this magnificent hotel, and he had stayed in some nice places in his time himself. He cast an eye around at the incredible designs done in marble and the use of fabulously extravagant décor and furnishings. A fantastic chandelier hung from the ceiling within the main hall which allowed shafts of natural light to enter from the glass vaulted roof. This was a place for the rich and it could be seen it was trying to recapture the aristocratic feel of yesteryear.

Marco left his charge appreciating the views whilst he checked in the Englishman. He called Falcon over to the desk to present his passport, but just as Marco had said, all other arrangements had been made. Nothing for him to sign, Marco took care of that. It was simply a case of collecting the key and escorting the guest up to his room.

"We've got you a nice suite. You can relax and admire the view over the Villa Borghese." Marco was obviously proud to be able to show off to his guest such a wondrous delight.

"Great," said Falcon most ungraciously. "Like I said, job done then I'm out of here."

"I know that Tony, but we need you relaxed so you have no excuses for not performing. So enjoy it while you can because tomorrow we start work."

Marco was trying to keep a level head with the ungrateful Englishman, but he knew inside it was all just a game to both. Despite the circumstances, he knew Falcon would at least be very comfortable here, whether he capitalised on the facility was down to him.

Marco opened the suite door and led the way inside. This was still in keeping with what had been witnessed throughout the rest of the hotel. More 'no expense spared' décor, and despite being a capital city, hotel space here had not been used as efficiently as it was in London where every square foot would have had the life squeezed out of it. This was really civilised.

"I bet this is costing you a pretty penny?" said Falcon, slightly warming to the environment.

"I'll worry about money Tony. Like I said, you need to be relaxed so you will be effective. In the scale of things, this will amount to nothing . . . so enjoy. I'll call you in the morning, not too early, and we can get started."

"Just how long will I be here? Any idea yet?"

"Get a good rest Tony, you'll be checking out again in two days. Does that answer your curiosity now?"

"Two days!" exclaimed the Englishman in disbelief.

"Oh, so now you want to stay longer. Well, with all the money you'll be making you'll be able to."

"Balls to that! What I mean is two days and the job's done? How the hell do you expect me to plan and carry this out in two days? I don't even know the guy's itinerary, his habits or the lay of the land. How can I decide in a day or two where this is going to happen?"

"Like I said Tony, relax. Tomorrow's going to be a busy day and a very important one. You need your thinking head on because, like you said, you've basically got a day to get this shit together."

Marco threw him a quick smile, turned and walked towards the door of the suite raising his hand nonchalantly as he went. "Tomorrow morning. By the way, there should be a couple of suits in the closet, just in case you didn't have the right clothes to blend in at the hotel," he said, the door closed behind the Italian and he was gone.

Falcon couldn't believe what he had heard. "Christ," he said aloud to the invisible audience. "How much more of my damned life are these people going to take over?"

He ventured to the wardrobes in question and sure enough inside was a collection of suits, casual and dinner suits. Clothing for all occasions he thought. He sat on the edge of the double bed in the suite, again adorned in luxurious linen, a red and gold covering further enhancing the palatial surroundings. There were doors opening onto a terrace, where breakfast could be served in total privacy if desired, but it was here where the spectacular views from the elevated position the hotel enjoyed, reached their pinnacle. The terrace looked out over the Villa Borghese. This was an area of unspoilt greenery of some eighty hectares, such a rare sight in modern cities. This was so surreal, he thought, how could he be somewhere so splendid in such circumstances? This needed resolving quickly.

The familiar sound of the ring tone of his cell filled the still Italian air. Falcon had forgotten about the phones in his bag so it was a timely reminder to get them out and ready for the inevitable use they would both receive over the next couple of days. He knew from the tone it wasn't the Italians which meant his old friend Mr. Brown was checking in.

"Well, do the clothes fit you?" was the Americans witty opening comment as Falcon pressed the phone to his ear.

A sudden rush of fear came over him as he realised the Americans were listening to everything that was going on. He would have zero privacy now for the next couple of days, so had to be aware of the invisible spy he would be carrying with him from now on.

"Is that all you've got time for. Can't wait until I go to the bathroom, then we'll see who's laughing." That was the best he could come back with on the spot.

"Alright Tony, just checking in with you, let you know we're right behind you. Now, we've got a couple of guys already in the hotel, don't worry you wont know they're there. So relax and let's stay on the case."

"Gee thanks Dad, I was starting to get worried."

"Good to see there's still a human in there. Now, just get us the game plan so we can make arrangements at this end."

"What arrangements?"

"You play your game Tony; you've got enough to worry about. Leave this side to the professionals."

"Hey fellas; I think I may need to know your plans as well, don't you?" asked Falcon quite pensively.

"You don't need to worry about that, need to know basis, for your own security. I'm sure you understand."

"Whatever you say boss; I'm in your hands. As you heard, I've not got a great deal of time. Looks like one day so you'll need to look into Ricci's schedule and see if we can get a head start?"

"We're already on it, now you can't do anything until tomorrow so why not just do as the man suggests and relax. Try on some of them nice new clothes."

"Screw you," said the Englishman who then promptly terminated the call.

Once again the intrepid Englishman found himself wondering how to pass away the hours. He had so much around him in this splendid sleeping palace yet he remained wholly uncomfortable within its walls. Not that it was somewhere he would never choose for himself, the fact was that it was chosen for him, and yet again the elements of being in control of his own destiny were being taken away. He unpacked his few possessions and meagre supply of clothes he had packed into his hand baggage, his ever faithful rucksack, and assembled his toiletries diligently in the marble clad bathroom.

"Well done Tony, that's passed a full three minutes of the night away," he said out loud to himself, although he was now conscious he had the ever present audience at the end of the airwaves emanating from his transmitters. It was still early evening, not even six o'clock. He decided he should take a walk around the outskirts of the hotel. Maybe it would help at some future time, he would never know, but at least he could pretend and that was all he needed to occupy his mind. After all he though, there must be some reason they put him here, maybe the job is to be carried out somewhere nearby.

He remained dressed in his casual attire and set off for the Roman streets that were waiting outside. Falcon enjoyed the race against the omnipotent hotel staff whose sole purpose for existing seemed to be to pamper to overpaying obnoxious guests, in trying to open a door or move a chair for himself. He browsed at a couple of leaflets that were by the main desk as he strolled through the foyer, in particular one describing the Villa Borghese adjacent to the hotel.

Night had already begun to fall yet this city seemed to be livelier than when he arrived a few hours earlier. The traffic levels had increased and more people were on the streets. Although it was the onset of winter, strangely in Italy it never seemed as cold as in the UK and Falcon managed to walk around with his overcoat unfastened. He still had two cell phones in the pockets, which was a bit of a chore, but a necessary evil he decided. It should not be for long now after all.

He ambled along the road on which the hotel was situated at no great pace on the periphery of the unspoilt greenery, why shouldn't he? There was nothing to race back for, when he came upon an arched entrance which passed him through to the Villa Borghese area. He had read about its attractions in the tourist leaflet he still had with him and decided to wander around its pathways, exploring the new found land with its exquisite architecture. This was the real area of wealth when the Italian traders were at their peak. Nowadays they housed fine works of art by many celebrated artists, but their grandeur remained. The parkland even contained Rome's National Museum of Modern Art. The whole place seemed so organised, as if there had been town plans in place for hundreds of years to allow the growth of the nation's capital without destroying its natural history and beauty. Very few capital cities could demonstrate they had stood the test of time as well as Rome.

Even facing such delights, did not take Falcon's mind off his reason for being there. There were still lots of people around in the Villa Borghese but he couldn't at all get into tourist mode. Nor could he possibly imagine what he was looking for as he strolled around the pristine grounds. How is this going to help me he thought, I don't even know what I'm looking for or at. Falcon decided that was enough for this evening. Even though he knew time would drag back at the hotel, he might as well go and enjoy a good meal and some wine on his new friend's account, after all, there was a chance it could be his last. He didn't allow that sombre thought to dampen his ardour for some fancy dining, if anything it increased his voracity. He headed back to the hotel and amused himself at the prospect of being able to describe some of the finest food and wine to his invisible partners, and just wondering what pre packed fast food they would all be dining on this evening. Yes, just a little glimmer of fun in these dark days helped lift his spirits, but as always Maria was never too far from his thoughts.

The Englishman dined well that evening, enjoying various sumptuous courses exquisitely prepared and presented, complemented with a fine Italian Chianti as recommended by the wine waiter himself. Falcon thought it might appear rude if he pushed for his favourite Spanish wines when in such good company of vintners, but he was not at all disappointed. He could sense the quality and smoothness in the rich fruity red which, he believed, justified the price Marco would be paying for it when he settled the account in the next day or two. Perhaps they will kill me, he thought, just for my expenses tab. There was still just less than half a bottle remaining when he had finished dining so that was taken upstairs to the suite to enjoy in his own company. Hardly a classy move, but Falcon was not prepared to waste such a rare beauty, especially as he wasn't paying for it himself. Besides, he was sure it would help him relax and that's what everybody had been telling him to do that afternoon.

It certainly worked for him, the following morning he awoke after seven o'clock, which was highly abnormal. He felt thoroughly refreshed and marvelled at the fact that the weight of the heavy ornate bed coverings made it look as though he had barely slept in the bed that night. He decided breakfast in the room, in private, would get the day off to a relaxing yet reflective start. Here he could get back to the personal contemplation and of course be able to take any incoming calls from the Italians or the Americans without any unwanted prying ears.

The breakfast was wheeled in by a service cart the size of a small car. There was everything a family of four could want, let alone an individual, all he had to do was sign, so easy. He sat there watching the city vibrancy surface again. The daylight had already started to break through and again the air was not too cold for an Englishman but it was too cold to take breakfast outside even wrapped up in the hefty towelling robes from the bathroom. He was slowly ploughing through the breakfast assortment when the first call of the day came in.

Falcon slowly raised himself from the table, chewing a warmed buttered croissant as he went across the room to the bedside cabinet where he collected the Italians' cell phone.

"Morning Marco," he said whilst still chewing, showing nothing but a lack of respect for his tormentors, "I trust we are well?"

"Mr. Falcon, I'm glad we have found you in good spirits today," came back the reply, but it was not Marco. He knew from the guttural sound it was the unmistakable voice of Gunther Menzies, the mastermind and financier of this whole sorry affair. "I trust you are enjoying my hospitality?"

"I thought I may as well relax a bit, yes. I can recommend the Chianti if you are interested . . ."

"No games now Mr. Falcon. You will be ready for nine o'clock if you please. We shall collect you then from the main hall area. Good day . . . Tony."

There was no time for further discussion. Gunther was gone. He said what he had to and left the conversation.

"Game on!" shouted Falcon, knowing full well his people were listening in. "Nine o'clock pick up from the hotel, possibly Gunther not fully sure yet. Just make sure you have enough guys out there to keep the tail on."

He was sure the NSA men along with help from Duval and his operatives would have plenty of coverage on the ground. There was always the tracker but that could not be relied upon as a cast iron guarantee they were always right there in the shadows. Falcon decided he would still have time to finish enjoying his lavish breakfast before showering and making himself presentable to his Italian friends, and so he did.

Priding himself on his usual punctuality, Falcon was awaiting collection by his escorts in plenty of time, leaving himself some fifteen minutes to spare before they were scheduled to arrive. At least that way he gave himself an opportunity to observe the comings and goings of people within the hotel and see if he could spot any of the bad guys, or the good guys for that matter. Finally, after the brief period of surveillance from one of the ornate chairs in the main hall, he spotted Marco. Falcon sighed with a little relief as he would far sooner have Marco's company than Gunther's, but preferably the company of neither would have been ideal. Despite his intense watching, he saw nothing out of place and set off to greet Marco as he strode across the patterned marble floors. The two greeted like old friends and were soon in the waiting car and the careful chauffeuring style of Francesco once again. Today they were in a black Jeep Cherokee, a change from yesterday's vehicle but Marco soon explained this was a better vehicle for casual observation and of course was bigger than most things that may want to get in his way. So it was a brute force thing, nothing else.

Chapter 23

Francoise Duval lit yet another cigarette. He was pacing up and down, outside the offices of Mr. Salvatore Ricci, waiting to see the prosecutor at the earliest possible moment. He was in awe of the quality and magnificence of the surroundings as they far outshone any office Duval had ever worked in. These were works of art and being used by the legal system as offices. Duval knew that in his service, the chance of an outside window was a status symbol showing authority and promotion, but fine architecture and sculptures he was not at all familiar with.

The heavy oak door of Mr. Ricci's office opened as he was shown through to a receptionist who was the last line of clerical defence to the famed prosecutor. Even she had a splendid office. No smoking in here, he thought, as he sank his feet into the deep plush burgundy carpets whilst he waded across the floor to the open doors of the inner office of Mr. Ricci himself.

"Good morning inspector, can I interest you in a coffee?" asked Ricci. He was a well dressed man wearing an Italian hand made suit, slicked back black hair and a bit of a suntan to his skin which wasn't bad for the time of year. He spoke eloquently with impeccable English and commanded attention as he soared around his office; clearly a man in control of his life.

Duval responded as he walked towards the prosecutor, "Good morning to you sir. A coffee would be very nice, thank you."

"Please, take a seat," said the Italian, as he showed several comfortable arm chairs to his guest from which he could pick. "So tell me Mr. Duval, what is so important that you needed to pull strings just to get in here today that could not be discussed over the telephone?"

"Well sir, it's a delicate issue really," replied Duval hesitantly, looking around to see if they were alone.

Ricci sensed the need for discretion, so closed the heavy office doors before returning to his own seat behind his large oak inlaid desk. A seat he preferred to take when in company so he could keep an eye on everything with no one to the rear. No sooner had he sat down than two cups of fresh Italian espresso arrived. He signalled that the door be closed, as his secretary departed, after leaving the aromatic brews for the two gentlemen.

"Right Mr. Duval, we are alone now. So what is the issue?"

"Sir," started Duval, "we have very good information I'm afraid, that there will be an assassination attempt on your life in the very near future."

Duval was almost afraid to reveal what he just had, but he felt the need to protect the attorney from what was being plotted against him, even though Duval was not in possession of any hard data.

Ricci let out a forced stream of laughter which took Duval by sheer surprise. The Italian composed himself, took a sip of the steaming coffee and placed the cup between his hands extracting the warmth from its receptacle.

"Mr. Duval, please forgive my out burst, but really, that's not news. Have you any idea just what sort of people I have to deal with through this office on a daily basis? To put it in perspective for you, if a day goes by when I don't receive a death threat I think the postal system is on strike again or the telephones are not working."

"With all due respect sir, I appreciate you do a difficult job, but we do feel this warrants precaution at the very least."

"I work with the vilest scum this country has generated, as well as other scum the crime families of this nation see fit to import to help them in their grotty little empires. I pursue drug dealers, murderers, pimps, bookies, debt collectors. You name it, you think of a vile crime, and I chase the organisations behind it. We've successfully broken up many such families and cartels, disrupted income streams of billions, yes billions of Euros here and abroad, yet there's still a long way to go. Tomorrow sees the start of another case we are prosecuting, against the alleged godfather and a dozen of his henchmen of the infamous Rialto family. I know these people want me dead for sure. All those we have put away over the years, they want me dead. Hell, there are people in the government who get their own salaries topped up by some of this scum that want me dead, yet I am still here. There have been several attempts on my life but I'm still here . . . and I won't be frightened off."

Salvatore Ricci became very passionate towards the end of his speech to Duval. Clearly he was fully committed to the cause, irrespective of the fact that he might pay the ultimate price for his loyalty to society.

"Signor Ricci, your achievements are well known, I'm just asking if we can make any other arrangements for your safety?"

"Like what Mr. Duval? Have you seen my security? I'm better protected than the Holy Father himself. What else can be done?"

"I can see that you have plenty of precautions in place, but what about postponing the trial for a few days? Would that be possible?"

"Never! That trial will go ahead as planned. There's many years of work gone into that trial. A whole lot of people are relying on a successful prosecution, lives have been endangered and some lost in getting to where we are now. I will not tarnish their memory by postponing the trial. What message do you think that sends out? Only one, the government is now running scared of the crime families. Well, let me tell you, I'm not running."

Ricci was now raising his voice, his obvious passion for his mission coming through once again as he slammed his hand hard on the desk as he finished. Duval looked sheepishly at the floor for a few seconds. He was lost for words. What could he do to help this guy? Clearly very little was going to get his support.

"What if you didn't make such a spectacle of your arrival?"

"Are you asking me to use the back door Mr. Duval?"

"More discretion would at least help us," replied the Frenchman, hoping that his pleas would at least be given a fair hearing.

"There will be no discretion. This great nation expects a stance on organised crime, they expect me to continue and force our way into these organisations and crush them into the ground. We do it head on in Italy Mr. Duval, no back doors, head on. These people will see me coming in the front door every time. Salvatore Ricci has no fear; he wants his enemies to have the fear. That's how it works. It's for the people, it gives them hope. As politicians, that's what we're here for."

Ricci stared at Duval who returned the compliment. There was a dreadful silence for several seconds before Ricci spoke again.

"What makes you so sure this is any more real than any other threat we get here?" he asked.

"Well, it's a little confusing at the moment, but we basically have a contact on the inside of the gang who are planning this . . . project."

"Who is this guy, can he be trusted? I mean, is he totally reliable?"

"From what I have seen sir, I believe so. He has some very influential friends."

"This contact you have, how did you manage to break him?"

"We never broke him sir, he's . . . well, one of our operatives I guess. One of the Americans' to be precise."

"So he's an American?"

"Actually he's English."

"Duval, this seems to be getting weirder by the minute. If you, or whoever has a man on the inside, why not just pick them all up? Hell, I'll even prosecute them for you if you want."

"We can't just yet. We're not quite sure of the extent of the particular cell or what they're really after."

"So what's your guy in there for. How did he break the ranks and survive to feed you back the information you now have, albeit minimal by the looks of things?"

Duval paused, realising he needed to be sure no operation was being compromised here by any revelations he might make. "They hired our guy, they came to him; otherwise we would not have even known this operation was going on."

"Hired him! For what exactly?" asked the curious prosecutor.

Again Duval hesitated in his response. He looked around the office again to ensure they were still alone before turning back to the Italian. He took a deep breath and then blurted it out, "He's the shooter sir."

"What?" You mean to tell me the Americans are involved in planning my murder?"

"No, the Americans, and ourselves, are out there trying to stop the assassination."

It was now Ricci's turn to reflect and ponder what had just been said.

"Is he any good?" he asked tentatively.

"They say he's one of the best alive. The way his skills were explained to me by the Americans, they were happy he was on their side. He's a specialist and capable of a very accurate shot from a long way out."

Once more, Ricci seemed lost for words and stared blankly at the office walls as his head seemed to be in an endless spin. Finally he snapped from his semi trance.

"Well thank you for your time today Mr. Duval, I appreciate you are a busy man. Now, I've got a lot of things to do before tomorrow so if you'll excuse me."

Duval knew his time was up at the prosecutor's office and no further dialogue was going to change anything. As he arose from the chair to make his way to the doors, he turned to Ricci, "Sir, with all due respect. What I have just told you, operationally, is strictly confidential. Please do not relay this information to anybody outside of your closest aides. Our man is the only source of information we have, we certainly don't want his position compromised."

"Do you not trust my staff Mr. Duval?"

"At times like this sir, I trust no one. Feel free to discuss the possibility of an attack on yourself with your closest security staff, but please, don't discuss the sources or the specifics."

"Your secret's safe with me Mr. Duval. Have a nice day," said the Italian as he ushered his unwelcome guest out of his office. He closed the doors and slumped backwards onto them in private. Perhaps for once the ice cool attorney was feeling a little heat. He returned to his desk and called his secretary to send in his Chief of Security If nothing else, Ricci felt he needed to share the salient points of the discussion with the Frenchman, even if it changed nothing in the way of arrangements for his forthcoming public engagement.

Duval meanwhile was heading back to the small command centre that had been set up within the Carabinieri headquarters, housing the listening equipment for the NSA to which they were all now privy. Duval had his own agents on alert and they were involved in the cross town tailing of Falcon and the conspirators along with a number of Brown's operatives. The Carabinieri were on full alert to offer what assistance was deemed necessary from Interpol under the leadership of Francoise Duval, although even Duval knew that the NSA were really calling the shots, even if not publicly. He would always take his lead from Brown.

Duval set about explaining the reticence on the part of the Italian prosecutor to make other arrangements to Brown, who was of course less than pleased. The last thing he really wanted was for Falcon to be put in the position where he needed to take the shot to save his girl. Unfortunately, Brown knew how the man functioned, so he was sure that Falcon would inevitably take the shot if the situation called for it.

"So why's this fella so dumb he won't take extra precautions?" he asked of the Frenchman.

"It seems to me the man's a celebrity more than a lawyer. He needs the camera to function I guess. Maybe he's planning on running for president some day and he's just building his case now."

"You're probably right. But sounds as though we're gonna have to stay on this guy as well now. I'll just have to leave you to get on his back again once we get some more info out of Falcon."

He turned to his team and shouted, "Tell me people, where's our boy now?"

"He's on a tour of Rome at the minute Chief. No indication yet where they're headed. Just idle chit chat coming out of the car, at least what we can hear. We've got a couple of cars on the tail as well and others out in front we're trying to direct in advance."

"Well keep on it folks. There are lives at stake here!"

Chapter 24

Unfortunately for Tony Falcon, this didn't start out as one of his luckiest days. There were now four of them in the vehicle, the fourth being of course Gunther.

"Good morning once again Mr. Falcon. I trust you are now well rested as we have work to do and quickly?"

"Really, well things aren't so bad after all."

"What do you mean by that?" asked Gunther.

"You know, if we're going to be done with one another very soon then we can all go our separate ways and perhaps, God willing, never see one another again."

"You talk boldly for one in your position Mr. Falcon. Still, have your fun if you wish. You know where we're going now Marco, let's do it."

Falcon was unsure about exactly what that meant. He sat there apprehensively, as the lunacy of continental city driving began to surface. Francesco was throwing the car across lane after lane with little regard of other road users, but they were all doing the same. The others didn't seem to mind the ducking and weaving as though it was the norm, but it was not right for the Englishman. Surely this was only going to attract attention, he thought, but it never did. It was just the way it was done and invariably smaller cars gave way to bigger ones, laws of the jungle. They drove around the streets for fifteen minutes before stopping, but Falcon knew, in terms of distance, they hadn't gone far from his hotel. Some of the same landmarks were still easily visible.

"This is it," said Marco, "everybody out."

That didn't really apply to everybody as Gunther clearly had no intentions of putting himself on the streets of Rome unnecessarily. The other three got out of the Jeep and assembled on the pavement. They left Gunther in the parked vehicle and set off on foot. Marco led the way and Falcon dutifully followed without question. The strcct was not as busy as the main thoroughfares they had just left but there were plenty of pedestrians around. Marco suddenly halted, causing Francesco and Falcon to stop sharply. He turned on Falcon and said quietly,

"See the guards over the road?" he then proceeded to act all casual by drawing a cigarette from a pack and lighting it.

"What of it?"

"Well Tony, that's your shooting gallery."

"My what?" said the startled Englishman.

"That's where Ricci will be tomorrow afternoon when you take the shot. This place is being converted into an Italian Fort Knox. It's a big Mafia trial and lots of additional security measures have had to be put in place before the start. There's going to be a lot of people in the dock tomorrow."

"Let me get this straight. This place will be crawling with cops and you want me to stand here and shoot a politician."

"Tony, even I could do that. Get real please. This is where Ricci will be; now you know, you've got today to pick out where you want to be. Look around you, see anything you like, any good vantage points?"

"You want me to do this in a day?"

"That's all we've got I'm afraid. I don't like it as much as you but that's the score and there's no changing it. As you can imagine, security will be tight. You'll do well to get anywhere within a kilometre of here, the whole place will be locked down. There'll be police helicopters circling as well as spotters and police marksmen in place. This is big Tony, this is for our cause, and we won't get a better chance or at least such a prolific chance."

Falcon looked around. He could see no obvious vantage point for his shot. He screwed his eyes up as he scoured the landscape, no hill tops, no church towers, and no buildings that seemed within a half decent distance.

"There's nothing here. There's nowhere for a good shot."

"This is why you were the chosen one. This is why you're getting paid what you are. This place was chosen for that very reason; it's as secure as it can get for close quarter attacks you see. You're the best there is, nobody disputes that.

You come very highly recommended and we know you take on some very special projects, we know what you earn, or at least part of it. We know you can take a long shot, well beyond a kilometre, and still hit the mark. What about the church tower up on the hillside there?" asked Marco, raising his finger into the low winter sun.

Falcon shook his head in disbelief.

"Have you any idea how far away that is. That's got to be a mile away, minimum. There's just no way. That's proper sniper rifle territory, very specialist military grade equipment."

"But there is Tony; we know you've done it before."

"There are long shots and near impossible shots. Have you any idea what has to be taken into account for a shot like that. First of all we need to consider the flight time. Even with the fastest bullets, we're still talking several seconds before the bullet will actually reach its target. So we need to predict where the target is going to be after that lapse. Then there are the physical constants to consider. The obvious one is wind, over such a distance any change in the anticipated wind speed could mean you will miss the mark. Remember we are talking minute angle changes here which are exaggerated by the time they reach the objective. Humidity will even play its part believe it or not. The humidity in the air will have different frictional effects on the bullet. Heavy humidity will slow it down which will in turn alter its trajectory. Then there's gravity. We can allow for that with the elevation but that's just another factor where micro adjustments will make all the difference. Hell, with the miniscule margin of error we're talking we may even have to consider the effect of the rotation of the Earth."

"Well said Tony, spoken like a true professor of ballistics, although a little too far fetched I think at the end, but nevertheless, well put."

"Far fetched!" exclaimed the startled shooter. "It would be interesting to see you make such a shot."

"Luckily for both of us . . . I don't have to. Now come on, let's go and have a look at the tower and see if you think it's a possibility. Unless of course there's anything else you see that may be suitable. I know you wanted to do the planning Tony but things have been sprung on us so just in case, we started looking ourselves, you know as a fall back position. But if you do see anywhere on our travels, just shout up."

The three of them walked back to the car, not a single word was spoken. When they got back inside the vehicle, Falcon let loose his anger.

"This was meant to be my way, don't you remember. I do the planning, that way I make sure I can get back out. I don't like being rushed, that's when mistakes come in. Lack of planning, and it's my neck in the damned noose if it all goes belly up."

"Don't be so dramatic Tony," shouted Gunther. "If you screw up then all our necks are in a bloody noose, including the lovely Maria's."

Falcon's blood was starting to boil inside but he knew he couldn't rip into Gunther just yet. He was still stuck in a position that he hoped was only occurring in a nightmare and he'd wake up any moment, but a reality check swiftly told him that wasn't the case. Marco jumped into the conversation to diffuse the tensions in the back of the vehicle.

"Tony, we just thought we would help out a little, save you the trouble. It's still your call. Let's go to the old church tower and you decide for yourself. If it's no then it's no, but you'll need to find somewhere else very quickly. Like I said, tomorrow is our only chance."

"Even if it could be done from there, I'll still need a suitable gun which will have to be zeroed and set today. How are we going to achieve that?"

"Don't worry about the gun Tony, that's all in hand," said the Italian with a slight curled up grin on his face. He felt that he had an answer for every problem Falcon could throw in his direction. The Englishman was quickly painting himself into a corner and running out of excuses. However Marco was always mindful of what a cornered rat is capable of, so tried his best to play Falcon diplomatically rather than be forceful with him.

Francesco weaved the burly vehicle up the narrow and winding streets, skywards towards the old church tower. Clearly there was little cause for people to venture into this area regularly which in itself made it a reasonable location to ensure privacy and discretion. The church was strangely remote with all the changes that had gone on around it over the years and there was little in terms of a congregation immediately nearby. It was still clearly in use and had minimum maintenance undertaken to keep it functional, but one would imagine it was rarely full. Access into the church tower was fairly easy; the doors to the church were not locked as no valuables remained on display in this house of God due to its remoteness, an unfortunate sign of the times.

This time all four ascended the stone staircase to the top of the bell tower. The clear day afforded similar views across parts of the city Falcon had enjoyed from his hotel. Marco handed him a small pair of binoculars so he could assess the surroundings and take sight of the target area from this vantage point. Falcon lost all sense of indignation at being there and was suddenly once again engrossed with the operation. This was the part he revelled in, physically planning the shot, the arithmetic and the zeroing in of the rifle, this was the real technicality. Once that was done, all that was required was a steady hand, albeit a real steady hand, and nerves of steel.

"Okay," said the Englishman. "This is not a bad spot, I'll give you that. But what about people, won't there be people about here tomorrow?"

"No, only Sundays and religious holidays this Church is used. Tomorrow we will be fine. Any other problems?" asked Marco.

"I only saw one way up here, how do we get away afterwards?"

"Well, we don't draw any attention to ourselves for a start. You leave the gun here. Make sure you give it a good wipe down. There's an old disused well in the church yard, and it's deep. Throw it down there. It'll never be found. Make sure you pick up any shell casings as well, but I guess I don't need to teach you all that do I Mr. Falcon?"

"But what about getting out?"

"Tony, Francesco will be here with you. He'll be your driver. There's a side road coming off to the left as you go back down the hill. That will take you away from the policed area and take you round the side of the hill through those old houses you can see." Marco raised his finger and pointed at the rooftops of the houses in question. "The road is hidden from traffic coming up the hill, that's why you never saw it."

Falcon pondered the route and could see how it was plausible but wanted certainty.

"I want to drive out that way, for my own curiosity."

"Of course," replied Marco, "I would have expected nothing less. Now, anything else you need from up here?"

"Well, I know you've just about thought of everything, but from this range, I need an accurate distance, scaling it off a plan just won't do?"

Marco just grinned. Without any change of expression Gunther produced from his inside pocket an infra red telescopic range finder. "I take it this should suffice," said the mono-toned German, still sporting dark sunglasses which seemed out of place for winter, despite the low sun, it was hardly dazzling.

Falcon was surprised at the production of such a piece of kit. He had to confess quietly to himself that they had done some proper planning for this venture. He would have liked a different location and more escape routes, but that said, in the time he had available to save his lady, and himself, this was not a bad set up. He raised the scope to his eye and started to zero in on the courthouse doors. It was ranged at seventeen hundred and twenty metres. There was also an elevation drop of sixty metres or so to also be taken into account.

"So what happens when your boy arrives then?" asked Falcon.

"Normally he would be surrounded by guards but he usually has a wave for the cameras and we expect a few words for the media on the steps before going inside, he's a real people's man."

"So the shot is at the top of the stairs, right?"

"We expect so."

"Do you have some paper and pen?"

Marco produced a pocket note pad and small pencil which he hoped would suffice. Falcon jotted down a couple of details in the pad, range and elevation and what he perceived the wind element to be today as he stood there in the open tower. At least the openness allowed a sense of the wind effects that needed to be factored into the equation. He drew a small schematic for his own benefit, tore off the pages, put them in his trouser pocket and returned the book to Marco.

"That's me done," he said. "Now let's see this way out."

The four climbed back down the stone staircase and into the church courtyard. Marco pointed out the well which Falcon duly approached to look down. Just as he was told, it seemed a long way down, he couldn't see the bottom. He picked a small stone off the floor and dropped it in and listened. It was several seconds before any sound of impact with water came resonating back up the innards of the tubular stone column. It was a good way down.

"That will do nicely," said Falcon, ". . . at least as long as they don't suspect the shot to have come from here."

"You worry too much Tony," said Marco. "Have a little faith, we've done our planning, and this is a sweet job for us all."

The pathfinder party climbed back into the jeep and Francesco obliged by demonstrating the exit route. Falcon realised that it was a good get out card; it should be quick and take him well away from any heat that the shooting would obviously attract. There would inevitably be an immediate lock down of the surrounding area, but if they were quick enough, these side streets would be superb. His only real concern was that there was only one way out. This was against the grain as far as he was concerned, but this time he was limited. After all, this was not a normal job; he was probably fighting directly for his own life. For now he had to go with the flow that his Italian colleagues had conjured up. Then there was the next immediate concern. Francesco would be with him, or at least close by when the shot was taken. Would the Englishman be the recipient of a subsequent lead projectile? Again and again such thoughts circulated his head whilst all the time wondering how he could get away with the shot and save Maria. Time was running out and his brain was working over time.

As the truck ventured back into main stream Roman traffic, Marco realised that Tony had spent the journey from the church with his face almost pressed against the rear side window and never said a word. Marco thought it time to venture into the Englishman's contemplations.

"Well what do you think then Tony, is it a goer as you say?" he chuckled as he said it, thinking he was trying his best to adopt an English persona.

"Why do you ask? You already seem to have made the decision for me, despite the agreement."

"Agreement!" shouted Marco. "What the hell do you think this is? This is no handshake and job done my friend. This is a business deal as you well know. We all win, but as for agreement, we had our ideas if you recall, and you flatly refused. So, I'm afraid, if you wanted a gun then this was the best we could come up with. You are stuck with it just as we are. You know what our preferences were. So, if you speak of deals, we have given ground on this one, as long as the result stays the same."

"I don't do car bombs. I told you that as soon as you threw it in the melting pot. Despite what you may think of me I will not take unnecessary collateral casualties, and a car bomb

I'm afraid does just that. Maybe even family members and I won't have that on my conscience," retorted Falcon with real conviction.

"A killer with a sense of justice, how nice," sneered Gunther, joining the conversation from the other rear seat.

"At least I have a sense of justice."

"Do you?" replied Gunther immediately with venom. "Do you really think that's the case? You're the same as we are only on a different side." He paused, "I'm bored with this, and I think we've already had this conversation on a previous meeting. Let's get back to the job. Marco wants to know if you are satisfied with the plan he has come up with for you. A simple yes or no will do. We don't have time for an autopsy. If yes then we can proceed to the next stage."

He turned to look at Falcon directly awaiting an answer. His eyes felt piercing through his dark glasses but Falcon could barely make them out, although he was sure they were just as menacing as they were when he was in his heyday, cold, calculated and evil. This was the one he could not trust, this would be the double crosser he thought, even if he wasn't the one to undertake the actual deed.

"I guess it's okay, but not quite what I would have . . ."

"Enough," shouted Gunther. "Enough," he repeated in a far softer tone. "So we are agreed that this is suitable, now let's get out of town so we can move on."

Marco and Francesco glanced at one another and started to grin. Marco then piped up from the front of the vehicle, but without turning, around as he didn't really want to face Gunther whilst he was still smirking at the outburst towards the assassin, "Now, if you could change anything Tony, what would it be? Just for curiosity's sake, bearing in mind we don't have much time."

Falcon thought for a few moments. These guys were just messing with his head, he was sure of that. The decision was already made, why bother asking. This was a mind game he was on the wrong end of and it was again unfamiliar ground. He quickly ran through the whole scenario in his head from the sighting of the target to the freedom into the open roads.

"Well, assuming that Signor Ricci will arrive on time and do as planned. The shot should be relatively straight forward, subject of course to the physical elements we have to combat against tomorrow. The biggest failing in the plan, as I see it, is in the time we have for the escape."

"Oh!" replied Marko, as though really surprised by this remark. "I sensed you were happy with the route and just how quickly we get away from the police activity. There will be a lot of activity you know."

"I'm sure there will. That's my point. What about a change of cars as we go through the houses. What if a helicopter sees us, I mean a big black truck like this one will stand out. The helicopters will be circling like fury after Ricci goes down, and this beast up in the hills by an old hardly used church may stand out. Why not just swap cars and come out in an everyday common car, Mercedes or Alfa, something that there's lots of zipping about Rome. By the time they get on the ground and realise the switch, we will be in the army of marching ants, just another car fighting its way around town."

Gunther glanced across the vehicle, from his staring blankly out of his window. He looked over the top of his shades then lifted his head back up.

"My my," he said, "we do have a brain. Why didn't you think of that Marco? You know Mr. Falcon, that's not a bad idea after all."

He nodded his head up and down several times with approval before continuing, "Marco, see that we take Mr. Falcon's advice on board."

He again turned to the Englishman. "You know Tony, are you sure you never want to see us again? I'm sure we could give you a very prosperous life after this job. You have a rare talent, an intellectual killer, I like that."

Falcon shook his head resolutely. "It will be a cold day in hell when that happens, I assure you of that. I am taking you at your word, a deal for a deal. Then we're through, right?"

"Whatever you say Tony, I just thought you may need another employer when this is all over. I mean, you can hardly go back to your old chums now can you?" Gunther then left it at that and turned back to watching the outside world in silence, knowing full well that he had started to get inside Falcon's brain, just where he liked to be, to facilitate control.

The vehicle continued its trek through the city. Falcon had no idea where he was now headed, he had lost site of any recognisable landmarks for a tourist some time ago. Soon they were on the autostrada which seemed to be the ring road around the city. He spotted a road sign for Lazio, at least he recognised that name, and realised he was now on the northern side of Rome. Soon they crossed over the Tiber River and dropped off the motorway at the very next junction. Again they were heading north on a smaller but still major road, constantly keeping the flowing Tiber on his left hand side, dotting in and out of view as they travelled. The journey took them beneath another autostrada then it was open road out into the countryside. Despite the time of year, it was still a pleasant sight to see the greenery that still existed there.

It didn't take long on the less trafficked road before they were again turning off the highway. Less than five minutes from the last motorway bridge thought Falcon, as he was trying to gain his bearings before the truck turned to the left and the road construction became somewhat inferior in quality. A further five minutes of steady driving brought the vehicle to an isolated farm stead. It comprised several smaller buildings and two large barns, as well as a reasonably sized farmhouse, which in its day must have been sufficient for a family of seven or eight, thought the Englishman.

"So where are we now?" asked Falcon.

"Where indeed?" replied Gunther, as he climbed out of the Jeep. "Watch where you step Englishman," he shouted, laughing as he left Falcon and the others to make their way into the main house whilst he strode ahead. A cigarette was in his mouth, even as he was climbing out of the car; he must have needed that thought Falcon.

"This Tony is what we call our little safe house in the country. This is where we will bring you back to tomorrow before we all go our separate ways, in a controlled manner, so we don't attract any attention," advised Marco.

"Why don't we go our own way after the hit, then I can get home and out of your hair?" he asked somewhat bemused.

"Tony, we trust you, but let's say . . . not implicitly. We'll do it our way."

"And you expect me to trust you?"

"You have little choice really. You're just going to have to."

"What's the point in bringing me here now? Now I know where you are, what if I went to the police now?"

Marco smiled that knowing grin which was enough to let Falcon know that he knew the Englishman simply wouldn't even contemplate such a move. After all, if he was the real intention he would have done it already rather than go through with this charade.

"Come inside Tony, let's make you a coffee and get you in the mood. Then I have something to show you which I'm sure you will appreciate."

Falcon was sure his observers at the NSA would know his exact location so he felt reasonably secure in taking the offer of going inside the building. Why would they want to harm him now after all the planning that's taken place. Surely they had got the picture so far, so why not continue to see it through. He followed Marco inside and was surprised at how the place felt like a home. It was not a run down damp decaying hiding place as he had suspected. There was warmth and the unmistakable smell of fresh coffee having recently brewed.

There were also a couple of others there that Falcon had not seen before. They seemed to be in very high allegiance with Gunther and were clearly conversing with him in German. Falcon could understand the basics of what was being discussed but it was mainly small talk, certainly nothing operational. The two new faces were one male and one female.

Both looked like they were hardened travellers and not the type that would blend in easily at parents' night at school. The female, who he surmised went by the name of Inga, at least in their company, was a tall and slim girl, probably aged early to mid thirties with long but untidily kept blond hair. Her hardened petrified features made her unattractive and she reminded Falcon so much of Gunther, they were certainly a pair. Clearly the interaction between them showed they had known each other for some time. The other male present was Karl. He by contrast seemed somewhat quiet and withdrawn, hardly the vicious terrorist demeanour yet very stony faced. He was shorter than Inga and sported a tight cropped black head of hair and wholly unfashionable black rimmed spectacles, more like a throw back of unwanted glasses from childhood. Inga seemed to call the shots in the group with the exception of Gunther. Even the Italians seemed to obey her wishes, whether out of respect or fear, Falcon could not decide.

Despite her harsh exterior, she still made the Englishman as welcome as she could. He sensed there could be no love in this woman whatsoever, or if there ever had been then something had happened in her past, to rip out her heart. She made all of the arrivals coffee and presented some sandwiches that were already prepared.

"This is lunch Tony," joked Marco. "Unfortunately we don't have time to get you back to the hotel. Besides this is a damn site cheaper." He chuckled as he chomped on a pastrami and cream cheese sandwich.

"Falcon wasn't too bothered about a mere snack; he was hardly in the mood for gorging himself again. In fact he was still fulfilled with the morning's breakfast, to the extent that any food was probably not going to be really appreciated by his palette in any case. The coffee though was another matter. He would rarely decline a fresh Italian coffee, whatever the recipe or circumstances.

"So what's the purpose here?" he asked.

The Germans and Italians looked successively at one another, and then all eyes fell on Gunther to break the silence.

Gunther got up from his chair and stepped out of the room into a room at the rear. A few seconds later he was back with an oversized briefcase, which he plonked unceremoniously onto the kitchen table, where the others were eating.

"That's for you" he said looking squarely at the Engllish-man. "The toys you've been waiting for."

Falcon knew immediately what to expect, although he wasn't sure what sort to expect. He laid the case flat on the table and slowly, almost seductively, flipped open one catch, then the other. Click . . . click. It was like Christmas morning and a child peering slowly into a mystery present, savouring the moment and stretching out the anticipation. Almost teas-ing the rest of the audience although he was sure they had all seen it before; and there it was in all its glory.

Pristine in condition, a slightly modified British made L115A3 sniper rifle complete with scope and bipod mount-ing, modified to allow the barrel to be disconnected from the main body of the weapon for ease of transport and more importantly concealment. Falcon was amazed at seeing such a weapon, he had not even had the chance to fire one in an-ger yet as this was only recently released to the UK armed forces, although he had been made aware of its capabilities. He knew of the weapons pedigree, having worked with it's predecessors, but was also looking forward to establishing whether the upgrade was as good as he was led to believe.

There was a gap in the foam lining where something was obviously missing, highlighted by Falcon stroking his fin-gers around the innards and halting at the obvious missing article.

"Oops!" said Gunther. "Almost forgot." He leaned over to his coat and removed the range finder scope he had offered to Falcon an hour earlier at the church. "I guess this belongs to you now," he said, as he handed it to Falcon.

Falcon stared at the beauty that lay before him. To many it was just another gun, but like all skilled craftsmen, he appre-ciated the quality tools of his trade, and this was quality. He stared in awe at what lay before him, modified by a specialist who loved his art. This wasn't just a sniper rifle . . . this was an assassin's precision tool. He stroked his hands over the weapon, feeling the texture of the wooden stock contrasting with the bitter chill of the cold blued steel barrel. There was even ammunition in the case; this was a self contained killing machine. There were bigger and better weapons available for his craft, but they were much more cumbersome. For the job at hand, although probably at the weapons capability limit, this was not a bad choice after all.

"Okay then Mr. Expert, set it up. Let's see what you're made of," said Gunther once again acting like a stern headmaster. "In answer to your question, you're here so you can set this beast up and mark your range. We are in the middle of nowhere so this afternoon is your preparation time. So put the puzzle together and let's get on with the show."

Falcon slowly removed the composite parts of the rifle from the padded cell in which it had been incarcerated. Piece by piece he assembled the weapon in a matter of seconds. At the end of the day, they were all the same irrespective of what model you use. A rifle can only be broken down into so many individual parts for quick re-assembly. The biggest concern would be to get the scope dead on parallel with the barrel; a minute fraction adrift would render the entire machine useless. He slid the scope gently into place along the upper sliders of the breach and felt it securely lock home with a comforting click. He studied the finished piece for a few seconds before being yelled at again by Gunther to get outside and set up the weapon.

They strode out of the back of the main house and behind one of the large barns. The view once more led down to the Tiber.

"We're roughly just less than a mile from the river as a guide so you set up whatever range you decided based on this morning's figures," advised Marco. "Once you find your mark, let us know and we can set up some specific targets for you to fine tune if need be."

There was an old hay cart which had been left in the field and started to show signs of decay through lack of use. Falcon decided to clear a space on its deck and placed the rifle on the bipod for support onto the cart. It meant he would have to stoop down a little while he made the mark but he did need a steady footing for him and the rifle if he was to accurately set the scope.

"You know, once I set this today, we can't break it down again otherwise the calibration will be off."

"Whatever you say Tony, you're the man now," replied Gunther. All five onlookers watched in silence as he set up his tools. "Don't you want to use the silencer?"

Falcon looked at the genius Gunther and thought he had found a flaw in this mentor.

"I will if you want me to miss. I'm sure you know how a silencer works Gunther; it slows down the bullet which means the trajectory won't be as flat. With that comes greater inaccuracy, more wind effects etcetera . . . etcetera. So, in answer to your question, no I won't."

Gunther seemed affronted by this and turned back into the house, quickly followed by Inga.

"He's a happy chappy today," joked the Englishman.

"I suggest most strongly Tony that you don't get on the wrong side of Gunther. Just do your job eh," replied Marco, still wanting to play the diplomat.

"Don't worry about me Marco, look I'm pissing my pants," he retorted sarcastically.

Falcon realised this was getting everybody nowhere. The Italian stopped talking and Falcon got about his work with more fervour than before. Micro adjustments with the scope, setting for seventeen hundred metres, that's near enough to the required distance he thought and wondered just how accurate his hosts were with their range advice. He scoured the river line for a suitable target and decided on a large tree over the opposite bank utilising the range finder. It was a little further than he needed but nothing to cause concern. If he could make his mark here, it would do fine for the object the following day. He readjusted the scope to the new range. He made no allowance for any wind effects that might occur and decided to take his first shot. He loaded the first shell casing into the breach of the Accuracy International rifle from the five round magazine and lowered himself almost passionately down onto the firearm. He spread his legs, virtually to an uncomfortable position, as he levelled his body and face behind the scope. Marco was looking through the finder scope at the tree Falcon had pointed out, to watch the projectile hit its mark.

Falcon was now in familiar territory. This was his domain. He felt his adrenalin start flushing through his veins as he took aim and sighted the cross hairs of the optical scope on his target. The Pine tree didn't stand a chance he thought as he caressed his finger tip around the trigger guard. Now he was set, the finger slipped inside the guard and onto the trigger. Slowly . . . slowly he squeezed, moving with surgical precision until BANG. The shot was away. There was clear surprise from behind but he remained focused on the scope to see if he could spot the spiralling lead shot hit its mark. It didn't but there was a telltale puff of earth approximately three metres to the left of it.

"Hell, was that what I thought it was Tony?" asked Marco.

"I guess that depends on what you were thinking about doesn't it?"

"See how far you were out though, and that's a stationary tree. What about a moving target, have you got it in you?"

Marco was testing the Englishman. He knew he had it in him, otherwise they wouldn't have sought his services, but he wondered if he could handle the job whilst flustered.

"You do the arithmetic old man. That's a fraction of a degree out, probably less than half a degree. Why not make yourself useful and do some praying that we can get this accurately set today. I suggest you don't get under my skin and let me do my job."

Clearly Marco knew he had hit a nerve. A professional never likes his quality being called into question, and Falcon demonstrated that even under these circumstances, he still wanted to ensure he could carry out the task as required, swiftly and accurately. Before he was expecting it, Marco heard the second shot away. That was even closer, now down to less than a metre.

"I surely hope we don't have a windy day tomorrow, otherwise this will all be a waste of time," said the Englishman as he again twiddled the adjustment screws on the scope. Time for him to pass a little worry back to Marco he thought.

A subdued Marco softly replied, "The weather is expected to be clear and no real wind expected tomorrow, although still cold, a bit like today. But that's only the weathermen guessing."

The third shot rang out in the valley, this time finding its mark in the tree. "That's my boy," exclaimed Falcon as he watched the bark fly off the tree as he kept his eye pressed to the sniper scope.

"Is that it done then Tony?"

"Hardly," he replied. That's the alignment or windage adjustment done, now we need to fine tune the elevation."

"Do you want some targets setting up?"

"Nope, I'll select something on the tree. That's easier now that we're almost there."

Again the sniper took aim and fired off another shot into the besieged pine, unable to defend itself against this onslaught of 8.59mm lead shots pummelling their way into its very soul. He chose the last point of entry as his precise target this time and was clearly honing in on the mark. This shot rattled into the tree less than twenty centimetres away on the vertical from the objective, still slightly low though. One more adjustment should do it he thought. He was as ever correct in such matters. The next shot sank into the tree adjacent to the mark. There were less than two inches between the two slugs and Falcon knew that even a machine would not be able to get closer consistency than that from this range, using such a relatively low calibre weapon.

He handed the rifle to Marco, "That's ready now, so treat it like a lady. Any knocks and it will be useless, understand, and don't be tempted to strip it down. It goes in the truck assembled like that."

"Yes sir," he replied walking away and back into the farm house.

Falcon was pleased with his relative success, but knew the witching hour was drawing ever nearer. He pondered as he trudged back into the building, with Francesco as always shadowing him, whether he would be able to shoot a good guy. That was not his usual modus operandi. Could he betray every ethos he worked and lived by for personal gain and save his Maria? His heart told him yes, that's why he was there, but it was competing with his brain which thought otherwise. He knew already he was in for yet another unsettled evening.

The conversation back inside the kitchen died as soon as the Englishman appeared through the doorway. Either they were talking about him or talking about something he wasn't to know, either way it was less than comfortable. He looked at the motley crew assembled before him, what a group. Hardened murderers, an apparently wealthy looking Italian who he thought had no real need to be mixed up in anything like this, and of course Francesco who probably had no real idea what he was fighting for, he was just added muscle.

"I guess that's me done, so is it back to the hotel for me?" asked Falcon, almost hoping it would be. Not for the regal lifestyle it offered but he could not comprehend spending the night with the terrorists.

"Francesco will run you back down and yes, I will take good care of the rifle," said Marco. "Francesco will collect you in the morning at around nine, I assume that's okay? You will need to get yourself in position a few hours earlier; the proceedings will start at around one p.m., so I suggest you bring a sandwich."

"I'll be ready. What about you, are you not coming back to town?"

"Don't worry about me; we have things to discuss here, things that don't concern you. See you tomorrow after your work is done. I shall call you some time to make sure everything is in place and let you know once they set out for the court."

Marco then nodded and Falcon knew it was time to leave. He turned without saying a word carrying his coat over his arm, and left the farm house. The return journey was eventless with the non communicable Francesco. Falcon tried to take some bearings as they drove but it was pointless. The night was already quickly drawing in and very soon they were just another vehicle in the hustle and bustle moving around the capital. A further fifty minutes passed once they crossed the outer ring road before they reached the hotel, and even then Francesco simply nodded and never spoke as Falcon climbed out of the Jeep.

It was only once he was alone, back in his room that the consequences of his involvement with the terrorists began to hit home with Falcon. Previously he was able to manipulate his conscience into the belief that his actions would be for the better good, somehow. For the first time since this began less than a week ago, he realised the reality. Could he really kill a champion of the people to save Maria? Would it even save Maria if he did, probably not? Would Maria be happy that he traded Ricci's life for hers, after all she was an Italian so probably thought very highly of Ricci herself? Lots of thoughts were now being generated but remained unanswered.

These people knew him and he knew them. Common sense dictated that they would not want him around after the job, he would be the only link back to the group, he and perhaps Maria. Falcon started to quiver and suddenly feel the cold, despite the overwhelming heat inside the suite compared to what it was outside. He needed to shower, try and cleanse his thoughts and make some sense of the entire situation. He left his clothes where they dropped and stepped into the oversized shower compartment and took a lengthy sprinkling of steamy hot water. He had no idea how long he bathed, but it certainly helped reduce some of the tension knots he was feeling in his neck and head. The only problem was that it didn't provide him with a solution. He dressed only in the complementary white bathrobe and paced once again slowly around the room. It was at times like these he wondered whether there was any merit in taking up smoking. So far in his life he had resisted that vice, but it wouldn't do him any more harm than the present danger he was in.

Somewhere in the room a cell phone broke the silence. Falcon knew instantly that it was his own phone and would surely be Brown, at least he hoped. He scoured the room to find the source; his clothes still littered the floor hindering the search. The coat which held the phone in its pocket was still located adjacent to the door of the suite. He pounced on the grey article and retrieved the phone.

"Hello," he gasped.

"Tony, Brown here. I take it you are alone."

"Of course, why? Surely you know that I trust you still have people here."

"We do, we're just not sure if anybody else is here as well. I suppose we'd better get down to business. Have you any idea what the deal is with Gunther and his crew yet?"

Falcon thought the question a little strange as he had already explained what he understood to be the plans back in London.

"I thought I told you all that, what's changed? Do you know something I don't?"

"Something's not right Tony, that's for sure. There's too much activity and too many people around Gunther for a simple hit. Are there any other targets they've spoken about? Any other jobs, anything at all?"

"I'm sure you heard it all, so why ask me?"

"We heard a lot of it, the transmission got a bit muffled for a while but we got most of it. We also know exactly where you've been. By the way I want the watch back when this is over, I've got to sign it back in." Brown knew this was a little light hearted humour and it was not that essential it be returned, but he sensed the tension in Falcon's voice and felt he needed relaxing.

"Oh, so no keep sake for me then. What if they kill me, you going to take it off a dead man?"

"Probably, at least we'll know where to find you. Now, was there anything untoward that you saw or heard today?"

Falcon tried to recount the day even though he knew the NSA and Duval would have far more detailed accounts of it than he had, even though he was the centrepiece.

"There's a woman with them, a right hard bitch if you ask me. Not sure what role she plays but I wouldn't want to cross her. She seems to have some pull in the group that's for sure." He paused a little while before adding, "Gunther says he wants to employ me after this job."

"So, you're already sending out resumes?"

"Get real James, he's pulling my chain, we both know he's probably going to pop me off as soon as the job's done. I know I'm the patsy here, so you've got to make sure I'm not."

Brown's speech tone turned a whole lot more serious now; his words were carefully chosen and spoken slowly and purposefully. "Tell me Tony, are you ready to take this shot? I mean, if it goes to the wire . . . will you be able to take it?"

Falcon allowed himself to fall backwards on the bed, looking blankly up at the ornate ceiling work. His eyes started to blur a little as the emotion of the whole affair took hold and water began emanating from his tear ducts, albeit only in small quantities, it showed a humane side to the assassin.

"I'm not sure," he said. "This is the first time in this thing I have to admit I'm not sure if I can take it. He's on our side fighting these bastards that are persecuting me. Can I do this for personal reasons? I always knew deep down that I should never get too involved in a personal thing. I tried to have rules you see, but with Maria I just lost them. She's my Achilles heel. I always thought that any relationship you needed to be able to walk away from in an instant, no notice, no warning and no regrets. Just walk and never look back. But I can't here. I just don't know what to do."

The fuzziness got more intense and the assassin needed to physically wipe his eyes as the water levels were about to flow over out of the eye sockets.

"Look Tony, if it was a bad guy, if you were working for me on this shout and he was a real bad guy, a nasty mother, from the church tower would you be able to make the shot with what you've got? Think hard now, is it possible? I know that if anyone can it would be you, but can YOU Tony make that shot?"

Falcon again thought this a strange question. He wiped his eyes and sat upright on the soft and bouncy bed, sinking deeper into the covers as he did so, shifting his weight.

"As long as the wind doesn't pick up a great deal or the heavy rains come in, I guess I could."

"You guess man!" hollered Brown down the phone. "You're the best in the world and I know you've hit targets further away than that. So you think really hard before I go on to the next phase. Can you hit the mark if you had to, forget all the other complications but can you do it?"

"Yes I can," he replied slowly and almost as forcefully.

There was a little sigh at the other end of the phone. "Good, I'm sure glad to hear that. Now Tony, I hope you're sitting down." There was another pause increasing the trepidation in the hotel suite. "We want you to take that shot."

"You what?" bolted back Falcon almost instantly. "Are you fucking crazy?"

"Calm down Tony. Duval has finally worked his magic with the attorney. He's explained everything, well not everything of course but everything he needs to know. He's prepared to be shot and he'll have a vest on so you make it a chest shot right. When he goes down his bodyguards will pull him straight into the building and sort him out. Then there will be sporadic news coverage about his condition which should give time for things to develop your end. At least we should see their plan unfold."

"It's insane. What if I miss the vest? What then?"

"If you miss the vest there'll be no need for the media to lie. It's all been explained, he knows the risks. This guy wants to be president some day. This publicity will take ten years off his campaign. Believe me, he'll be doing News-Week before you're back at your apartment. He'll be a bloody hero. Only rub is . . . you can't afford to miss."

"I can't believe this conversation. Up to five minutes ago I was thinking maybe you would be the one to put a slug in my brain. Everything's changed again."

"For the better though I feel. You wanted your way out, there it is. We're giving you the go ahead so now you don't need to fight with your conscience, just do what you do best."

Falcon's head was spinning. This had become so surreal all of a sudden, with an escape route that he hadn't even dared contemplate. Authority to take the shot was never even dreamt of as being an option.

"What about protection for me? What's your game plan?"

"We've already started spreading resources. It's difficult to physically stake out the place you were at today, as there's nowhere to hide, but we have got the Carabinieri going in there tomorrow morning early to stake it out. They'll go from the river so shouldn't be seen. They will provide the heavy artillery if it comes down to a dog fight. There will also be one of my guys with Ricci. Duval's operatives will be the vehicle tail on you so we see where they decide to take you tomorrow after the job. There will be a few cars spread along the route you took today so they won't look conspicuous as they change tails. Most importantly of all, the Carabinieri will also have their own marksman in a nearby vehicle keeping an eye on your back. If it looks as though this Francesco fellow is gonna pop you then we'll just take him out, no question."

Falcon was astonished at what had been put in place that afternoon in a matter of only a couple of hours. He was almost speechless, which was evident when he managed to fumble out his next sentence,

"You have a lot of bases covered there for sure. Let's hope it goes to plan."

"See how a watch can save your life Tony, neat gizmo eh? You take it easy this evening. We'll still be listening in case

Marco calls but chill out and be fresh for tomorrow. We've got you covered."

"So it would appear, catch you later . . . and . . . thanks."

"No problem brother," came back the reply from the American. "By the way, a small word of advice. Do us a favour, when you're next in the John, leave the watch on the bed or something, I thought you were kidding before."

Falcon laughed out loud and shook his head in disbelief. "You guys have some job, out."

He pressed the appropriate key on his cell and ended the call, lobbing the phone to his side. He fell back into the splendid softness of the bed covers feeling better than he had all week. Maybe, just maybe, this was now coming together and everybody could come out a winner he thought, except of course the bad apples.

Chapter 25

Falcon dined in his room that night, just in case Marco called; and he did. There was nothing great to discuss, more of a courtesy than anything else, in making sure the hired gun was primed and ready for the following days activity. Of course with his newly created verve he convinced the client he was firing on all cylinders and they agreed the pick up time the following day.

The Englishman slept well despite retiring to the bed early, he knew he needed to be fresh for the upcoming events, that meant no alcohol, not even at somebody else's expense. Brown's people were also good for their word and had him delivered by room service a padded envelope which contained the small hand gun as promised. It wasn't his usual weapon but might yet prove invaluable. It could be easily concealed using the ankle holster that came with it. He was not sure as to whether he would risk taking the weapon but it was certainly reassuring to know he had the option.

The morning chorus had already commenced in the grounds of the Villa Borghese before Falcon awoke. It was only seven o'clock and he had plenty of time but he thought it prudent to be fresh and ready. He arranged for breakfast again in the room as he showered. Today's breakfast was a substantially lighter affair, opting for the simple continental. He knew it might be a while before the next meal but the last thing he desired was to be lying in wait with a full stomach. Instead, he would take a little fruit from the room to see him through. This scenario was nothing new to Falcon, and in reality this was probably the most civilised preparations he had ever been allowed to make on the day of a hit. It was just the overall circumstances that soured the moment. Still, hopefully at the end of the day he would have all the necessary reassurances that Maria would be left alone, he would be left alone and he would be substantially richer. However at the back of the mind was the doubt that it would be as simple as that with these people. Still there was Duval and Brown with their assault teams on stand by. He thought about the Carabinieri stakeout team behind the farm, not being able to enjoy the same preparations as he could.

At around quarter to nine the Englishman decided the time was upon him. He could now sense the perspiration levels start to build up, nervous tension starting to rise as the muscles around his torso began tightening. The knot in the stomach started to appear but he fought it. He stopped at the large wall mirror before he left the room and took a long hard look at himself before he started speaking. "It's for Maria, you know you can do it sunshine," he spoke in a hushed tone even though there was nobody else around. "Let's go and nail these bastards!" With that, he was gone and straight outside to await his taxi driver. To his surprise Francesco was already there and once again in the black Jeep.

"Morning Francesco," he said as he ascended the kick boards of the truck and climbed into the cockpit and closed the door.

Francesco simply nodded and smiled. Then he put the car into gear, pushed the throttle and moved off from the hotel with little regard to any traffic that was behind as he did so.

"That could have been an interesting start to the day," said Falcon knowing he wouldn't get any reaction from his apparently mute chauffeur.

"I take it we have the rifle?" asked the gunman wondering whether that would get a response. Again Francesco looked over at him and simply smiled.

"This is going to be a long day," he muttered under his breath. That again brought no reaction from the driver. He was concentrating so intently on his weaving technique through the Roman morning traffic. Falcon knew it was to be a busy day in town so was prepared not to be surprised if Francesco adopted any unusual routing. He had watched the local TV news in his room and had already seen Mr. Ricci this morning in all his glory. He was certainly the showman

Brown played him out to be. Today's trial was big news and there was plenty of media coverage.

The obvious way to the church was to back track through their escape route, that way they would avoid any police checks or road blocks as they neared the court house. Luckily the Italian had already worked this out and they made their destination overlooking the turkey shoot well before ten o'clock. Francesco swung open the rear door of the Jeep, pulled back a large picnic style blanket and revealed the weapon which had been stored in the back of the jeep on numerous plush sheets and blankets so it had an easy ride. It was the Englishman's turn to simply nod his approval.

He removed the weapon carefully, gave it a thorough looking at, up and down, and then pointed to the church. They closed the Jeep's door and set off inside the church yard to the vantage point in the tower.

After climbing the stone steps, Falcon set the gun, still deciding to use the bipod that was still affixed to the barrel, on top of the tower wall. This was necessary so he could develop a suitable comfort position to take the shot. It would be best if he could lie down but that was not going to be practical from here, so the next best thing would be to be able to stand almost upright. He checked his posture and felt that it could easily be achieved if he chose one of the higher parts of the castellated walls. He lined up the weapon and pressed his eye to the scope just to get the feel of the objective site. This was now real. He surveyed the area through the highly powerful rifle scope and there was a lot of police activity. Still, they should be outside the zone of scrutiny from where they were, so as long as the escape route was clear, they should be fine.

He removed Marco's telephone from his coat pocket and set it on the ground. Now it was just a waiting game. He and Francesco would be up in the tower for several hours, not speaking, getting cold just waiting for the call. Marco had agreed to call when Ricci was en route and if he could, give him pre-warning as the target was about to arrive.

Francesco turned out to be a little better than Falcon had given him credit for, after all he had the foresight to bring a flask of coffee which they could share, which was more than he had. It was well received as the winter chills set around the church tower. Fortunately the wind had not picked up since the previous day, so there was no additional complication there, but he was still unable to get any conversation out of his voiceless Italian comrade. The shooter was sincerely hoping that when the call came, Francesco would be by his side and not behind, as that would be unnerving to say the least.

Periodically he would pick up the rifle and assess his target zone, only to reveal the ever increasing presence of the security forces. Road blocks were clearly now being set up and the armed guards much more visible. Still several hours to go . . .

Chapter 26

There was a nine man crew donning their working gear ready for the operation, although man would be an inaccuracy since the crew actually comprised six men and three women. There was no apparent dress code for this rag tag mob although some were dressed in black trousers and shirts and all had available black balaclavas as part of their attire. The black suits would have passed for any Special Forces unit from most militarised nations, but they were not. This was a special force of a different kind. The leader of this motley crew was one Gunther Menzies, notable terrorist wanted in several states and now on the loose in Italy. Gunther made sure his crew meticulously checked and rechecked all of their equipment before loading it into their respective vehicles.

The squad was heavily armed with a mixture of hand guns and sub machine guns. They even sported between them numerous hand grenades along with an explosives specialist armed with several kilos of C4 plastic explosives. They were certainly on a mission for sure. Between the crew was one small lorry around seven and a half tonne size and two Fiat panel vans. The truck was white and detailed the hirer from whom it had been rented for a month. The two vans however were different. One was totally unmarked and in blue, the other was also white but sported the signage of a specialist local tyre repairer.

"Now people," started Gunther. "this is a very important day for us all. It will change your lives . . . for ever. Be aware of that, and if you're not sure you're ready for that change then speak now."

Nobody would dare speak out at such a time. They all knew of Gunther's quest for undying loyalty. Anyone who was unsure and owned up would very quickly find themselves either in an unmarked grave out in the woods or at the bottom of the Tiber. No, this crew had been checked before and all were game.

"We know the route the target will be taking. So, when we hit, we hit hard. We've been over this dozens of times people and there's no time for errors. Are we all clear on that?"

A muffled crescendo of agreement with Gunther's sentiments arose around the enclosure.

"We hit the truck at around two fifteen so make sure your watches are all accurate. We need our truck in place just as soon as the courier is stopped and we get the back doors open. Now, if anybody gets in your way, don't hesitate. You take them out, CLEAR." he shouted.

Again nods of agreement.

"Now for one last time, Inga will go over the details so be sure you are all clear. Inga."

Inga pointed to the paper plan that was taped to the wall of the enclosure where the crew was gathered.

"The truck will leave the airport at around one o'clock this afternoon. It won't be breaking any speed records so we expect it to get into the city where we can track it somewhere around two o'clock. The route should take it along the autostrada E-80 which some of you know as the Roma—Fiumicino road. Near the end of this road we believe it will head north along Via le Isacco Newton. Our point of interception will be the underpass beneath Via Portuensa, approximately two kilometres after leaving the autostrada." Inga relayed the script like a seasoned professor, well versed in her subject, and delivered it with authority. All eyes and ears were attentive on her delivery.

"Karl, what's your role?" she snapped as she turned to one of the male operatives

"I follow the courier van as soon as we pick up its trail then I drift my van into the middle of the road just before the exit slip off Isacco Newton and have a break down to hold up any traffic behind," he replied, having done his homework.

"Very good," replied Inga, "but what else?"

"To make sure the side door is facing north when I turn the vehicle."

"Very good Karl. That will give you just a bit more time to get the passengers out, every second counts. I shall be under the bridge with the truck and white van. As soon as we see the courier approaching we throw the stinger across the road and take out the tyres. Remember there will also be an escort vehicle, probably only one and probably police and it will be behind the courier. You may have no choice but to eliminate them so do not hesitate, otherwise it will be you lying in the road. That's why positioning of your vehicle will be key to the success here Karl. We'll deal with the courier truck at the front end."

Gunther listened in admiration to his dedicated team reviewing final preparations yet again as though this was some exciting adventure. In a way it was but it was also deadly. They might never come back, any of them. There were still unknowns out there that could not be accounted for.

"How much time do we think we really have before back up arrives?" asked Karl.

"You will have sufficient so long as we're not sloppy," replied Gunther with a cold steely gaze in Karl's direction. "Just have a little faith. There'll be no shortage of chaos today and everybody will be running around like headless chickens."

The undercover Carabinieri stake out team had no idea about the vehicles currently being made battle ready within the barn. Neither did they have any idea of how many people were actually present. This aspect of their detection only became apparent as the vehicles rolled out of the farm outbuildings on the predetermined schedules that had been set. The truck was to go first shortly followed by the blue van. The blue van would wait on a side road off the autostrada opposite the airport and tail the courier truck back into the city, relaying to the advance party the route as it developed. Meanwhile the truck would go and simulate its breakdown beneath the underpass. Shortly afterwards, the tyre repairer would follow suit such that he was in position ahead of the courier truck. Unfortunately for the observing authorities this was certainly an unexpected turn of events.

When Brown got the news about the vehicle movements it was already after midday. He couldn't contact Falcon as he was already set up in his own poaching perch awaiting the arrival of the State Prosecutor. Even if he could, he was convinced Falcon had no idea what was going on, otherwise surely he would have said so, rather than set himself up like that. No one could make a move on the farm as there was no cause to do so yet and it would blow the surveillance operation wide open. The Special Forces operatives decided though to try and edge closer to the premises in readiness for anything that might imminently erupt.

Brown requested Duval to speak with the locals and see if they had any vehicles in the area that could possibly try and locate one of Gunther's vehicles, but it was a very long shot. Almost every available unit would be tied up for the day on the protection requirements for the forthcoming trial. This was Italy's biggest priority for the coming days at least, as many feared the mobsters would never see the inside of a court room, no matter how secure a facility had been created.

Brown quizzed the local officials about the movements of any other senior dignitaries, any politicians visiting Rome today but there was nothing. They were powerless for now to do anything, other than react once it started to unfold. Brown's and Duval's own direct resources were busy looking out for Falcon, so they couldn't possibly be relocated, and besides zero hour was fast approaching for the arrival of Mr. Salvatore Ricci. The whole area was already a media frenzy, probably just how the attorney liked it. There was going to be some votes won this afternoon for sure.

Brown despised the uncertainty that was unfolding yet he was powerless. All the planning, all the scheming and double dealing could amount to nothing. Was Falcon just one assault on the famed prosecutor and his cause, perhaps a side show whilst Gunther was to spearhead a full on attack. Had Falcon been compromised? Brown's head was spinning with possibilities but the bottom line was he just did not know. He was now the one to sit biting on the fingernails until events dictated his next move.

Chapter 27

Time was dragging immeasurably for Falcon. No entertainment whatsoever and no interaction with his associate in the isolated church tower. Boredom interspersed with flashes of how he was to pull off this coup this afternoon. He was to pretend to kill a guy from over a mile away. He needed to pull off an illusion that would have even mystified the great Harry Houdini. The chances were, in truth slim, too many variables outside his control, but Falcon knew he had no choice. Everybody had their backsides in a sling. Brown could wipe him out in an instant if he felt his own operations had been compromised. Gunther was highly likely to burn him after the operation. Whether this was by simply shooting him in the back of the head when the deed was done or whether he was to be the patsy for the assassination on Ricci was not known; but all were credible possible alternatives.

His throat fluctuated from desert dryness to severe salivation. His internal emotions were in freefall. The only solution was still, even now at the eleventh hour, to try and go with the plot as hatched by his NSA friends. Perhaps they had a motive of their own in risking Ricci and setting up Falcon. Unlikely, but he knew the pool in which he had swum in recent years, so most things wouldn't surprise him. In fact, the only thing that had surprised him was the knowledge Gunther and his associates had on himself and Maria.

Falcon munched his way through his fruit to help pass the time, exchanging an apple with his Italian friend for a coffee. Waiting, that's all he could do, wait. Marco was to call when the time was right but that call was a long time in coming. The air was still and cold today but at least visibility was excellent. Falcon repeatedly clasped his hands together as he exhaled sporadically into them for warmth. This was more nervous tension than a real need for warmth, his thermal gloves saw to that. If nothing else, the master craftsman knew that the main tools of his trade were his fingers, they needed the touch of a surgeon so they must be kept pristine and ready for immediate action.

Finally Falcon's mobile phone rang out, breaking the usually unnatural silence in the church tower. Unnatural because this was Rome, the capital city of life, it should not be so still. It was Marco of course, who else. Not even a wrong number had graced the cell phone since it had been in the Englishman's possession. Francesco glared at Falcon wondering whether he was going to answer or not. Sensing the concern he allowed it to ring a couple more times, just for sport, before taking the call.

"Hello again Tony," came the suave and elegant voice of the Italian. In another life he could have been a movie star, unfortunately it was this life which was of more immediate concern.

"I trust everything is in place?"

"Everything's set to go here Marco. The only thing missing is the mark. It's a pity you couldn't join us, we're having a ball."

Marco allowed the Englishman his finite moment of humour before starting again. "Glad to hear it old boy. Now Salvatore Ricci has set off from his offices, he should be there in around thirty minutes which takes it to around two o'clock. As we get nearer, I'll fill you in on current progress but you just make sure you're ready."

"Marco . . . I am ready, alright. I just want to get the hell out of here and on my way. You worry about that, not the shot; I'll take that on, that's my responsibility." Falcon's uneasiness made it difficult for him to conceal his inner frustrations.

"Glad to see your revitalised interest in our project Tony, it's very refreshing."

"It's all to do with focus. That's my control strategy, everything else gets shut out. I can't focus on a job that my hearts not in. We're past that stage now. I've agreed to do the job so let's just get on with it without the mindless distractions."

"Right then, I'll see you later at the farm. Speak to you shortly and . . . don't miss."

Marco terminated the call before Falcon could even think of a reply, never mind blurting one out. He was sure it was more of a ruse. He wondered whether Marco, as an Italian, really wanted Ricci out of the way or whether he was just playing along with Gunther's games. The whole set up was riddled with doubts. He sought comfort in the fact that Brown's people were listening to most of the conversation, at least he did not feel fully alone. Soon he would, hopefully, be back with Maria as though nothing had happened, but as he sat in that church tower he knew life could never be the same again.

The sniper started to caress his rifle, gently wiping it with his gloved hand as though he were caressing a baby. Tender and gentle he stroked it and checked it for several minutes; then a look over the tower wall at the activity in the kill zone. There was lots of it. The street had of course been cordoned off and throngs of journalists and media crews were penned in behind secondary crowd barriers that had been erected across part of the street. Police activity was now very prevalent and the sole chopper circled above the city, centring on the court house. Of course they could not be seen in their vantage point by the chopper due to the roof over their heads, but it could be an issue when they made their escape. That was a problem for later. It was time to get prepared.

He again checked over the rifle, checked there was a shot in the breach and made sure the scope was still in focus on the court steps. There would not be a great deal of time to take the shot although everybody knew Ricci would want at least a few photographs taken by the media for his news file. This was going to be one of the biggest days of his life and he would want to milk it for all that it was worth.

The cell in Falcon's jacket rang again. He stood the rifle against the wall of the tower as he removed the phone from his jacket pocket.

"Less than five minutes and he'll be there. Time to make ready Tony, good hunting."

That was it. No further exchange, no banter, no antagonism. A cold sharp message; it was time.

The Englishman's heart started racing. He was in unknown territory and had no idea how the next few minutes, let alone few hours or days, was going to unfold. He removed his gloves and carefully ensured they were returned to his pocket. Then, like a skilled craftsman, he laid his most precious tool delicately, and with pride, out onto the parapet of the tower and knelt down before it. It was almost prayer like although there was likely to be little forgiveness from any quarter if this went wrong. This could also be the worst moment of his life. It made the time in Africa seem a picnic now as it was so long ago. The pains and haunting from that escapade started to flood back to his mind. What a time to start thinking all the bad stuff he thought. He tried to focus his mind on the good side of his life: his beloved Maria, his home in the mountains, his passion for fine wine and skiing. This helped but could still not detract him from the real significance of what he was about to undertake. There were lots of people's lives at stake now and their fate could be decided in the next couple of minutes.

He sensed where Francesco was, which fortunately was to his left. At least he could be seen most of the time and Falcon would not have the worry of trying to make the shot, with what could be his own assassin standing right behind him.

"Now don't move an inch," said Falcon to his Italian cohort. "I don't need any distractions whatsoever, so just stay right where you are."

He was sure this was essentially falling on deaf ears due to the language barrier, but he felt Francesco got the message, ably assisted by the hand gestures from the Englishman.

Falcon was now pressing his cheek to the butt of the rifle. His right hand enveloped the trigger guard as he zeroed in the scope to the flurry of activity that was unfolding on the court steps. People were now being ushered and pushed back in the press area and various barriers were being repositioned, or opened across the road, due to the impending arrival of the prosecutor. The police presence, both visible and invariably under cover, was suddenly heightened. Several military style dressed officers paraded the vicinity with their canine friends looking hungry for a kill of their own.

The sudden flurry of exploding flashes of light were the tell tale sign that the paparazzi and other members of the Italian media circus had spotted the arrival of Ricci's car. It was like a November the fifth display as the black chauffeur driven vehicle of the state prosecutor slowly pulled alongside the court house. The car remained stationary for a few seconds amid the unrelenting flashing lights, but for Ricci the showman, this was part of the overall allure. He loved it and as predicted he was going to milk it. Falcon imagined that at this very moment Ricci was inside the car with his personal stylist ensuring every hair was in place ready to meet his public. The truth was that Ricci was himself ensuring his Kevlar vest was fitted correctly and not evident.

Falcon watched the activity intently through the scope of the rifle. A sudden flurry of what were most likely protection officers or body guards sprang into the steps forming a secure cordon for the prosecutor as his door was opened and he stepped out into the lime light. He waved to the media as he rose from the car and proceeded up the steps in a most controlled manner for a man that was about to be shot. Francesco never took his eyes off Falcon once he knew the stage was set and the Englishman could feel his penetrating gaze, but right now he could not say a thing. He focused on the task at hand. Falcon's forefinger took its place on the trigger exerting a minute fraction of pressure, but enough for the seasoned hand to know it was on the tools and ready to get to work. Watching through the scope as Ricci slowly turned to face the publicity Falcon drew a breath then held it. The trigger finger stretched one last time and came back to rest in the firing position. Ricci had fully turned and started to raise his arm to the crowds as Falcon controlled his breathing and squeezed ever so gently on the trigger in an effortless motion, releasing the lead assassin on its lengthy journey through the Roman skies. The thunderous crack was deafening in the confines of the overhead roof and startled the Italian but Falcon remained transfixed on his subject. The couple of seconds once more seemed an eternity but he knew the bullet would land before the shot was heard at the receiving end. Ricci stood waving like a famous rock star to his adorning fans, as the lead projectile pierced effortlessly through the designer suit, purchased especially for this trial, and into the Kevlar jacket. The impact and momentum lifted the attorney off his feet and backwards a couple of metres. The sheer pain and shrill stabbing he felt as the bullet hit home made him sure the jacket had not worked and he came crashing down to the ground with an almighty squeal of pain. The bodyguards instantly realised that he had been shot and pounced around him dragging him backwards into the building just as they had planned dozens of times in training. The sudden surge in police activity was tremendous and looked in total disarray. Officers and combatants in different forms and colours of uniform were running seemingly haphazardly in all directions. Guns were drawn by everybody who seemed to be carrying one, screams were coming from the media section from many female journalists, but many just kept the cameras rolling. The flashlights started popping furiously once more as everybody ducked and dived for cover, not knowing if anything else would happen. Would there be another shot?

Reporters scrambling for live news feeds to announce the assassination, or at least shooting, of their most eminent politician. The country would be in immediate shock as this was the man of the common people. To most Italians, this would be their JFK, and it would hurt.

Behind the closed doors and away from the melee outside the courthouse, Ricci was still writhing in agony. The searing pains in his chest were crippling and despite reassurances from his aides that he had not been shot, it sure as hell felt so. They ripped open his crystal white shirt to reveal the Kevlar vest and the compacted lead slug mushroom it retained. The assistants and medical staff rushed to remove the vest and try and comfort Ricci in his pain. On removal, a huge bright red patch was revealed on his chest, in the heart area, which had already started to change colour as bruises were forming almost instantly. The doctors checked him over and advised he had what appeared to be a couple of broken ribs, hence the pain. His vital signs were checked and predictably the pulse and heart rate were both racing.

Relieved at not physically having the bullet penetrate his torso, the psychological pain eased, however there was no mistaking the fact that a couple of broken ribs probably hurt just as much as a bullet. The doctors insisted that he go immediately to hospital and this was to be under a massive security blanket. Ricci's security staff, only those closest to him, actually knew what was to happen, told the entourage that he must go to the hospital out the front door and be fully covered with the sheet over his face on the stretcher. It was essential that nobody saw him. The attorney was given a shot of morphine to help quell the pain and reduce his squirming.

It was decided he would be put on a rigid stretcher to help contain him as he was revealed, shrouded, to the outside world. The media needed to transmit that he had, in fact, apparently been assassinated. There would be no formal announcements as he would be rushed away, the media could make their own assessments in that regard. That way he could never be accused of duping the media in the future when his bitter rivals turned on his political ambitions. After ten minutes or so inside the building, the morphine had started to work on the prosecutor and it was felt a good opportunity to get him out and under heavy security into the hospital.

Ricci was covered with the sheet as he closed his eyes and tried to dream away the pain. He knew it was time to be still but despite the stabbing pains still circulating his chest cavity, he marvelled at his own performance today, and even more so felt the self satisfaction at having played a part directly in the capture of some rather dangerous people. It would turn out to be a good day after all. The media frenzy was still there as the doors swung open and the awaiting ambulance was readied at the foot of the steps. The motionless sarcophagus was swiftly carried down the stairs and into the waiting ambulance. Only the doctors that were present inside the building were allowed in the back with a couple of security guards.

The on looking reporters were still in turmoil and the hordes were shouting questions wildly at the entourage of security personnel and staff surrounding the stretcher, yet in reality it was highly unlikely that any would ever get an answer. The rear doors of the ambulance were slammed shut and it sped away with what was one extremely large police escort. Now police activity was immense across that part of the city. Police cars were running everywhere cordoning off streets to try and give the ambulance a clear run to the hospital. There were outriders everywhere clearing a path. Police cars with sirens travelling side by side clearing the way, and back at the court house the traffic was just the same. Cars were moving every which way, the police helicopter making endless sweeps across the area at low level and police and Carabinieri officers starting to roam out away from the court building. Even a few blocks away police cars were still being heard streaming towards the incident zone. The city had never before seen such activity in a single act.

Falcon watched part of this drama unfold but knew he could not hang around for long. Once he saw Ricci take the shot, he remained as focused as he could to see if there was any blood but was unable to do so. The dark suit would have hidden it, at least in the initial stages. But he knew the attorney certainly played his part to the full. If he was still alive, and right now that was a big if for the Englishman to contemplate, he would be in a great deal of pain for sure. Once Ricci had been dragged into the court house and the doors closed it was time to depart.

Falcon turned to Francesco who was still gawping at the Englishman in awe. He was a good testament to the success of the shot and would be more than capable of adding credibility to the media coverage whilst the next few hours unfolded.

"Come on," screamed Falcon, "time to move."

Francesco snapped out of his trance and regained focus. They hurried down the tower steps and, just as planned Falcon gave the rifle a wipe then dropped it down the well. As long as they don't work out where the shot came from he should have a bit of a start. The pair then made it back to the Jeep and swiftly set off along the route they had selected previously. Francesco revved and spun the Jeep around the narrow streets like a seasoned rally driver knowing every little twist and turn bouncing his English colleague from side to side as they went. Suddenly the vehicle stopped as it pulled along side an extremely plain looking white Fiat Grande Punto.

Francesco stopped the engine and jumped out, signalling to Falcon to do the same. He locked the vehicle and produced from his pocket the keys for the Fiat. Falcon was a little bewildered at first but realised they must have taken on board his suggestion. Somewhat impressed by his Italian mute Falcon started to believe he may yet see this day out. He climbed into the somewhat smaller vehicle, patting his ankle as he did so to ensure his comforting pistol was still with him. He was glad he decided to bring it after all; surely it was better to have it and be caught than to need it and not have a chance. That was the logic that went into the decision.

The pair pulled away from the Jeep and continued on its way. This time a lot more sedately as it wound its way around the narrow streets. There was no other traffic in the vicinity. Probably the residents were either down at the court house or watching up close on TV the local drama as it unfolded. The crescendo of sirens was very evident as the pair drove back to the farm. As they left the narrow streets and found their way onto more major roads, the disturbed traffic was highly evident. The authorities flying here and there taking precedence over other road users, was having a profound influence on the rest of the traffic. It was utter chaos.

Chapter 28

The armoured truck left the airport as planned, and to the schedule as outlined by Gunther, to within a couple of minutes, followed as anticipated by a lone police escort. Nobody ever questioned where Gunther got his information. Some of the crew he was working with here had previous operational experience with the German, what they did know was to appreciate the usual accuracy of his information. He had a way of getting things out of people, finding their weak spots and subsequently exploiting them. Some never even realised what they were getting into. Inga was herself not destined for a life of terrorism. She was well educated, from a good family but unfortunately her previous career as a PA to a very prominent industrialist whose empire had been set as a target for Gunther's campaigns, meant she would inevitably cross his path. Her fate had been set and nothing she could do would change that. She fell for the German's charms and ultimately betrayed her own position of trust for her employer, leading to his ultimate departure from this life. Once the deed was done, she had been so transformed by the German's idealistic views and attracted to his ways of expressing them; she never showed any remorse for her sins. She had quickly become just as cold as her mentor and the mutual attraction had remained between the pair ever since, although never as lovers solely professional mutual respect.

The blue van had, as ordered, been laying in wait near to the airport exit to pick up the tail of the target vehicle. The van with its two front seat occupants casually drifted onto the autostrada several vehicles behind the object truck and contacted their leaders advising them that it was on the move. The co driver traced her finger along a road map which had been highlighted with the planned route of the armoured truck to highlight any changes that were suddenly experienced that would need to be relayed back to the team at the underpass. It was meticulously planned and not anticipated

340

to change, but there were always acts of God that could not be anticipated.

Gunther had remained at large for so long due to his planning and his cunning so he was not anticipating any surprises, but always remained aware of their potential arrival.

The traffic was busy, although it was always is in and around Rome. It was easy for the truck to simply sit back and follow their prey in accordance with their instructions. The two occupants were in uniform with the all black attire but the balaclavas were not being used, not yet. The pair would surely have attracted attention in standing traffic had they been worn. These were reserved by all players for the moment they exposed themselves and their artillery to the waiting world. Nobody knew what cameras would exist, CCTV, passers by, mobile telephones and even tourists. Cameras were everywhere so the face covering was essential. Constant communication from the blue van to the squad's commanders was maintained in order that schedules could be refined for the setting up of the broken down vehicle at the underpass to allow for slight changes in timing due to the traffic being heavier, or even lighter, than expected. The last thing that the crew would want was to be positioned there for any length of time before the arrival of the target vehicles, attracting unnecessary attention.

It was time. Gunther made the decision to set down the white lorry and jumped in with Inga. He drove steadily along his prescribed route as planned having advised his colleagues to start taking their position behind the police escort as the assault time was nearing. The blue van commenced a steady climb through the little amount of traffic it had allowed to build between it and the object vehicles, but nothing that made it stand out, drifting steadily in and out of the centre lane maintaining constant visual contact.

Gunther and Inga did not speak to one another as he slowly manoeuvred the truck around the infernal Italian traffic. He hated traffic of this magnitude, he felt claustrophobic due to its very nature of entrapment should he need to

escape in a hurry. He preferred open assignments but this
one was different, a little more unusual than most he had
undertaken. This was not for a greater cause; this was all his
own planning so he had to go with it. His hands were getting clammy as he laboured with the impatient Italian drivers who fervently seemed to believe that honking horns and
waving hands would have a similar effect as Moses did with
the Red Sea. Unfortunately for them it did not and Gunther
was not in the least concerned with who he might be upset-
ting to his rear. Despite his anxiety at the traffic tightness, he
still had a plan and would stick to it like a true professional.
The only conversation within the vehicle was the messages
relayed between the three terrorist transports. It was all going like clockwork.

Inga got the regular news-feed from the blue van regarding
its position and it would be very soon time for them to com-
mence with their partial road block. Too early would cause
such a traffic back up the target vehicle might re-route at the
last minute, so this was essentially the most difficult aspect
of the whole plan, the timing. Gunther slowly hauled his vehicle onto the slipway for the Via le Isacco Newton and joined
into another chaotic traffic stream. His size helped his vehicle
nudge its way into the inside lane. Fortunately he would not
have too far to travel to the underpass and at least the traffic,
although dense, was still free flowing. Indications were that
the object vehicles and their support truck were only around
fifteen minutes away. It was now time to get the tyre repair
truck with its additional crew into motion. It had been parked
up a few blocks away monitoring the relative movements of
the terrorists' vehicles, lying in wait for its own call to battle.
The estimate was of the order of ten minutes or so to be at the
breakdown site, but if all went well this would put the white
van ahead of the targets. The call came and it too set off and
joined the traffic tracing the route Gunther had meticulously
followed only a few minutes previously.

The truck of Gunther and Inga came to a grinding and
juddering halt beneath the underpass and pulled over to the

road side as though the vehicle were experiencing a problem. This met with even further honking of horns and irate Italian gesticulating, all of which the pair were of course oblivious to. They went around to the near side of the truck and Gunther made out he was on his cell phone whilst pointing furiously at his front tyre for visual effect to passers-by. It was merely confirmation to the tyre repairer he was in preliminary position.

The blue van placed himself behind the police escort and needed to stay there as long as possible for now. Once he got onto Via le Isacco Newton he would have to stalk his prey closely not permitting any other vehicles to get in between them, as this would provide severe and unnecessary complications. The driver's focus was intense as his greasy palms slid around the plastic covered steering wheel. It was another hot and humid day in Rome, humidity fuelled by vehicular frustration by all local inhabitants. The cheap van that had been hired for the job was not full of luxuries, such as adequate air conditioning, compounding the build up of stress as the assault neared its climax.

The traffic was still steadily flowing past Gunther's truck, albeit a little slower as the onlookers tried to catch a glimpse of the driver's misfortune. The tyre repairer was there ready for action but the personnel remaining generally out of sight from curious passers by. The rubber-neckers slowed the traffic themselves which could be to the advantage of the terrorists as the armoured truck approached. They had the call from Karl that the convoy was exiting onto Via le Isacco Newton. This was it. Gunther shouted to the crew waiting inside the tyre truck to make ready and the tyre bursting stinger was already out of the van and inconspicuously between the two vehicles awaiting the deployment order.

Karl was doing a fine job stalking the police escort and the armoured car. It was now time for Gunther to stem the traffic flow a little further. The mechanic from the tyre truck stood in front of Gunther's truck and so he could be clearly seen by the slowing oncoming traffic, edged the truck out into the inner lane. This was much to the great consternation of the furious drivers who in their fancy Italian vehicles would be no match in an impact competition with the truck, yet the purpose was simple. It reduced traffic flow now to a single lane which could be much more easily controlled. Suddenly the truck came again to a grinding halt. Vehicles braked even more sharply from behind and the crescendo of different tones of car horns was deafening. Vehicles crept past, ranting, raving and profusely swearing in several cases staring straight into the cockpit of the German's vehicle. He was alone for now as Inga was outside still behind the white van. The mechanic waved his arms in pretend disgust as he looked bewildered at the sudden collapse of the truck yet again.

The targets were seconds away now, edging closer to their destiny. The occupants of the white van donned their balaclavas and fighting equipment and just waited for the signal. Then it came, like a thunderbolt smashing into the side panels of the truck.

"GO GO GO," were the cries from outside.

Simultaneously the stinger was deployed, a matter of inches in front of the armoured car as it too scuttled past the mêlée that had been contrived. The distinctive sound of the two front tyres popping on the vehicle was well received as it veered off to the right with the sudden loss of steering control. Fortunately the speed did not send it out of control but the sudden onset of the ensuing assault took both driver and mate by surprise.

The blue van was now at the back of the commotion and it too turned sideways as ordered, blocking further vehicular movement but also allowing its own task force of a further five combatants in all to disembark with strike force speed.

From the front one operative smashed a chunk of plastic explosives into a pat and stuck it to the front of the windscreen. This was followed by the placing of a radio controlled detonator within the explosive which clearly startled the drivers simply with the speed of the activity from the attackers as their truck lay momentarily paralysed. Weapons of a varying nature were now pointing at the truck with several shots being fired by Gunther at the door and window simply for effect. He knew they would be bullet proof but wanted to show there was no messing about here. He shouted they had only five seconds to get out of the truck before they blew it up along with its occupants.

Meanwhile the police vehicle had come to realise there was a problem, but those valuable few seconds of disorientation gave Karl all the time he needed for his people to be in place. Without care two of the crew opened fire with automatic weapons peppering the police vehicle as its occupants tried in vain to escape from the rain of lead they were now suffering. Unfortunately that would not be possible, for them there would be no escape. No time for calling for back up or any last farewells, the two police officers ended their lives in a hail of murderous cowardly bullets on the Via le Isacco Newton. Confusion reigned behind as the now stationary traffic began to realise something more sinister was taking place. Karl rallied a salvo into the vehicle that was right behind his truck as a warning and the startled driver jumped out of sight beneath his dashboard as his windscreen shattered into millions of tiny shimmering glass crystals, showering him as he lay uncomfortably wishing he was somewhere else right now.

The commotion at the rear would buy a little time and the race was now on to get the drivers out of the truck. The explosives operative held up his transmitter in plain view of the panic stricken drivers whilst Gunther could be clearly seen counting down with his fingers from five. These drivers would be unarmed and underpaid for this so would be unlikely to die for a cause that was not theirs. As Gunther reached the count of one the doors flew open and two screaming armoured truck drivers leapt from their potential casket. Their hands were held high above their heads as they were ushered muttering and pleading past Gunther by two others from the crew to the side of the road, where they were mercilessly beaten around the back of the head with a weapon butt rendering them unconscious. At least that would be better than them dying.

The explosives were removed from the windscreen and swiftly replaced on the rear doors of the truck. Everybody stepped aside and sought cover away from the blast as the plastic explosives were detonated in a display of short term pyrotechnics. As the smoke cleared it revealed through the mist that the rear door had successfully been penetrated. The door was yanked open to reveal a multitude of boxes and cases.

"Take all we can," yelled Gunther. "Karl, make sure there's no heroes back there."

Karl was still at the blue van and once again let a wild burst of gunfire loose at random into the throng of cars that was now spewed in all directions and orientations across the road. They could go nowhere so it was nothing more than a turkey shoot.

"Nobody needs to get hurt," he shouted, "just stay down."

Gunther opened the rear roller doors of the white truck as the rest of the crew began removing boxes of various sizes and vastly differing weights from the armoured car. A series of roller conveyors, only a metre or so long each with drop down legs were pulled out of the truck. These had been fabricated to be the same height as the truck to facilitate speedy loading. It would not be pretty but certainly effective. Two operatives worked the armoured car placing the booty onto the first set of rollers. Others moved them along the rollers, from one to another as they turned through ninety degrees, then a third up into the truck. There were two more men in the truck removing from the conveyors and throwing as far back into the truck as possible.

"Move it . . . move it," shouted Gunther. "We're losing valuable seconds here."

He got back into the truck and started the engine so it was ready to roll as soon as loaded. Meanwhile the other two vehicles that had been used were having themselves a dousing of petrol as they were to be left behind. That would not only help eliminate as much forensic evidence as possible but would also delay any clearing of the road or possible heroes following on. But all was not to plan.

A solitary passing patrol car passing on the opposite carriageway saw what was happening and threw its sirens into action as it braked sharply and pulled over to the roadside opposite. The two officers jumped out and started firing at the robbers. A hail of bullets were exchanging whilst the robbers were still trying to work on clearing out of the truck. Cars were screeching to a halt and running into one another on the opposite carriageway as the gunfight unfolded. The police officers were ducking and diving between the car wrecks which were themselves suffering peppering from the attacking force of Gunther and his crew.

One of the police officers was hit but not killed, as he lay on the warm Roman tarmac he called in to his controllers the incident that was currently in progress. The gunfire kept on and on, most of it coming from the automatic fire of the terrorists which did well to keep the heads down of the pair of officers that were trying to thwart a daring operation and getaway. One of the crew was shot on the conveyor loading and she fell to the floor. She was hoisted up into the back of the truck most unceremoniously but Gunther would not really want to leave any leads behind him.

"Time to go," he shouted. "Everybody in, leave the rest let's go."

With that, a hand grenade was lobbed into the blue van by Karl, who, as he turned away from the truck took a bullet in the leg which brought him crashing to the ground by his van. Within a couple of seconds the van exploded with a thunderous roar and a huge fireball which not only engulfed the vehicle but also the unfortunate Karl. Gunther knew that Karl would have no tale to tell after undergoing such treatment and would be lucky if he could even be identified relatively quickly. The second truck also burst into flames as the last of the crew jumped aboard the white truck and set off.

They pulled down the rear roller doors as they set off yet the lone police officer remained undaunted and continued to fire passionately at the truck, discharging round after round from his service revolver.

The shots pierced the side of the truck and everybody in the back threw themselves onto the floor, sliding around, mixing with the booty when another of them took a shot to the back. The bullet pierced the man's chest cavity resulting in his almost instant death. Almost clear and a freak shot ended his life. This was the unfortunate Paulo. He was a close friend of Marco's who was not on the raid today as he was stalking the attorney Mr. Ricci, for the hit man Falcon. Paulo had never been in trouble with the law but had succumbed to Marco's leanings in recent years and now was thought to be the time to bring him on board with Marco's own political aspirations, although this was somewhat a very large project for the novice to become involved in.

Inga checked the youngster over but she knew he was dead. His scarlet blood seeped through his clothes and started to spill onto the lorry floor. She then moved to the girl who had been shot. Her wound was in the stomach and when Inga revealed her midriff found that it was quite severe. She knew this one would not survive either; it was only a matter of time. She tried to comfort the girl but knew it was in vain. She was in so much pain and the blood flow seemed relentless . . . she responded to nothing.

Gunther drove like a crazy man for a couple of minutes before realising he had no company behind him and he slowed to a less conspicuous pace. He knew his route well and now needed to head back to the farm as quickly as possible.

Gunther's mind was now also racing, he grinned as he thought of Tony Falcon, the great Tony Falcon sat in that church tower assassinating Italy's most prominent politician. How he had duped the great man, and so cheaply. Emotions can be expensive he mused to himself, but at least the plan had worked. There was no police activity this side of town getting in Gunther's way and very soon he would be safely back inside the barn from where he could disappear into the sunset never to be seen again. Gunther started whistling to himself as he drove the truck towards its resting place, although his front seat passenger had little knowledge of what lay behind that great smile of his and thought the celebrations a little premature, especially after losing some of the squad.

Chapter 29

Falcon's journey back to the farm was sedate and uneventful due to the tremendous traffic congestion, so it took the twosome well over an hour. Still Francesco failed to communicate with Falcon and concentrated on duelling with his countrymen, fighting for that extra yard of carriageway, whenever it appeared. Falcon's solitude once again allowed his mind to wander. He could still feel the small handgun strapped to his leg and in truth was somewhat surprised his tormentors hadn't bothered searching him at any time these past few days. That was his sole comfort right now. The chaos that lay before him only reinforced the chaos in his mind. His whole life had turned upside down in such a short time and would never be the same again, whatever the final outcome of the day's events. In fact, his whole life might well come to a sudden end sooner than planned as he still had no real inclination of what was in store for him back at base camp. Would Gunther really want to pay him the balance of their deal, highly unlikely? Would he ever get to see Maria again, right now that was just as doubtful? He could feel himself slump down in the passenger seat oblivious to the scenery nonchalantly passing him by. Even at that pace the outside world was a mere blur as he concentrated on his inner focus. He had to be strong and anticipate the unexpected.

Francesco took out his cell phone and made a call. Obviously this was to either Marco or Gunther and Falcon was pretty sure it was notification they were almost back. Sure enough that was the case.

The car had travelled the route across the river and away from the throng of the city into relative serenity yet Falcon had not even noticed the change. As they drove the car along the road to the old farm, one of Francesco's colleagues was waiting to swing open the barn doors and allow the old Fiat to get out of sight. Falcon was surprised whilst the car drove in, as there was Gunther and a host of others hurriedly shifting boxes of a variety of sizes out of a white truck into smaller vans and cars. The activity was not what had been expected by the shooter, it looked as though somebody was on the move, but who and why?

The Englishman's curiosity in that direction was short lived. Unsurprisingly for him, as the car was brought to a standstill, Gunther gestured with a pistol in hand for him to get out of the vehicle. Falcon shook his head in apparent disbelief as he slowly alighted, ensuring he didn't make any sudden moves. There were several men around the car all holding weapons so any attempt to dislodge Gunther's would be futile. He may get a few of them but he himself would ultimately lose out.

"I thought we had a deal Gunther?" shouted Falcon above the commotion that was taking place in the background with the banging and shouting from the movers.

Gunther looked down the top sights of the automatic pistol and aimed it at Falcon's head.

"Bang bang," he said before allowing a false laugh and very rare smile crack open his taught face, waving the pistol sideways indicating for Falcon to move slowly in the direction of the side door.

"Who said we still don't have a deal Tony?"

"So why the gun? It's not the usual way deals are concluded in my experience."

"Ah, well you see Tony old boy. That's what you English say isn't it . . . old boy? Well Tony, this is not an ordinary deal, is it? Hell, you might be an assassin sent to kill me for all I know, this is just my insurance policy, nothing more. So just do as you're told and we can all be on our way."

Falcon slowly moved across the barn floor as directed, looking around at the activity trying to fathom out what was going on although obviously still apprehensive at Gunther's reassurance.

"Curiosity got the better of you Tony?" asked the German in his now normal patronising manner.

"I guess you could say that," he replied, still looking around.

"All in good time my friend, now, in the house if you please."

They left the barn, one of Gunther's men first, followed by Falcon, then two others with the German ring leader at the rear. As Falcon entered the kitchen where he had taken tea only the day before, an almighty blow came crashing down on the back of his skull. A searing pain that shot straight through his body to his feet bounced back again like an eternal spring. Gunther's pistol whipping from behind was more ferocious than the Englishman could have ever anticipated and it sent him limply sprawling like a downed grouse in shooting season.

Very quickly one of the aides took Falcon's arm and dragged him to the next room, where Inga was tending a bleeding comrade on an old tubular iron bed that had been dragged from one of the rooms. Falcon was promptly handcuffed to it, even in good form he would not be able to pull it around and be mobile but with his own disability and half blindness with pain, he was at their mercy and to all intents and purposes incapacitated.

The girl was curled up in the foetal position wincing and sobbing with pain yet barely conscious. Inga could only try and calm her with cold towels on her head and hold her bloody hand for comfort whenever she was able to. She had tried cleaning around the wound and the bowl of water by her side used for washing resembled more of a summer fruit drink than a cleaning fluid. The cloths simply soaked up the blood, it was unrelenting.

"How's she doing?" asked Gunther, as Falcon tried to regain some sense of what had just happened to him. The pain didn't clear but his vision was becoming less blurred as he brought himself slowly to his knees, quite a task he found when chained up with one hand like a tethered dog. He Slid his face up the side of the metal tubes to try and gain some height above the floor.

Inga looked at the German and simply shook her head. "Nicht gut, nicht gut".

"I guess this is it then Gunther? Is this how you do business with all your comrades? Leave no trace. I don't blame you really, I'd do the same," said Falcon, trying to sound coherent, as he rubbed his head where the pain seemed to originate from, only to reveal in his palm as he did so, a slow red river still flowing from his skull. He could now sense the gentle warm trickle as it irritatingly dropped onto his bare neck, almost tickling had it not been for the excruciating pain he was trying to combat.

Gunther put his gun down on the table and pulled up a chair to be a little closer to the Englishman, but remaining out of reach from any lucky wild swing he may feel the urge to land.

"Tony," he said in a quiet and delicate voice, "it's a pity we were never really on the same side. We could have done things you and I, changed the world, but I guess deep down you always had your bloody stupid morals. Just look where that got you now. It could have been so different. So what's it to be? Should I kill you, like you say, no traces no comeback. Even better, you're now a wanted man. One call to the police, they find the weapon, match your prints and hey presto, case solved. But deep down, you know that will still only work if you're dead so I guess your options right now are a little limited, wouldn't you say?"

Falcon glared at the smug German and shook his head as his lips parted as though growling like a snarling lion. He paused for a few moments pondering his next words, he thought that wise as they may prove to be his last.

"I guess you win Gunther. You fooled me, I did what you asked and you still have me. You win all ways. I trust the girl will be left to get on with her life, as part of the deal. You can take me but at least promise me you will leave her out of it. She's nothing to do with my business, just leave her get on with her life; please." The Englishman himself was now in a position of pleading. He realised his own outlook was bleak but at least knew he should fight for Maria's rights. That was now uppermost in his mind. He wasn't afraid of dying; he had come close in the past and always believed that if his number was up then so be it, fate would see to that. But Maria was not part of his ultimate destiny, he had dragged her into this mess unwittingly and now had to use his last moments trying to save her.

"That's sweet," said Gunther. "You plead for that girl in what may be your last moments. Well, I'm not all bad you know Tony. I have been in love myself you know."

Inga rose from the bed and stood behind Gunther, the bed rose a little as she stood up, stirring the bleeding patient back into a state of semi awareness letting out muffled groans as she squirmed. Gunther smiled at Falcon although even Inga couldn't bring herself to do that, and simply stared blankly at the gyrating bleeding parcel that lay on the bed. Falcon sensed the need to turn around and there it was; a sight he could never have imagined seeing in his wildest nightmares. A face so etched with pain and hair so matted with blood that had gone so dark it was clotted black. The face was empty of life, life savagely and prematurely removed. The once beautiful face was suddenly so gaunt, yet he knew, he knew straight away this was his love. This was Maria.

He stroked her matted hair away from her eyes so he could see her face, not as he ever wanted to see it but he still needed to. Emotions were racing around his body in every direction, emotions of love, fear, hate, anger, pain and joy; all at the same time. He wanted to grab her and squeeze her fragile femur little body for one last time but the chains of captivity prevented that. He could see her trying to make him out yet he could not find words to speak. He was dumbstruck. Fear had silenced him, fear of losing his beloved and this being the last vision he would ever have of her. It wasn't meant to be like this. He moved her strawberry coloured hand from her stomach where she had been clasping at a small towel only to reveal the true horror of her injury. Falcon had seen wounds like this before. Sure, the patient could live perhaps if treated timely, but a stomach wound would do so much internal damage that without any quick treatment, there would be so many complications, torn organs and the mixing of toxins into the blood stream, survival chances were slim. His heart seemed to momentarily stop. He put his hand over hers and back onto the wound as tears welled up in his eyes and started to roll down his cheek.

He swiftly turned and lurched at Gunther but to no avail, unless he ripped his own arm off, there was no way he was ever going to reach the German.

"Why you bastard, why?" he screamed. "She's done nothing; she didn't even need to be involved. I'll personally see to it you die a fucking slow death and if not in this life I'll haunt you in the next and the next until I make you pay." Falcon was screaming his words through tears yet Gunther seemed almost unmoved.

He suddenly felt Maria's delicate touch once more from behind so he turned away from Inga and her man to face Maria. He dropped himself back to the floor so he could get closer to her and rest his cheek on hers. What more could he do. His only solace was that at least they would both die together and if there was another life, then hopefully they could be together very soon, but this time for an eternity.

As he lay there gently sobbing into Maria's ear whilst running his hand gently through her hair and stroking her head, Gunther piped up in the back ground.

"For the record Tony, and for what it's worth, we didn't do this. She is a casualty of war, of the cause. She was with us all the time."

Falcon raised his head, "I don't believe that for one minute. I knew her and she was no terrorist."

"You never really know anybody Tony until it's too late. She's not a terrorist in the sense as you associate me with terrorism. Your choice of words, not mine. I see myself as a freedom fighter, but we'll go with your words for now; but she was part of a movement. Her parents were part of the same movement as were her grandparents. Sure, not bomb throwing and plane hijacking but certainly separatists out to undermine the government, albeit usually in a more civilised manner. They are all German Austrians by birth right and since their homeland was carved up by the allies and handed to the Italians after the war, they have been silently fighting for it back ever since. Mussolini didn't treat them well so they strove for independence. Never successful of course as there were too many factions, consolidation was so ineffective, but she was still part of it. It's almost hereditary, passed down through the families although, just like most causes, they're a dying breed. The world's becoming smaller and capitalism will invariably win through, so the participants in the fight become fewer and fewer until ultimately everybody just accepts the hand they've been dealt and don't look for change."

"So how did she get mixed up with a bunch of international murderers if she was not really an activist?"

"You can put that master stroke down to Marco, he knew her father so it was easy to reel her in."

"But why, what could this child possibly offer you that you couldn't find anywhere else? She's no cold blooded killer, she was innocent. What could she possibly give you?" asked Tony, in bewilderment whilst still caressing his Maria.

"You don't see the irony of it yet do you Tony? She's a catalyst, that's all. We wanted you and when we tracked you and found your connection with Maria, well Marco saw the opportunity straight away and cultivated it. She knew nothing of your past or what you do for a living, she didn't even know you were involved until a few moments ago, but the whole thing just fell in our laps, a gift from the Gods. This was surely divine intervention, after all the hard work that had gone on over the years fighting for the people's causes, those people who now just as quickly turn their backs on you as though you never existed. This was my finale."

Falcon could was unable to take any more of this right now, he wanted to focus on Maria. She was barely conscious and her attempts at speaking were little more than a whisper. As his head again met with hers, he could hear her softly call out his name.

"Tony, I hear my Tony, is it you?" she spluttered exhaling globules of blood with saliva as she struggled to speak.

"I'm sorry my darling, I didn't mean to get you involved in this, please forgive me."

Her words were slow and obviously strained, working hard on every syllable but still showing that dogged determination right up to the very end, a trait the Englishman would always remember her for.

"You've nothing to be sorry to me for. This is my doing, not yours."

"Come on Tony, we both know there isn't long. I'm thankful to God for giving me this last opportunity to see you. It makes everything seem a lot easier. The pain has eased now, you're already spreading your magic on me."

Falcon pressed against her a little harder for the extra comfort, hers and his, as he heard her labouring over her words.

"You just take it easy now and we'll get you fixed up, save your energy."

"Tony, whatever you are, you can't lie to me, I see through it. I know this is my time now, God's calling for me and I've got to go. It's his will. But I'm glad that I could see you this one last time and tell you how much I have always loved you, you gave me a wonderful life of joy and happiness and I loved every minute of it."

A sudden pain seemed to rifle around Maria's body as she shot into a brief spasm. The air rushed from her mouth as she did so.

"Tony," she said softly as she squeezed his hand as hard as she could, "I'm going now, I know it, good bye my love . . . I'll wait for you on the other side. I love you Mr. Tony . . ."

The whispering stopped and Maria's grip loosened on Falcon's hand. She had gone. He could not immediately come to terms with what had just happened. Behind his back even

Inga had a tear rolling down her face. Gunther was less sympathetic as he simply took a cigarette from his pocket and put it to his lips.

Falcon squeezed Maria's bloody body as best he could with only one hand free whilst allowing his emotions to get the better of him and tears started free flowing from his face and falling onto hers. She looked different now somehow, no more in pain and some of that beauty that had attracted him to her in the first place was starting to return. Maybe this was her soul on its way to the next existence. It was several minutes before the sound of the Englishman's gentle sobbing over his beloved was broken by Gunther's guttural voice.

"I'm sorry it came to that Tony, really, that was not part of the plan."

"What plan, you still plan on taking over the fucking world with your ideals. She's dead through you, dead; and all for what, a politician? There'll be ten more behind him waiting to fill his shoes, then what?"

"Ideals, you talk to me about ideals Tony! I already told you, there's no space for radicals any more, the world's gone soft. It's dog eat dog nowadays, no great causes left to fight for. Even if you win they are turned over by capitalist greed."

"Oh really, so why kill Ricci? What's the political motive there?

"None."

"None!" cried Falcon in total disbelief. "What do you mean none? He's the number one man in politics right now; surely you didn't kill him just for sport?"

"Well," replied Gunther. "I guess you could say we did. Or to be correct, you did."

"Why, you take a man away from his family for a game."

"It's all in the plan Tony. How many police cars did you see when you were leaving, hundreds I bet? That's the plan. You had virtually all the law enforcement vehicles and officers over that side of town looking for an assassin. They came out of the woodwork I expect. That meant there would be very few over our side of the town when we hit the armoured truck."

Falcon's eyes shot open. He glared at Gunther in disbelief for a moment, his eyes searing the air like lightning strikes.

"You mean this was all for a robbery, a bloody robbery, and people are dead for it. No great cause other than to line your pockets with dirty money. You killed my Maria for a fucking robbery you slimy little shit . . ." Falcon was yanking at the bed now and shaking with rage, snarling and spitting as he spoke. If only he could free himself of the chains holding him down he knew he would physically tear Gunther apart limb by limb. The adrenalin flowed through his veins fuelling his rage.

"This is why we needed to restrain you Tony, it really wasn't my doing but for security's sake, I had no choice."

Suddenly Francesco came bounding into the room and announced, much to Falcon's shear surprise in near perfect English, that Marco was on his way to the farm right now and would be here in a couple of minutes. Falcon could not believe that for all this time the Italian mute had been seemingly able to understand his every word, yet refrained from any form of communication whatsoever. He simply grinned at the trussed up Englishman as he lay bound to the bed, still clasping a hand on Maria's, feeling her warmth as it slowly ebbed away.

Gunther turned to Inga, "I guess you had better go and make everybody ready to depart. Don't forget five or ten minutes between them yeah, don't attract any attention."

"I guess that's it now Gunther is it? Turn and run and get back under your rock somewhere."

"You can't rile me today Tony. You can't steal my greatest triumph from me now. I'm rich beyond my wildest dreams. I can hide anywhere on the planet with that amount of money and nobody will ever find me. Hell, with that cash I could walk the streets of London and be incognito as you say."

"After all of the charades, it's all about cash. The world's greatest self proclaimed freedom fighter is nothing more than a common thief."

"Tony, unless you want another lump on your head I would watch that mouth of yours. There's nothing common about what we achieved today. There's over two hundred million Euros in that truck today in various forms. Cash, bearer bonds even a bit of gold bullion, not bad for a days work. Now with even fewer in the pot to share it with then there's more to go around. Seven is a better share than nine don't you think. Sorry to be so cold about it but that's reality I'm afraid," said the German with clinical and unnerving precision.

Marco then bowled into the room and saw both Falcon and Maria's lifeless body. He clasped his hands and drew them swiftly to his mouth and shook his head in disbelief. He bent down to touch the young Italian goddess but was swiftly rebuked by Falcon.

"Don't you lay a single hand on her you filthy shit," snarled the prisoner. "You got her into this and she has paid the price. I hope you can look her father in the eye and tell him all about the just cause she died for."

Marco was clearly shocked by what he had seen and was led back out of the room by Inga, with an arm of solace from her around his shoulder. He was definitely mourning yet that cut no ice with the Englishman. Marco was just as guilty as Gunther for Maria's death, and no amount of crocodile tears would save him from the Englishman's revenge if the chance ever arose.

Gunther rose and clasped his sidearm as he did so.

"I've just got to visit my team and wish them all farewell; this will probably be the last time we shall all meet. Don't worry, I shall not be gone long, you just make yourself comfortable."

Falcon was at last alone in the room with Maria, how peaceful she now looked. He tried his best to lay her out with some dignity, outstretched and not screwed up. He carefully brushed her hair once more off her face, revealing her beauty and tried with the towels and bed coverings that were around, to wipe away the blood that had gathered on her face as a result of her internal bleeding and speaking. His swollen bloodshot eyes told the story of the love he had lost. Despite the circumstances, he would love her always, no matter what she had done. Just as he was sure she would have him, if she had ever discovered his true profession.

Chapter 30

Gunther entered the barn to a rapturous round of applause from his comrades in arms. He nonchalantly raised both hands accepting the plaudits, before dropping them again to signal his colleagues to quieten down.

"People, we have all played our parts here today for which we shall all be well rewarded. My only advice is to spend it wisely otherwise you may attract the wrong attention. You know the agenda now, just make your way to Zurich and the bank will take care of you and help keep you out of trouble. We've negotiated a pretty good deal on your behalf," he chuckled as he told his crew this fact, but the truth was that for fifteen percent of the turnover, their banking associates would launder the funds through off shore entities and back into Switzerland, as clean money for disposal at their leisure.

There were three more vans in the barn to be utilised by the robbers for their escape. These had clean number plates and would not attract any unnecessary attention. The plan would be to take a steady run through to Switzerland over the next day or so and meet up outside Zurich where the contents could be transferred over to a security warehouse for collection by the bank, once all was in place. In theory quite simple but the trick was ensuring they did not attract any interest when crossing the Swiss border, hence the need to travel different routes and times. Three cars in convoy may not attract attention but three vans might do.

Gunther shook hands and embraced his colleagues in turn as they each got ready for their departure. The first three operatives would go in a white panel van and take a steady drive up North and across the Italian-Swiss border some time the following day. The second van to leave would be Francesco and Marco who would head back inland and up towards Verona. They would then cross into Austria towards

Innsbruck before heading west into Switzerland. Gunther and Inga would take the coastal route around Italy and head into France first before crossing back into Switzerland.

After the first van had left, Gunther again shook hands with his old friend Marco.

"I'm sorry about the girl Marco," he said, ". . . and you know I don't often make statements like that so I must mean it."

"Thank you old friend, I know you do. What do we do now eh?"

"I'm sure you'll find some way of passing the time. Right you two, it's time you left so we can all get the hell out of here."

"What about the Englishman?"

"I'll take care of business this end Marco, you just be on your way," replied the German with his ever proficient manner.

The two men nodded acknowledgements to one another as the Italians jumped into their van and set off down the farm road towards the main highway and into freedom.

"Right Inga, I guess it's time for us to leave now. Just do a sweep and make sure we leave nothing behind and we'll be on our way. I'll just go and bid farewell to our English colleague."

Gunther came back into the room and found Falcon gazing once more over Maria's lifeless corpse. He slowly turned as the German entered the room, but wanted as much quality time as he could get with his beloved, before he himself was despatched to face his own judgement day with the almighty.

Gunther returned to his chair overlooking the bed and placed his pistol back on the side table. Falcon glanced at it but knew it was well out of reach. Gunther saw the look and smiled knowingly back at him.

"Feel free to take your chance my friend; I would do in your position."

Falcon's head just bowed as though in deep shame as though he was pouring out his wildest sins in confession to his priest.

"Come come Tony, don't be so gloomy. She's gone to be with the angels, you know that." Gunther halted a short while to see what reaction he could get from the hired assassin, but there was none. Had he broken the legendary Tony Falcon, perhaps so? He had discovered the great man's weakness after all.

"I guess you're expecting the worst now, I mean . . . with just you and me here? There must be a lot going through your mind right now."

Falcon raised his head slowly and stared squarely at Gunther, "Just get it over with and be on your way, you've taken everything I ever loved, you can't hurt me any more."

Gunther nodded and picked up his pistol, "I guess you're right. But just out of interest, aren't you just a little bit curious as to how we landed you in the first place? Not even a little?"

This got Falcon interested of course. "I guess so," he said, "not that it'll do me much good now."

"I guess not, other than answering any loose ends you may still have. It's always best to go with no unanswered questions, don't you think?" replied the German in philosophical mode.

"Okay then, how was it done?"

Gunther again smiled and started to laugh out loud.

"Well Tony, you see your friend Wilhelmson at Credit Suisse is also our friend Wilhelmson. He's been doing our finances for many years through one organisation or another within the Bank and as he climbed the ladder his customer knowledge increased, as did his circle of influence. He worked out you do business for the NSA because he knows some of their fronts that use the Swiss Banking system and traced funds from them to you on the international wires. Switzerland, Bahamas, Cayman's, it was all there and easy for a banker to follow if you know where to look. Clever eh?

Just from a money trail, but they left a trail that would embarrass a slug, they hung you out to be picked up and never knew it. That's when we put tabs on you ourselves in the UK, and . . . well . . . the rest you know I guess."

Falcon listened intently to the brief he had just been given, mulling over how he would ever extract revenge on the Swiss betrayer, even the banker was collaborating with terrorists. How did that get through the net? He had forgotten that he himself was staring death in the face. Tethered to an anchor block he had no chance of escaping from, his life in tatters with the loss of his beloved who lay motionless behind him and Gunther sat lording it over the Englishman occasionally waving his gun around then putting it down again as he eloquently expressed himself with the aid of his hands.

The two men glared at each other for several seconds, Gunther in his chair overlooking his trapped quarry, Falcon still resting half on the floor and against the old iron bed. Falcon's eyes remained glazed as he tried to quell the emotional flow that was building up inside him. This was not the time to release the flood gates, he would go with dignity. It would be Gunther who would lack the dignity he thought as he would be the one executing a man who was tethered, he saw Gunther as nothing more than a lowly coward and refused to give him any satisfaction over his next murder.

Suddenly there was a commotion from outside. Screams from Inga could be heard along with tremendous crashing noises coming from the barn area. A sudden burst of automatic gun fire caused Gunther to lurch from his seat like a startled rabbit. Bewildered he looked at Falcon then at the door leading outside. He dashed towards the closed door but as he was nothing more than a couple of metres away it was kicked open with such a ferocity it forced Gunther to leap aside and avoid it crashing inwards. He fired blindly his automatic pistol into the opened doorway but there was nobody standing there at the time.

Panicking, Gunther suddenly felt under threat for the first time in many years. He fired five or six shots from the automatic pistol into the void yet still there was no response. He had no idea where these were landing yet there was still a silence from the other side. He could not hear Inga nor could he hear anything else. The sound of silence unnerved him. He turned on Falcon with gun half raised yet as he spun round he was greeted with a sight he was least expecting.

The Englishman had recovered his pistol from the leg holster he had been sporting all day which to his amazement had not been discovered or even suspected. Thank God for Mr. Brown he thought. Gunther froze for a fraction of a second when he was staring down the cold blue steel of Falcon's handgun.

"You betrayed me Tony? I guess I under estimated you after all."

"You betrayed yourself Gunther. You could have remained a nobody, but your greed took over. You exploited these people for a cause that was no nobler than lining your own pockets. You've sunk to a lower depth than you were when you were nothing more than a bloody cowardly murdering terrorist."

Falcon cocked the trigger on the pistol letting Gunther realise that he was now only half a squeeze away from discharging justice of his own.

"I won't let you take me Tony. You know that, I'm not going to any prison I assure you."

"Who said I want you to? You owe me Gunther, big time. You think I'd get enough satisfaction knowing you were in jail and would be out some day, I think not."

"I'm sure we can come to an arrangement Tony. Have you any idea how much is in the van right now, I can help you disappear and never want for anything again."

Falcon looked as though he was contemplating the offer.

"To many people that could be tempting Gunther, but I guess I'm not many people. You owe me and I want paying, but there's no amount of cash you could pay to buy back that debt."

"Ever the idealist Tony. Well, I guess we managed to get away with something even if you managed to nail me. It'll still be one of the biggest hauls in history, that's something I can take to the grave."

A flurry of activity behind Gunther caught his attention. He remained still semi poised with his pistol, but deflected his gaze momentarily to the activity now behind him, as several black clad members of the Carabinieri accompanied by James Brown and a couple of his associates appeared.

"I wouldn't bet on that Gunther," said Brown in his traditional American drawl. "I think you'll find we pulled both vehicles in and your comrades, along with the loot we believe. So I guess you actually got away with nothing by my reckoning."

Brown assessed the two adrenalin fuelled alpha males squaring each other off a matter of a few feet apart.

"Alright Tony, we'll take him now. Drop the weapon Gunther, there's enough armour trained on you to turn you into confetti, so let's go."

Falcon saw that evil smile of Gunther's begin to appear, starting from the corner and slowly emerging across his lips. He knew what was coming; Gunther was planning to go nowhere alive. Falcon was ready. As soon as Gunther's fingers started to move on to the trigger Falcon let loose his first round. The lead slug tore through Gunther's sweater and into his right shoulder sending him reeling backwards into the wall. The Carabinieri guns suddenly trained on the German as he slid a little down the wall leaving behind him a trail of smeared blood as he did so.

He still managed to retain his weapon as he shook his head in Falcon's direction. He was not a quitter. Yet Falcon knew his adversary wanted the Englishman or his associates to finish him off.

Brown started to move towards the German when Falcon intervened.

"Leave him be James." He paused for a couple of seconds, "This one's personal."

Brown stared at his freelance employee. "I appreciate that Tony, but we could make some good use of him. I'm sure you understand." His voice was softer than usual as he tried to almost plead with Falcon's better side. However, Brown knew that if it came to it he would not interfere with Falcon's intentions for the German; he would be able to tie up the loose ends somehow.

Gunther saw this reticence on both parties and again raised his weapon. Falcon was as ever alert to the event and fired a second shot into the German's other shoulder. He remained resting against the wall now bleeding from both sides. The weapon was still in hand although hung limply by his side. Falcon knew it would be unlikely he could draw again yet he still felt cheated. He could not finish the job if Gunther was not able to fire but he also wouldn't simply assassinate him, despite the loathing that he felt. There was nothing for it, if the German refused to bow down and surrender, Falcon would have to make him. Without a second thought he fired two more shots into Gunther, one in each leg, the second catching the German in the left knee cap bringing him screaming crashing to the floor. This time the weapon was yielded and the game essentially over.

Falcon clasped his pistol by the body and held it out for his friend from the NSA to retrieve, letting all know that the shooting was over.

Gunther lay screaming on the floor cursing and spitting as the law enforcement officers ensured he was fully disarmed and sporting no other concealed weapons before allowing the medics access to his wounds. He turned his head across the cold floor to Falcon, eyes squinting and face wrought with obvious pain.

"Why didn't you finish the job you bastard? You're a coward Tony, a bloody coward."

"Oh the temptation was there believe me. But I know you'll suffer in a cage for the rest of your life. That will hurt you more than giving you an easy exit. Besides, there may not be much left of you when these guys have finished with their debriefing, now there's something to look forward to."

Brown set his people to releasing Falcon from his chains. Once free he turned to Maria who now looked so peaceful on the bed. He once again tried his best to make her look at ease, placing her in a more respectful pose for her onward journey. He tenderly touched her face and passed his fingers gently over her closed eyes, before allowing his hand to fall sideways and once more run his fingers through her hair.

The medics moved in to formally take care of Maria's body and received an icy stare from Falcon as they went to lift her from the bed. Brown sensed this anxiety and shouted at the paramedics

"Be careful what you are doing, you treat that girl with the greatest of respect you hear. She's earned that right."

Falcon turned to his old buddy and nodded in appreciation for the gesture that had been made, although this didn't relieve him of any of the pain he was feeling for his loss. That would be insurmountable, he knew that.

"You alright buddy?" asked Brown, as he put an arm around his friend as they together walked to the open doorway, leaving the fracas behind them for others to clean up. They stepped outside where Falcon saw the blood stained body of Gunther's female companion laying in the courtyard.

"Don't get involved. Rule number one . . . don't get involved. I broke it and paid the price and took an innocent life as a consequence." Falcon managed to squeeze his solemn words out but was in a minor state of trance and would need some recovery time. It was whether he would ever recover that was the question for Brown.

"It's a pond of shit we peddle in Tony, and we don't come across many nice guys. We all know the score and it's not pretty but don't be hard on yourself. I'm very sorry about Maria. I wish we could have helped but we had no idea what was going down, you know that."

Falcon gazed upwards into the setting afternoon sun. He felt he could now allow his emotions to escape and a small raft of tears began to emerge from his eyes and the warm trickle flow down his face.

"Yep, it sure is a dirty pond James," he wept.

"You'll need time to recover my friend, we'll help you get sorted you can be sure of that. We'll wait for you until you say you're ready, if you want to come back. You're our best solo op, we'll miss you if you don't return but you'll still have our full backing whatever you choose. The lord himself will be behind you I'm sure. I'll make damned sure."

"A solo op. These guys called me a Sole Trader somewhere else recently, it's starting to stick!" exclaimed Falcon. "I think I've done enough dirty dealing for the lord almighty to not be interested in me James. I'm pretty sure I'm somewhere well down his list in the forgiveness stakes."

"There's good in you son and don't underestimate it. You serve a purpose for the better good; it's just that most people don't care to admit it. You do a shitty job but somebody's got to do it and I don't see a queue behind you," Brown reassured the Englishman.

Falcon exhaled slowly and loudly. "You got the rest of them did you?"

"Yea, Duval's team picked them all up without a shot being fired. It's a good result for law enforcement. By the way, Ricci sends his regards and thanks for being such a good shot. He did ask me to tell you though that he hurts like hell, he's got a few cracked ribs and he'll be sore for a few weeks yet, but as he says, that's far better than a hole in the head."

"Looks like he's on his way to the presidency then."

"Guess so," replied the American.

"What's next for Gunther?"

"Duval's team could really do with a session with him. I expect that once he has finished singing he'll be taken to Algiers where he's wanted for murder and bombings, given a fair trial, then they'll hang him I guess. That's if there's any real justice in the world," stated the American with the dignity of a preacher delivering a sermon. He stopped the walk with his friend and turned to face him.

"Don't worry about Maria's memory Tony. We'll get the police to say it was an automobile accident; nobody needs to know about her involvement here. We'll see to that. She can be buried with dignity. It's the least we can do; she was no villain, that's clear to see."

"You know I appreciate what you can do for her, I still remember her for what she was to me, and not this artificial existence she was sucked in to."

Falcon walked a couple of steps away from his American friend, "Don't worry about me, I'll return some day. Besides there's not a lot else I can do. I just have a loose end to tie up first, I'm sure you understand."

The American nodded knowingly, "Sometimes ignorance is bliss Tony, and I can be blissfully ignorant sometimes. You do what you've got to do, then drop me a mail through the usual channels when you're ready. We'll clean up this end. The guys will escort you back to the hotel where you can sort yourself out then go at your will. We'll settle the account if it's not already paid up. I know you rarely carry cash . . ."

Chapter 31

It was early evening and the snow was again falling in down town Zurich, as Heinrich Wilhelmson sat in his ornate office, on the upper most floor of the Credit Suisse building in Paradeplatz. The surroundings were one showing he had made it to the top of his profession, original works of art and exquisite antiques adorned the oversized office. The room itself was the size of a typical apartment and contained separate dining and seating areas, surrounded by leather sofas, away from his series of desks and computer screens. Yes, this was comfort that probably exceeded what he attained in his own home. But the prize was of course the elevation. The higher up the building then the greater your prowess within the organisation, it was not just the better view across town, but the stigma that went with which button you pressed if you were ever in the communal elevators. Wilhelmson had now made it to the top floor after a life with the bank; the only moves now were sideways, physically. The objective once here was to move along the corridor towards the main board offices.

Through his years at the bank he had often made an impression within the different departments and divisions in which he worked. In his youth he showed flair as a dynamic trader on the floor and his ability to squeeze additional margin points out of clients by flipping transactions was incredible. A smooth talker and fast thinker, ideally suited to the hustle and bustle of trading, but that was not enough. He knew if he pushed himself there he would make the dollars but probably burn out in no time at all and he wanted more. From a very early age at entering the business he observed the respect that went with the top floor and that was where he set his sights. He had achieved it faster than most did and that was in no small part down to his ability to attract inward investment, often luring clients away from other institutions. Sure he had to work for it but with the banks infrastructure, moving money around the world and losing traceability was relatively easily done.

It was whilst doing such trading for lesser legitimate monies that he saw a niche. He saw how cash could be wiped clean, laundered, even in this day and age of bank scrutiny and legislation, of which the Swiss Banking Fraternity were also obliged to adhere to. He developed a way of cleaning money that did not attract any attention from his superiors, and even if it did they would probably have turned a blind eye due to the sizes of deposits being attracted.

Once he got into this circle of trading, Wilhelmson needed not to sell his wares, his customers came to him. Not only was he rewarded by the bank for his results but, of course his wealthy patrons also showed their appreciation financially. He always dressed well, drove nice cars and dined wherever he wanted without need to see a price list. The banker had married although unsuccessfully and now enjoyed as best he could the bachelor lifestyle. His works took him on many travels around the globe and often returned having secured more cash deposits for his employer. He was a made man and didn't really need to work during the day any more, the operation with his team was self running almost. The others had no idea what was really going on behind the scenes with the more secretive characters he dealt with, it was all merely seen as asset protection, just what they were in the business of doing.

The telephone in Wilhelmson's office sprang into life, disturbing his moments of solace when he relaxed, listening to Puccini, allowing the world go by; still business was business and Puccini would always wait.

"Heinrich Wilhelmson," he replied into the receiver

Nothing came back, just silence.

"Can I help you, hello . . .?"

Still nothing; Wilhelmson replaced the receiver and returned to his music, once again closing his eyes as he did so. He would give himself another half hour or so before leaving the bank for the evening, for yet another so called business meeting that needed to initially take place outside of the bank's walls, whilst he set up the relevant systems for his new client's needs. He poured a small brandy, from the personal cocktail cabinet that was common place on the top floor, and sat back down to relax. He could do no more preparation for tonight, he felt he was ready. He closed his eyes and allowed the music to be absorbed.

Twenty minutes or so passed, when he decided he should make himself ready for this evening's meeting. The banker visited the private washrooms allotted to the senior executives, where he took a brief wash and freshened up before returning to his office. He returned once again to the soothing sound of Puccini and started nodding and humming the tunes, as he closed the heavy oak door behind him.

As he turned into the room the banker was presented with a vision he never thought he would have to endure. There, in his very own chair was Tony Falcon, a man he had thought was killed by armed police and special forces in a shoot out in Rome only the day before. He had not even bothered emptying the Englishman's accounts yet until he had received formal notification, but was anticipating doing so over the coming days. This was a resurrection from the grave. This was suddenly a nightmare. The banker's heart was racing, with every sweat gland on his body starting to pump out, making his crisp and clean shirts somewhat damp almost instantly. The body secretions were now profusely running down his face which had gone ashen with fright. His fists became clenched as he wondered what to do next, what to say. The few seconds lasted a epoch.

"Lost for words Heinrich? That's not like you," said the Englishman, who for the first time in days suddenly felt as though he was again where he preferred to be, in the driving seat. Falcon's tone was calm and collected, no emotion, just direct.

"Sit down then Heinrich, I think we need to talk, don't you?"

The banker slowly sidled across the floor to the leather sofa nearest the door. Falcon decided he would also move over to the seating area and sit on the sofa opposite his trapped prey. It would be good sport after all. Wilhelmson fidgeted most uncomfortably and almost without control as the Englishman came closer.

"Now, what shall we talk about Heinrich, any ideas? I know, let's talk about Gunther."

The banker was visibly trembling and obviously struggling to get his words together. He was salivating at the side of his mouth as he tried to retain composure in his speech but that was going to be impossible, he could only bubble his words out at best, and they were far from coherent.

"They forced me to give you up Anthony, surely you know that. I've been loyal to you for many years. I never questioned your business, I trusted you." The whining voice was pleading in its tone. "Gunther threatened to kill me, he knew about you. He knew you banked with me. They got me to set up the meeting with you in the first place, I promise you."

"So you know what I do for a living do you?"

"Of course Anthony, of course. But you are not only my customer I think of you as my friend. I wouldn't want to harm that special bond, but they would have killed me." The pleading was incessant and starting to annoy the Englishman. He remembered how Maria died only yesterday with such dignity, in a world that was not of her making. That innocence stolen and abused for the purpose of others and yet Falcon could see this miserable banker, with clean hands and clean money living off the backs of other's dirty work, now pleading. It was sickening.

"So you believed Gunther would kill you, why? I mean how do you know he had it in him?"

"I've known Gunther for many years, I know what they are all capable of," said the banker in defence of his actions.

Falcon sat opposite the frightened Swiss Banker and nodded his head showing his quarry he understood the predicament he was in. The Englishman stood up and started to walk away from Wilhelmson towards the long window behind the banker's desk affording views across the darkened Zurich night sky.

"I see what a position you were in Heinrich, I'm so sorry you had to be so. But answer me this, if you will."

"If I can, I will do anything at all to clear this unfortunate misunderstanding, anything at all."

"You've known Gunther for many years, more than me yes?"

"That's correct, probably near twenty years or so now."

"If you knew what he was, and you knew what I was, as your friend, why didn't you come to me for help, instead of turning me over to them? Surely, as your friend, you know I would have helped you, just as you would have helped me."

The banker had begun to start feeling at ease but the shakes were once more returning. He knew he could not answer the question satisfactorily.

"This seems to be one big mix up Anthony. The main thing is you're safe, nothing's changed."

"My whole life has changed," shouted Falcon, putting the banker even more on his back foot.

He had to think quickly as he fervently believed time was running short.

"You have your whole future ahead of you Anthony. Think of this as a new beginning. I have a lot of clients who would gladly pay for your services, and pay handsomely. A lot more than you could expect from the American's I'm sure."

The banker thought he may have a line here. Perhaps he could win over the Englishman, after all everybody was only in business for money, weren't they? Maybe such a presumption is where it went wrong.

Falcon turned away from the window and now faced his prisoner once more, this time he had gun in hand equipped with silencer.

"My life has changed because of you and your greed. The only girl I ever truly loved has been taken away from me and

I hold you responsible. Yes you, no matter how you look at it, it was you who set me up with Gunther and in the process got Maria killed, and you want to repay me by acting as my agent."

The Englishman promptly raised the gun to Wilhelmson's direction and shouted in his own controlled rage, "Fuck you!"

"No!" came the long drawn out cry from Wilhelmson as he saw the gun raised and the trigger pulled back.

The distinctive whistling sound of the lead warhead leaving the barrel of the handgun was enough to strike fear into any man, but it had already impacted the banker in the stomach before his hands were barely raised. The impact in the spleen area caused a greater pain to the victim than he could have ever imagined. The explosion of red, emanating from the now shattered spleen onto the white shirt, resembled a spilled paint tin more than a bullet wound, the volume of liquid being so profuse. The banker lurched forward on the sofa as the bullet penetrated his body and the piercing pains instantaneously shot around his frame. He screamed with pain again pleading for mercy.

"Please Anthony, I'll make everything right, I promise you."

"That one's from Maria, that's how she died but a lot slower. Unfortunately I don't have the time to wait and watch you go too slowly, I guess you could say this is your lucky day."

"You won't get away with this. You can't murder me; they'll hunt you down like a dog. There's CCTV in the building, everyone will know who did this. You go and I promise you, I'll swear I didn't see who did it. For God's sake Anthony, let it be."

"Forget God, this one's for my sake."

He raised the firearm a second time and emptied a single shot into the banker's forehead. That was curtains for him for sure. The limp body of the once proud and successful Heinrich Wilhelmson now lay trussed up, like an overgrown turkey, on his highly expensive furnishings. Falcon watched the motionless body for a few seconds, the only signs of motion being the blood that continued to flow from the carcass.

"No loose ends old man, no loose ends," said the Englishman in his own hushed way as he leaned over the flaccid corpse. He removed the silencer and returned it and the handgun to his pockets. Then, just as he had when he came up the stairwell, Falcon donned a full head ski hat which was way too large for his head and flopped well down on all sides, but did a very good job of hiding any features that may show up on any surveillance cameras, whilst not attracting the attention a balaclava might.

He slipped out of the executive's office just as quietly as he had entered them and made his way to the less fashionable fire escape stairwell, at least this way he would be unlikely to meet with any other employees. This afforded him the opportunity to slip outside into the now crowded streets, mingling with people just as equally wrapped up against the winter cold. Now he was just another anonymous faceless person among the crowds.

The following morning, Falcon returned to his bank at Paradeplatz just as he had done on many occasions. He announced himself at the private banking entrance and requested a meeting with Mr. Wilhelmson.

"Do you have an appointment with Mr. Wilhelmson for today Mr. Falcon?" the receptionist asked as she picked up her desk phone to speak with the relevant secretary.

"No, I was just passing really. I am leaving today, it was just a flying visit and I wondered if I could sort a few things out while I had the opportunity. Still, if he's too busy could you tell him I should be back next week and we'll meet up then." Falcon was a good actor and carried this off to perfection.

"It's alright Mr. Falcon, one of our directors is happy to see you, a Mr. Klaus Kramer. I'll escort you to his offices."

Falcon was escorted in the private elevator to the top floor, where he was greeted by yet another pretty young receptionist looking all official in a very smart and well fitting business suit. He had to admire the suaveness of the Swiss. He was shown into an office that was even more palatial than that of Wilhelmson's, but a few doors away from the one he was in the previous evening.

"I see the decorators are in down the hallway, I thought the place was only done last year. I guess you guys are making plenty of money?"

"Mr. Falcon, I'm afraid I have some bad news. I'll come straight to the point. You see, Mr. Wilhelmson suffered a massive heart attack at home last night and sadly passed away. So for the time being, I shall be looking after his client base until we reallocate them across the business. I know it may sound blunt and heartless but I assure you we have our customers' best interests at heart. We are very sorry if this causes any inconvenience. So, now you are aware of the situation, please feel free to discuss with me any problems you may have or anything we can do for you, as we shall make this transition for you between account managers seamless, I assure you."

Falcon made out his shocked expression and shook his head with mock disbelief.

"I'm very sorry to hear that about Heinrich, I guess my issues are not that relevant today after all. I'll call back in a week or so."

"Mr. Falcon, we are still in a position to help, although I guess you may be a little shocked."

Kramer handed Falcon a couple of his business cards.

"Please Mr. Falcon, feel free to call me any time, for anything. My personal numbers are on that card and trust me they are not in general circulation. You're a well respected customer of ours, and long may you remain so. I will most likely be handling your account when the restructuring is done."

Falcon shook hands with the banker and told him he would be in touch in the not too distant future. Very soon he was back outside the ornate building, in a state of disbelief himself as to what had just transpired. How could the bank make such a statement and be so quick with decorating a dead guy's room? Clearly they themselves thought he was playing a dirty game, and maybe, it was one of his client's in that game who they thought could have done the deed. The cleaning up operation turned out to be even easier than he had hoped; someone else was actually doing it for him.

He strolled along the Zurich streets with a great burden now lifted from his shoulders. He still mourned for Maria and would be back in Italy soon to attend her funeral, but this matter of business took greater precedent over being around her grieving family. He could easily make excuses for his absence in so far as wanting time alone, but still he knew seeing her buried would be a very difficult time.

One thing was for sure, he could never again break the golden rules. There would be no more emotional involvement and no career change. He knew he was trapped in a career cycle he could not really get out of. Perhaps slow down and gradually drift away in the later years but retire from, that was too formal and would never be allowed to happen.

Epilogue

As expected the funeral was a very sombre and highly emotional affair. The tributes to Maria were tremendous, both verbal and floral, but that still didn't ease the pain Falcon felt for his loss. He spoke to her in silence as she was laid to rest for the last time, promising to be a regular visitor, but also knowing she was after all with the angels and would keep an eye out for him, just in case he couldn't look out for himself.

Once the formalities had ended, the Englishman returned to his own villa in the small Italian village. It was just as he remembered he had left it that day when he came in searching for a shooter to take to Venice; the only difference now was that there was no Maria. The atmosphere of the whole villa had changed but he knew it would be difficult for him to leave this place, with it holding so many memories. Would he ever let go of the ghost or would he need it for his own comfort? Only time would tell; but today that decision could not be made.

The Englishman poured himself a rather large fine scotch whisky and downed it in one as he stood at his front windows again admiring the views of the Alps, which first attracted him to this magical place. He could hear Maria in his head, all the good times they had had in this house, she would always be present.

A second whisky was poured as he went to the study and sat at his computer and fired it into life. There she was again as large as life as the wallpaper on his screen, there was no getting away from her.

Falcon started the email service for his Cayman Islands front, Apollo Holdings.

There was only one address in the address book, so it was not too difficult to find. The address was selected and the mail was written. Simple and concise, but to the recipient one Mr. Brown, it would be just about the best news in the world.

"I'm back . . ."

Lightning Source UK Ltd.
Milton Keynes UK
06 July 2010

156602UK00001B/71/P